Split

by **Arushi Sood Joshi**

Llumina
Press

© 2009 Arushi Sood Joshi

Requests for permission to make copies of any part of this work should be mailed to Permissions Department, Llumina Press, PO Box 772246, Coral Springs, FL 33077-2246

ISBN: 978-1-60594-336-7

Printed in the United States of America by Llumina Press

Library of Congress Control Number: 2009906209

Dedicated lovingly to the three most important people in my life—my daughter, my husband, and my mother.

H, thank you for painting "Split." You are a genius.

Prelude

Good Morning Amrrika

Normally the purveyor of soft rock, this December morning the FM radio station playing in Aradhana's bedroom as she got ready for work warned of gloom. With the wind chill factor the temperature was predicted to drop to minus twenty degrees Fahrenheit by nightfall, with twenty-four inches of snow expected by the next morning. Newscasters were anticipating it to be the worst snowstorm since the historic "Great Blizzard of '78." Horror stories of that fateful storm that paralyzed New England a little over three decades ago were being recounted on every local media source at the slightest provocation. Back then, seventy-five people had been killed and over 500 million dollars worth of damage had occurred. Boston alone had seen nearly twenty-seven inches of snow, which had been an all-time single storm record. This time around the chief meteorologist on the radio advised listeners to stock up on essential supplies and signed off by asking people to be safe. There was no telling how badly Boston would be affected this time.

Aradhana nonchalantly brushed her hair as she listened. The storm warning should have put her in emergency stock-up mode. She should have stocked up on her standard essentials like "I Can't Believe It's Not Butter," eggs, bread, milk, pasta, instant pasta sauce, and of course—frozen goodies galore from the Indian grocery store. However, after over eight years in the United States of America (or *Amrrika* as she endearingly liked to call it in a put-on thick Indian accent), Aradhana knew this storm too would probably would be a false alarm, or at least grossly exaggerated.

As she turned away from the mirror, she was face to face with a bright yellow and blue silk comforter on a dark cherry queen sized bed. The paisley print in yellow illuminated a memory of eight and half years ago, when Gauri, her mother had insisted on stuffing it in her bag on her maiden voyage to America. The comforter looked rather lonely in the master bedroom of the small two bedroom Cambridge apartment. For alumni of that distant land the room held few touches of home, save for a quartet of yellow and blue silk pillows, and a grey stone statuette of Lord Ganesh, the elephant headed god. The rest of the bedroom was bare.

As she proceeded to make her bed, she held on to the comforter for a few minutes longer than required, and then almost abruptly finished the task with unprecedented speed. With the same momentum, she made her way to the kitchen and poured herself some milk and Honey Bunches of Oats cereal. The real breakfast of her favorite *poha*, the Indian rice flakes or *upma*, the semolina porridge, were treats reserved only for weekends.

While she munched on her cereal, the radio continued to play in the background.

Looking outside her window, Aradhana saw the snow from the night before and let a shiver pass down her spine as she anticipated what the cold outside would feel like. The winters seemed to drive the sometimes distant and cold exteriors that most people seemed to sport, especially during this season.

Existence during the winter was exhausting, as everything required planning. The season was characterized by layers—layers of clothing, layers of moods, and layers of snow. The sheath of white generally appeared at night, when you were most oblivious. Mornings would greet you with the warmth of the sun reflected on an endless pool of snow. Splashes of snow would be strategically dispersed like some secret code of the gods on the remaining vegetation from fall. Winters saw the roofs cozily wrapped in a comforter of white.

This attempt at secret communication by the snow god would, in due course, demand its price. *Of course*, thought Aradhana, *if this was India, there would be a snow god.* This god would either be wrathful or benevolent depending on how he or she felt about our deeds. Aradhana was almost sure that this god would be a "he." He would be in the same fraternity as Indra, the rain god; Vayu, the wind god; Surya, the sun god; and all the other pantheons whose names she could barely keep track of but feared and respected all the same.

One of the mundane retributions of the snow was shoveling the driveway, or in her case, the walkway. She'd also have to deal with the inches of snow clinging stubbornly to the windshield and mirrors of her silver BMW 525i. With a cheap shovel and a seven dollar ice scraper from AutoZone as her only weapons, she'd have to go to battle.

• • •

As she went into the master bedroom to pick up her laptop, Aradhana checked her reflection in the full-length mirror, and was pleased with what she saw. At five feet six inches, she stood taller than most Indian girls, and had straight dark hair that rested gently at her shoulders. She had a strikingly angular face with high cheekbones, an olive complexion, brown eyes, and a straight nose that rounded at the tip. Individually her features were merely attractive but combined together, they drew attention. She had the type of look that made people want to turn back at least once. She exuded a strong confidence and a lost look both at the same time.

Today, she wore a black pantsuit from Ann Taylor with a burgundy silk top, accessorized with a single string of white pearls and matching earrings. This was her professional look; one she loathed but was used to creating at this hour.

It was on days like these that she really missed India. Growing up, even a few inches of rain had meant no school. Of course, in an ongoing pursuit for excellence and efficiency, much had recently changed in India. However, Aradhana preferred not to think of the changes that had taken place in every facet of life as she knew it—especially the ones that didn't sit well with her memories—as she found some masochistic solace in thinking of how great things were back home.

Today, however, she had no choice but to trek to work.

"Thank God it's Friday," she said as she grabbed her laptop. The most revered day of the week for Americans. When she first came to the United States, she didn't understand all the fuss about "TGIF" — Thank God it's Friday. Just how stressful could the other days of the week be? However, when she started working six years ago, she got her answer. Now she was a believer in TGIF, long weekends, sick days, vacation days, and just about any other day away from the routine of office life at Swanson and Well. Swanson and Well or S&W was the prestigious human capital consulting firm where she was Senior Manager of Employee Management Services.

Her job description included bringing new business into the firm as well as servicing her clients' policy and training needs as it related to employees. Take away the big words and it meant that she needed to train management and staff so that they didn't do or say something stupid, which would cost the company big bucks in the highly litigious United States. She also helped clients develop shallow rhetoric that would save their behinds should something they had no control over happen, such as discrimination lawsuits and disgruntled employees. Her services were window-dressed in terms such as Employee Morale, Diversity Training, Crisis Management, and Policy Development but what that really meant was fluff that gave the appearance of propriety and inclusiveness. In the short time she had been working, she had been quite successful. Aradhana knew that her success came not from the fact that the company liked her, but from the fact that the clients loved her. In her time with S&W she had generated significant repeat business with the clients with whom she had worked. She still hadn't been able to pinpoint what they liked about her though. A client once suggested that it was her non-intrusive but take-charge personality. Others had suggested she had an edge and was an "out of the box" thinker. Her company didn't really care as long as she continued to sell the fluff and bring in the bucks. To ensure that the upward trend continued, they had begun hinting at partnership for her within the next three years.

As a first-generation immigrant, people were always interested in what she thought of the United States. If she had a penny for every time she had been asked over the years if she'd ever go back home, she'd be really rich by now. As she walked out of the bedroom, she stopped to glance at the undisturbed side of the bed. He'd be back soon, but it didn't feel like soon enough.

Roots—The beginning

Not So Humble Beginnings

*A*radhana celebrated her eighteenth birthday on hot and dusty Indian summer day. It was a big birthday as it was the official coming of age birthday in India; a green light to adulthood. An age at which she was legally allowed to vote and get married. She got a lot of cards that highlighted those privileges and welcomed her into adulthood.

So far she wasn't particularly excited about the special privileges that came with this so-called adulthood. As if she was waiting to turn eighteen just so that she could get married, or vote for leaders who were too old or too corrupt to make a difference. Like her billion or so fellow citizens, she too was frustrated with the "system." Sure, a billion people would put a strain on whatever resources however good, but the government ought to have been doing more. Colonialism had ended over half a century ago but the colonial mindset hadn't. When would they learn to be proud of what they had and who they were? When would they be able to come out of the shadows and reclaim their existence? Everything was blamed on the system and the people. When would people start taking ownership for their fate and who they were? She was as passionate about her country as anyone could be. She often quoted Sir Walter Scott's poem "Patriotism," she didn't want to die "Unwept, unhonour'd, and unsung." She challenged everyone who said they couldn't make a difference. She was a fierce, dramatic, and idealistic eighteen-year-old.

Aradhana woke up with a smile on her face that morning. She couldn't get over the little cabaret that Abhay, her sixteen-year-old brother had done for her at midnight. Without permission, he had borrowed her brand new powder blue off-the-shoulder smock top that she had planned to wear with a dark blue denim skirt to her birthday celebration. At midnight she had been pretending to be asleep, but in reality, even at eighteen she couldn't help being excited about her birthday. It was a Kapoor family tradition to wake the person of honor at midnight whilst he or she feigned sleep. Abhay had been the first to enter her room. He was wearing overly tight jeans that engulfed his slight physique. He seemed to think it was very fashionable and made him look macho, much to his three sisters' chagrin. The family, however, accepted his fashion statement and had grown used to seeing him dressed that way. That night, as he watched his sister comply with the ritual of feigning sleep, he had tugged at her blanket.

1

"Happy birthday, fatkins! See how sexy I look!" he had declared.

Aradhana could not contain her laughter as she watched him pucker his lips and suggestively slide the shirt off his shoulder. Although on the small side, he was quite good-looking and extremely charming. Having three sisters had given him an in to the privileged sorority of his sisters and their friends. Through his extremely honest relationship with them, he had learned the secrets to a woman's heart, and the do's and don'ts that all men should follow to keep a woman once he got her.

Although Aradhana had lost her baby fat in her mid-teens, Abhay never let her live it down, and still endearingly called her "fatkins." When he did, she would chase him around the house, but the truth was she really didn't mind, as it made her feel close to him.

Abhay and Aradhana went to the same high school. She was in the twelfth grade or what Americans called a "senior." Abhay was in the eleventh grade or a "junior." At first she had hated the fact that she had to go to the same school as her younger brother, but she knew in her heart that it was Abhay's school first. He had spent over ten years of his life there, while, up until that last year, she had gone to a prestigious all girls' convent school with her older two sisters, Amrita and Aasma.

Abhay's midnight birthday wishes were followed by the duo of her older sister, Aasma and her mother Gauri. Ashwin, her father was notably and expectantly absent. He had turned in for the night, and Aradhana, didn't expect to hear from him till morning, that too at Gauri's prodding.

Gauri had pecked Aradhana on her forehead, and blessed her with her hand on her head.

"I hope you are successful in whatever you do," she had said half hopefully and half authoritatively.

Aradhana uncomfortably accepted the blessing, as she thought about how everything with Gauri was about success. Then with guilt she wondered why she always read too much into what Gauri said. Why was there always this undercurrent between her and Gauri? The next statement gave her a clue.

"I wish Amitra was also here to be a part of this. She always made everything so special, isn't it?," Gauri stated rhetorically.

Within minutes of her comment, the phone rang. As Gauri excitedly answered the phone, her voice lit up.

"Yes, Amrita *beta*, you are going to live for a hundred years. We were just talking about you. We all miss you so much. Yes, yes, your little sister is here. She is finally becoming a woman. Let's hope that she starts to act like one. Yes, yes she is so different from you and Aasma. I just hope she matures."

Aradhana listened uncomfortably as she waited for the phone to be handed to her. It was the prodigal daughter at the end of the line. Amrita, the oldest of the Kapoor siblings was a winner all right. At five feet eight inches, with thick, long jet-black hair, and distinctive blue eyes, Amrita had model looks. Married to the son of a famous Delhi businessman, she had been playing the part of the wife par excellence for the past five years and resided in Delhi. She had gotten married when she was only twenty-two through a match suggested by a distant family friend. Amrita had veto power about the marriage, but Kiran, the prospect groom, seemed decent enough. Without anything to compare him to, Amrita gave her consent. It was obviously for the best, as Amrita had never seemed happier than she was after her marriage.

"Thanks, Amrita *didi*," Aradhana said using the endearment "didi" or elder sister, half out of respect and half out of habit. "Yes, mummy has planned something for this evening. I have a few friends coming but the rest are those numerous uncles and aunties that we all love so much."

Gauri playfully slapped Aradhana on her back spotting the sarcasm right away. "You all think everything is so funny. None of you appreciate all that I do around here," Gauri continued in the background while Aradhana was still on the phone.

Aasma was the next in line to wish Aradhana happy birthday. She had been her quiet self all this time, albeit smiling and reacting appropriately to the numerous comments being made.

Aasma looked lovely as always and wore a peach negligee with a matching house coat. Younger than Amrita, but older than Aradhana, she held a special place in the Kapoor family. Her shy demeanor won her no enemies. But the demeanor was not to be confused with her lack of intelligence or skill.

Aasma could have been anything she chose to be. She was a certified chartered accountant or the equivalent of a CPA. She had passed her exams with minimal effort and now worked in a reputed accounting firm. However, the job was considered a filler until her true dreams of getting married were achieved. She had forfeited an offer to go to the United Kingdom for further training.

Aasma had a perfect profile to achieve her true dream and was very much considered "marriage material."

Five feet three inches, Aasma at twenty-three years old had a curvaceous figure, an ample bosom and prominent buttocks. Like Amrita, she also had jet black hair and a fair complexion. Unlike Amrita, however, she had traditional black eyes. She was more of a conventional beauty; one every Indian man would be proud to show off.

Now the Kapoors were looking for a suitable match for Aasma. The ideal man would be as prestigious and as good looking as their son-in-law Kiran, and needless to say, he would come from the same Punjabi community as the Kapoors.

Aasma's birthday wishes surprised Aradhana the most.

"Ary, always stay the way you are," Aasma had said sincerely.

Aasma and Aradhana seemed to have so little in common. In fact they couldn't have been more different. Aradhana always thought that Aasma didn't care much for the way she was. Aasma's comment, in light of Gauri phone remarks to Aradhana, suddenly filled her heart. She hugged Aasma rather comfortably, considering it wasn't something they did often.

• • •

Aradhana considered herself the black sheep of the family. She had not been a pretty child and was always on the pudgy side. It was only post-puberty that her transformation had begun. Her sharp features were beginning to show, and her baby fat was melting. She was passionate and principled to a fault. From the ripe age of thirteen she had become firm in her values and beliefs. She intended to execute the rest of her life's journey defending and living by them. She had been a real tomboy, always preferring to hang out with the boys rather than the girls. She was a lot stronger than she looked and got into physical fights often. Growing up, the boys didn't judge her, so she liked them. After her transformation, her relationships with the boys had changed. The boys had started taking more interest in her than she liked and they giggled and whispered a lot more around her. She had hoped they'd continue to see her as the Aradhana that they'd call out to play cricket, football or hockey, but things changed, and so had Aradhana despite her own resistance. She was becoming a woman. A savvy woman who had learned what she knew from playing rough with the boys, and watching her sisters from a distance.

Deep down Aradhana was in awe of her sisters. They seemed to be content with whatever was handed to them. On the other hand, Aradhana seemed to fight whatever came her way. They were blessed with simplicity that Aradhana believed set them free. As far back as she could remember she overanalyzed things. She fought hard with Gauri to get the same rights that Abhay did, which included being allowed to stay out as late, wearing shorts, and just about anything that Abhay was entitled to by right of his sex.

Her internal strife was exacerbated by her experiences at the all girls convent school that she attended. The same Saint Thomas Convent School that had churned out genteel ladies like Amrita and Aasma had also churned out someone like herself. With her tightly cropped hair, belligerent attitude, and tomboy personality she was not a success story for the school.

There was little to remember of her convent life save for the experiences that taught her exactly what little girls were made of. It wasn't sugar and spice and all things nice. The nuns from the convent looked nothing like those from *The Sound of Music*, Aradhana's favorite classic movie. They had oil-greased hair and hailed mainly from the south of India. There was, however, a token Italian nun thrown in for authenticity—the principal, Mother Florence. Mother Florence caught unsuspecting girls by their pigtails and accused them of being Satan's daughters. In her ominous voice she'd condemn them to burn in hell. Aradhana was not raised Catholic, but she was beginning to believe there was some truth in her being Satan's daughter given the things that she had envisioned doing to Mother Florence. Aradhana was picked on for being a "little troublemaker." Among her faults were that she tucked her tunic too high under her belt, exposed her knees, and rolled her socks too low. Twice, her hemline was publicly opened and her socks pulled up high. She spoke in an unladylike manner and asked the nuns too many questions. In her defense, even if the nuns were Jesus' brides, they definitely didn't act like it.

It was after her tenth grade that she broke down in front of Gauri and said she would not go to that school any more. She was somewhat surprised when Gauri honored her wishes and enrolled her into Abhay's coed school Desh Vidhyalaya. Abhay was happiest at being able to ride tandem with Aradhana on Bambi, the rusted 75cc dream machine or truthfully an excuse for a motorbike. Still he preferred it to riding the bus, even if he had to push Bambi for at least twenty to fifty feet whilst Aradhana peddled furiously before Bambi decided to grace the world with the sound of her motor.

Balle Balle—The Hurrahs

*A*fter scanning several matrimonial ads for Aasma, it was ultimately someone from Gauri's numerous *kitty* groups who suggested Pankaj Khanna. A *kitty* was like combination of a bank or fund scheme and an adult sorority except it wasn't as selective. Pankaj was twenty-seven years old, tall, fair, and had a well-defined physique. The fact that he was an engineer made him even more impressive. Aasma had a photo portfolio that had been shot by a professional photographer in anticipation of such an event, namely the selection ritual that happens in arranged marriages. It served the purpose well, and Pankaj's family loved Aasma. Pankaj also got the seal of approval from the Kapoor family. The Khannas were also from Delhi, a fact that comforted the Kapoors since Amrita was also settled there with her husband. The engagement took place a month after Aradhana's eighteenth birthday in a quiet ceremony at the Kapoor home. It was all done very quickly as Aasma was already twenty-three and the Kapoors did not want to wait much longer to marry her off.

The wedding was to be at an elite Country Club in Delhi. Amrita and Kiran's large Sainik farm bungalow served as the venue for the close friends and family to stay during the festivities. In addition, the Kapoors had several relatives in Delhi, at least a dozen who played host to their guests as well. Since they were given five months notice, and the winter vacation was at hand, the turnout was better than anticipated. Also, since RSVP requests were not generally complied with in India, there were a lot of last minute guests added to the list. Several cars were deployed to pick up the guests at the airport, railway and bus stations. In addition to hired cars, several friends and family members had loaned their second cars as well. It wasn't considered a favor, as you were expected to return it in due course. Anybody and everybody with a valid driver's license or any driving experience was expected to shuttle the guests. Thankfully Aradhana, although eighteen and therefore old enough for a license, had a phobia about driving cars. Her 75cc motorbike was as big a vehicle as she could handle. Unfortunately, she still had to accompany the hired cars in order to help identify and escort the guests back to their designated host homes. She hated the task. Not only did she not recognize half the people from the extended families, but she hated being smothered in their embraces as somehow her nose always ended up being trapped inches away from their armpits.

Some of the guests had traveled in an air-conditioned three-tier coach with all expenses-paid status. Among the guests who had accompanied them from Hyderabad were a few of Aasma's friends and two of Abhay's high school buddies. Aradhana was especially fascinated with Abhay's buddies—one, short and plump with permanently greasy hair and the other tall and thin with a broad forehead and a slender moustache as his only signs of manhood. Abhay's thin and tall friend Nirman had been eyeing Aradhana with boyish adulation since they were introduced a year ago but she hadn't given him much thought. Aradhana had not bothered inviting anyone to the wedding because she wasn't sure what drama was likely to erupt.

Indian marriages are a time of festivities, bright new clothes, lots of gold jewelry, and a time for young boys and girls to indulge in the sport of flirting—first coyly and then shamelessly. Delhi was quite full of eligible candidates to play this sport and Aradhana's cousin Sanjeev who lived in the city provided a pool of candidates for his female cousins to draw from.

While Aradhana lacked the feminine guiles her sisters had, she couldn't help but begin to feel an interest in men. From the background, she had been observing her sisters skillfully excel at this sport. She was adamant to try her hand at it too. Like a jungle cat staking out its prey, she had been eyeing Sanjeev's friend Ritik. She savored the thought that Ritik would have been a challenge even for her sisters. He looked older than what his barely adult license proclaimed. He was clean shaven with a sharp masculine jaw line. The ruggedness that his looks and physique proclaimed, his eyes denied. She wasn't sure just what she wanted to do with Ritik or what victory would look like, but she wasn't thinking that far. This new sensation was quite intoxicating, and she was enjoying it.

During the week of the wedding, there was a party every night. Generally initiated by the hordes of relatives, the guests would show up religiously each night. The women were the first to start the festivities. They demanded the *dholak*, an Indian drum, and a spoon. If not, there was always a loud well-girthed *uncle* in a safari suit to demand that the festivities be started. There was a lot of drum playing while the adults would sing old Punjabi songs that were beyond Aradhana's comprehension. She was able to make out that they were flirtatious, insulting, territorial, and bold. Generally, the men and woman formed separate groups. So as to facilitate eavesdropping, neither was too far away from the other, but interference was limited. The men would be a few feet away from the women's contingent, never without a glass of whiskey in one hand and a plate of tandoori chicken in the other. They would not miss a single chance of jumping in into the song with an "Ahooye" or "Shawa" or "Balle Balle," none of which meant anything. The women, on the other hand, would be holding a soft drink and the ubiquitous chicken leg. They often walked up to the men and indulged them with *aap bhi na* or "you're so...." at their not so funny jokes.

The children were encouraged to dance, and sometimes even received money for their performances. Punjabi tradition involved setting aside such money from the dancing to be given to the help, but it was generally distributed among the youngsters. The drunker the male contingent got, the more money the youngsters could expect to make. The boys over eighteen were encouraged to drink to highlight their manhood and capacity for drink, while the girls, if they were caught doing such a thing, would be chastised with whispering and pointing by the older women to the girl and her mother.

• • •

During one cold night full of festivities, having recently come of age, Aradhana asked her cousin Sanjeev for a Vodka and Limca. It would not be the first time she was trying alcohol, but she had never done it in front of her parents, and definitely not at her sister's wedding. Sanjeev had the drink made in a plastic disposable glass in order to disguise it and brought it over to Aradhana, who was watching Aasma sit in the middle of the women's contingent and blush coyly (as was expected of her) at the song references to her displacing her mother-in-law as the new "woman" in her husband's life. The kids sat at a distance, waiting to be dragged into the festivities in due course. For now, they were watching the fun and making small talk. The huddle of guys laughed at something Ritik said. Aradhana leaned closer to hear what was so funny. Apparently, Mahlotra aunty's ample cleavage was in their direct view as she bent over to beat the drums. Ritik and contingent appeared to think that this voluptuous thirty-five-year-old mother of six-year-old twins would actually be a hoot to do.

"Surely, Mr. Mahlotra can't handle that hot package," someone said, pointing to a heavy, unattractive man.

"Come on," Sanjeev said, challenging Ritik, "I bet you can't get her attention."

Having had one too many "screwdrivers", Ritik took the challenge, "I'll do you one better—what will you give me if she kisses me?"

"Shut up! You're full of crap," cried someone else.

"Want to bet? Before the night is done, she will kiss me," said Ritik.

Aradhana's eyes interlocked for an instance with Abhay's thin and tall friend, Nirman. He gave her a look that said, "I'm sorry, but I'm not with them."

After some deliberation, the reward was determined to be all the winnings of the night's dancing. The only condition was that Sanjeev would trail Ritik for the proof. Aradhana thought this highly immature, but could understand why a twenty-one-year-old would find it challenging. She didn't particularly like the fact that she seemed to find Ritik quite attractive in that instant. His rebellious, bad boy image coupled with his chocolate face was quite enticing. She imagined Ritik sweeping her up in his arms and kissing her long and hard. Ritik, for his part, seemed preoccupied with devising a plan. Then it hit him.

• • •

Some twenty minutes later, it was finally Sanjeev who narrated what happened while handing over the day's earnings.

He was in awe and kept repeating, "I bow to you, man. You are the master."

By this point Aradhana had walked right into the middle of the boy contingent and promptly sat herself down to hear what happened. By now, everyone knew she had heard everything, but dismissed it, saying it was "only Aradhana." Aradhana felt herself getting excited as she heard how the plot played out. What surprised her most was how easily Mahlotra Aunty complied. *She must have really been frustrated*, thought Aradhana, but a single glance at Mahlotra Uncle made it understandable. He was almost the same height as Mahlotra Aunty, and was plump, mustached, and balding. He was also obviously very drunk. He was nothing in comparison to his wife who had kept her looks even after two children.

Ritik's plan had succeeded. The girls had been requested to call Mahlotra Aunty's twins into one of the guest rooms. Ritik went over to Mahlotra Aunty and whispered loudly enough for the other ladies to hear that one of her daughters was looking for her and needed some assistance. Mahlotra Aunty excused herself and headed with Ritik into an empty guestroom where Sanjeev was hiding in the bathroom.

The bathroom door was open enough for Sanjeev to peer out. After Ritik shut the door behind him, he grabbed Mrs. Mahlotra in his arms.

"Don't worry, the children are fine. I lied," he said. "It's just that I have never seen anyone as sexy as you. Ask me to stop and I will. It's just that I could not go on, knowing that I didn't try."

Mahlotra Aunty was apparently too shocked to respond, but didn't pull away. Ritik gently moved the hair from across her face that had created a natural veil. He felt her knees buckling under his strong but gentle touch. The strong Armani cologne emitting from him was a powerful aphrodisiac. She looked at him dolefully, imploring his lips to seek hers. He took her cue, and his lips gently made acquaintance with hers. She responded with such a strong passion that it caught Ritik by surprise. He caught Sanjeev's gaze through the door and winked at him. Sanjeev was too shocked to respond. As he continued kissing her, Ritik decided to see if his good luck would last and began to gently move his hands down to her ample breast, and massaged it gently.

She groaned in utter delight.

"Don't stop," she commanded.

He gently unpinned her *saree paloo* and unbuttoned her *saree* blouse. The same blouse that had been the focus of so much attention was now off her shoulder. Like a child unwrapping a gift, he worked his way to her imported bra. She was hiding quite a treasure inside, thought Sanjeev as he peered through the partially open door. Ritik gently caught her nipple in his mouth and moved his tongue across it. In response she groaned and reached out to his bulging crotch which was hidden inside his traditional Indian attire, the kurta pajama. Just then they heard Amrita calling for Sanjeev and it sounded as if she was heading directly towards the guest room. Mahlotra Aunty looked like she was going to die.

"Get out, you idiot," hissed Ritik toward the bathroom. Sanjeev took his cue and ran out the door and right into Amrita.

Mrs. Mahlotra turned red with embarrassment, fear, shame and anger.

"You bastard," she said to Ritik, "I'll never forgive you."

"What's your first name Mahlotra Aunty?" he asked earnestly.

As he narrated this to the group, the boys showed no remorse or emotion but Aradhana felt sick not to mention really sorry for Mrs. Mahlotra.

All her dreams of flirting with Ritik were now gone. She wasn't really sure why she was taking it so personally. She chided herself for not having better sense in picking a prospective interest. She could never play the game like her sisters. As far as she was concerned, she didn't really even know how to choose. As if to not leave any doubt in her own mind, she announced, "I'll never let anyone make a fool of me like that."

Remember the Roses

*B*y all predefined criteria, the wedding was a huge success. Food and drinks were plenty, at least two other weddings would come out of it, and only one major fight broke out between the relatives. The festivities that had taken so much planning and time seemed to end too soon to Gauri.

With Aasma gone, Gauri became engrossed in her housework, fanatically task-driven, and even more focused on finding herself new projects. She found herself a project in Aradhana's education. Gauri had greater ambition for Aradhana than she seemed to for her other daughters. She had always wanted Aradhana to become a doctor. She supported the belief of a majority of Indians that a successful career meant either medicine or engineering; anything different was generally considered the result of a failed attempt to pursue the other two.

One day Gauri came to Aradhana and gave her eight different medical entrance forms.

"I ordered these forms for you," she said. "You are very intelligent. Why are you wasting your life always playing with these boys? Both your sisters are married to good boys and are well-settled. Your father and I are counting on you to become a doctor so we can find a good boy for you too."

Aradhana filled out the forms with her mother hovering overhead like a plane desperately waiting for permission to land.

Over the weeks that passed, Gauri would periodically track Aradhana down to inform her of the previously unidentified medical schools the children of her *kitty* party friends were applying to. The declaration was followed by a frenzy of frantic calls to relatives within a fifty-kilometer perimeter of the targets in order to pursue a military-style mission of acquiring the forms. Strategies for dealing with any resistance by the identified target, such as irrelevant obstacles as missing the application deadline were devised. Typically, this involved identification of additional resources, known or merely heard of, who could exert influence. If all else failed, there was a resource pool of cash that could be used to institute treason.

Suddenly even Ashwin, the Kapoor family patriarch who had shown little to no interest in all things familial appeared to care about how the medical entrance preparations were going. The Kapoor's master bedroom was on the same floor as the four rooms that were allotted to the children. It seemed like whenever Aradhana opened her bedroom door to make a trip to the kitchen or family room, Ashwin would accost her and, in his deep-throated, no-nonsense voice say,

"Your studies are going fine, no?"

No! she desperately wanted to respond, but Aradhana like every true Indian knew that "no?" at the end of a sentence was a non-negotiable "yes"—or it least it had better be. To get him off her back, she'd nod from left to right in an affirmative. This again was understood as a "yes" only by other Indians. As she would learn after she left India for the United States, anyone else would forever be confused as to how the violent head swing from side to side means yes.

Every morning at 4:30 a.m., Gauri would wake Aradhana so she could get to the medical preparation classes, which were held at the ungodly hour of 6 a.m. Aradhana couldn't exactly remember which demonic *aunty* had suggested the merit of these preparation courses, but she hated her all the same. Since she didn't like any of the aunties, the additional effort of identification was moot.

She was expected to head to her regular high school classes after the tutorial classes. For one week Aradhana dutifully dragged herself to the tutorial classes, but somewhere between the cerebral cortex and the theory of relativity, she lost interest. These topics that she once found challenging, she now approached with disdain. The disdain was not as much for the William Harveys or the Einsteins of the world—it was for everything around her. Why did they all suddenly care about what she did with her life? Had anyone once asked about what *she* wanted to do? Sure, she loved medicine and had seen every episode of *E.R.* and *Doogie Howser M.D.* In fact, had someone asked her what she wanted to do, she would have said medicine. But this blatant disregard for her views deeply offended her sense of self. The truth was that it should not have come as a bit of surprise to her. These were the rules of the game and she knew it. Somehow, though, there was a fire in her that had been lit and couldn't be ignored. Two days into the second week of torture, she began cheating.

• • •

She'd dress and leave home, but instead of heading to the "Surya Medical Preparation Tutorials," she headed to the *Goddess Saraswati* temple.

The temple was relatively small, and less ornate that many others in the area. The external structure consisted of a single pyramid-shaped tower over the main shrine. At sunrise, the sand color exterior glowed with the warmth of gold. The exterior was adorned by intricate carvings of mythological and sacred figurines. The tower stood in the middle surrounded by a compound. To the right was a courtyard. At the entrance of the court yard was a place for the devotees to remove their shoes before they entered. A little further ahead was a trough on ground level for devotees to wash their feet before entering and leaving the temple. To the left was an open space at the center of which was a Tulsi or Holy Basil plant. The inner sanctum, consisted of a life size idol of the Goddess Saraswati dressed in a white saree with a gold border, riding a swan, and playing the veena.

Aradhana felt some guilt and shame in the realization that Goddess Saraswati was the goddess of knowledge. But she absolved herself from this guilt by justifying that it was the only place that was open at six in the morning, and she was pretty sure she would not bump into anyone she knew there. When she arrived, she would seek forgiveness for using the temple as a sleep slanctuary and then a few minutes later, she'd sit cross-legged on the floor and rest her head against the sacred pillar at the entrance of the temple tower and fall into a deep sleep. Anyone who happened to pass by would have paid no attention as she looked like a devotee deep in meditation. After a two hour nap, she'd head to her high school that started at nine.

A week into this ritual without having been struck by lighting, she heard a familiar voice call her name. At first she thought it was God, calling to pass judgment. Within a second she rationalized that God was late because there were a billion or more Hindus in the world to judge, many who had committed crimes of much greater severity. In her mind she hadn't given God a human form, but she always referred to God as He/She. If God was a woman, she did not want to face the fury of a woman scorned. And if he was a man, he'd understand the confusion and forgive it.

Her thoughts were interrupted by a gentle tap on her shoulder. She reverently opened her eyes, while instinctively clasping her hands together in the *namaste* position. Reverence and pleading was going to be her strategy. Seeing it was only her brother's friend Nirman, she unfolded her hands, suddenly feeling very foolish. She hadn't seen Nirman since Aasma's wedding—and since she had ignored his obvious interest in her. Abhay's thin, tall, awkwardly mustached friend was looking very different.

Nirman had shaved his slender moustache and looked surprising striking in his school uniform. The navy blue pants, white half sleeve shirt and blue sweater vest made him look both elegant and erudite.

She looked at her watch groggily. It was 8 a.m. and she would be late for school if she didn't leave shortly. She was in her pink-and-white checked school shirt and navy blue tunic. As per the temple rules, her shoes were outside the building so she had her socks on, folded down close to her ankles.

"Nirman! What are you doing here?" she asked a little defensively.

Coyly, he responded that it was his birthday and that he liked to start the year by seeking blessings at the temple. While he was politely exchanging pleasantries, he seemed a little distracted which made him all the more interesting to Aradhana in that moment.

"Oh, happy birthday," she said politely and then added patronizingly "So how old are you, sixteen?"

She was surprised to find out that he was almost a year older than her, especially because he was in her brother's class.

"Did you lose a year or something?" she asked.

"Sort of. I'll tell you about it some other time. I need to get to something now, but lets catch up soon," he said indicating the conversation closed.

Aradhana took her cue and mumbled something about being in a rush herself, and headed to the courtyard where Bambi, her motorbike, was parked. Alone with Bambi, she kicked and pushed, but Bambi refused to start. Frustrated, Aradhana kicked the bike, only to slash her calf with the spike protruding from the pedal. As it started to bleed, she yelped like an abandoned puppy. She left her bag by the bike and went back into the temple to find Nirman. She looked by the pillars where she last saw him, by the nine planet gods, by the Shivling, and every other deity positioned in the temple but he was nowhere to be found. Dejected, she walked out of the temple and saw him serving food to several dozen people of all ages sitting in a circle around the temple.

She stood at a distance and when he was done, she approached him and asked if she could ride with him to school. Her grimaces told the rest of the story and a concerned Nirman steered her into the temple courtyard. In the courtyard, he led her to the community washing area. The copper tap gushed warm water to the stone trough at Nirman's slight touch. Aradhana rested her hand on his shoulder and he helped her wash her calf which was still bleeding profusely. Their actions elicited more than a few stares from fellow devotees. Several who made their way to the tap, asked what had happened. Nirman politely, but authoritatively let them know that things were under control. Once clean, he bandaged the wound with his white and blue bordered handkerchief. He then led her to a slightly beaten Fiat parked in the temple courtyard. They drove in silence to school.

For the next seven days he met her at the temple every morning and drove her to school. Every day they talked more and more. She found herself sharing with him more feelings than she had with anyone in such a short time. She spoke of her near perfect sisters, her emotionally absent father, a mother she didn't fully understand. In return, he told her about how he had recovered two years ago from bone marrow cancer after undergoing a year of painful chemotherapy and a bone marrow transplant. He was forced to take a year off from school and went through a severe depression.

On the seventh day, Nirman came to the temple with a dozen long stemmed yellow Dutch roses. Slightly embarrassed and surprised that he knew her favorite color, Aradhana accepted them. During the ride to school, he asked her whether she knew why he had given her the flowers and she admitted that she didn't have a clue.

"It takes us one hour to get to school from the temple and an hour to return. That's one rose for every hour I have spent with you. Yellow is for our blossoming friendship and the full bloom is how fulfilled I feel being with you," he said hesitantly.

Extremely corny, but pretty sweet, thought Aradhana. As they reached the school parking lot, she did something she considered very bold: she reached over and kissed him gently on his lips. At first Nirman didn't know how to react. It looked to Aradhana like he had never really kissed someone before. But neither had she and she seemed a lot more confident than him. She would have liked for him to make the first move; perhaps grab her in his arms, kiss her first gently and then passionately. Instead, their first kiss was a little awkward—at first not enough exploring and then too much. She tried not to focus on the specifics. They both would need practice. It wasn't what she had expected her first kiss to be: A rather awkward tryst in the school parking lot with her younger brother's best friend and the school watchman doing what he was hired to—watch.

The day Aradhana kissed him, Nirman told Abhay that he liked Aradhana and that if it was okay with Abhay, he would like to go out with her. Abhay reacted maturely and told her it was fine with him as long as his sister wanted it, too. Like a good brother, for good measure he added,

"You hurt her, man, and I'll tear you apart."

Dream Sabotage

*A*radhana was first in her school on the crucial board exams. Her mother's joy knew no bounds as she told all the neighbors and friends how well Aradhana had done. She would start off with the seemingly harmless question of asking how their child had done, and no sooner did they answer would she attack them with Aradhana's results. The medical entrance exams were a few months after the board exams and tickets were booked for remote locations so that Aradhana could attend them. Gauri, who had previously never been interested in Aradhana's style of studying, would now sit everyday across from Aradhana, trying to look busy with her book while Aradhana studied. She would make Indian-style tea, complete with spices, and put it in a silver flask that she would perch strategically on the study table by sundown. Every morning she'd ask Aradhana how late she studied while verifying her responses by visually measuring the amount of tea that remained from the night before. Once she caught on, Aradhana started emptying the flask of tea down the drain so that she wouldn't have to answer the additional question of why she didn't drink the tea. She hinted a couple of times that she didn't need the tea but Gauri would hear none of it. Plus, it gave her another task on which to focus.

When she wasn't buried in her books, Aradhana was with Nirman. Since both of Nirman's parents worked late hours, they found it easier to meet at Nirman's home. Gauri didn't question Aradhana much since she left with her books, under the pretext of studying with some friend or the other. She didn't like lying to Gauri, but she knew Gauri wouldn't approve. Sometimes Abhay would accompany Aradhana to Nirman's home. At times, they'd all sit together and discuss their futures. At other times, Aradhana and Nirman where by themselves. Even in private, their academic futures assumed center stage. Aradhana was more than a little surprised to learn that Nirman's prirmary goal was to move to the United States. He wanted to be a car design engineer. The concept of leaving India and moving to another country was alien to her. No one in her family had ever left the country even for a vacation. She wasn't clear on why anyone would.

She proposed if it was for the pursuit of education, surely there were more than enough opportunities in India. Also, why limit himself to the United States? Couldn't Nirman consider Japan or Germany?

Nirman however was clear. The United States, it had to be. That is what he had always dreamed of since he was a little boy.

Ideology aside, Nirman's plan had caught her more than a little off guard. During one such academic planning session, Aradhana asked in an uncharacteristically soft tone.

"I'm not in your future plans, am I, Nirman?"

Nirman was taken aback.

"Of course you are," he said defensively.

"Then how can you decide to go to the States when I have to spend the next five to seven years studying medicine here? We will never have a chance to take this relationship anywhere," she said, her voice rising.

"It's not like you can't come with me," he replied. "You don't even want to practice medicine. And even if you did, why can't you do it there?"

Aradhana looked hurt and confused. "How do you know what I want to do? Why is it that everyone knows what my plans should be except me? You know, I don't think we should see each other until I figure out what I want to do with my life."

"You can't be serious. But if that's what you want, why don't we talk when you are ready," Nirman conceded as she walked out of his house.

• • •

Aradhana spent the next two weeks before her exams single-mindedly focused on her studies. She did exceptionally well in the medical practice exams and felt confident enough that she'd be admitted into at least three of her top five school choices. Even though she had skipped the tutorials, she paid attention in high school and had spent significant time studying. Still, she was far from clear on what she wanted to do.

Everyone's interest in her future was getting progressively more bothersome. Aasma and Amrita had been calling every other day to keep the motivation going. The worst part was how Mr. Kapoor insisted on telling even his contractors that his daughter was going to be the biggest cardiac surgeon in the world.

The first test she took was for a medical school in the southern town of Chennai not too far from home. The first three and half-hours of the test were on biology and botany which she was sure she nailed. After lunch would come physics and chemistry. During lunch, Gauri was there with a prep test, yogurt for good luck, and cucumber sandwiches.

"Eat enough so that you're not hungry, but not so much that you are full and sleepy," she advised her daughter.

Aradhana looked around the room—almost everyone had well-oiled hair and was accompanied by a parent or guardian. Some were in groups quizzing each other and others were still learning the periodic table out loud. Aradhana's head was spinning. Something didn't seem right. This wasn't her dream. Even if it once was, it was now other peoples' dream. If only those who seemingly cared for her could see her for her ideals and beliefs instead of as the future doctor which "every family should have."

In the afternoon session, she marked "D" for every response.

A Plan to Secure the Peace

*A*s expected, Aradhana wasn't accepted into a single medical school, a fact that embarrassed her mother so much that she missed three of her kitty parties. Her sisters gave her the pity pep talk while Abhay pretended like nothing had happened. Aradhana felt unmotivated to defend her cause so she just ignored it all.

Though Nirman and she hadn't yet reached an understanding of what direction their "lives" were heading, she caved in and reached out to him. She told Nirman that she respected the fact that atleast he knew what he wanted to do. While she was hurt that he planned to leave the country, she recognized his passion. For his part, Nirman apologized for not having brought it up sooner. He also said, that he always assumed that Aradhana would be interested in joining him. They both agreed to take things as they came.

After a soul searching summer, Aradhana felt like she was back to square one. She had started a war but without a plan to secure the peace; a thought that would come back to her in regards to a certain global leader several years later. Why wasn't she like people who knew exactly what interested them and what they wanted to do?

Half the time she seemed to make decisions out of rebellion. If someone expected her to do something, she preferred not to do it. This was her decision and yet it didn't feel right or good. She kept telling herself that she didn't want to be a doctor but she knew it was a lie. As far back as she could remember she had wanted to be a cardiologist. When she was a child, whenever she played "doctor," she had insisted all the other children play patients with chronic illnesses.

When reading the Mills and Boons romance novels as she was growing up, she had had an affinity for the doctor-nurse series. Only in her dreams, the roles were reversed—the nurse would be a dedicated, muscular heartthrob with a Florence Nightingale touch and steaming with passion. Despite his millions in inheritance, he would work out of his desire to do good for humanity.

Aradhana knew she would make a good doctor. She was very good at the sciences. She could solve any chemical equation, identify any body part, and dissect anything without flinching. Would this be the biggest mistake of her life? Had she sabotaged the only thing she had dreamed off for so long for no good reason? The piece that she felt good about was making the decision herself. Like a lioness wounded during a chase, she felt both great triumph and pain at the same time. After her wounds healed, she could take on the world again but if they didn't, it would change her life. While she sat licking her wounds, she resolved that she'd let nature take its own course. She didn't yet have to decide what her next hunt was; she just needed time to heal. What she was made of was more important than what career she pursued. Surely, a respite to her dilemma would come.

Respite came in a three-year undergraduate degree, the default choice for most undecided college entrants. The program was called Bachelor of Arts, and the college was less than ten kilometers from her home. Her family was horrified at her choice. It was bad enough that she was pursuing a three-year degree at a no-name college, but a Bachelor of Arts program crippled the last bastion of hope they had for her. They contended that theories of the mind, language, and society were for those with no future and no other options, but never the pursuit of a keen mind. Unlike medicine and engineering, which were recognized as professional degrees, these were unprofessional. Even the unprofessional degrees had a prestige ranking; the least offensive of which was the Bachelor of Science, followed by a Bachelor of Commerce degree. Aradhana's choice was the lowest on the totem pole and in her family's eyes, the ultimate blow to their standing in society.

For the next three years life went on quite relaxed for Aradhana, with the family mostly ignoring her intellectual ambitions. Once she went to college, she floated through it as it required minimal effort on her part and was interesting enough. She read several books related to psychology, anthropology, and religion outside of what was required. Life was moving along.

• • •

There were two major developments during those three years. The first occurred when, during her first year of college, Nirman left India for the land of his dreams. The elusive U.S of A was now his home. Until his departure he worked hard to master the SAT exams and showed a dedication and sincerity to his studies that Aradhana had never seen from him before. His focus was on acing his SATs. For all her presumed knowledge of the world, Aradhana had never really heard of the Scholastic Aptitude Test. There was really no reason to, as no one she knew had ever taken it. While preparing for the test, Nirman had taken the trouble to explain the components of the exam to her. He went into great detail about the types of questions in each of the sections. He made Aradhana try to answer questions in all the sections—math, verbal, critical reading, and writing. Nirman enjoyed quizzing her on his tests, a fact that Aradhana didn't particularly enjoy. She was convinced that many times there was more than one right answer to each of the questions and was sure that if given a few minutes, she could convince someone of why she answered the way she did. The multiple-choice format for logic-based questions did not bode well with her.

Aradhana tried to be as supportive of Nirman as she could, but she struggled with the fact that his success meant that the one person she could talk to would be gone. However, because Nirman seemed so driven and excited, she ultimately began to support his dream. Remembering her exams and how Nirman had supported her through that period, she often checked his practice exam responses and gave him many "you're capable of achieving whatever you set your mind on" pep talks.

When the examination day came, she insisted on driving him there on Bambi, her pride and joy. Given Bambi's infamous history, he was a bit nervous. If Bambi broke down and he missed his exams, his dreams would be crushed; at least until the next time they offered them. Bambi however, knew when she was being assigned a responsibility. When the stakes were high, she was in top form. That day she started on the first kick and provided a smooth ride all the way to the test center.

Aradhana was in Nirman's house weeks later when his SAT results were delivered. As usual, both his parents were at work, and they were alone. Since her abysmal performance on the entrance tests, Gauri had stopped asking for Aradhana's daily itenary as before.

After signing for the letter, Nirman went into another room to open it. When he returned, he looked Aradhana straight in the eyes and said that his dreams were now crushed. He even let out a tear, saying that with his marks he would never get into any school. Aradhana hugged him, her own heart sinking as she felt Nirman's dream shatter. After spending a few minutes against her bosom, he pulled out his SAT scores—2300 out of a possible 2400. While she was mad at Nirman for pulling the prank, she understood the thrill the drama added to his experience. Admission to any university in the country was virtually guaranteed. Two weeks later he received a full scholarship to the automotive engineering program at the California Institute of Technology.

Net Lovers

*T*he time spent away from Nirman was easier than anticipated. In fact, Aradhana would later define her time in college as a "blast." The days seemed to fly by as memories were woven into the fabric of youth. The days were filled with friends who were trying to find themselves as much as she was. Together they used the backdrop of the college as a setting where ideas gave way to ideals. They gathered to debate, to reason, to discover, and to live. The little cafeteria where *"khatas"* or debt logs were opened and closed was cherished for more than the one item on the menu. The three tables it housed were the recipient of both in sync and out of sync drumming of Bollywood movie tunes and sometimes, the odd English rock number.

Things with Nirman couldn't have been better either. He called her every week and they spoke for lengths at a time. Aradhana used to keep a cheat sheet during the conversations to ensure she covered all the important topics and events that had transpired during the week. Based on their structured rapid-fire conversations, she suspected that Nirman maintained something similar. The relationship became stronger as they chatted on the internet daily. She had used her savings to buy a Pentium One desktop computer with a 56K modem. What she did not have was enough money to pay for a monthly internet connection so Nirman sent her a two hundred-dollar wire to pay for the connection for a full year.

She awoke religiously every morning at 6 a.m. so that she could chat with him before he went to his evening class. Sometimes Aradhana would ask Nirman to come online during her evenings so that speaking to him was the last thing she did before she fell asleep. During the next two and a half years, she saved the text of every one of their chat sessions. She had ten floppy disks titled "Love Floppy 1 through 10." Often she would put one of them into the computer and sigh as she read its content. Unlike the telephone conversations, the net conversations were more spontaneous and served as a window into Nirman's world.

It appeared to be a utopian world where Nirman had it all; where success greeted him every morning and life was simple. The streets were clean, money was plentiful, and people were happy. It was also in these conversations that she got a glimpse into the culture he had so openly embraced. She learned of new foods such as PBJS or peanut butter jelly sandwiches, falafel, and BLTs. She learned about how cool Cartman from *South Park* was and who Apu from *The Simpsons* was. Nirman thought that both the politically incorrect cartoon characters were "too funny." He added in short order that Aradhana ofcourse might not approve of the stereotype that Apu was cast as.

She also learned a whole plethora of irrelevant but enjoyable trivia. Once Nirman came online to tell Aradhana that he got "laid."

Aradhana responded with, "What?!!!!! Does 'lay' mean, what I think it means? How could you? We agreed….I never thought you'd let me down," and fifteen more minutes of typing amid tears.

They had promised each other celibacy until marriage. Would Nirman really do that to her? Sure, American girls were supposed to be fast, but she had thought that Nirman had more restraint than that.

In his response, all he wrote was

"Finished? ABAHHH!" he declared in capitals, "You're such a tease. Did I say "laid?" I meant "leid." Leis are just colorful beaded necklaces that they use during Mardi Gras and I got *leid.*"

They laughed both virtually and individually for a good few minutes.

"I love you and miss you too much," she typed.

"Well so do I," he typed back. "I want you to come do your Masters here. I don't want you to say no."

"Can I really do my Masters there? Will I get into a college? Where will I get money? What will I do?" she typed furiously.

"Chill, babe. I have a plan," he declared triumphantly.

The Next Big Thing

*T*he next big thing and the second major development to happen to Aradhana was her own journey to an unknown land. She still wasn't sure of what exactly she wanted to do. She was enjoying her Arts program, especially the subjects of philosophy and psychology. She figured she'd do a masters program in one or the other and then decide what to do after that. Surely there had to be some money to be made in one of those fields.

She prepared for her GRE but halfway through the process was hit by a cold fact: she only had a three-year degree and most colleges in the U.S. would not consider her without a four-year degree. Her only hope was that some small school would look at her good grades and make an exception. She had already taken money for the GRE application from Nirman and knew that he was stretched to his limit. Since her parents knew nothing about this plan, she couldn't ask them for any money. There was no easy way to earn money in the small city she lived in without getting the rumor mill started about her family's financial stability. Teenagers from "good" families were not expected to be on the streets earning a living—all such responsibilities fell on the parents. It was considered unacceptable for a child within a decent family to work. As Aradhana was almost 21, she was by no means a child, but as long as she was still single and pursuing her education, it was the responsibility of the Kapoor family to provide for her. It would be a sacrilege if one of Gauri's kitty party friends or Mr. Kapoor's business colleagues saw Aradhana working. Aradhana thought this idea to be rather ironic in a country where child labor was openly ignored and even employed. Aradhana was given a small allowance to cover her petrol costs and other expenses; however, even with the savings she had accumulated, it did not go far when converted to dollars.

She felt terrible about taking money from Nirman but he was insistent. Even after some assistance, she could not apply to any more than the complimentary four colleges to whom the GRE scores were sent as part of the GRE application fee. Her choice of colleges was not based on either interest or knowledge of their offerings—they were selected because of their proximity to Nirman. She chose three colleges in California, one being Nirman's college. Then randomly, she selected a little known college in Massachusetts. In true Aradhana style, there was no good explanation for it, just an inclination to do something that didn't fit. It was Sienna Fione College in Cambridge, Massachusetts.

Given that she had less than a month to prepare and the fact that quantitative reasoning was not her strong subject, she still did reasonably well on her GRE's—a score of 1450 out of 1600, which would get her into a decent school. She did what she thought was a kick-ass job on her essays. As directed by her professors, she wrote her recommendations by herself and had them sign it. She thought she did a great job on them as well. She gathered the transcripts of all her various diplomas and the short-term courses she had done in addition to her college degree to make up for not having a four-year degree. Two of the California colleges suggested that she apply as an undergraduate transfer for the fourth year and the third one sent her a cryptic email apologizing for the mistake they had made and were now withdrawing the offer for admission because of her lack of a four-year degree. The offer of acceptance must still be enroute to her, she gathered.

"Not everything works as smoothly in the U.S of A as people give credit for," she declared in an email to Nirman.

Using her limited knowledge of the US, she asked Nirman if she could sue them.

"Clearly, the mental trauma and the emotional setback, not to mention the funds dispensed as a result of this judgment must present a case in America's litigious society," she wrote to him, adding a winking emoticon at the end of the sentence. She knew she would never do something like that. Plus, it was probably their prerogative to offer and withdraw admissions from whomever they pleased.

The big surprise came when she got the acceptance letter from Sienna Fione College in Cambridge, Massachusetts. She waited several days for a withdrawal of this admission offer as well and when it didn't come, she e-mailed them to confirm her acceptance. It was true—she had been admitted. She had limited knowledge of where Massachusetts was and how far it was from California. Nirman's e-mail said it all: to him, it may just as well be a separate country. Did she know how much coast-to-coast flights cost? Whatever prompted her to select Massachusetts? Did she even know anyone who ever lived in such a cold state? Did she know how much it snowed there and how cold she'd be?

"No to all." she responded.

Clearly this was not the most optimal solution if the idea was to be close to Nirman. However, Aradhana was beginning to get excited. Moving to America represented no more being told what to do, what to wear, when to come home, what to eat. No more nosey kitty party aunties, annoying fat-bellied gregarious uncles. No more answering to anyone. For once in her life, she would be able to do just as she pleased without being made to feel guilty about it. She was even beginning to feel distant from Abhay. Suddenly his focus was on gelling his hair and pumping iron. Hanging around his older sister who had stolen his best friend was clearly a style-cramper, so he was not particularly sad to hear that she was leaving.

Surprisingly enough, her parents reacted quite calmly upon hearing the news. In a very un-Kapoorish manner, there was no melodrama, no attacks on how she had cheated and gone behind their backs. All they presented were some good questions such as "How do you plan to pay for this?" An interesting question and one for which unfortunately Aradhana had no answer. Mr. Kapoor then did something that surprised Aradhana more than anything—he offered to pay for at least one semester with the promise that he'd help her with additional semesters if she needed it. For the first time in a very long time, Aradhana hugged her father.

Road to America

There were several steps that needed to be taken before Aradhana left for America. On her list of "Things to do" were getting a medical clearance, getting a visa, arranging for foreign funds, buying a ticket, shopping, and securing a place to live in the U.S.

The first step was getting her medical records in order. The hardest part of this task, was not taking the vaccinations, but coming up with proof of the vaccinations she had already gotten in the past. No one in India kept track of their medical history with such precision. Record keeping at smaller medical establishments was generally lax, and procedures informal. Even prescriptions didn't need to be documented. Most pharmacies handed you medication without prescriptions. Thankfully, after several visits to the doctor and consultation with her family physician, Aradhana was able to get a somewhat accurate picture of her medical history together.

After that, she applied for her visa at the Chennai consulate. She had heard of several stories of visas being denied but for some reason she wasn't worried. Her case had merit and she was going to see Nirman, so surely no one would stop her if her parents had approved her going. She needed a lot of paperwork from her father, including property papers, business title, proof of funds, a sponsorship statement, and a demand draft for some ungodly dollar amount. The proof of funds was to be for two years of college or $50,000 dollars, which included boarding. No one in their society had that kind of money in their pockets. There were three popular shades of money—white, black and grey. White, was the clean rightfully earned funds. Black and grey on the other hand were the questionable sources of funds, mainly illicit gains that most people kept buried deep away from the income tax piranhas. Everybody had some, and everybody kept it a secret. There were elaborate ploys to turn grey or black money into white. Property transactions were top of the list. The details were too complicated for Aradhana to understand. Aradhana sometimes wondered who decided "white" was the good kind of money and "black" the bad type, but she never got to the bottom of it.

It was strange to see Mr. Kapoor arrange for the funds. He had a tidy sum lying around but most of his savings were invested in his construction company. This was a time to lean hard on friends. There was little shame in seeking help not only because of the time constraints, but also because many had been forced for one reason or another to take part in this kind of elaborate scam over the years. Some needed to show funds for loans, others to inflate earnings, and, of course, to send their children abroad.

The ploy involved depositing the accumulated funds in the requisite bank account, keeping them there for fourty-eight to seventy-two hours and then drawing up a statement of funds. Once the verification was completed, the funds were returned to the rightful—albeit unlawful owners of the black money.

After the paperwork was completed, she and Gauri made arrangements to go to Chennai. They stayed with the same friends of the family that they had when she took her disastrous medical entrance exams. The appointment was set for the day after their arrival. Aradhana dreamt up various scenarios that would be played out at the visa counter. Would they ask to see all the paperwork? Would they interview her? Would everyone be dressed in suits? She was confident but nervous. The appointment did not specify a time, but only indicated that applications were accepted on a first-come, first-serve basis until 10 a.m. Unknown to her, Mr. Kapoor had arranged to have one of his employees travel separately and get in the visa line at 5 a.m. When Aradhana got to the Consulate with Gauri at eight, she was shocked to see that had it not been for her father's foresight, there would have been a few hundred people in front of her. Some had even camped there overnight. It was the first time she truly understood the desire and drive of people to get to the "land of milk and honey." The light in their eyes was something she would never forget. She, for one, was sanguine—driven by love and by adventure to an unknown land. These people had a dream while she was just escaping. Some would have their dreams shattered today, but she knew they would come back. While in line, she heard some say they had waited for ten years for their green card and now the moment had finally arrived. They were going to sell everything they had and go to the U.S. to change their lives forever. Then there were people she hadn't expected to see: priests, people in *dhotis* that didn't speak a word of English, people with rubber slippers and untucked shirts. She wondered about them as she stood in line. *What business did these people have there? How could they afford to make the trip? What would they do once they got there?*

Before she knew it, she was asked to go inside alone with her papers. She wasn't sure what she'd find there. She had expected to be seated across a table from the Counselor General but instead she found that it looked an awful lot like a bank. People were called up to a window, answered a few questions, and were done in less than five minutes. She saw a lot of Indian people working administrative tasks but all the people behind the counters were white. She hadn't ever seen many white people face to face before. For all its diversity, there were few foreigners in India. The only ones she had seen were backpacking tourists or on television.

Ahead of her were two women who seemed to be mother and daughter. The mother spoke little English but from what Aradhana could make out, it seemed she wanted to go visit her older pregnant daughter. The girl, who was around Aradhana's age, put her file through the skinny slot between the counter and bulletproof window. The man behind the counter flipped through it. In a tone more rude than required, he asked her several questions about their family and assets in India which the girl answered politely.

He then quizzed the woman, who, in her limited English, kept repeating,

"My daughter pregnant, first baby."

Aradhana was shocked when she heard the girl plead over what seemed to be a "denied" stamp on her paperwork. The man would have none of it and asked them to leave. Apparently they had been rejected for a lack of assurance that they would return. The woman had tears in her eyes, but remained stoic. Aradhana was still trying to catch their conversation on their way out when she heard the man call "Next!"

She had taken the Test of English as a Foreign Language or TOEFL and watched many English movies, but when the sharply dressed, clean-cut gentleman spoke to her from behind the glass, she didn't respond. It was a different accent from what she was used to—she half-expected him to speak the way an Indian would. Still distracted from having watched the mother and daughter, she found herself saying "Sorry," the second time he repeated "Next."

The visa officer asked her something about her graduate program, whether she had any family there, and something about her funds. The next thing she heard him say was to come back in the afternoon to collect the visa.

As she walked out of the room, everything began to sink in. She was going to an unknown land where she wouldn't understand people at first, and they wouldn't understand her.

When she and her mother returned home, there were celebrations all around. A five-year student visa had been granted. Funds for the first semester were secured. As to a place to stay, a distant relative surfaced in Boston. A cousin of a cousin, who was said to have good values, would host Aradhana for a week until other accommodations were finalized. Aradhana hated the thought of imposing on this individual she had not known had existed until then; however, her guilt lessened when she saw the super deluxe grade A strand of pearls with matching gold earnings and the heavy maroon and gold *saree* that her parents were sending along with her as a token of thanks for the woman's hospitality. Aradhana figured she didn't eat much, and would soon be out of that aunty's house. *How hard and how much of an imposition can staying with the woman be*? she thought to herself.

Gauri had packed two huge suitcases for Aradhana. One had all the lentils and spices a person could ever eat, along with heavy packages of rice and flour. There was also a ridiculously large leather jacket that the salesperson had assured Gauri was an export item. The shapeless jacket with drawstrings was apparently in fashion and coveted by all girls traveling abroad. More importantly, it had been tested in subzero temperatures (as evidenced by no complaints or returns), which would come in handy in Massachusetts. Gauri had filled the second suitcase with clothes and shoes, lest it turned out the United States didn't have decent western wear. Having spent most of their lives disagreeing, the one thing both Aradhana and Gauri seem to be equally concerned about was how difficult it would be for Aradhana to buy anything in the United States.

• • •

Gauri called Aradhana to her room a few weeks before Aradhana was to leave. She sat across from Aradhana on the bed. She wore a pink and white salwar kameez with paisley print. Her hair was tied into a loose bun, and her face looked radiant. It had a "just washed" sheen to it. Her almond shaped eyes focused gently but deeply on Aradhana. Aradhana, looked expectantly at her mother. She wore a pair of dark blue jeans, along with a mustard tee shirt that clung to her frame. Her hair was loose, and she tucked it behind her ears as she sat waiting for Gauri to begin.

"Aradhana, I know you think that I don't understand you," she said.

Aradhana wasn't quite sure how to respond to her mother who was sitting less than a foot away from her on her bed. She looked down as a sign of respect, not sure of what to say next.

Her mother continued.

"Amrita and Aasma have always followed my lead. You on the other hand have always had your own mind. I· know it may have seemed to you that I haven't always supported you, but I was only trying to protect you."

Aradhana found her voice again.

"How can making me feel judged and always comparing me to Amrita and Aasma be protecting me? You never accepted me for who I am. You always wanted me to be like the rest. Well, I am not them and I never will be."

Gauri interrupted.

"That's the thing, I don't want you to be like them. The same things that I was afraid of you for are the very things that will make you successful. I know that you are extremely independent and have your own mind. But don't forget, I am also your mother. I know how sensitive you are. You are more like me that you know or would like to admit. If nothing else, just remember one thing. Always, follow your mind and not your heart. The heart will come to accept what the mind thinks is right. It's one sure way to stop from getting hurt."

"Can we please not be pessimistic all the time? I am not going forever. You can give me the life lessons when I come back in two years. For now, all I know is that I have absolutely no idea of what to expect." Aradhana chimed.

"All right, all right," Gauri smiled. "Just don't think I am deaf or blind. I may not have said anything, but I know what's going on, and why the US has suddenly become so attractive for you. Also, don't think I had'nt realized for all these years, who you were spending so much time with."

Before Gauri could finish her sentence, Aradhana, jumped off the bed, and hugged her mother. Partly, because she couldn't believe the conversation she was having with her mother and partly because she wanted to end it on a good note.

• • •

Mother and daughter were joined at the hip until Aradhana left. They sampled every restaurant in the city. Aradhana had never seen Gauri let her hair down before. Gauri insisted they take *Bambi*, instead of the car. Apart from the usual fare of Chinese and Indian food, Gauri had insisted they eat American food. Since neither was sure what American food really was, *fast food* that included pizza, burgers, and fries had to suffice.

They watched her favorite movie, "The Sound of Music," together. They even watched the latest Bollywood flick at a nearby theatre. It didn't disappoint with its clear dichotomy of good guys, and bad guys, the forbidden love between the rich girl and poor guy, a rain song, thrashing of the bad guys, and the typical off screen intermission experience where they had the usual *Thumbs Up* cola and samosas.

Aradhana felt closer to her mother than she had in a very long time. As the day to leave approached, her heart was filled with a strange heaviness. An uncomfortable tingling sensation gripped her whole body. Both Aasma and Amrita were flying down to Hyderabad to see her off along with their extended families. All the wheels were in motion. Suddenly though, she didn't want to go.

The Legacy

Gift of the Magi?

*A*radhana had never understood just how much Gauri loved her, nor had she realized that she was more like her mother than Gauri let her know. In fact, that was the reason Gauri was so strict with her—she would die before she let Aradhana feel the pain she'd felt. How helpless she felt in not being able to express herself to her own daughter. She had hoped that the bond of blood between them would have allowed Aradhana to understand her but Aradhana didn't. Amrita and Aasma were different. They trusted her and did not question her whereas Aradhana was always confrontational. She knew that Aradhana was not to blame. Living in Amrita and Aasma's shadow had been tough for her. That was the reason she had drifted more towards her brother Abhay. She seemed to have made a resolve to prove that she was different, and better than her sisters—just not at the same things.

Aradhana had barely even spoken to her about her decision to go to the United States. Gauri knew nothing about the country beyond the few Hollywood movies she had seen. These were limited to the classics like Sound of music, and the Wizard of Oz—she insisted that all her children saw them too. She had also rented every Disney production that the local video store had. However, neither the classics nor the Disney movies truly gave her a sense of what life there must be like. The American dream of a house in the suburbs, beautiful children, a white picket fence, and a couple of dogs had caused significant turmoil within her. She had a nice big house and beautiful children but she kept thinking that something big was missing: a loving husband and inner peace. She had been struggling with her identity for so long that she had forgotten who she had once been.

Since her marriage, Gauri had lost all identity as an individual. All she was ever perceived as was someone's daughter, or wife, or a mother. She avoided any opportunity to think of how her life metamorphosed. It hadn't always been like this but it was like this for as far back as she chose to remember. Nobody cared to ask her about what she liked or wanted. It was implicitly agreed that her likes and dislikes were subordinated to those of others. She was still an individual with needs but no one seemed to recognize them. Her relationship with her husband was a farce. The last time he invoked any feeling in her was years ago. They had sex but only for his satisfaction, never hers. She wished she wasn't so acutely aware of what she was missing. Did he not see the total void in her eyes? Probably not, seeing that he never bothered to make eye contact with her. It was all about *his* needs. There was nothing more to it. How could he, of all people, assume that she didn't have desires, especially after all that he knew? She was so tired of this life and what it represented. While the physical element was significant, in the grand scheme of things, it was still too small to her. There were other things she missed more in this life.

She had several talents that she had suppressed when she got married. She was an excellent painter and wrote poetry. But in the end, these did not seem to matter. Her paintings were too bold and abstract to appeal to her husband. She had tried to share her feelings with him when they got married but it quickly dawned on her that they were very different.

It began with a painting of the goddess Durga, considered by many Hindus to be one of the manifestations of *shakti,* or strength, the female cosmic force and energy that sustained the universe. Goddess Durga's name literally meant "beyond reach or inaccessible." She symbolized the victory of good over evil forces. According to Hindu mythology, the gods created the goddess as they concentrated their powers to win the long battle against the *asuras* and demons. She was shown typically in the Hindu world to have between four to twenty arms. The most common renditions showed her with eight to ten arms. Each hand had a weapon or symbol in it given by each of the gods from whom she was created. Common forms showed her as holding the trident, discus, bow, arrow, sword, dagger, shield, conch, lotus, rosary, and the *kalash,* or divine cup. Gauri's rendition showed the goddess with eight arms; however, unlike the other versions that showed the goddess bearing arms in each hand, her rendition tried to capture the essence of the goddess as a woman. The goddess's arms slowly faded and evolved into different animals. In Gauri's mind, each figure was symbolic of a woman's role or conflict in life. They included the cow, the nurturer; the lioness, the provider; the mare, the breeder; the fox, the intellectual; the snake, the manipulator; the dog, the loyalist; the mongoose the protector; and the cat, the loner.

Gauri had been very passionate about trying to show several things that were going on in her mind at the time she had painted it. She wanted to show how even a goddess of strength and vanquisher of evil was not immune to the challenges or different forms a woman needed to take. Surely, despite her strength and greatness, the goddess would face similar challenges in a mostly male dominated world. It was saddening to her that in the Hindu culture where several female goddesses were represented as symbols of strength and intelligence, their mortal forms struggled to hold their own. She used the goddess Durga to highlight this fact. She also wanted to demonstrate that despite the numerous forms or roles a woman needed to take, she essentially kept her form while incorporating all elements into herself. The normally radiant and victorious Durga looked tired in her oil on canvas, but not lost.

Gauri's husband had looked at the painting with great disdain.

"What are you trying to say?" he asked. "This is rubbish. You should paint beautiful flowers and landscapes."

But Gauri wasn't interested in painting flowers or landscapes. She did not even bother showing her poetry to her husband as she was sure he would neither understand nor appreciate her poems. These too were full of symbols and metaphors that expressed discord.

Gauri found it both fascinating and ironic that her own name represented an incarnation of the goddess Durga, the ultimate symbol of strength. Nobody knew Gauri for who she was—not her husband, not her children, and not her kitty party friends. Instead, she showed them what they wanted to see. It was easier to live with the status quo than to rebel and she knew she would drive herself to madness if she tried. The more she wanted to fight off certain characteristics, the more she took them on. She thought of her relationship with Amrita and Aasma. She had made them into perfect women so they would not have to struggle with their identities as she had. She had believed that maybe, if they had been taught from the beginning not to have any identity, they would not question things and become unhappy when they discovered the world wasn't as fair as they were taught to believe.

• • •

She was a generation ahead of them but although she had been brought up to believe in equality, expression, and self-conformation, she knew now it was all a lie. She wished she had been programmed in her early years to believe that it was her role to suppress her identify for the greater good of her husband and family.

As the only child of a senior army officer and a strong woman with a Ph.D in English, Gauri had been brought up with a strong identity. Her father, Colonel Sidhant, had taught her everything he would have taught a son, including how to fire a rifle. They practiced in the backyard using oil tins and any other cans they could find for targets. He also taught Gauri how to run and long jump. When she was sixteen years old, he let her drive the army jeep. Gauri had been extremely athletic while growing up, but even the slightest examination of her physical self at this point fooled even her into believing it was a lie. She still didn't know whether her father had taught her these skills because he wished he had a son, or whether he truly believed that she should be liberated. He always let her believe it was the latter. He used to tell her,

"I will teach you all I know. What you choose to do with it is your decision."

For a man who had seen half a dozen wars, he was as soft as could be. When he came home, he made requests rather than barked orders. Gauri had seen him give training to junior officers and interact at the army officers' club. There he seemed like an entirely different person. He was strong, firm and commanded respect. At home, though, he seemed to melt into his wife's arms.

Her mother, Savitri was the ultimate symbol of sophistication. While she could easily have been a trophy wife with her tall stature, sharp oval face, and deep dark eyes, she was anything but that. While she proudly stood by her husband's side at every opportunity, she never did anything she didn't want to do. Though she never vied for the spotlight, she was always the center of attention. Regardless of where they were posted by the army, she always taught English at the local army school. Gauri often saw the look of pure awe in the eyes of the students, who constantly looked for excuses to talk to her mother. Gauri's mother had taught her to have confidence and believe in herself. When Gauri wrote her first poem at age five, her mother stuck it on the refrigerator and gave Gauri a gold star, promising her any gift for every poem she wrote. Gauri became a prolific poet and, keeping her promise, her mother always gave her whatever she asked for. She carefully saved all the poems and catalogued them in a binder that she called "Gauri's Collection."

Gauri adored her parents and admired them more than anyone else as they instilled such confidence and love of life in her heart. Winning their approval was more important to her than anything else. She had been genetically gifted with their brains and talent. Their constant encouragement just added fuel to the fire within her and Gauri excelled in what ever she did. Because of her father's postings from the army, the family never spent more that five years in one city and traveled all over India. Gauri missed having a stable life and a permanent group of friends. Her only consolation was that she was not alone as there were several other army officers' children who were in the same boat. Initiation into their circle was fairly easy. The only friends you made were also children of army officers and you saw them both in school and socially. The Indian Armed Forces took great pride in being the only institution devoid of corruption. They viewed their strict rules and guidelines in great superiority to the anarchy that enveloped the rest of the country and the fraternity tended to stick close to their own. All Gauri had seen was life within the Armed Forces. When she became a teenager, she met other teens through the private army clubs and socialized liberally. There was a code of behavior and everyone respected it. If there was a dance in the army club, the young gentlemen would first seek permission from the girls' fathers for the dance, even before he asked her.

Gauri had blossomed into a young attractive woman; however, she lacked the savvy that her mother posessed. That being said, her mother always made her feel like she was the most beautiful girl in the world. However, like all teenagers, suddenly what her family said wasn't enough. She needed affirmation from the world outside. Gauri wanted to be all that she was led to believe she could be. She could no longer respect the confines of the spirit of competition and independence with which she had been brought up.

• • •

She was eighteen years old and had just finished high school. She still socialized at the army club and attended all the events. It was the Christmas Eve dance. Even though a very small population of the Indian Armed Forces was Christian, it did not stop them from celebrating the event with pomp and splendor. Any reason to drink, eat and make merry was good enough. At that time, while alcohol was not widely available to the general population, it was available to the Indian Armed Forces.

He was twenty-six and a Captain in the Army. He came up to their table and asked to dance with her. He had fair skin, blue eyes, and was sharp and attractive as many of the young officers there were. His eyes were the ultimate attraction—they were rare, forbidden and mischievous. There were several other single women there that night, but he came to her. His name was Captain Rajeev. Gauri always discounted young men who approached her, as she thought they just wanted to impress her father, who was their commanding officer. However, they knew not to mess with their commanding officer's daughter—a simple dance and that was that. It turned out that this officer was only visiting for a short training course and would return to his hometown in a week. As etiquette required, he came up to her father and requested permission to dance with his daughter. Colonel Sidhant was in a good mood that night, as he always was when his beautiful wife Savitri was next to him and gave the young man his assent.

She had never met anyone like him. She was not a good dancer, but he kept tandem with her every move. He made her feel like the best dancer on the floor. He smiled at her sometimes confidently, and sometimes mischievously. She tried to look down a few times, anything to avert his magnetic gaze, but his eyes commanded hers to make contact. After a few dances, they joined a few other officers and their dates at a table that was within plain view of the other ranked officers who occasionally used their trained vision to check on their daughters. Colonel Sidhant did the same. Gauri seemed to be having a good time even though he knew she was going through an awkward stage. He had planned several battle strategies and was an expert on complex psychological warfare techniques but when it came to dealing with his eighteen-year-old daughter, he felt ill-equipped. He relied on Savitri's judgment when it came to tightening or loosening the reins. On this occasion, Savitri had whispered into his ear that he had better call Gauri back to the table but Sidhant was feeling liberal that night. Gauri seemed to be having such a good time that he didn't have the heart to call her back. If they could not let go of her in an army club, how could they possibly watch her get married, he joked to his wife. Savitri was pleasantly surprised at Sidhant's stance. She knew that sometimes she was too possessive of Gauri. She had been fortunate enough to find love and now she had to let Gauri do the same thing. She let Sidhant's judgment prevail.

Gauri was discovering herself. Men were expressing interest in her not as a commanding officer's daughter but for who she was as herself. They laughed at her jokes and took interest in her views. Captain Rajeev was especially indulgent. When he offered her a drink, she evaluated her options. She could either continue to let her hair down or she could be as righteous as she always was, and act like the commanding officer's daughter. She decided to let her hair down. Out of respect for her father, she asked that her drinks be mixed with

Coke so that no one would know. After two drinks, she was quite tipsy. She had tried alcohol before, but it was in tiny quantities and under the watchful eye of her father. She felt the drinks relax her further and giggled more liberally. For his part, Captain Rajeev was a real charmer. He encouraged her to relax, showed great interest in her opinions from everything from Kashmir to the world wars. But he also made her feel like a woman—an attractive, intelligent woman that he was very interested in. Gauri couldn't remember the last time she had laughed so much and was surprised when she heard the clock chime 11 p.m. Gauri's parents were ready to leave so Colonel Sidhant made eye contact and with a nod of his head, indicated for Gauri to join them. Captain Rajeev and Gauri went over to the table and Captain Rajeev requested permission to let Gauri stay a while longer. Colonel Sidhant refused, but Captain Rajeev persisted, promising that he would personally take responsibility and ensure he and the others at the table would get Gauri home. Her father hesitated for a bit, but Gauri pleaded—she was an adult now and could take care of herself. Plus, in such a tightly knit group no one took advantage of the commanding officer's daughter. Her father agreed, saying that she had to be home by midnight. After some bargaining, he agreed to let her stay out until 12:30 a.m.

After her parents left, Gauri continued to drink and called her new suitor Captain rather than Rajeev as she liked the sound of it. There were three other couples at the table. As the slow romantic songs started, one by one, they left for the dance floor but Gauri and the Captain stayed put, continuing to talk and flirt.

They had a table under a tree in a dark corner. At first he held her hand and she didn't pull back. As they sat at the table, he touched her thigh under the white tablecloth. Gauri had not anticipated this, but she wasn't ready to pull away from her first experience at physical intimacy. She looked around to make sure no one was watching. As she smiled at him, he continued and then gestured for her to follow her. The club was big and the lighting was mostly limited to the main club area which included the officer's club and a few dining room options. Once outside, he began walking her away from the club. Not having really experienced alcohol before, she was giddy from the three rum and colas she had consumed and was therefore only faintly aware of what was happening. She remembered that he whispered something into her ear that made her giggle as he took her to an area covered with rocks. Looking around, he assured there was no one in sight. There were several trees and a walled compound between the rocks and the road. Within minutes, he had her pushed up against the rocks. She was still giggling as she had never been touched before. He lifted the pastel dress with the sash that she was wearing and yanked her panties down. She was delirious as his tongue tickled her down below and continued to giggle. This time he stifled her giggle and told her to be quiet. Before she knew what was happening, he was inside her. As he held her tightly and moved deep within her, she suddenly realized what was happening. It hurt greatly and she was bleeding. She wasn't ready for this—she had thought they'd have fun and then, when she was ready, they'd stop. She started to cry and begged him to stop.

"Please, Rajeev STOP. Please, I don't want to. Please it hurts. Please don't do this," she bellowed.

He told her she wanted it. She wasn't really sure of what she wanted, but she knew it wasn't this. As tears flowed from her eyes, she continued to beg him to stop. Everything was hurting, including the rock behind her back. Then, just as suddenly as he started, he stopped and she felt very wet. She wasn't sure if it was her blood or his semen. He told her to put on her clothes. As she did, she wiped the blood off her thighs with a handkerchief from her purse. Her dress fell into its position again, but her legs were hurting and she was still crying. He took his handkerchief out and gave it to her, telling her to stop crying and informing her how she should feel—it was fun and she enjoyed it. If she wanted to be a woman, she should stop acting like a baby. This is what grown people did, and they enjoyed it. Didn't she want to be a woman?

Because she feared him, she stopped crying as she didn't want this to happen again. He made her promise that she would not mention it to anybody. He warned her that if she did, everyone would think she was a whore, and nobody liked a whore. When she said she wanted to go home, he told her that he'd drop her with the others because otherwise the "old man" would freak out. She hated hearing him call her father that. By that point, she hated everything about him. Here she was in pain, and he didn't once ask her how she felt. They went back to the table and spent the longest fifteen minutes of her life. One couple was giggling, and whispering sweet nothings into each others ears, while the other discussed merits of foreign education. Rajeev drank his whiskey and soda and looked at the sky with great intensity as if looking to discover a new star. Gauri felt wet,

cold and dirty. She wringed her palms and spent fifteen minutes trying not to howl.

"Time to drop you home, old girl", Rajeev said jovially, as others
smiled.

When she entered the house, she was grateful to find that all the
lights were off. She knew that if her mother or father saw her, they
would know and even if they didn't, she would burst out crying. She
felt humiliated and sick. What had started as playful fun had ended
with a feeling of disgust and violation. Was she really a whore to
have allowed it to go that far? Her parents would never forgive her.

"Gauri?" her mother called out from her bedroom.

"Yes, it's me," she replied with a cracked voice.

"Is everything okay?" her mother asked worriedly.

Gauri knew that if her voice cracked again, her mother would be
out of bed in a flash and there would be no escaping the truth. With as
much strength as she could muster, she kept her voice even and assured her that everything was okay.

Over the weeks that followed, Gauri felt sick. She wasn't sure if it
was just shame or whether she had physically fallen ill. She continued
to feel lightheaded and vomited often. When she missed her period,
she knew something was very wrong and that she needed to figure out
what was going on very quickly.

She could not risk going to the army doctor, as everyone there
knew her family. She took a bus into the city and went to see a gynecologist. She spent the entire hour's journey dreading what she would
discover. She was hoping she was wrong as she could not afford to be
right. She was just eighteen—she had a long way to go before she
could even imagine the unimaginable. She hadn't heard from Rajeev
since that day, not that she had expected to or wanted to. All she had
heard was that he had returned to his base camp.

When she got to the doctor, she immediately sensed her appre-
hension and easily guessed her age. Presumably Gauri was not the
first person to come to her with this question. When the test results
came back, her worst fear came to pass—she was indeed pregnant.

Gauri could not hide the fact anymore and needed her mother. If
there was one person she trusted to guide her, it was her mother. She
was struggling with several emotions and couldn't make sense of anything. During the bus ride back, she went over in her head several
times what she planned to tell her mother, but it never seemed right.
There was no right way to describe what had happened to her. Guilt,

fear, anger, and betrayal burdened her soul. Gauri decided she'd tell Savitri what happened word for word. If her mother thought she was at fault, then maybe she was.

When she got home, Gauri put her head down on her mother's lap and told her exactly what happened. She choked on her words several times and avoided eye contact. What if she saw disgust in her mother's eyes? What if she had let her mother down? Gauri had expected to be yelled at and cursed for her stupidity, but she couldn't have been more far away from the truth. When she was done, her mother lifted her head from her lap and hugged her tightly. Wiping the tears from Gauri's eyes, she looked directly into Gauri's eyes and assured her that it wasn't her fault. She was just a child. It was not a sin to have sexual feelings, but taking advantage of someone *was* a sin. Gauri showed no signs of her tears drying up, so her mother let her cry for what seemed like several hours, running her fingers through her hair. When Gauri was done, her mother told her to find courage within herself. Her family would always be there for her, but she also needed internal strength. Her mother told her she loved her more than anything else but that even she couldn't feel the real pain that Gauri was feeling. There was no easy way of erasing what happened. First she needed to understand that she had been violated against her will. It was not her fault, so one emotion she should not feel was guilt. For the first time since that night, Gauri believed that was true. Her mother was her pillar, and she knew that she would always be there for her. Her mother vowed that she would find out all she could about Rajeev, but Gauri made her promise that they would not beg him for support. In fact, as far as she was concerned, if she never saw him again in her life, that would be too soon. A man who could walk away saying such horrible things as he had would not come through. Savitri, however, felt a little differently—what if Rajeev was sorry for his actions? What if there was some redemption on his part? She needed to talk to her husband and see if there was some way to right this wrong. If Gauri had this child, then it needed a father. She wasn't really sure what they could expect from Rajeev, but they had to try. All they knew about him was that he belonged to the second armored battalion and was posted in the northeastern center in Assam. Other than that everything else was unknown—Gauri's father would have to find out more.

After she spoke to Gauri, Savitri had a long conversation with her husband. He was outraged, and promised he'd make Rajeev pay. Like

Gauri, he felt a tremendous heaviness in his heart, as if somehow he was to blame. He had let his poor little girl down, the one he protected with his life. He hadn't let so much as a scratch pass unnoticed up until now. Now, the biggest violation possible had been perpetrated on his daughter and he could do nothing to undo it. He was usually a good judge of character, but his this time his judgment had let him down. If he hadn't given Gauri permission to stay out late, this would never have happened. He didn't even know what to make of Rajeev. The idea that he had violated the daughter of a commanding officer within the secure confines of the officers club was unthinkable. He promised Savitri that he'd hunt Rajeev down and shoot him even if it meant ruining his own career. Savitri reasoned with him; maybe Rajeev was sorry for his actions. If he heard Gauri was pregnant, he may want to redeem himself. It was a chance worth taking as they had nothing to lose at this point. After great agony, he conceded his self-respect and agreed. He would call the commanding officer of the brigade that Rajeev was stationed at and inquire about him.

The call did not go well. Savitri stood by her husband the entire time and watched him tactfully dodge any direct questions on the reason for his enquiry. She saw that her husband, who was usually very direct, was having a hard time with the delicacy this conversation required. But this was for his daughter—his ego did not matter, his rank did not matter, and what this commanding officer or anyone else thought definitely did not matter. After some questions about Rajeev that were innocuously presented, her husband became silent. After that there were some monosyllabic responses before her husband abruptly excused himself from the call and hung up. His normally controlled face had fallen and he looked like a mouse that had been cornered. His horrified eyes stared at Savitri, as if asking for help. Savitri knew this wasn't good news. As they sat down, she learned that Captain Rajeev was married and had a two-year-old son. In fact, he was married to the daughter of another commanding officer. Not that it mattered anymore. This man, who had violated his daughter, was already a father. Perhaps if Rajeev had a daughter instead of a son, he could have imagined the outrage of his act, thought Sidhant as he quivered aloud. For once, Savitri had no answers. Both wondered silently how they would tell Gauri this news. Savitri knew it had to come from her, but she also knew that Gauri would be expecting some guidance. Just a few hours earlier, she had told her daughter not to lose hope and now, here they were without any. Within minutes of deliberation, Savitri knew what had to be done. She discussed it with her husband, who agreed. All they had to do was make sure Gauri was in agreement.

When Savitri informed Gauri that Rajeev was already married, Gauri stared blankly at the wall and showed no emotion. Unlike before, there were no tears. Savitri was afraid to see her beloved daughter who was usually so highly emotional show no signs of life. As she walked towards her, Gauri did not even blink. Savitri shook her, and told her that she had to react, otherwise she would never deal with it.

It was only when Savitri told her that both she and her father thought that she should have an abortion did Gauri let a single tear fall. Worried that this might not be what Gauri wanted, Savitri told her that, in the end, the decision was entirely up to her. If Gauri wanted the baby, they would support her in that as well. She was about to go on to explain the pros and cons of both when Gauri silenced her with a single dismissive wave of her hand.

"I don't want to have anything to do with this baby or Rajeev. They can both die," she said hollowly.

Savitri chose not to respond to her daughter's harsh words. Though she herself had suggested the abortion, she did not think of it as death or murder of a baby. As far as she was concerned, the fetus was still developing and not yet quite human.

Savitri tried to explain the merits of the choice with a philosophical discussion. "A child not conceived of love is doomed from the start. It's better not to bring a child into the world than resent the child for no fault of its own," she said. "Every time you looked at the child, it would only bring up feelings of resentment and hate, and memories of an unhappy time. It would be better for everyone if the child were not brought into the world." Her words had no impact on Gauri. For the first time since Gauri's own birth did Savitri feel that her daughter was distant from her. Gauri, who had cried her heart out only a few hours ago, was now not letting her hurt show. Savitri thought maybe it was for the best. Her daughter had moved from denial to pain to anger—hopefully she was on her way to recovery.

Still, Savitri knew that Gauri had always cared about what people said about her, as she craved social acceptance. There was most certainly fear in Gauri's heart that Savitri knew she wasn't admitting. Savitri wanted to give Gauri the time that she needed to heal, but she couldn't walk away yet. She knew that Gauri wanted to be alone, but this pain that she was feeling watching her only child stare into the void was greater than anything she had felt before. She sat with Gauri until night fell, neither saying anything during the hours that passed. Her husband stopped by twice but could see that there was scarcely any room for a third person, so he did the unselfish thing and let them be.

The silence was finally broken when Gauri cried that she wanted the baby gone as soon as possible. Savitri assured her that it was the right decision—Gauri had the support of her family and that was all that mattered.

Over the next week Gauri kept her distance from everyone. She created an invisible wall between herself and the outside world including her parents, whom she revered. It was hardest for Savitri. At a time when she wanted nothing other than to be close to her daughter, her daughter wanted to have little to do with her. Savitri believed that once the abortion was over, she would have her daughter back. Yes, the pain and anger would continue for some time, but she had faith in the love the family shared. Savitri set up the appointment with the doctor and waited in anticipation for the day that the pain growing in Gauri's womb would become no more.

Savitri though of the cruel irony of the fact that her daughter was violated on Christmas. The Magi brought gifts for the baby Jesus but what had they brought for her sweet innocent daughter?

Broken Wings

*G*auri's life was about to change forever, and no one saw it coming. It all happened too quickly and then time stopped. Despite what anyone said, Gauri couldn't help but hold herself responsible. It happened just a day before a new chapter in her life would begin.

As was her usual routine, Savitri was on her way back from school at 3:15 p.m. Being the wife of the commanding officer, she had the luxury of having an army jeep drive her to and from the army school. Gauri and her family had been in this town for a little over five years, which was longer than they had been in any other town. The driver of the jeep, an army employee, had been in the town for over fifteen years. He had traversed the route between the school and the house more often than he could remember. He was especially fond of Savitri or "Savitri madam" as he referred to her. She was not snooty like some of the other commanding officers' wives. She didn't bark orders. It was more like she was making a request when she asked him to pick her up at a certain time. He respected her immensely for the respect she gave to everyone and the respect she commanded. The ride back started like any other ride between the school and home.

Savitri sat thinking of her daughter. Poor Gauri—how hurt she must feel to shut the world out like that. Gauri liked people—she felt things, and she showed her emotions. This wasn't like her. She was changing from inside but that had to stop. She was too good a person to fundamentally change herself. Savitri tried to imagine what feelings Gauri was experiencing and what was driving a person like her who needed company to become so isolated. Savitri shut her eyes and tried to feel what Gauri was feeling in a way only a mother could do. There was guilt; a heavy burden for things that she could have possibly done differently. What if it really *was* her fault? *No!* Savitri said to herself. There should be no guilt. It wasn't her fault. It wasn't her baby's fault. And then there were other feelings. There was fear—fear of losing control, fear of losing innocence. She imagined Gauri thinking that she would never lose control ever again in her life. Then there must be an internal battle for the unborn child that Gauri was to lose. Even though, she was trying not to bond with the baby, surely Gauri must have felt something. This was probably the strongest emotion inside Gauri, Savitri imagined. She had seen how maternal Gauri had been since she was a little girl. Gauri never had any brothers or sisters of her own, but had always gravitated towards other children. She was incredibly patient with them and Savitri knew that some day she would make a great mother. Savitri's thoughts seamlessly migrated between Gauri's mind and her own. They were, after all, one. It was a divine feeling, and someday Gauri would experience it with her own child. *But not too soon if I can help it*, thought Savitri.

Gauri was planning to attend college just outside town. It would be the first time she would be attending a civil institution. So far every school she had gone to was under the protected walls of the army.

"Those walls had been unable protect her. Maybe she would be better off in the outside world," thought Savitri.

She smiled thinking of how much Gauri was like her and how much she wanted to be like her. She wanted to do her BA in English literature just like her mother. Because Gauri would still be living at home, her commute would be long. But Savitra trusted her driver to bring Gauri to and from college safely.

Savriti's mind wandered off to her husband as well. For the first time in twenty-five years of their marriage, they had nothing to say to each other. Guilt too painful to articulate enveloped them. They both felt that they had let their daughter down. Either of them would have taken Gauri's pain if it meant saving her from it.

As the jeep stopped suddenly, Savitri's thoughts were interrupted. In front of them was a roadblock. A military vehicle had overturned, blocking their regular route. They needed to take a detour which would take them out of the cantonment area. There was no cause for concern as they had taken this route before. It was just not very scenic.

The noise and pollution were significant and the traffic was horrendous. Her husband always joked that if India were under military rule for a decade, it would be returned to a clean and uncorrupted nation. The driver turned the jeep around and got on the main road where traffic was worse than usual. As the vehicles challenged each other for space, Savitri wondered why cars continued to honk when clearly there was no room for more than one car in either direction. By laws that defied physics, multiple cars were squeezed into a space meant for two and cars honked endlessly even when there was no room to pass. Savitri couldn't help but compare this pandemonium to the scenic route they were accustomed to taking. She realized how protected they were in the military environment—at least until one of their own betrayed them. She was not one to hate, but she felt such an overwhelming emotion towards Rajeev that it must have been hate. It was all she had been able to think about since they found about the incident. She had to stop letting this drain her and be strong for Gauri.

When their jeep got on the bridge, Savitri had an ominous feeling. The bridge was built more than forty years ago over a river that remained dry most of the year, and sometimes for years at end. All that remained to be seen from the fifty-foot drop was parched ground as far as the eye could see. As she stared at the veins created by the dry earth, a white Ambassador car packed with eight people drove up behind them. The driver was intoxicated and honked endlessly at the Jeep in front of him in hopes of passing. When he didn't get the signal to pass, he decided to do it anyway. He did not see the large oil truck that was quickly approaching from the opposite direction. As they both tried to make space on the narrow bridge, they ended up pushing the army Jeep off the bridge. As the car toppled through the air, Savitri's last thought was of Gauri, and how much she loved her.

"God, please take care of her," she thought as the car hit the ground.

• • •

Both Gauri and Sidhant went to identify the body, even though the corpses were charred beyond recognition. The police had removed some jewelry from the body and it was positively identified as Savitri's. Despite that, Gauri and Sidhant would have recognized Savitri as even in death and destruction, she exuded a distinct aura. This was not a fitting goodbye for a woman like her—she deserved a more poignant and poetic death. A death without pain. Gauri would never really know how Savitri died or what her last thoughts were. The woman who had kept a family so happy for so long was no more, nor was her strength and courage. How could she have alienated the one person she needed more than anyone else in the last week of her life? Gauri was devastated. First she was given this unplanned child and then her mother's death. It had to be a punishment from a previous life. There was nothing left for her now. She was close to tuning out the whole world but an invisible force made her look at her father.

Sidhant was shattered to the core. There was nothing left in him but his physical form. He showed no emotions and had gone into shock. Gauri realized that his mind and heart were not on a plane that she could reach. He could hear no one and experience nothing. If she had let him, he would have stayed with the charred body until his own body gave in. There was nothing left for him. For a man that had seen untold deaths, this was the one that destroyed him. He would never be the same again. It was then she decided to be unselfish. She was going to support the man who had supported his family all his life. As she gazed at Savitri's charred body she knew it was up to her to make arrangements for her mother's funeral. She knew she had to take her father home so that no one could see this strong man crumble like this. Friends offered to arrange for the funeral, and Gauri consented. Sidhant was unwilling to meet or talk to anyone and kept himself locked up in his room all day.

The funeral took place the next day. There were rituals to be performed and Gauri and Sidhant let the priest do what was necessary. Because the body was charred, it was left covered with a white sheet before it would have to be burned per Hindu tradition. Gauri accompanied the body with her father to the cremation ground. Daughters did not typically light the funeral pyre as it was a right reserved for the sons. Gauri knew her mother would have wanted her to do this and she held her father's hand as he set the pyre aflame. As they watched the body go up in smoke, their minds wondered about the irony of burning someone who had been burned to death but they both knew it had to be done. It was said that an improper funeral would mean that Savitri would be caught between this world and the next.

In their own selfish ways Sidhant and Gauri wanted Savitri to remain with them in this world. Savitri was not done with her responsibilities in this life. It was believed that if a person had not completed their duties in this life or had left something midway, they would remain in this world until the work was taken care of. However, both knew deep down that more than anyone else, Savitri deserved to be set free for her devotion.

A month and half after Savitri's death, Gauri had not heard her father say anything more than the few monosyllabic words that were absolutely necessary for communication. When Gauri forced him to eat, he ate; but only enough to exist. Gauri spent her hours taking care of the house and trying to remind her father that life went on, a fact that she did not believe herself. She had almost forgotten about the child growing inside her. At three months into her pregnancy, she had significant nausea and vomited constantly. Although she tried not to focus on it, it was becoming unbearable. She knew she had long missed her appointment and neglected to take care of the once pressing need, but it just didn't seem like a priority with all the things that were happening around her. When the pain became too much, she decided that she would find the courage and tell her father that she still wanted to abort the child. She wanted to dedicate her life to her him. She felt that she had brought her mother and father whom she loved so dearly great pain and therefore believed in her heart that it was her responsibility to keep her father alive. She knew that Sidhant would never abandon her. So what if he wasn't there for her through her pain? He did love her; he just didn't know how to express it when he was going through his own pain. Even though Gauri and Sidhant were bound by pain, they become distant in their expression of it. She worried about him more than she worried about herself. How could they both be expected to fly with broken wings?

It was in a dream that Sidhant saw Savitri again. She looked just as beautiful as she had in life, but had a sad aura. Sidhant remembered everything about the dream clearly. He remembered laying his head on Savitri's lap and crying until he couldn't breathe anymore. He told her that he wanted more than anything to be with her. This life meant nothing to him, as his soul was with her. When he asked her why she looked sad, Savitri told him that she was sad because of him. Sidhant begged to know why. Why was the love of his life saddened by him? He would do anything to change that. Savitri reminded him that he still had their daughter to think of and that Gauri needed him. Even in death, the responsibility of Gauri was still a burden on her soul. She wanted to leave this world and go into the next, but this fact wouldn't let her. Gauri was a child—*their* child—and she needed her parents. As Savitri was gone, the responsibility of Gauri fell on Sidhant. Gauri was the ultimate symbol of their love, and she needed care, comfort and guidance. Sidhant remembered being filled with guilt and remorse in the dream. He had neglected their child because he was too busy grieving himself. If he was dead and Savitri were alive, that would never have happened, as she would have found the strength for their daughter. After he promised Savitri that he would take care of their daughter and make things right, he begged Savitri not to go but it was then that he awoke.

The first thing Sidhant did when he awoke was go into Gauri's room and sit by her bed and kiss her forehead. She looked so innocent and peaceful in her sleep, unlike the sadness that permeated her face when she was awake.

"I'm sorry," was all that he could mutter softly, but Gauri's ears were too eager to get comfort to miss it. She awoke from her sleep and hugged her father tightly. They cried for what seemed like forever in each other's arms. She told Sidhant about her wish to go forward with the abortion, and how it was already late. He promised her that they would go to the doctor the first thing the next morning.

Despite not having an appointment, the doctor sensed the urgency, and agreed to see Gauri again. After she had examined her, she asked to speak to Sidhant privately. She told him that she was willing to perform the late-term abortion but that there were some complications as there were some moral and physical considerations to be considered, such as Gauri's long-term fertility prospects. She also informed Sidhant that Gauri had something called Hyperemesis Gravidarum, a medical term for excessive vomiting during pregnancy. Though mostly innocuous it could be serious if Gauri didn't take care of herself. Even when the risks were discussed with Gauri, she remained adamant about her decision. She told Sidhant that they were all risks she was prepared to take, but Sidhant found himself strongly opposing Gauri's choice. He had lost Savitri and could not risk losing Gauri or the chance for her future happiness. He was firm—she would have the child and they would take care of it. It did not matter what the world thought.

By this point Gauri found herself happy with her father's persistence, as the woman inside her found herself becoming attached to the life forming within her. While she had but a moment ago, sought to terminate the pregnancy, she had sleepless nights thinking about the flutter in her womb. The womb and what was growing was already depending on her. She had convinced herself that she didn't want the baby. It was the right decision for everyone. Hearing Sidhant however, let an emotion flow that she had held back for too long. She wanted to be a mother. Perhaps she'd be even half as good as her mother. Since she found out that she was pregnant, Gauri had lost the will to live. This would give her a reason to live again. She would live for the baby.

Mumbai Dreams

$\mathcal{S}$ idhant made a solemn oath to now put his promises into action. Within a few weeks, he took a voluntary retirement from the army and moved himself and Gauri to Mumbai, a city in which they had no roots. Many felt Mumbai to be the Mecca of anarchy and chaos. It was an enigma, but many couldn't help but be drawn to its success and anonymity. It was easy to get lost in the labyrinth that defined the city, which is exactly what Sidhant and Gauri wanted. They moved into a small two-bedroom apartment in the heart of the city. Although it was a significant downgrade to their quality of life, there was something about the anonymity of the city that made things easy to deal with. Life was moving along and Sidhant did what he could to ensure Gauri's life remained as normal as possible. He made several trips with Gauri to a nearby small Catholic college and arranged mid-semester admission for her.

In the few weeks that Gauri was in Mumbai, she began to feel violently sick. She would vomit continuously and could not hold in any meal. They got in touch with a gynecologist who confirmed what the earlier diagnosis was. Her Hyperemesis Gravidarum ensured that Gauri had a very hard time during her pregnancy. Her body continued to reject food. She got most of her nutrition intravenously. She was too sick to attend college. Even when she did, she felt terrible; not just physically, but also emotionally. The students and teachers had viewed her suspiciously. She knew what they were thinking of her. They judged her, and probably made their own stories up about how she got pregnant. She had no friends at the college and spoke to no one. Some girls tried to reach out to her but she pushed them away too. The principal of the college, a stern looking nun had called her in when she was about five months pregnant, and her pregnancy was obvious. Despite her stern appearance she was kind; one who it seemed had seen much pain in her life. She asked Gauri, whether she was married. She knew the answer because Gauri's application had clearly said she was unmarried. She asked Gauri whether she had the support of the child's father. Gauri found herself crying before the kindly nun. She told her that this was not a child of love and explained her circumstances. The nun told her that she should take time off until the baby arrived, and then return back to college. She promised her that she would ensure that she lost no additional time and would let her make up for lost time through coaching. Gauri was happy to have this direction. She had been very close to dropping out. The promise of a fresh start made her think that maybe all was not lost.

After she took a leave of absence, Gauri tried to focus on the small joy she felt about the child that was growing inside her. Both she and Sidhant began reading books on parenting, as it had been some time since Sidhant's own firsthand experience and even then he had relied on Savitri's judgment and natural maternal instincts. Their little world was beginning to reflect some hope. There was an unspoken promise that the child would come into this world and make things better. Although Gauri continued to feel ill, she had moments of good health where she found herself enjoying the experience of being a mother. She found happiness in the expeditions with Sidhant to buy baby things, such as a crib, sheets, toys, and other utility items. She also enjoyed the long walks she and her father took whenever she was feeling well. She thought about how her life would have been without her father's support and realized she would never have survived. Suddenly he had assumed the role of the pillar of strength in her life and become the voice of reason.

They didn't know yet whether the child would be a boy or girl, but Gauri found herself hoping that it was a girl so that they could share the special relationship that she and her mother had shared. One day during her seventh month, Gauri fell violently ill and had to be rushed to the emergency room by ambulance. An immediate procedure was done and at two o'clock in the morning, the cries of a baby girl could be heard echoing through the hospital corridors. She was tiny and weighed less than three pounds, but everyone marveled at her sparkling blue eyes. She was put in an incubator and Gauri and the baby were in the hospital for a month. Both recovered miraculously and looked healthy. Gauri and Sidhant named the baby Amrita after Savitri's mother. Their lives were replete with new hope.

• • •

What Gauri had been too busy to notice during her evening walks before the baby was born was a tall, slightly built, wheat complexioned, mustached man who followed her everywhere. With Amrita in her arms and significantly more aware of her surroundings, she now noticed Ashwin for the first time. She viewed him with great hostility and felt he had no business looking at her or her daughter. She was used to some stares but his was more than a passing stare. He seemed to be observing them, sometimes from a distance, and sometimes close by. Once, when leaving her apartment, her eyes caught his. Gathering her courage, she confronted him. What business did he have to follow her around and stare at her and her child? She threatened to report him to the police.

"I'm sorry if I offended you," was all that he said.

She didn't see him for a few months after that.

Gauri started attending college again. The kindly nun had kept her promise and personally tutored Gauri to help make up for the time she had been absent. She gave her tough assignments but Gauri loved every minute of the challenge. College was good. Post-pregnancy, Gauri began to open up and realized that there were a few girls that she really liked. College was beginning to remind her that she was just a young girl like the rest of them. Things were really beginning to look up. Amrita was an angel. It was as if she had felt Gauri's pain throughout the pregnancy and heard and absorbed the conversations about life and fate that Gauri had with her belly during that time. Sidhant's life also had new meaning. He loved the role of a grandfather and father rolled in one. He always scolded Gauri if ever she was upset at Amrita.

"Don't you dare say anything to my princess or I will take her away," he would chide.

Time flew by. Amrita was already a year old and Gauri was in her second year of college.

Gauri began to see Ashwin on the street again, but he kept his distance. Gauri knew that he was watching her but now came to see him as harmless. In fact, she began to find the idea of having him around as somewhat comforting and familiar.

One day when Gauri returned home from college, she found Ashwin sitting with her father in the living room playing with Amrita. Gauri's first reaction was to grab Amrita from his arms, ignoring the disgruntled look her father gave her. However, Amrita did not appear to be in the mood to be taken away yet. Nevertheless Gauri persisted and grabbed Amrita tightly and took her to her room despite her cries. Sidhant walked into Gauri's room to confront her. Why was she being so rude? He knew Gauri was very protective of Amrita, and that was expected, but he didn't understand why she was creating such a scene. Gauri explained her previous encounters with Ashwin, including the confrontation.

Sidhant listened patiently, and then explained that Ashwin lived next door with his sister after having lost both his parents in a car accident. He had just graduated from his final year of civil engineering and was in the process of looking for a job. He had already told Sidhant about how Gauri had confronted him the year before. He also confided that he seemed drawn to Gauri and felt an inexplicable need to protect her from any harm. Gauri couldn't believe that Sidhant was buying into the mumbo jumbo that Ashwin was feeding him. Why did her father trust Ashwin? Sidhant insisted that she was being rude and that was no way to greet someone who had come into their home. He reminded Gauri that in their culture, a guest was equivalent to a god. He insisted that if Ashwin's intentions were bad, he would not have come into their house. By the time they finished their conversation and Gauri went back into the living room, Ashwin had left. Despite Amrita's cries, he had heard everything they had said. Gauri felt a little guilty, but thought that it was for the best. As far as she was concerned, she didn't have any room in her life for any man and probably never would.

Marriages Are Made in.....

S ix months had passed since the incident and Gauri had not seen Ashwin around. One day she got a call while at school telling her to go to the hospital immediately as Sidhant had had a heart attack. The kindly nun at the school arranged for a van from the convent to drive her there. During the ride, various questions rushed through her mind. What if something happened to her father? What would become of Amrita and her? Suddenly her heart skipped a beat. What had happened to Amrita? Where was her baby? Who had taken her father to the hospital? When she got to the hospital, she was shocked to see Ashwin and his sister Preeti there.

Preeti had Amrita in her lap, and had managed to get her into a calm state. Ashwin immediately ushered Gauri to Sidhant's room. As she went, she turned to look back at Amrita, and was reassured by a warm smile from Preeti that her daughter was okay. Over the next three days, she put her complete trust in the two strangers who took care of all her and her daughter's needs. Because the child was not allowed in the hospital overnight, Ashwin forced her to leave, promising that he would call if anything happened. He insisted his sister stay with Gauri and take care of her and the baby. In the mornings when Gauri came back to the hospital, she learned from the nurses that Ashwin had never left her father's side. Sidhant was showing signs of recovery, but he continued to be weak.

Gauri was scared beyond belief. She didn't want to think about her father's mortality. She was so helpless in the world without him. On the fourth day, Ashwin came and told Gauri that they could take her father back home. Ashwin took care of everything from that point on, always ensuring that there was someone with Sidhant every day. The three of them, including his sister, took turns during the day with him but he insisted that Gauri continue to go to college. He had managed to get a job with a major construction firm and was drawing an enviable first salary of 10,000 rupees per month. Despite being in the job for less than six months, he took several days off to care for Sidhant. Gauri was beginning to trust Ashwin and his judgment. Gauri wasn't quite able to identify when and why this was happening, and why she let herself be directed by him but she did know that all his decisions were being made in the best interest of Sidhant, Amrita, and herself. She was not oblivious to the sacrifices that he and his sister were making. They were both god-sent and she was not going to tempt fate by driving them away. Amrita also took strongly to Ashwin. Like any mother, what was most important to Gauri was not how she was treated, but the treatment of her child.

Sidhant was back on his feet in less than a month. He was grateful to Ashwin and his sister. If Preeti had not heard Amrita crying uncontrollably, and if the door had not been open, Sidhant probably would have been dead. It was Preeti who had contacted Ashwin and called the ambulance. Over the next year, Ashwin and his sister became a permanent fixture in their lives. Gauri was in her final year of college and Ashwin was moving up rapidly in the construction company.

One day, Ashwin asked Gauri to come over. Sitting her down in his dining room, he asked her in his signature matter-of-fact style if she would marry him. Gauri spat out the water in her mouth. She didn't know what to say, so instead mumbled "Sorry" and ran out. When she got home, she discovered that Sidhant knew exactly what had transpired as Ashwin had already asked for his permission. Gauri couldn't believe that her father had hid that from her. She never wanted to get married. It didn't really matter that Ashwin had brought stability back into their lives. Even though Ashwin cared for Amrita, there weren't any guarantees that he would treat her like his own daughter once they were married.

Sidhant didn't pressure Gauri as he knew this would not be necessary. The mother in Gauri would want a better life for Amrita. A week later he sat her down for a talk. He had already had one heart attack and would not live forever. He wanted Gauri to find happiness and have a normal life. Gauri owed it to her daughter. Gauri relented. She agreed to marry Ashwin under the condition that she first graduate and that her father live with them. After graduation, Gauri and Ashwin were married in a courthouse in the presence of Sidhant, Amrita, and Preeti. They broke the wall between the two small apartments and made it into one large one.

Marriage was very hard for Gauri. She realized that she felt no enjoyment in sex and that the rape had made her frigid. Because Ashwin was so practical, having Gauri in his life was enough. Having a strong sexual relationship with her was not necessarily a priority for him. He was a man who took his responsibilities seriously. He was a good father to Amrita, a good brother, and a good son-in-law. He was the textbook definition of a good man but he was not necessarily a good husband, as he was a man of few words and few interests. He was not the type to give weight to feelings and emotions. Gauri was still young and didn't really know what she was lacking. She just felt that she got what she deserved. He did not abuse her and he did not pressure her to have sex, at least not in the beginning. He provided for them and gave her daughter a last name. More than anything else, he took care of her father and respected him. Wasn't that what life was about? Was she a wretch for expecting more? It was only much later in life that Gauri would fully appreciate what she was missing. Gauri never let Sidhant know or even sense her unhappiness. He asked her if she was happy a few times and she responded that she was. She even went as far as to say that she had never been happier in her life.

Two years after Gauri and Ashwin got married, Sidhant had another heart attack. This time he did not recover. It was almost as if he felt that he had done his duty and could now go to his beloved Savitri. Not a single day had gone by that he had not thought of her. Upon Sidhant's death, everything from Gauri's past was erased. All that remained in her life were relationships that had begun less than three years before.

Gauri had completely forgotten what happiness was. She viewed her life as a chore. She dreaded waking up each morning and often wished she would die in her sleep. She wasn't really sure why she was this depressed, but she was and she didn't like it. Savitri and Sidhant would never have let her sink so deep—they would have checked the depression in its early stages and forced her to come out of it. She needed that push to get out of it but no one seemed to care enough, especially Ashwin.

Her relationship with Ashwin was also changing. Though he had always known Gauri's history, he started resenting her for it. She struggled to pinpoint exactly how Ashwin felt about her. Sometimes she was quite sure she saw hate in his eyes. The irony was that Ashwin was the kind of man who held grudges—he never forgave and he never moved on. Even though he had married Gauri out of his own free will, galloping in and saving her like a knight in shining armor, he never forgave her for having been raped. He held Gauri responsible for whatever had happened to her that night. Gauri sometimes wondered why he had followed her around, and pursued her. In the end she attributed it to attraction and Ashwin's need to rescue people.

The fact was that he was too righteous to confront her or not be a good father to Amrita. That bothered Gauri. It would have been much easier to handle if he had confronted her with his feelings; if he shouted at her and they fought it out. But theirs was not a relationship that could survive confrontation. It was too weak to withstand the outcome of raw emotions. Moreover, Ashwin was fundamentally an unemotional person. He had few desires in life. Gauri had hoped that he would bring some zest back into her own life, but the truth was that Ashwin lacked zest even for his own. Gauri has no idea of how to make a fundamentally unhappy man happy, especially since she herself was battling depression. The only thing he was good at was his responsibilities. Ashwin was the most committed man she saw. She knew that no matter how unhappy he was with her, he would never leave her.

Gauri didn't want to have any children after Amrita, as she felt that it would be unfair to her. To Ashwin's credit, he treated Amrita as if she was his, but Gauri knew he longed for a child his own. Gauri wanted to give him that one gift to repay him for all that he had done for her family. But fate wasn't done testing their relationship. Tried as they may, Gauri could not get pregnant which made Ashwin resent Gauri all the more. He was sure that her fertility was in question. Neither brought up the subject of testing and determining the problem. The topic hung like a heavy grey cloud, waiting to burst.

Two years into the marriage, their barren relationship looked like it was too parched to yield any hope. Suddenly one fateful night changed that and Gauri became pregnant with Aasma. Ashwin's happiness knew no bounds. It was as if his manhood was validated. He cared immensely for Gauri during the pregnancy and made sure she was not lacking for anything. When Aasma was born, Ashwin dedicated his days to his daughters. It was Ashwin's idea to never let Amrita or the world know that Amrita was not his child. As far as he was concerned, he was her father.

Preeti had gotten married shortly before Aasma was born. Preeti had fallen in love with a Christian. Ashwin was dead set against the alliance and had threatened to kill Preeti if she pursued it any further. It was Gauri who often lied for Preeti and let the relationship blossom. It was ultimately Gauri who convinced Ashwin to bless the union and have them married. Soon Preeti and her husband moved to Australia and they rarely heard from them. Ashwin had one more thing to blame Gauri for now that Preeti had another man in her life, Ashwin was no longer the one who made decisions for her. His entire existence and self-worth was based on his ability to control people and be their savior. All his energy was now focused on Gauri, Amrita and Aasma. With Preeti out of the house, only a nuclear Kapoor family remained. However, Gauri and Ashwin soon found out that a child was not the answer to their lack of companionship. Preeti had served as a buffer masking the fact that they hardly spent time together. As Ashwin and Gauri now had to spend more time with each other, how little they had in common was suddenly out in the open. However, like Ashwin, Gauri was also loyal. She did everything that a good wife, mother, and sister-in-law was expected to do.

As Ashwin spent even more time with the Amrita and Aasma, he spent even less time with Gauri. By the time Aradhana was born, Ashwin was bored with fatherhood. Moreover, having one more girl was not what Ashwin had planned. By this time Ashwin had started his own business and focused his entire energy on growing the business. The material status of the Kapoors was steadily increasing, and Ashwin had an opportunity to do some large projects in the south. The family left Mumbai, and headed for a more suburban life in the southern city of Hyderabad. Abhay was born in Hyderabad. While Ashwin was happy to have a son, he was not a good father to Abhay. Whether he was overwhelmed with children or the fact that Abhay was not the boy he had hoped for was not clear. Growing up, Abhay was more sensitive and emotionally needy than all the others. Ashwin's interactions with Abhay were marked with constant taunts and bullying.

Ashwin never left any of his children wanting for material things. As he moved up in society, he expected Gauri to play the part of an affluent content wife. Gauri was grateful for her children as they truly brought joy into her life. She felt that she wasn't as good a mother or as elegant a wife as Savitri had been, but she was a decent mother. She put aside her depression for the sake of her children and made their lives hers. She devoted herself to their class projects and plays. It didn't matter if they had the smallest part in a school play, Gauri could not have been more supportive or complimentary.

She did, however, try to mold the girls into being conservative and reconciled to a woman's duties. Amrita and Aasma were both more than eager to please her but Aradhana was always the rebel. She always got into fights with the neighborhood boys, especially when they bullied her brother. She wasn't domestic like the two other girls. Aradhana had a zest for life that reminded Gauri of what she could have been. Aradhana was deeply in touch with her feelings. She was also the one who was most affected by the arguments between her parents. That being said, she was also the one who was happiest when things went well. Gauri worried about her, as she didn't want her life to turn out as hers had.

Gauri tried to protect all her daughters from the hurt that she felt when she realized that gender roles do exist. Parents raised their little girls with a sense of equality and a "can do it" mindset. Little girls believed believed it and took on every challenge. They entered marriage with that same false sense of equality and soon learned that their parents lied. The same parents who taught them about equality expected them to compromise later in life. It wasn't fair, Gauri had experienced it first hand. Gauri loved Aradhana too much to let her hurt like she did, which is why she was sometimes so hard on her. But deep down, Gauri was proud of Aradhana's rebellion. Maybe Aradhana would be the one to break the cycle.

Abhay, sweet Abhay, was so gentle and sensitive. He tried so hard to win his father's approval. Ashwin, however, wanted Abhay to be a man and not show his emotions. Abhay would start to cry when Ashwin yelled and screamed at his sisters or at him. Abhay felt deep anger at his father for controlling the family and exercising such authority. As time went by, Ashwin became more distant and aloof from his family. The closer Gauri became to the children, the further he distanced himself. He cared very little about what the children were doing. However, when it came to parading his family socially or making decisions for them, he was in the forefront. It was strange that Gauri and Ashwin had spent so many years with each other. Habit, however, was a strange thing.

Fresh Off the Boat

Maiden Voyage

*M*any people came to see Aradhana off at the airport. Aasma and Amrita were there along with their husbands and in-laws as were Abhay, Gauri, and her father. Gauri's kitty party friends and their big-girthed husbands came, as did her father's employees. Added to the mix were a dozen friends from various stages of her life.

Gauri had insisted she eat some sweet yogurt, which was considered auspicious, before she left home. Now, as they made their way to the airport, she was paying the price for it. She desperately wanted to get inside and use the restroom, but it seemed that the goodbyes would be prolonged due to the fact that the entire contingent had bought the twenty-rupee tickets that would get them into the waiting area. That was as far as they were allowed to come—ticketing, baggage check, and security were on the other side of the metal railings. There was little point in actually buying the twenty rupees ticket but it made people feel connected for a bit longer.

There was no direct flight to Boston from Hyderabad. She would have to go to Mumbai, formerly called Bombay, and connect to a flight to Boston from there. She was dressed in a black and white double-breasted pantsuit with a black lapel. Gauri had had it custom-tailored for her but it fit awkwardly. She looked like a chef in a fancy restaurant who had accidentally grabbed part of a magician's outfit. In her mind, the only piece missing was a hat and the rabbits coming out of it. The only consolation was that it seemed that almost every other passenger also thought that an international flight required formal attire. Evidently, they too were making their maiden voyage. That or they thought themselves and their business very important. There were a few who had made a concerted effort to look like they didn't care. They were going back home, and they intended to dress that way. It appeared quite strange to Aradhana at that time that someone would deliberately dress shabbily in oversized or too-tight track suits.

Aradhana's contingent was there well before the stipulated time. Gauri was afraid the baggage would be overweight and they would need to make alternate arrangements. Aradhana instructed that the goodbyes be expedited but the people who had traveled long and far would have none of it. Additionally, they weren't planning to leave until they had consumed twenty rupees' worth of air conditioning. Defeated, Aradhana decided to at least check her bags and then come back for the goodbyes. The airport was so small that the group behind the railing could observe the entire process.

The bags were forty kilograms overweight. Unless she paid a fine of one hundred and seventy five dollars, she couldn't bring them on the plane. In her mind she cursed the lentils and spices liberally, but was a little more respectful about cursing Gauri even though she wanted to hurl the rice and flour across the railing. She couldn't get over how much her family embarrassed her. They didn't even consider that this was her first time flying abroad. Now people all through the airport were staring at her, or so it seemed to her. As she sized up the nicely-dressed lady behind the counter about how best to handle the oversized luggage issue, she was interrupted by one of the Kapoors loudly demanding in Hindi to know what happened. *Great— and there's the frosting on my burnt cake,* thought Aradhana.

Gauri demanded the bags be brought back to her. It seemed like the whole airport was now focused on the Kapoors' drama. What they did next Aradhana would never forget. Squatting down, Gauri laid the bags on the floor and opened them while the remaining contingent formed a circle around her advising her how to best lower the weight. When all of her belongings had been exposed—including her lingerie—Gauri took out a five-kilo bag of rice and flour and then transferred what seemed like fifteen kilos into Aradhana's carry-on bag. She then stuffed Aradhana's purse with underwear, handed her three heavy text books and wrapped the ugly oversized leather coat around her body. "Just shoot me, please," Aradhana said loudly which seemed to amuse everyone. She, however, was not kidding.

As if her suit wasn't bad enough, she was wearing a three-kilogram leather jacket in what was thity degrees centigrade weather. She was instructed to keep the carry-on baggage close and try to hide it at the weigh-in counter. For what it was worth, their intense space management worked. The lady behind the counter looked amused, but not surprised as apparently the Kapoors were not the only ones who thought that purchases could not be made in America. The woman checked the bags in and gave Aradhana the okay signal. However, Aradhana was now carting along an over-stuffed and heavy carry-on bag and a purse filled with panties. As far as she was concerned, it was a ridiculous load to be balancing, but she wasn't going to put up a fight in front of all those people. Finally it was time for goodbyes. Time had flown during this fiasco, and she was now running late.

The goodbyes were rushed but she had to go through everyone one by one and say an appropriate farewell. This whole thing had exhausted and embarrassed her and she wanted to get as far away from them as possible. The goodbyes did not seem hard in the moment but as she walked away, she heard Gauri sobbing and her father chiding, "Not now."

Once past the metal railings, she made her way to the restrooms and relieved herself of the spoonfuls of sweet yogurt that everyone insisted on feeding her after Gauri had fed her the first spoon. After that, it was time to start the journey, which was a brand new experience for Aradhana. Although she was twenty-one, she had never taken a flight alone, let alone gone on an international flight. She tried to look cool and immersed herself in *The Bourne Identity* by Robert Ludlum as she waited in Mumbai, but she was so excited that she could barely finish a page. Staring at the book, she imagined what it would all be like. Three times she fished out Priya Aunty's address from her suit pocket. In case her host did not show up in Boston, she was to call the phone number immediately.

She barely ate or drank on the flight. Because she had been so busy for the last week, she had not talked to Nirman once. He knew she was coming, though, and seemed thrilled. She thought of little else but seeing him again. If the country would be only half as nice to her as it had been to him, she'd be happy. In three days it would be his birthday. She smiled as she remembered their first meeting on his birthday several years ago. She was making the trip sooner than necessary just to be closer to him on his birthday. She had butterflies in her stomach. She was flying Air France and the flight would stop some eight hours later in Paris. The cheap ticket that had been purchased required a six-hour layover at the Charles de Gaulle Airport.

The flight attendant spoke in French and then translated it into English and Hindi. Aradhana had been quite excited upon hearing they would be stopping in Paris. She had taken French in college and had been practicing very broken French and limited phrases with her friends ever since then. It was considered cool to say your hellos, goodbyes, and thank yous in French. In her mind she practiced "What time is it?," "Where is the bathroom?," and "When does the flight leave?" over and over; however, she was very upset when the flight attendant first spoke in French and she understood nothing other than "Welcome," and "Have a good flight." She realized she had never spoken to anyone in French who had an authentic accent before. All she had going for her during her wait in Paris was that she could read the signs.

Once they landed Aradhana moved about like someone in a drug-induced state. A couple of people on the flight tried to befriend her but she had too much going on in her head to be social. They had been given breakfast and lunch coupons for the airport restaurant and she ate her *petite dejeuner* of orange juice and croissant. After that she went to the duty free shop and spent thirty-five dollars on Calvin Klein One cologne for Nirman. This was the first—and to her, very expensive, purchase in dollars she had ever made. She thought about it for a good two hours before buying it—smelling other colognes before deciding. Once she was done, she bought some lunch: a flavor-less roasted vegetable sandwich that she doused in pepper and ketchup.

She chided herself for not eating her vegetarian meal on the plane. After being frisked through security and asked questions about her business in the United States, she found herself back on the plane. The final leg of the journey to the U.S. of A was now in motion. This time she was a little more relaxed and befriended the young blond French gentleman who took the seat next to her. She was pleased to learn in his broken and heavily accented English that he was going to visit his girl-friend who was studying at an American university. As they discussed France and India, she got to practice her French with him and was humbled by the fact that he responded politely to her questions about school, favorite foods, and hobbies even though she was sure her grammar was wrong. She was also surprised to find herself telling a stranger all about Nirman and her first trip abroad. She had been given clear instructions by Gauri to not let anyone know that this was her first trip, to keep her purse close, and to not talk to strange boys and yet she found herself breaking all the rules all at once.

At some point she didn't even care as to whether her seatmate was interested. It just felt good to verbalize all her excitement. After their fulfilling conversation, a good Indian meal, a Hindi movie, and a couple of hours of sleep she was almost calm when the flight atten-dant announced *"Bienvenue aux Etats Unis."*

Of Breastfeeding and Strange Welcomes

*O*nce in the immigration line, she and her French companion were separated. He had apparently been born in the United States and was an American citizen, while she was directed to a humongous line full of people of all shapes, sizes, and colors. This was the line for the people with the non-immigrant visas—the ones who were only allowed to stay for a short duration before having to leave.

As she looked around, she was awed by the diversity of people. Flights from Malaysia, Saudi Arabia, Germany, and Nigeria had landed at approximately the same time. She was ashamed to admit it but she had never seen what people from these countries looked like except on television. If it hadn't been for the break in Paris, this airport would have overwhelmed her completely. She found some solace in repeatedly checking out the "aunties" with the big dots on their foreheads, and the "uncles" in safari suits and rubber slippers from her flight. If they could survive this then she was determined she could as well. She knew for a fact that some of them did not speak a word of English. As she made her way up to the front of the line, the debacle in understanding the American accent at the Chennai consulate played in her head.

To her pleasant surprise, a smiling green-eyed gentleman only a few years older than her and in an official blue uniform greeted her. "Welcome to the United States," he said pleasantly. She checked out his smile and wondered if he was this nice to everyone. After he asked her some innocuous questions about the school she was to be attending and whom she would be staying with, he stamped her passport.

"Have a wonderful stay, and enjoy school," he said with the same smile as he handed it back to her.

As she looked around, she decided that the water in the United States was full of some euphoria-inducing tablet because all the clone-like immigration agents were going through the same ritual. There was no shoving or pushing at all in the very structured lines. The same people who would have trampled you back home were now being kept in line by some invisible mechanism. The joy of the immigration agents was infectious and she found herself smiling without cause. Everyone in line before and after her seemed to be full of gratitude as they thanked everyone from the customs agents to the baggage handler to each other. When Aradhana got to customs, several Indians' bags were being opened and pickle bottles and sweets were being removed. She hoped her bag wouldn't be opened as well as God knew there were a lot of things in it she didn't want on display. Another smiling agent asked her if she had any fresh fruits or edibles. She wanted to say "yes," but found herself saying "no." *Great*, she thought—she had started her stay with a lie. She justified it by telling herself that everything she had was dried and purely for personal consumption.

As the customs agent took her declaration card, he asked her if this was her first trip and what she was here to do. She answered his questions politely, again wondering about the water in the country. He also bid his goodbye with "Have a good day. Enjoy your stay."

After she was finished with customs, a kind gentleman from Africa helped her load her luggage on her trolley. She saw some baggage handlers but rightfully suspected that they would charge her for the help. She pushed the unbalanced and overweight cart through the automatic doors, awkwardly balancing her oversized jacket and handbag on top of them. When she made her way to the greeting area, she was surprised to see many Indians and realized she had no idea what Priya Aunty looked like.

The crowd was rapidly dispersing as they each claimed their friend or relative. There were big hugs, loud shrieks, and sounds of joyful unions all around. Aradhana stood uncomfortably in a corner, feeling a little unwanted. Where was this "Priya Aunty" and how was she to find her? All her mother had said was that she was average height, had long hair, and a three-year-old son.

Some ten minutes later, which seemed like an entire day, she saw a woman with cropped curly hair making her way towards her. As there were no more Indian greeters or visitors left, this had to be Priya Aunty. After confirming her identity, she formally shook Aradhana's hand. Suddenly Aradhana found herself missing the "armpit hugs" she typically loathed. A nice warm comfortable armpit would hit the spot. This greeting was super formal and Aradhana feared it would set the precedent for her time in America. Next to her, Priya Aunty had a three-year-old little boy in a pram, which she referred to as a "stroller." The kid seemed too tall to be pushed around in it. When Aradhana leaned down and pulled his cheeks as every Indian was taught to do, he said something in loud protest that reminded Aradhana of a dog snapping after being unwontedly petted.

"Sanjay, honey, say hello to Aradhana," his mother pleaded.

74

As Sanjay was apparently not feeling social that was the end of the conversation.

As they made their way out to the car, Priya Aunty apologized in advance for something she called the "Big Dig" and the obnoxious parking situation at Logan Airport. Aradhana nodded where she thought appropriate even though the conversation made no sense to her whatsoever. As they loaded the luggage in the car, Priya Aunty made some comment about how large it was which made Aradhana squirm. They had to put one of the back seats down all the way so little Sanjay had to share his space with her bags. As Priya Aunty strapped him in his car seat, to Aradhana it seemed like he was being strapped into a space-age capsule that would soon detach itself from the mother ship and make its way home. This was, after all, America, where everything was expected to be super modern and space-age.

Unfortunately for Aradhana the capsule didn't launch and the little brat kept kicking her front seat all the way to Brookline, the suburb of Boston where Priya Aunty lived. Aradhana tried to ignore him and take in the surroundings but the journey seemed endless. First they had to wait at the toll booth, which she found quite strange. Cars had to stop and pay money to a person in the booth or zip through other lanes that had signs that read "Fast Cash." Apparently, they were charged three dollars just to pass. Including the money that had been paid at the parking garage, Aradhana realized in a rush of guilt that Priya Aunty had already spent six dollars on her behalf. She figured that to compensate, the least she could do was let little Sanjay kick away at the back of her seat.

She tried to soak in the sights and the smells (or the lack thereof). It was the first thing she noticed. America didn't smell like anything. She did see a lot of construction, and figured that all that dug-up area which was clearly big, was the "Big Dig." She peered out of her window and made a deliberate attempt to sketch her memory with what she passed. She was expecting a clutter of high rises. Instead, she saw several grey stone and brick buildings. The buildings had more character and detail than her eyes were scanning for. She didn't capture all of the details, instead she sized their geometry. She saw a water body with some boats in it. She saw another town on the other side of the water. Priya Aunty saw the sparkle in her eyes and said something about Cambridge and Boston. There was so much around her, but Aradhana couldn't get herself to focus on it. She was tried, and hungry. Overwhelmed and sleepy. Uninformed and being kicked.

Their destination turned out to be a small two-bedroom house in what Priya Aunty called a "two-family home." The bedroom given to Aradhana was tiny but she was grateful to have a roof over her head. A few hours later at 6 p.m., Priya Aunty's better half, Brigesh Uncle, arrived home. When they were introduced, he instructed her to call him Briggs. *Briggs*, thought Aradhana, *how awful—a perfectly nice Indian name abbreviated for no reason.* Priya Aunty also took the opportunity to tell Aradhana not to call her aunty; that Priya was sufficient. She was then given her first lecture on how no one called anyone "uncle" or "aunty" in America. Instead, they referred to each other on a first-name basis. The privilege of calling someone aunty or uncle was restricted only to true aunt and uncle relationships.

Aradhana helped Priya set the table for dinner and prepare the salad. Dinner was to be spaghetti with marinara sauce and meatballs. Aradhana told Priya she was vegetarian, but that she would be quite happy to just have the tomato sauce that was being served.

Basil was chopped and put into the sauce, and served on a bed of spaghetti. As she ate her first forkful she thought of how to politely let Priya know that it was in desperate need of some spices. Apparently her expression betrayed her and Priya bought some salt and pepper to the table. While she tried to roll the spaghetti onto the fork so that it wouldn't drip across the sides of the mouth, the phone rang. Aradhana was surprised when Priya answered it and then said that it was for her.

It was Nirman, who had gotten the number through directory assistance. Although she was thrilled to hear his cooing voice, Aradhana, who was already feeling quite out of place, didn't really want Priya or Briggs to share this moment with her. Also she thought it very rude to be on the phone during dinner. Nirman instructed her to get a calling card from a convenience store and call him as soon as possible. She promised she would. When she returned to the table, they silently finished their meal. Afterwards, Sanjay begged to be taken to Baskin-Robbins and the parents complied. When Aradhana tried to share the backseat of the car with him, he burst into a fit of tears, declaring adamantly that he did not want Aradhana to sit with him.

If he were a true Indian kid, he would have gotten a slap right then and there or at least a stern admonishment for throwing such a tantrum. But he wasn't and this wasn't India, either. When cajoling failed, Priya requested that Aradhana come up front and sit with Briggs while she shared the back seat with Sanjay.

The ride took less than ten minutes. When they got there, Aradhana was surprised to find that they were they only customers. They had the full attention of the two young girls behind the counter. She looked uncomfortable as Briggs took three different samples before settling on plain vanilla. When it was her turn, she said she'd rather skip having ice cream. Aradhana was already feeling guilty that so many of the revered dollars had been spent on her. The thought of spending over three dollars on a scoop of ice cream tightened her stomach and gave her a sensation of being full. Briggs however was insistent.

"It's your first day in America. What do they say in Hindi? Ah! Yes, *Moo meetha kar lo*, sweeten your mouth," he said impressed at his attempt at Hindi and his translation. Aradhana knew the auspicious significance and the implication that having something sweet to celebrate good news. She was sold on the idea. She wanted this time to be as auspicious as possible.

"Thanks. I'll have a scoop of vanilla too," she said, not wanting to select anything more exotic. Even the ice cream names where making her head spin. She wanted to try some flavors, but was uncomfortable asking. What if she mispronounced something? What if they didn't understand her? What if they refused to give her a sample. Vanilla was international. No confusion there.

When they got home, Aradhana wanted nothing more than to sleep. She was full from eating and more dazed that she had ever been. But before she called it a night, she saw one other thing that made her believe that this indeed was another world. After they returned home and Sanjay got into his pajamas, he made his way to Priya's breast and, much to Aradhana's surprise, started sucking on it. She knew for a fact that Gauri had stopped breastfeeding her children when they turned one. She wasn't really sure why she was so uncomfortable by what she knew in her heart was the most pure and natural bonding between mother and child. She wasn't narrow-minded, and was a fanatic about all things natural. Still, she felt like she shouldn't be there. She felt like an intruder.

Dollars and Cents and Making Sense

*P*riya had closed the last conversation of Aradhana's maiden night with a firm advice.

"You should sleep. Tomorrow will be a long day of apartment-hunting and initiation."

The next day, with bratty Sanjay in the back seat of the car, they went to Sienna Leone College to check out the boarding situation. Once again, Sanjay took devilish pleasure in kicking Aradhana's seat. She wondered if she should say something. India promoted community child rearing and therefore it was considered okay, if not desired, to correct a child when wrong. She remembered chidings from several uncles and aunties for breaking windows, being rude, or throwing tantrums. For now, she decided against it. She was grateful for the support, and figured that if his parents didn't care about his manners, why should she?

Half an hour into the drive, Aradhana found herself very queasy from the car ride. Priya attributed it to the high speeds and recommended chewing gum to alleviate it. Aradhana humbly accepted whatever was being offered, and clenched her fists all the way to school. When she got there, however, all thoughts about her stomach disappeared when she got a glimpse of the beautiful campus. As far as her eyes could see, there were trees with leaves of every different color from yellow to crimson. Tucked between the trees were sloped-roof brick buildings with dark long glass windows that were a perfect blend of modern and traditional. For a minute even bratty Sanjay was quiet, seeming to take in the beauty as well.

The landscape was like nothing Aradhana could have ever imagined. As they walked through the campus, she felt like it was at least twenty times bigger than her college back home which had gloated about its six buildings and twenty acres of land.

During the twenty minute that they toured the campus, Aradhana thought of nothing but the beauty. Her reverie was interrupted when they went to the residence life office to inquire about on-campus housing availability and costs. She didn't know what pained her more—learning that they had no availability, or learning that, even if they had some, she would not have been able to afford the four thousand dollars a semester that it cost for room and board. She felt faint as she realized that the eight thousand she had brought would barely help her pay for the first semester in this expensive private school. She would never be able to afford to live anywhere.

Just when she thought all was lost, Priya pointed to some "Roommate Wanted" ads on the bulletin board. Although there were several, one in particular seemed too unbelievable to be true: two other Indian girls were looking to share their apartment with a vegetarian Indian girl for a mere $330 dollars per month. Although Aradhana would have to share a room, Priya touted the inclusion of heat and hot water in the rent as a big advantage. They scribbled the address and phone numbers on yellow sticky sheets of papers, which Priya referred to as "Post-its." Shortly after, they called the number from Priya's cell phone and a girl with an American accent answered and confirmed it was her posting. The apartments were close by and it was decided that they would stop by a few hours later when the second roommate was in.

This gave them some time to figure out what to do about the money situation. Like a veteran, Priya ushered her to the student employment office and requested to see a summary of all the open job postings. Many were disqualified, as they required a commitment of more than twenty hours, which would have been a violation of the student visa. There were only two that Aradhana was eligible for. One was in the cafeteria and the other in the Gender Issues Council. Since the new semester had not yet started, the school was running on a limited schedule basis which meant that the cafeteria was open, but the Gender Issues Council was not. Aradhana wasn't even sure what the council did. They made their way to the cafeteria. As they entered, Aradhana's nose was overwhelmed by strange smells she had never experienced before. The cafeteria was entirely different from the benches under trees that she was used to in her college. Back home, the college cafeteria was subcontracted to an army officer's wife who ran the cafeteria mostly on credit and prepared the food in her home. The system worked quite efficiently, though rumors had circulated that the canteen was running at a loss and may soon shut down.

This cafeteria was like a fancy restaurant, and had separate counters for different types of food. Not all the counters were operating that day, but nonetheless it was quite impressive. Aradhana had no idea about what type of job she'd be asked to do here. She had never worked a day in her life for money. It wasn't that she was lazy or arrogant—it just hadn't been something she had had to do. Moreover, her father would never have allowed it. Priya led Aradhana into the cafeteria management office where the gentleman behind the counter gave her a form. After Aradhana filled it out and handed it back she was surprised to find that that was it. There were no questions asked, and no discussion about her previous work experience. In fact, seeing that they weren't busy at that point, the man suggested that Aradhana give it a shot behind the counter right then and there. She was extremely excited and asked Priya if she minded. Priya said that would be just fine as Sanjay was hungry and she could get him a snack while Aradhana spent a half hour or so behind the counter. According to the gentleman, she already had the job.

Aradhana was paired up with a much older lady who didn't look like a student. It turned out that she was one of the few permanent employees on the campus not related to the school. She had dirty blonde hair and round glasses that were at least two sizes too big for her. She was much taller than Aradhana and didn't particularly appreciate being given an apprentice. Aradhana spent the next ten minutes watching her sometimes swipe cards for students and sometimes take cash from the small trickle of students and parents who came in. Suddenly, without warning, the woman looked at Aradhana and said she needed to go out for some fresh air. She told the woman next to her to keep an eye on Aradhana, and in an instant Aradhana found herself alone behind the counter.

With fascination, Aradhana studied the different keys on the cash register. There was also a cheat sheet next to the register with a list of codes of the specials. Suddenly it seemed that the trickle turned to a stream as a summer class for undergraduate students had just ended. The students made their way to the different food counters and then to Aradhana's cash counter. As the first student stood in front of her with fries, a cheeseburger and a Coke, Aradhana looked helplessly at the lady at the next register who yelled for Bob, the man who had taken Aradhana's application. While Bob manned the other register, the lady—who introduced herself as Betty—directed Aradhana on what to do. The cards were apparently something they called Eagle dollars which were prepaid meal cards. As Aradhana rang up the customers, Betty stood behind her looking over her shoulder and correcting her where necessary. She was just getting used to processing the prepaid cards when one student presented cash. Aradhana fumbled. She had to return eighty cents, but she had no idea what eighty cents looked like. Picking up three quarters, she studied them closely to make sure she had the right amount and then looked for five cents. Because five cents was smaller than ten cents, she naturally reached for the ten cents coin. Betty smiled and told her that the ten cents was a dime, and five cents, a nickel. Luckily, people in the line seemed extremely patient through the ordeal. When the other lady returned from her fresh air break, she reeked of cigarette smoke which earned her a dirty look from Bob. Aradhana looked at her watch. Thirty minutes had passed and she had had the time of her life. She said goodbye to them all, promising to be back when her semester started.

Having worked for the first time, Aradhana was on a huge high as she joined Priya and Sanjay and they made their way to the Franklin Hill Apartments. It was a town home community on a hill. For some reason, it reminded her of her favorite movie, The Sound of Music. That alone made her feel warm and familiar. As Priya parked the car in the visitors' parking spot, Aradhana spotted a rectangular swimming pool with a semi-private wood fence. Green hedges added to the privacy. Wooden steps adjacent to the pool led to two tennis courts protected by tall metal fencing. Aradhana had goose bumps—the community was perfect. As Sanjay was getting cranky, Aradhana was afraid they would have to turn back and leave without visiting the apartment. She kneeled towards Sanjay and thanked him for cooperating. She also promised to watch two Disney videos with him upon their return home. Her efforts were not wasted and Sanjay seemed to quiet down.

Flights of stairs lead to a cluster of townhouses surrounded by trees. Each was a gated unit with a small stoned front yard. When they rang the bell of apartment number 1701, a tall, skinny girl with tightly cropped hair, shorts and a tank top opened the door and invited them in. The living room had wood floors and was bare except for a blue striped couch. The living room included a dining area that was connected to the kitchen through a serving window. A narrow hallway led to a bright, spacious kitchen that looked like it was seldom used. The large windows in the kitchen looked out onto a panoramic view that included the silver steeple of a church and a view of the clocktower attached to the school library. The girl, who had introduced herself as Alaya, led them down a hallway and up a flight of wooden stairs where there were two bedrooms and a single bathroom. One of the bedrooms had nothing in it except for a comforter on the floor which was being used as a makeshift bed. Alaya's room was the only room in the house that was furnished. It had a large bed, green checked curtains, and a couple of abstract paintings with green as the primary color.

It turned out that Alaya was a molecular biology major who had been born and brought up in New Jersey. At some point during the tour, a petite girl with jet black hair and matching eyes came home. Her hair was in a braid and she wore an oversized T-shirt, loose-fitting jeans and a light windbreaker. She introduced herself as Laxmi. Laxmi was a second-year graduate student studying advanced mathematics. Laxmi was the girl with whom Aradhana would have to share the bedroom, something Aradhana had not done since she was eight. She valued her privacy, but she had little choice in the situation. Laxmi had a thick South Indian accent and was from the city of Chennai. Alaya and Laxmi seemed like unlikely roommates. Apparently, Laxmi was the one who had requested that the third roommate be vegetarian and had several questions for Aradhana about her eating, sleeping, studying, and music habits.

After ten minutes of grilling, Laxmi and Alaya excused themselves and went into the next room to discuss if Aradhana would be an acceptable roommate. They returned with an affirmative decision, and Aradhana found herself an accepted resident of 1701 Franklin Hill.

A Day to Forget

*A*radhana was so excited that for the rest of the day she hardly saw, thought, or heard anything. She did not even mind Sanjay's constant "I wanna go home" and other whining. It was, however, a strange excitement. She had a sense of achievement and self, yet she felt disconnected from everything around her. The day had been surreal. She was glad about how things were falling in place, yet nothing seemed real.

When they finally reached Brookline, it was already evening. Before they got to the house they stopped at a store called Healthy Harvest. Aradhana would later realize that this was the type of high-end supermarket she would not be able to afford to go to for several years. As they walked through the aisles, Priya picked up a whole array of fresh vegetables and fruits. With the processed foods, she religously read the label of every item. This was Aradhana's first time in such a big supermarket. Little ones had been popping up throughout her town at home, complete with aisles and scanners, but this was very different. Everything here was pristine and everywhere she looked there was a vivid display promoting some product or other. Her head began to spin from looking at the prices. Sanjay picked up what looked to be a popsicle from the refrigerated dairy section, but it turned out to be something called a "string cheese." By the time they made their way to the counter to purchase such strange-looking vegetables as broccoli, brussel sprouts, asparagus and butternut squash, Sanjay had already finished his string cheese which made Aradhana wonder how anyone would know what happened to it.

The first thing Priya did, however, was turn over the empty cheese straw wrapper to the cashier. The total came to 105 dollars. Aradhana tried to appear cool, but was quite fazed, as that was over 4500 rupees. She thought of how many months of her 200 rupees in pocket money that came to. She was beginning to feel like a country bumpkin. Not the kind that bumped into people and said the wrong things, but the one that walked around with a slightly perplexed look on her face wondering where to go next.

Priya planned to make butternut squash soup, buttered asparagus, and garlic bread for dinner. Aradhana had read about succulent buttered asparagus in a cookbook once but had never eaten them.

When they got home, it was time for Sanjay to have some real milk. Aradhana tried not to look uncomfortable when Priya popped a breast out. While Sanjay's lips attacked Priya's breast voraciously, Aradhana volunteered to start helping with dinner. She had no clue where she'd need to start with a menu she had never tried. Garlic bread seemed the easiest so she started slicing up the big French roll. After that, she peeled and cut the garlic into tiny pieces. Then she had little left to do in the kitchen for lack of knowledge, so she set the table. It was about then that Priya finished breastfeeding and made her way to the kitchen to chop leeks for the soup. Aradhana watched with fascination as the butternut squash was cooked in the oven before being mixed with the leeks that had been sautéed in olive oil and thyme. All was tossed into the blender, pureed, and presented with a sprinkle of pine nuts. She then watched as Priya cleaned what she called the thorns off the asparagus, before throwing in a pat of butter and some sesame along with ground fresh salt and pepper.

When they were about done preparing dinner, Briggs walked in. As Priya gave him a "hello" kiss on his lips, once again Aradhana tried to look away. She definitely didn't think of herself as a prude. Infact, she always prided herself at being quite the opposite, but it was all happening too quickly for her to absorb. Dinner was served at 6:30 p.m., which was baffling to Aradhana as she couldn't remember eating dinner once before 9 p.m. back in India. Snacks at 6:30 p.m. and dinner at 9:30 p.m. was generally the practice.

As she ate the soup and asparagus, the new tastes tickled her palate but jet lag made it so that she was going to have to leave her gastronomic assessment of the experience for later. Politely she picked up the plates and washed them in the sink. Priya protested, but Aradhana knew that this was the right thing to do. After she had cleaned the table and the dishes, she excused herself and went to bed even though it was only 8 p.m.

She did not rise until 1 p.m. the next afternoon when Priya woke her up for lunch. Once they were done with lunch (leftovers from dinner), Nirman called. Aradhana felt warm when she heard his familiar voice. For the next fifteen minutes she told him about her first day at work, the experience at the supermarket, dinner and anything else she could remember, but he only made a few sounds in acknowledgement and was cold and distant. When Aradhana confronted him about his behavior, he said something that made Aradhana's knees buckle.

"What's the date?" he asked.

Suddenly she realized it was the day after Nirman's birthday. She had been so wrapped up in this strange experience that she had forgotten the reason she came here early! No matter how much she apologized, Nirman remained cold. He attacked her with the accusation that she would never have forgiven him if the tables had been turned. For once, Aradhana had nothing to say. She begged for forgiveness pleading that she'd been a zombie for the last three days, but he said he needed time to think and hung up.

Aradhana cried herself back to sleep, wishing she had never come to the United States.

A Roof to Live Under

*W*hen Aradhana woke up the next morning, she remembered Priya trying to wake her up for dinner. She also remembered that she had protested and demanded she be left alone. One look in the mirror told her that she'd have a lot of explaining to do. Her eyes were bloodshot and swollen from crying. She wondered if it was possible to be fully asleep and still cry. How she wished Nirman would understand.

When she got downstairs, she asked Priya for directions to the nearest convenience store. She absolutely needed to buy a calling card and call Nirman. Before leaving for the store, she tried calling once from Priya's phone. She didn't want to rack up long distance charges, but she felt compelled by her need to ask for forgiveness. When she got his answering machine, she hung up. Aradhana and Nirman had an unspoken ritual of speaking to each other first thing in the morning on his birthday and then going to the temple. The first time she ever met Nirman was in the temple, so she thought the ritual both spiritual and romantic. She wondered if he had gone to the temple at all yesterday. She knew he had found a Hindu temple, twenty miles from where he lived. She was too ashamed to ask him that yesterday. Today, however, she needed to know. A sinking feeling in her heart told her that he didn't go. That somehow meant she had wronged God. While she felt miserable, she didn't know how she could have avoided it. This entire experience had been harrowing for her, especially living with an aunt whom she hardly knew. She felt like she was imposing, and Sanjay did everything he could to assure her that she was.

It was a modestly warm day and she wore her blue jeans, black short-sleeved T-shirt and a denim jacket. On her way to the store she passed a Dunkin' Donuts. It seemed crowded, and she could smell the strong scent of coffee as she passed. She would have liked to have stopped, but there were too many other things on her mind. As she continued, she saw signs for a children's hospital and heard ambulance sirens whiz past her. She noticed almost instantly how the other cars pulled over and let the ambulance pass. She tried to absorb her surroundings while wiping the stray tears that came to her eyes. She longed for a friend's patient ear. As she walked, no one seemed to notice her. She found it strange how people did not stare here. In India, she was always used to someone staring at her. Occasionally someone would make a pass, but regardless, you could be assured that a dozen eyes would be looking in your direction. Whether their motivation was fleeting curiosity, lust, or just boredom, there were always eyes on you. Here, people seemed to look away even before they made contact. Those who did make contact smiled politely or greeted you. During her walk, she smiled back at the two women who walked by her as well as an older man, but ignored a middle-aged man. He moved along nonchalantly.

She reached what was called 7-Eleven. She saw a familiar looking face behind the counter. It wasn't a face she knew, but it was the familiar face of an Indian. As he stared at her, she felt warmth in the familiarity of a stare. She walked around the store, but didn't find what she was looking for. She almost cut into the line as she was often used to, especially when men were before her. She stopped when she saw an older woman wait in line behind a strangely dressed boy whose pants were almost falling below his hips. The crotch area extended several inches below where it was supposed to and his shirt was four sizes too large. Aradhana felt a little uncomfortable in her extra tight jeans, which were all the rage back home.

She asked the man behind the counter for a calling card.

"You want to call India?" he asked hopefully.

"No, California," she replied.

He seemed disappointed, but gave her a card from behind the counter. Apparently five dollars would get her over 200 minutes.

Over the next two days she left ten messages for Nirman, but he didn't call back. Priya sensed Aradhana's pain and asked her if she was all right. Aradhana did not fight back her tears and let them flow. The tears flowed for more reasons that she realized. Not only was she upset about Nirman, but she was missing the sights and smells of the only home she knew, India. It hit her that it would be a long time before she went back home. She cried because she missed the constant concern and interference from Gauri. She cried because she no longer felt special. But she cried the hardest for Nirman. She had left everything to be with him. What if things never got better? What if this was all a mistake?

Priya let her cry and confided a story of her own. Briggs was her second husband. She had married her college sweetheart, and within a year of their marriage she caught him in bed with an American colleague. Priya said she let him go, which was the hardest thing in the world to do. She quoted a popular proverb, "If you love something, set it free. If it comes back to you, it's yours. If it doesn't, it never was." The words resonated with Aradhana and she developed a new-found respect for Priya. She also stopped calling Nirman. It was hard to take Priya's advice of letting go of the one she loved. What if he didn't come back to her? She found herself struggling with how quickly her life had taken a turn for the worse within just days. In her heart, she knew she hadn't lost Nirman. If she knew him—and she did—he'd call as soon as he was over the hurt.

She turned out to be right. Nirman called her a week later to say he was over the hurt and he accepted her apology. She was glad for Priya's advice. She had a lot to thank Priya for.

Priya took Aradhana shopping. They bought a twin bed set with a metal frame and an unfinished wooden desk and chair. Priya offered to buy the desk, but Aradhana declined. With significant difficulty, she forked over the four hundred dollars in cash. The delivery was to be made directly to the apartment. Priya also told Aradhana that as they were about to upgrade their dinning room set, she could have the old one.

This was the first time that Aradhana had ever lived anywhere but her childhood home. This would be her first home as an independent person. She had all ready started making plans for the new apartment. She decided that she and her roommates would live like family. They would shop together, cook together, and eat together. They would decorate the home together. It would be like the dorm lives she read about in books while she was growing up. Her favorite was the *Claudine At St. Clare* series by Enid Blyton. The girls in the hostels shared a divine sisterhood, and so would she. On the designated Sunday, Briggs, Priya, Sanjay and Aradhana made their way to the apartment in Briggs' large Ford Expedition. Sanjay still wanted his back seat solitude and mother's breast, so yet again Aradhana sat in the front.

Franklin Hills seemed to be alive with movers' trucks and foot traffic. It appeared that many people were using the weekend and the beginning of the new month to move in. Aradhana had limited luggage with her. The same bags that she thought were too many now seemed like too few. Briggs helped carry the bags up the steep stairs. Laxmi opened the door and just barely acknowledged their entry. There was too much happening for Aradhana to take notice. She asked Laxmi if it was okay for her to take the bags up to the room. Laxmi nodded from left to right, in what Aradhana understood to be a yes. The room was large, but like any other place, it would be too small with two women in it.

It was almost noon, and they hadn't eaten yet so Priya suggested that they grab an early lunch. They went to the town square, which also buzzed with activity. The entry to the square was signaled by a low bridge over the river, which Aradhana learned was some tributary of the Charles. In the river were several ducks of varying shades of brown. There were quaint shops on either side of the road. There were several restaurants of varying food types and Aradhana couldn't believe that there were four Indian restaurants on the same street. There were also several Chinese restaurants. She also noted the presence of several pubs, which Aradhana assumed served American food.

To Aradhana's pleasant surprise, they stopped at an Indian restaurant. It had be over a week since Aradhana had eaten a good Indian meal, and she looked forward to offerings where she wouldn't have to keep salt and pepper handy. The restaurant was called Tribute To India and it had a buffet. Aradhana unabashedly went back for two helpings, while conscious of the fact that Sanjay barely touched his plate. She knew that Priya would probably get him pizza on the way back.

After the much relished meal, Priya, Briggs, and Sanjay dropped her at the apartment and said their goodbyes. As Aradhana made her way to the apartment, she realized that from now this was going to be her home.

A Dose of Mediocrity

Aradhana quickly learned that Laxmi was not much of a talker. She stayed buried in her books, and only nodded from left to right when spoken to. She had no desire to learn any more about Aradhana than she already knew. She spent the entire afternoon downstairs while letting Aradhana unpack her bags. Some time during the evening she told Aradhana that when Alaya returned, they should all sit down and discuss the logistics of how things were going to go. Alaya, it appeared, was the one who was the decision maker of the two.

When Alaya returned, she greeted Aradhana warmly and shortly afterwards summoned a meeting in the kitchen. Clear instructions were given on the sequence of bathroom usage (Aradhana would use it last), and sharing of the common spaces. Groceries were not to be shared. Each would be responsible for their own groceries and cooking. Since there was no television in the common area—the only one was in Alaya's room—they didn't discuss television viewing hours. They did, however, discuss entertaining hours. Boys were not allowed after 8 p.m., and nobody was allowed after 10 p.m. Never having lived in a shared rental space with strangers and not knowing her rights, Aradhana consented to all the rules. She was surprised, though. It seemed that even Gauri gave her more freedom.

Having heard the instructions clearly, she took the cue and made her way to the grocery store. Fortunately, the store was less than a kilometer from the apartment. Unfortunately, Aradhana lived on top of the apartment complex which meant she'd have to carry her bags up the stairs.

When Aradhana saw the price of fresh fruits and vegetables, she realized that she wouldn't be eating them for a long time to come. In the frozen foods section, she found burritos at less than ten cents each and picked up about two dozen. She didn't really know what they tasted like, but the detailed list of ingredients on the back of the wrapper gave her comfort that in addition to the numerous chemicals, they also contained beans and cheese in a flour wrap. She also picked up some frozen vegetables and ten bottles of pasta sauce that were on sale. She had never made pasta before, but surmised that this would be a good reason to start. She also bought large quantities of ramen noodles.

She noticed three other Indian boys who spent longer than usual staring at the burritos. She correctly guessed that they were new as well. After paying close to twenty-four dollars, she made her way back home. She calculated that as long as she kept her monthly maintenance bill to under sixty dollars she would be fine. Anything more would mean trouble. The burritos and ramen would last her for at least the month. That would mean that she could probably survive this month under thirty dollars. As she walked back, she saw the three boys she saw at the counter also making their way into the Franklin Hill complex. They stopped short of the steep hill, and made their way into an apartment. Aradhana stopped once to drop the bags on the asphalt and flex her wrists. When she finally reached the apartment, she saw the marks the plastic had left on her wrist. She rested the load by the door and rang the bell and made a mental note to get a duplicate set of keys. Laxmi opened the door sour-faced, and walked away before Aradhana had a chance to say anything.

It was time for dinner and Aradhana was famished. Walking down all the aisles of food had made her hungry. The sweet smell of curry that Laxmi was cooking teased her nostrils. She longed for home-cooked Indian food. She may have stared at the curry a little too long, or followed the scent a little too desperately, because Laxmi offered her some. As much as she wanted to accept the offer, she resisted. She stuffed the burrito into the fridge until Laxmi told her that they went into the freezer. She had been assigned a cupboard above the cooking range. It was not particularly convenient, and she used Laxmi's stepper to put the pasta sauces in it. Again she made a mental note to get this thing called a "stepper."

She realized she had no utensils except a couple of pans and a cooking pot that Gauri had forced her to bring. Laxmi pointed her to some paper plates saying that she could share those as long as she bought more when they were gone. *Why was she being so stingy, they were only paper plates,* Aradhana thought. Thankfully she had some real silverware courtesy of Gauri. She learned that the microwave came with the apartment so she could use it without feeling she was intruding. She struggled with it for a few minutes before it appeared that the burrito was being warmed. She had of course used a microwave in India, and more recently at Priya's home. But it was just that she seemed to be struggling with everything she touched. She was feeling stupid. Her need to eat the burrito further hurt her pride. She didn't even know what a burrito was but it didn't cost much and definitely didn't taste like much. And everyone seemed to be so aware of what they offered you, as if mental notes of all transactions occurring were made. Aradhana found herself constantly feeling obligated towards others.

Aradhana couldn't afford a cell phone. However, she convinced Laxmi to accept her proposal on splitting the costs and usage on the existing landline. Alaya, wasn't a part of the deal as she had her own cell phone. Aradhana shared with Nirman everything she knew or had experienced so far with her roommates.

"I am not sure what to make of them," she summarized.

"You and everyone who's ever had a roommate," said Nirman jokingly.

"I am just so tired of having to take favors from everyone. First there was Priya aunty, then Alaya, now Laxmi. Will I ever get to a point where I don't have to rely on others?" said Aradhana rhetorically

"You'll get there before you know it," answered Nirman.

"I am really not so sure. I've never been more out of place," said Aradhana.

"Relax. I'm here for you. For now, get a good night sleep," closed Nirman.

The bed was to be delivered two days later. Aradhana chided herself for not having thought through sleeping arrangements in the interim. She knew Gauri had included some bed sheets and pillow covers, but without a bed or pillows, they would be useless. She saw that Laxmi had a comforter that she used as a base and one she used to cover herself so using that as an inspiration, she folded several piece of clothing into the bed sheet and used it as a base. She used some sheets to cover herself and since it was beginning to get cold, she also put on two sweaters.

For the first time since she arrived, she slept like a baby.

• • •

Alaya had a car and since it was Aradhana's first day, she volunteered to drive both Laxmi and Aradhana to school. Aradhana knew that this was an exception and asked how she could get to school normally. It turned out that a shuttle bus made a roundtrip to school every half hour, which was about the time it took to get there given the stops the bus made. If the journey were made without stops and through the direct route that Alaya took, it took less than ten minutes. Aradhana asked Alaya where she could get a duplicate set of keys made. Since there was no easy way of getting to the town center, Alaya offered to get it done for her on her way back. As they left the apartment, she saw several people from various backgrounds with backpacks standing outside a car garage. They looked like students. Alaya confirmed that this was the bus stop. As they passed, she noticed the three boys from the supermarket.

Once they reached college, which every one referred to as "school," she followed the signs to the new student orientation. In Aradhana's mind, school ended after high school. She quickly learned that what she considered "college" was "university" to her British peers, and school to Americans. This was just the beginning, as there were going to be many other words that meant different things to different people.

Orientation was unspectacular, with videos highlighting the value of diversity and the success that lay ahead followed by a few professors and former students echoing the same message live. The underlying theme was success could only be achieved after hard work and many sacrifices.

Aradhana had taken the first empty seat she found available and was seated next two Venezuelans, who introduced themselves as such. She was surprised to see that they were blonde and fair-skinned as opposed to the darker complexion she thought all South Americans have. She had a lot to learn about different nationalities and cultures and she had a strong feeling that this place would teach her a great deal.

Lunch was served in what was referred to as the "foyer." It consisted of sandwiches with some strange sauces labeled "hummus" and "tahini." In addition, there was a huge fruit salad that again held mysterious fruits and some non-mysterious pizza. After debating her choices, Aradhana loaded up on the strange fruits and generous portions of the hummus and tahini but not before confirming with an amused server that they were meat-free.

Students walked about uncomfortably in the foyer thinking of ways to introduce themselves. Tables were set up all around and people gravitated towards seemingly friendly faces or people from similar cultures. Mostly people stuck to their own kind or the people they sat next to in the orientation. Aradhana gravitated towards the Indian table and shortly thereafter, the three mysterious Indians from the supermarket joined them. It turned out they were roommates. Asad, the oldest, introduced himself as an engineer from Dubai. Since he felt that he wasn't really going any further in his career he chose to do a Masters in Business Administration. The other two were from Mumbai and looked liked twins and soon acquired the nickname of T1 and T2 respectively. They dressed almost identically and gelled their hair back in the same style. They were not related to each other, and, in fact, hadn't met until they put ads on the school website about sharing a room.

Shortly after lunch, the new students regrouped in what was called the atrium and were provided with a list of administrative things that required completion. On top of the list was getting social security numbers followed by setting up bank accounts. From this point on they were on their own. The Indian contingent stuck together, as did the Latin American Contingent, the Far East contingent, the Middle Eastern contingent, and the European contingent. Individuals from the North American contingent disappeared and went in different directions.

The next two days were hectic. Everyone stuck together and the tasks were accomplished. On the third day, the newfound camaraderie seemed to dissolve as people started heading their own ways. Aradhana soon learned they were making a beeline for the job postings in the student employment office. Others who knew the system better were making a beeline for the Department Assistantships and Graduate Assistantships as those would help them pay for tuition. Some would even get a stipend that would help pay for their living expenses. There were a handful of students who had been offered scholarships along with admission. These students seemed the most relaxed. All others were competing for a handful of open positions. The jobs being offered in lieu of these assistantships were not particularly difficult. Most involved doing research for professors and other responsibilities included correcting multiple-choice exams and supervising a handful of undergraduate classes.

Not knowing the system and having little assistance from anyone else, Aradhana didn't do so well. She ended up with ten hours a week in the cafeteria job and ten hours working in the Gender Issues Council. Apparently, she could work only twenty hours per week on the F1 student visa, which was yet another detail no one had bothered telling her before she got to the US. Doing the math, she realized that she could barely survive on the apparent minimum wages she would get in both her jobs. The money she had would soon disappear into the first semester's tuition. The thought of reaching out to her family for more money was unfathomable.

Every time she applied for a graduate assistantship or department assistantship posting, it seemed someone beat her to it. If she did land an interview, there was always someone with more experience and skills than her. Being mediocre was a new feeling, and it definitely didn't feel good. She vowed that by the next semester she would have one of these assistantships that would pay all or part of her tuition.

Life wasn't turning out close to what she imagined. Her routine consisted of spending anywhere from ten minutes to an hour waiting for the bus in the morning. Sometimes she walked to school which took her forty-five minutes. After her daily two classes of an hour and half each, she would spend a few hours in the library before working in either the cafeteria or at the Gender Issues Council. She never seemed to have enough money and therefore could not join the other students when they went to explore Boston. Many spent their weekends clubbing and attending parties. She, along with a few others, spent it trying to find a third or fourth job.

She was amused by the questions people asked her about India. First there were those who only knew India as it was represented in the movie *Indiana Jones and the Temple of Doom* or documentaries about snakes and elephants. One asked her how they dealt with snakes at her house. Then there were those who were seriously surprised as to how well she spoke English. She felt indignant and one time responded, "I'm just so smart. I just learned it in the last two weeks." Like most Indians, Aradhana took pride in her command over the language as English represented the language of the educated elite. Over time her view on this would change drastically, but at that point she still felt that way.

• • •

Aradhana started to keep a diary that she called "Beantown Blues." She didn't fully comprehend why they called Boston "Beantown," especially after she tried the baked beans in the cafeteria. To be fair to baked beans, though, she now detested everything in the cafeteria. The diary noted all her experiences in Beantown and recorded one failure after another. It was turning out to be a real mood damper. Aradhana couldn't believe she was whining so much. It had volumes about how no one understood her and she wanted to go back home. Her first few impressions were that all Americans were cold. Seemingly friendly, they were all distant and self-consumed. They didn't really care about the "culture shock" that a foreigner might be experiencing. Even if they did politely greet you or sit with you in the cafeteria, they would never invite you into their home or their lives.

95

The other international students formed their own clans. There were natural affinities. People came together either because of race and culture or financial standing. Then she had to fight stereotypes, most of all from other Indians who seemed so eager to conveniently slot their fellow Indians into categories. Either you were the fumbling, heavily-accented coconut-oiled FOB (Fresh Off the Boat) or you were the rich American-Born Confused Desi (ABCD) who couldn't decide if they wanted to be all rapping black or white. She had heard the new Indian students call the ABCDs "coconuts" meaning they were brown on the outside and white inside. She heard people like her not only being called an FOB, but also a "chickoo" or Sapodilla fruit, which was a brown flesh fruit resembling a kiwi on the outside, but a fleshy fibrous brown on the inside.

She wasn't quite sure which group she fell into. She was not a fumbling heavily-accented coconut-oiled eager Indian immigrant and the last time she checked she had not come to America on a boat. But she wasn't a fancy car-sporting, American-accented, cash-rich immigrant or resident American, either.

It was best to describe herself as a confused cheeko, she thought.

New Friends and New Opportunities

One afternoon Aradhana was doodling in her statistics class, as they were still covering the basics of mean, median, mode. "Doodling" was another fascinating word she had added to her vocabulary since being in the United States. Of late she had picked up a useful arsenal of words and sentences, but rarely venturing beyond that. There was "I really appreciate it," "How's it going?," "What's up?," "Awesome," "Great," "Good," "Cool," "Later," and "All set." She thought that with those, even if she never learned anything else, she'd still be all right.

Her train of thought went from words to names. *What's in a name? Would a rose by any other name still smell as sweet?* She wrote, questioning Shakespeare in her three-subject notebook. Probably, she philosophized, but it wouldn't sound as sweet. Names! Ah! Those fascinating words we are called, she thought. Her name was difficult, or so she had been told several times. She was glad it had meaning. In fact, all Indian names had meaning. She wrote the names of everyone in her family with their meanings beside them: Amrita—nectar; Aasma—sky; Aradhana—worship; Abhay—fearless; Ashwin –strong horse; Gauri—gold, the Goddess Durga. She mindlessly scribbled further and smiled when she saw what she had written.

"When is Robert, Rob and when Bob? When is William, Will and when Bill?

When is Michael, Mike, and when Mic?

When is Margaret, Maggie and when Marge?

When is Joseph, Joe? When's Charles, Chuck!

Oh! How confused I get with no real system,

What's in the name you say! Well, try calling Holly, Ho, and discover your foe.

Oh! I miss Sirs and Madams; at least I wouldn't get into a jam.

'Say it again they say when I introduce myself.

I need to spell my name three times over again

And even then they miss at least two syllables

Oh, what's in the name! Let's just call each other numbers."

Aradhana was so caught up in her scribbling that she didn't notice the attractive guy next to her. At the break he had smiled politely at her, but no more than that. She had returned it with her own polite, unconnected smile that she had learned to greet people with. He had taken the seat next to Aradhana on the first day of class, only because it was the only one in the last row that was open.

Over the next few classes, however, he regularly took the seat next to Aradhana. With each passing class they spoke a bit more, starting with introductions and moving on to background. He introduced himself as Scott. Scott had a boyish face, curly dark hair and blue eyes like Aradhana had never seen before. He was around five feet eleven inches and lean. He looked a little like a wandering minstrel or an angel having a bad hair day. Aradhana could easily picture him with a harp.

Scott, Aradhana learned, was a third generation Irish immigrant whose last name was O'Donnell. He had graduated with honors, aced his GREs and had a full scholarship to this program. He wasn't quite sure on what he wanted to be when he grew up. Aradhana was surprised to learn that he was twenty-six, a good five years older than she. After he finished his undergraduate studies, he had managed his uncle's Irish pub in Coolidge Corner. He had helped grow the business significantly and made an investment in two other pubs, one in Quincy Market and one in Harvard Square, but after four years, he grew bored. Since he didn't really have a plan and money wasn't a constraint, he decided to go back to school. It didn't hurt that he was bright enough to get a scholarship even without being sure of what he wanted to do.

Scott drove a black Lincoln Navigator. The car was bigger than anything Aradhana had ever seen. One evening after the anthropology class, Aradhana was waiting as usual for the school shuttle. As Scott made his way to the exit, he stopped and offered Aradhana a ride. As was the unspoken tradition amongst the international students, anyone with the good fortune to receive a ride was to earn good karma by further extending the offer. It was a difficult way to earn good karma as it wasn't really your prerogative to pass on the good fortune. However, Aradhana managed to convince Scott to take along six more people. Since most of the students lived in or around Aradhana's community, they were all dropped off at the gate, except for her—he insisted on dropping her off closer to her apartment.

Aradhana truly appreciated the favor, and, as was the practice in India, invited Scott in. After all, he had gone out of his way to drop her home. The least she could do is to offer him some water, if not some food, as most Indians would do. Scott looked quite baffled and declined the invitation.

When Aradhana recounted the proceedings to Nirman, he laughed heartily but Aradhana was still unclear as to what her faux pas was.

"The poor guy thought he was going to get lucky. Decent enough of him though to turn down your offer. Can't say the same about you," Nirman jokingly chided Aradhana.

"Shut up. You know that's not what I meant. It would have been impolite to let him leave without calling him in. Anyhow, I guess that goes in my Beantown Blues diary as one more cultural faux pas," concluded Aradhana.

Aradhana was doing well in school, but the jobs were draining her. She often wrote in her diary that she felt like a zombie. She was good at going through the motions but wasn't really absorbing much. She had worked through almost every section of the cafeteria including the grill. At first she struggled with handling the beef, but then it became just one more motion she needed to go through. In India, the cow symbolized the ultimate symbol of motherhood. When people asked her why Hindus didn't eat beef, she'd explain the maternal symbolism and challenge them by saying, "You wouldn't eat your own mother, would you?"

One of the twins who worked in the cafeteria had thrown up when he handled beef for the first time. The grill was closed for the day, and the manager hastily cleared the mess before the students could freak out. After that incident, the manager made it a point to ask any immigrant who worked the grill if they were okay with it. Aradhana didn't throw up, but she didn't touch the meat. All handling was done with gloves or tongs or the spatula, which was okay as it adhered to the sanitary code. Aradhana's second job didn't involve food or cultural inhibitions, but involved new experiences as well.

The Gender Issues Council was the focal point for addressing all gender issues on campus. The GIC as it was called organized lectures with guest speakers on topics such as date rape, women in politics, and global perspectives on women's rights. Aradhana's job so far was to produce flyers announcing upcoming lectures and putting them up across the campus. She also had to work out the logistics of lectures such as ensuring the hall was booked, and the speaker had directions. Although she had considered herself reasonably aware of gender issues, working at the GIC made her aware that she had much to learn.

Towards the end of the semester, Aradhana totalled her finances. After having dipped into her funds from back home, she had less than one hundred dollars left in her bank account. Nirman suggested that she get another off-campus job. Aradhana naively asked him whether that would be legal. Nirman laughed and assured her that if she didn't get an off-campus job, she would be one of the few international students without one. Most worked in ethnic restaurants or stores. The process of looking for a job wasn't all that hard. It just required that you leave all ego and self-pride at the door. You basically went to all the stores and restaurants and asked if there was a job available. You then had to study the person and determine whether to broach the topic of getting money under the table. If the person looked that they wouldn't bend the law, then it was better to just thank them and walk out.

There were two types of international students. One was the BMW sporting students who didn't have any sort of job, either on-campus, or off. Money came to them easily and they liberally spent whatever was available to them. Most Americans seemed inclined to put all international students in that category. They seemed to view the international community with some disdain and only a very mild curiosity. The second type of international students comprised the majority. They had to do a minimum of two jobs either on or off-campus to make ends meet. They generally came from reasonably well-to-do families but the steeper costs of everything in the U.S. plus the foreign currency conversion rate left them disadvantaged. Aradhana fell into the second set. After talking to Nirman, she decided to look for an off-campus job. She needed to work for at least twenty more hours each week. Her plan was to go with Asad to the Indian restaurant where he worked and see whether she could be a hostess.

During her Introduction to Anthropology class, she had mentioned to Scott that she desperately needed to find a job but she had merely been venting. She had however underestimated Scott's predeliction for practical action. He shocked her the next day by asking if she was willing to work in an Irish pub. At first Aradhana thought he was kidding but soon realized that he was serious.

"What do I know about alcohol or bartending?" she responded.

"It isn't rocket science. You can learn whatever you need to in a week tops," Scott said. Seeing that Aradhana was still hesitant, he added "Plus, you could help out with the kitchen operations rather than the bar until you're comfortable." The fact that Coolidge Corner, where the pub was located, was in one of the areas the city now had legislated as smoke-free, made Aradhana seriously consider the option. Aradhana asked what the job would pay.

"The boss thinks ten dollars an hour plus a share of tips is fair," said Scott in a boss-like voice. "I think we could get you to work Friday nights, all day Saturday and Sunday evenings. That would make up the twenty hours you're trying to get," he surmised.

Aradhana could hardly believe what she was hearing. Aradhana Kapoor, daughter of the god-fearing Kapoor family working in a pub! Her mother would hang herself if she ever found out. She may as well have taken a job as a call girl. The offer seemed very decent, though, and Aradhana had no other offers. Scott mentioned that the tips could really add up, which would help her out. She was extremely nervous, though. How did someone who had never even been to a pub work in a pub? Moreover, she was aware that going over the twenty hours would be a violation of her visa status. She had mentioned it to Scott as well, but he didn't think it was an issue.

Bars in Bollywood movies were always represented as houses of vice. Only "bad" people went there and they all had "evil" intentions. Of course, pubs had begun to spring up all across her town too. They were considered trendy hotspots but girls rarely frequented them alone. And they definitely didn't work in them. She couldn't stop herself from asking Scott if it would be safe. She was quite sure Scott thought it a stupid question, but if he did, he didn't show it. In a very matter-of-fact way, he let her know that it was a family establishment and most of their customers were regulars. The O'Donnells knew many of their customers on a first-name basis.

"The Irish are fun-loving people who love their drink, food, and music. My cousin Kelly works there too, as do two or three other staff members. Uncle Jim manages the place, and you won't find a better boss. Plus, I'm in one of the bars during the weekends. Aradhana, I wouldn't suggest it if I thought it was inappropriate. If you want, you can start off with the kitchen or serving and only bartend if you want to," he said.

Aradhana asked Scott how long his offer would stand, as she wanted to double check with Nirman before she committed.

"No worries. It's an open offer," he replied.

Aradhana was conflicted. A part of her was pysched and really wanted this opportunity. Another part though didn't want to work in a place where there of so much stigma attached, even if it was in her own head. She was eager to get Nirman's take on it. She knew she could tell no one else. She could not confide in Asad and the twins who she hung out with quite often now. She couldn't tell Alaya or

Laxmi either as she feared she might be judged. Worse, she didn't want anyone to jinx this for her. So far she had lost several opportunities for a break. Several of the newcomers had managed to get assistantships or well-paying jobs. Somehow she hadn't played the game right. This was to be her secret. She might tell someone once she started the job, but not now. Deep down, Aradhana was hoping that Nirman would come to her rescue. Maybe he'd chide her for even considering working in a bar. Maybe he'd tell her that Indian girls didn't do that sort of thing. That would make him a typical protective Indian man. She would counter his arguments and exercise her individuality by telling him how hard it was for her here. She would ask him what she was supposed to do. Nirman would find the perfect solution and she would never need to worry about silly things like this. She was definitely out of her mind, and Nirman would fix it. He would never let her integrity be compromised. Good Indian girls didn't work in bars. He was, after all, the reason she came here.

She called Nirman, but he wasn't around so she left him an urgent message to call her back, telling him that she had something very important to tell him. He called two hours later and told her that he had been out with his friends at a local Mediterranean restaurant. After telling her about the poor service that was so typical of "all these ethnic restaurants" he said, "What's up with you?"

Aradhana told him about the pub job.

"Cool. Good for you," was his response.

"That's all you have to say?" asked Aradhana.

"What do you want me to say? I think it's a great opportunity, and it will be fun." Then in a matter-of-fact tone he stated, "And by the way, I think this Scott guy has the hots for you."

Aradhana wanted to scream and shake Nirman. Why was he being so cold? Why didn't he care? Why was he trying to hurt her? This wasn't the reaction that she had been hoping for or expecting. Why did she have all these expectations of him? Why did she want him to react in a specific way? Did his reaction indicate that he didn't care, or was it possible that Nirman was truly happy for Aradhana. Maybe he really thought it was a good opportunity for her and that it would be fun. Wouldn't many women appreciate this hands-off response? Would someone else interpret this as a supportive response? Why was there such a disconnect? What Nirman saw as being supportive, Aradhana saw as coldness. She was truly conflicted. She wanted wings to fly but she also wanted Nirman to be afraid to let her fly lest she injure herself. She wanted to fly but only after she convinced Nirman that she wouldn't hurt herself. She was struggling with her modern traditional values. She wanted to do this job but she also wanted to have someone tell her not to do it. She wanted to prove she could take care of herself, but she wanted someone to take care of her. Was she grappling with this paradox because she was a traditional Indian immigrant struggling in the United States or because she was just a typical woman struggling with her need for protection and independence?

Fighting with Nirman was in vain. He didn't understand what she wanted from him. She wanted security but Nirman didn't fell ready to give it. Whose fault was that? Were they just heading in two different directions? Nirman was all she had. She could not afford to lose him. She wanted to reach out to Gauri, but she knew Gauri would'nt approve or understand. She felt alone. She needed Nirman. He was her only connection to a part of the world that defined her soul.

King of the Hill

H is shop was on Main Street. Aradhana would get off the bus and walk up a steep street to get to his store. His last name was *Baadshah*, or king, and he shared the name with his store. Aradhana assumed that it was his alias but she was afraid to ask.

It was Asad who had heard of an opening at Baadshah's antique rug store. Since he was already working overtime he passed word of the opportunity on to Aradhana. Aradhana had decided that she wouldn't take Scott up on his offer yet. Working at a pub would have been a very hard sell to everyone around her. She easily could explain working at a rug store.

When she first walked into the store, a tall, thin, unkempt dirty blond-haired young man was rolling what seemed to be a new consignment of rugs. When he saw her enter, he unenthusiastically asked if he could help her. She told him that someone had suggested that they needed help. He didn't seem pleased with her. Aradhana wasn't sure why but she stood there stubbornly while he sized her up. Without a word to her, he turned and ducked into the small kitchenette at the back of the store, calling for Baadshah. A short man only a few inches taller than Aradhana walked in. He had dark curly hair, distant hazel eyes, a hawk-like nose, and thin lips. It appeared to Aradhana that he probably weighed a few more pounds than she did. His voice was strong and authoritative. He ordered the young man whom he called Brian to move his truck to the back of the store.

As Aradhana said hello, she extended her hand but instead of shaking it, he moved his hand towards his head in what Aradhana easily understood to be an *Adaab*, or Muslim, salutation. Having lived in close proximity to the Muslim culture, she surmised that he was not comfortable shaking a woman's hand so she politely returned the greeting. She told him that she was looking for a job. He didn't say much other than to tell her how much she'd be paid. He then handed her the keys and asked her to open the store at 8:30 a.m. the next morning. He wrote down the security code on a Post-it note that he found on a little table that held an old computer and handed it to her. Aradhana thought it best to forewarn him that she knew little to nothing about antique rugs but quickly added that she was a fast learner and would work hard to learn. Baadshah said that Brian would teach her what she needed to know and would join her at 10:30 a.m. the next morning.

Aradhana thanked him profusely and left. She had no idea where this man was from or why he was willing to give her this job without asking her any questions. She thought that he was either the nicest or the craziest man on earth.

The next morning Aradhana struggled before she got the security code punched in right. As she opened the door the alarm beeped faintly. She made her way to the alarm that had been pointed out to her by Baadshah the day before. As she entered the numbers from the Post-it, she confused the one with the seven and the alarm started to beep even more loudly as the grace period expired. She tried not to let it intimidate her and held her hand and the paper steady as she entered in the password the second time. This time it worked and the alarm stopped beeping. It was only after the noise died that she heard her heart beating. It was loud and she was shaking.

It was bright outside but the store was still dark. There was something eerie about the place. It was small and looked more like a living room than a store. She left the door open while she tried to look for a light switch and wished that Baadshah had given her a tour of the store. She had been afraid that if she asked too many questions, he'd withdraw the offer. She walked the length of the store twice, but didn't find the switch. Finally she made her way to the tiny kitchen that had a small stove, three steel pots and some plastic containers that had seen better days. There was a switch at the end of the kitchen but it only switched on a solitary sixty watt bulb over the stove. Aradhana was beginning to get scared. She walked around the store once more, aided by the daylight from outside and finding solace in the sixty watt bulb that glowed over the stove. At the entrance she found some tall rugs rolled up against the wall. Even though they seemed to place all their weight on her slight frame, she managed to shove them aside and saw the switch behind the rug. Unfortunately she wasn't exactly sure how to free herself after that to switch the light on. She let the rugs rest on her frame while she extended her left hand to the switch, heaving a loud sigh of relief when the fluorescent lights flickered on. It wasn't a good way to start the morning but she convinced herself that the hardest part was over. Now with the alarm off and the lights on, she tried to acquaint herself with the merchandise around the store so that she'd seem a little better versed if a customer walked in.

At first she thought she was reading the handwritten tags wrong because many of the rugs seemed to be over four figures and some even in the fives. To her, they looked quite unattractive and beaten-up. She couldn't understand why someone would pay those prices for them. She found some copies of *Hali: The International Magazine Of Antique Carpet & Textile Art, Rug Insider Magazine* and some other periodicals featuring antique rugs. A quick browse indicated that they were all guides for carpets and rugs. When she put them down, she felt none the wiser. She looked at her watch and saw that it was ten. So far no one had walked in. Then, at about 10:15 a.m., a tall un-shaven man with a dark beard walked in. His beard matched the texture and color of his shoulder-length hair. He looked to be at least six feet two inches tall and his skin was brown, but much lighter than hers. He wore black pants and a matching hooded sweatshirt. He seemed to be in his late twenties but he could just as easily have been in his forties. He was bulky, but not heavy and looked like he exercised on a daily basis. Greeting him with enthusiasm, she asked if she could help. He ignored her, and moving around as if he owned the store, looked into the kitchen. Seeing no one else, he asked where Baadshah was. Aradhana said that she didn't know when he'd be in. He then asked about Brian and she told him that he was expected in fifteen minutes. He didn't say much else but pulled up one of the little seating stools that were scattered around the store and sat down. With his deep, dark, and what seemed to Aradhana—angry eyes, he stared directly at her.

The fifteen minutes that it took Brian to arrive felt like a lifetime. The man unsettled her to no end. If she weren't responsible for the shop, she would have left. She knew so little about the store and eve-ryone associated with it that she didn't feel comfortable asking him to wait outside. As far as she knew he could be anyone from the owner to a very special customer. She walked to the kitchen and stood there, but his eyes followed her there as well. She wanted to keep him in her sight too, as she had been assigned responsibility for the store and she took the responsibility seriously. When Brian walked in, he kissed the man's hand, and called him *bhai jaan,* or brother. He then shot Arad-hana a dirty look. Aradhana felt as if snakes were crawling up her skin as something about the situation made her feel very uncomfort-able. The two men then walked to the back of the store and out through the back entrance that led to a small private parking area. It was then that Aradhana noticed an old white minivan. She noticed that the man had parked his Mercedes SUV next to it. They moved some large rolled-up carpets to his car, but Aradhana could not get a clear look at the proceedings outside as she was afraid to stare, especially since Brian had already given her a dirty look.

The same routine continued for a month. Each day was stranger and more intimidating that the one before. So far she had received no money for her services. She had asked once and Baadshah simply said, "End of the month." Sometimes Baadshah was there and when he was, he often spoke to himself and referred to himself in first person. Making tea was a sacred ritual to him. He had fresh herbs and spices that he boiled for hours. When he was ready to have tea, he would announce "Now Baadshah will have tea." The first few times Aradhana thought he was talking to her but that wasn't the case. He had little to say to her. When she asked him where he was from, he said he was a Kashmiri. He didn't say India and he didn't say Pakistan. Once in a moment of weakness he told her that he wasn't allowed to go to India as he was on some wanted list because of a liberation movement.

She asked him about his name. He said it was an assumed name that had stuck so long that no one called him by Ali Bin Kashmiri, his real name, anymore. He took this opportunity to educate Aradhana on why he thought both the Indian and Pakistani governments were useless and needed to be a taught a lesson. At some point Aradhana began to feel her blood boil, but more importantly began to fear what Baadshah was insinuating. His language was crass and his tone angry so Aradhana changed the topic as tactfully as she could. She loved her country and had her own views on where Kashmir fit in the geographic landscape. At the same time, however, she didn't think that any piece of land should be so important to be tainted with the blood of its own people for geographic boundaries. The beautiful state in the Northern part of India was now a hotly contested piece of property between India, Pakistani, and the ethnic Kashmiris.

The beautiful land that was once called a paradise was now torn by rape, bloodshed, and displacement. The pure fanaticism in Baadshah's eyes and words frightened her. She suddenly understood from their conversation that Baadshah hated her and where she came from. He hated women and thought they had no business outside the home. He hated Indians. She was both. She wasn't sure why he had given her the job.

Brian seemed to be an American who had converted to Islam. Like most converts, he was more passionate and zealous than the born believers. Everything about the situation that she was in gave her the creeps. She got the sense that something unseemly was cooking and shuddered to think what it might be. The man referred to as "Bhai jaan" came to the store often. He also appeared to be a Kashmiri. When he was there, he and Baadshah spoke intensely in what seemed to be Kashmiri or Arabic. The only words that Aradhana picked up were *azaadi,* or "independence" and *jihad,* or "holy war." Either they were planning something dreadful or financing it or just having impassioned discussions—she was not sure which. She was also not sure of what her role in this situation should be. Would anyone be interested in her conspiracy theories about Kashmiri liberators? Freedom fighters or terrorists, whatever she called them, no one would care. Moreover, she hadn't heard anything directly. She had shared her fears with Nirman but he told her that she was being paranoid.

After a little over a month of working at the shop Baadshah called her into the kitchen and handed her a check, telling her he no longer needed her services. She was a little afraid but more than anything was happy to have been offered an out. It was a decision she had been contemplating every single day since she worked at the store. Unfortunately, her financial situation was such that she hadn't allowed herself liberty of leaving. She took the check and walked out of the store and to the nearest bank.

When the check bounced a few days later, she was too afraid to go back. After one month of agonizing pain, intimidation and humiliation she did not have a penny to show for it.

When she got back to the apartment the first thing she did was call Scott and ask if the offer at working at the pub was still open.

Honorable Trade

$\mathcal{S}$cott invited her to meet Uncle Jim at O'Donnell's at Coolidge Corner the next day. Sierra Leone had a shuttle that made an hourly trip to Harvard Square. The shuttle ran until 11 p.m. on weekdays and until midnight on weekends, including Friday. Aradhana could take the Red Line from Harvard Square to Park Street and then take the Green Line to Coolidge Corner.

That Friday morning she went to O'Donnell's for the first time. Although it was cold and November, it hadn't snowed yet. That morning she had stomach cramps not unlike the ones she had before her exams. After Baadshah, she was very nervous about this opportunity. She thought a lot about what she should wear. As it was cold outside, she was sure she needed a jacket but other than that, she really didn't know what people who worked at a pub wore. Her general rule was to dress up rather than down. However, instinctively, she knew that she didn't want to dress too "up" in this case. She thought of wearing jeans but dismissed that idea. She had not come to terms yet with the ubiquitous status of jeans. They still represented overly casual attire to her. In the end, she settled on straight black pants and a lemon-colored turtleneck sweater. She wore a t-shirt under the sweater convinced that she wouldn't have to take the sweater off. She wished she had asked Scott what she should wear. Today however she just had to take a chance and hope she didn't look too dressed up or down. Still not accustomed to the cold, she wore her ugly leather jacket which made her look much heavier.

Her first impression of O'Donnell's was totally different from what she had imagined. From the outside, it looked more like a cottage than a pub. The faux stonewall arches of the entry separated the pub from the rest of the commercial establishments. A large gold embossed sign on a black background and dark green edging indicated that she was at O'Donnell's. The sign was posted above a dark green door with a latticed glass framework that extended three-fourths down the length of the door. It was a two-story building and the windows on the two levels were separated by green window boxes that brimmed over with cascading foliage. There were matching black and gold Guinness signs on either side of the door. A sign on the other side of the door read "Closed." It was around 10 a.m. and she had been told to come anytime between 9:30 a.m. and 10:30 a.m. She wondered if she had missed her appointment. Not willing to walk away from the job prospect and the hour and a half commute, Aradhana summoned all her courage and pushed the doors. The doors were lighter than they looked, and since she expected some resistance she was propelled inside with greater velocity than planned. No damage appeared to be done because no one was in sight.

With the light that gleamed through the open door and glass windows, she could better take in the surroundings. Lined along the walls by the windows were rectangular wooden tables between what looked like cushioned leather benches that Aradhana would soon learn were called "booths." There were four booths on either side of the door. The layout of the room appeared perfectly rectangular. Like a spotlight, light shone on a dark wooden bar that backed up against the left wall from where Aradhana stood. It was hexagonal, and extended one-third into the establishment. Some fifteen square leather-backed bar stools lay invitingly around the island. There was plenty of seating against the open right wall and green-cushioned chairs were arranged like flower petals around dark wooden square and rectangular tables. Bric-a-brac adorned the walls—everything from old bicycles to framed posters, clocks, jugs, and signs listing stouts and lagers. There was a double door some twenty feet from where the bar ended which had frosted glass with a set of stairs that led up to another seating area.

For a couple of seconds, Aradhana wondered what she should do. She guessed the double doors led to the kitchen but thought it might be presumptuous to find out. She called out a hello, at first softly and then louder. Suddenly, like the host of a game show making a grand entrance, a man rushed out from the double doors and declared triumphantly, "You must be Aradhana!" He missed the "h" in her name like most Americans did. Almost as suddenly he put his arms around her and gave her a hug.

"I'm Jim, as you may have guessed by now," he said.

Aradhana hadn't really guessed that this was Scott's uncle Jim. His warm embrace had taken her quite by surprise and she was still trying to figure what to make of it. Her guard had become perennially up since she had arrived in the country. She had just about reconciled to the fact that people were not demonstrative. They shook your hand and that was that.

She said the first thing that came to mind.

"Is Scott around?" she asked. She wished something more social or intelligent had come out of her mouth, but it was a little late for that.

110

Split

Jim didn't seem to notice.

"No," he replied warmly, "but he'll be here shortly." He gestured for her to follow him to one of the tables by the door.

"Let's chat, shall we?" he said while leading the way. As he took a seat, he called out "Kelly, come here, will you?"

Aradhana followed Jim's gaze to the double doors he had emerged from to see a petite girl with an oval face, a small, round nose, and straight black hair emerge. She had the same blue eyes as Scott and wore jeans, a white T-shirt, and a green apron like Jim. She was probably only five feet two inches but she stood a lot taller. Aradhana also got the impression that she was a lot stronger than she looked. She appeared to be around Aradhana's age.

As Jim introduced Aradhana to Kelly, the girl warmly shook her hand and welcomed her to O'Donnell's before settling into the chair next to her father.

"Scott talks so much about you," Kelly said, stealing a glance at Jim.

Aradhana was both pleased and embarrassed by the remark.

"Nice things, I hope," she replied, trying not to sound like a bumbling schoolgirl.

As she said it, she wondered what Scott possibly could have been sharing with his uncle and Kelly. She hoped he didn't make her seem like a desperate international student who needed a job to sustain her existence. She wasn't even close enough to Scott to reprimand him as theirs was a friendship that had just begun. In her mind she went through several justifications: he may have referred her for entertainment value or purely for information purposes. She was probably his only brown-colored friend from a land of mystics and gurus.

Almost as if she knew what Aradhana was thinking, Kelly jumped to her cousin's defense.

"All nice things. He thinks very highly of you and knows you'll be a very hard worker. An opening recently came up so this works out perfectly."

Jim appeared to be happy to let Kelly navigate this awkward situation. Kelly, Jim explained, had recently graduated and was taking a couple of years off to manage the family business. Like Scott, she too, would decide what else she wanted to do in life when the time came.

"But let's talk about you now—I understand you've never done this before," said Jim.

111

Aradhana conceded that she was not much of a drinker and had never done a job close to this.

"Oh, it's easy. There's nothing to it," he replied, using the same reassuring voice that he probably used when he taught Kelly to ride a bicycle.

"Since there's plenty to do in the kitchen and back room, you don't have to work the bar unless you want to. Kelly loves to work the bar. Peter works full time, and Paul works weekends. Scott bounces between this location and Harvard Square. This is my life."

Aradhana listened intently, trying to engage her gaze with both Jim and Kelly.

Kelly smiled at her and said, "Dad, will be happy tell you all about his life if you let him. However, dad before you get to your life, can you first tell Aradhana about O'Donnell's?"

"All right then. You will be working with Patrick in the kitchen. We also have dishwashers and other kitchen help. Depending on the time of the year, we hire extra help. People like to see people they know, though. The three P's as we call them have been with us for a long time. Especially Patrick—he's been here since O'Donnell's opened ten years ago. Everyone loves Pat. His Shepherd's Pie and Guinness recipes are famous around Boston. The guy we just lost ordered the nectars, stocked the backroom, and helped in the kitchen. Of course, that job is open if you want it. Otherwise we'll figure out where else to use you."

"Thanks dad, always good at giving a summary," Kelly joked.

As this was all new to Aradhana it didn't matter to her what her duties were as long as someone held her hand for a bit. She told Jim she'd be happy to fill the existing role and help out with whatever was needed. She added that while she didn't know much, she was really eager to learn. Then she instinctively used a sentence she didn't particularly like because she thought it reeked of insincerity and was overused, but in this case it came from a place deep within her.

"I really appreciate it," she said.

Learning the Trade

*A*radhana's American experience took a new turn the day she accepted the job at O'Donnell's. After that she no longer was observing the society from the periphery—she was now in it and she was able to observe close-up the interactions between regular Americans and their families. The couple of months that she had spent on campus prior to taking this job suddenly made more sense to her. She understood Americans better. They weren't really that different from the people she grew up with. They felt the same joy and pride in their families as she did. The only difference was that their families were a lot more nuclear.

At the pub, she was able to watch the exchanges between several families. She saw how parents interacted with their children, especially very young ones. At the core of their relationship to their children were respect and the right of the children to express themselves. She couldn't remember once ever being asked by her mother or father for her opinion on what she wanted, even if it was only from the menu at a place like O'Donnell's.

She realized that before now, she had held some deeply ingrained opinions about what Americans were like. She always thought them to be focused on themselves and very little else. The Americans she now observed confused her about what exactly their priorities were. They made great sacrifices for their children, whether it was driving them to soccer practice or ballet or anything else. But just as easily, once the children reached a certain age they abandoned them under the guise of experience and let them struggle on their own. Few children of Aradhana's age lived with their parents and even fewer seemed to have parents who paid their college tuition.

Apart from families, Aradhana also observed interactions between single men and women. She was not new to flirting, but these American mating rituals were in a league of their own. Of course, her exposure to these rituals was limited to O'Donnell's. However, that didn't stop her from sometimes letting her imagination roam. Though Aradhana resented stereotypes—especially when they involved what other people thought of her—it didn't stop her from typecasting people. There were the bold ones, both men and women, who determined their strategy for the evening. They spotted their object of desire and readily made their attraction known.

She observed the bold ones with special interest. Some eschewed small talk and directly went to bolder propositions. Then there were the coy ones who went through the entire evening before making a move. Aradhana could never imagine herself alone at a bar. Even if she did find herself there, she couldn't imagine introducing herself to someone. She wondered how she'd respond if anyone approached her. Most of the people who frequented O'Donnell's though, were couples and families. Sometimes there were large groups of men, especially during baseball season. Such stag crowds were especially boisterous during Red Sox-Yankees games which they watched on the two 42-inch televisions that floated above either end of the hexagonal bar. In India she was a huge fan of cricket, and regularly watched the matches. However, she still didn't fully understand the game of baseball and found herself distant from the agony and celebrations. While she was observing the society and its rules from close quarters, she still felt like an outsider.

She was acutely aware that she stood out at O'Donnell's. Apart from the two Guatemalan workers who washed the dishes and cleaned the kitchen, she was the only person of color who worked there. The clientele was mostly white. Occasionally there were people of color— sometimes even some Indians, but it was rare. She had heard somewhere that people came to an Irish pub to enjoy the Irish experience— the Irish drink, the Irish food, and the Irish people. She obviously didn't resemble an Irish person and her accent gave away any chance of going unnoticed. When she waitressed, she tried hard to put on what she thought was an American accent but many people told her she sounded British. She was just happy if they didn't stare at her as if she were an alien or ask her to repeat herself. She was especially conscious during the standard greeting at the tables, "Welcome to O'Donnell's. My name is Aradhana and I'll be your server tonight. Can I start you off with something to drink?" She could tell that they didn't get her name. She struggled before asking Jim for a nametag that said "Ary" and began introducing herself as such. She had always been overwhelmingly proud of her name and heritage and this concession felt like she was not being true to her identity. However, the tips were very good and the job was working out much better than she expected.

Whether or not she waited tables, she got a share of the tips. The tip jar or the "magic piggy" as the folks who worked at O'Donnell's called it, worked on trust. All tips regardless of whether they were received in the restaurant or the bar went into the magic piggy.

Aradhana's primary responsibilities were stocking the backroom with alcohol and the mixers for cocktails. She called the distributor to order the kegs of beer and cases of other alcohol whenever the quantities fell below pre-established levels. However, she did more than just order based on what had been set. She monitored consumption levels of different drinks, factored in any specials that they would run, and regularly polled Peter, Paul, and Kelly on what they needed. She also helped Patrick in the kitchen where she learned a great deal from him. Unfortunately almost all of the cooking involved meat. She had got accustomed to seeing bloody pieces of fresh meat, which O'Donnell's proudly featured. There was also a large freezer with meat and seafood.

Restaurant cooking was so different from cooking at home. Everything here was precisely measured whereas Aradhana personally had never made a dish twice that tasted the same. Patrick was extremely creative within the confines of precision. He took great pride in sharing his recipes with Aradhana. Many were traditional Irish recipes, which he had modified with his "secret" modifications. Every table ordered at least one of his Shepherd's Pies. He did wonders with potatoes and cheddar cheese and incorporated them into almost all his recipes. Many of the appetizers, especially the intricate varieties were pre-made and frozen. When ordered, they were put into the oven and baked to perfection. Aradhana helped prepare many of these appetizers in advance. She also helped present many of the dishes. She herself never tried any of the meat dishes. Often times the pungent aroma of meat expertly cooked teased her nostrils, imploring her to drop her guard. She wasn't sure why she resisted it so much. She was vegetarian by choice. The only food that her religion really prohibited was beef. But it seemed to her nonetheless that giving in and eating meat would deprive her of the righteous status in which she held herself. Already she had made concessions that pricked at her conscience, such as letting everyone at O'Donnell's call her Ary, a right she had reserved for very few in India. She resented the fact that that most people assumed she had anglicized her name after coming to the U.S.

Once again Aradhana struggled with the new paradoxes America generated within her. The irony was that the individualism she strove for in India, she wanted to abandon here for community. She had rebelled against most rules in India and here she fervently tried to hold on to those same rules. She had worn Western clothes all her life and never volunteered to wear the Indian *salwar kameez* at home. However, here, she seized every opportunity to wear the tradition Indian attire that much resembled loose pants with a long tunic and long scarf that was either draped as a "V" around the neck, or hung on one side. While many people complimented her, she knew they viewed her more with curiosity than any other emotion. She had never worn the Indian dress to O' Donnell's and had no plans to do so. She wanted to stay as far away from exacerbating her already obvious differences. But the truth was that she was still struggling with her job there. Although she felt significant pride in what she was doing, she still harbored some embarrassment. She knew that any Indian or Asian who walked into the bar viewed her with strange curiosity. She occasionally saw the same look in the eyes of the regular patrons who had any experience with her community.

The job at O'Donnell's defined her in more ways than she thought possible. She was extremely nervous the first time she worked the bar. Paul was sick at home and the place was buzzing. Jim, who was helping in the kitchen, asked Aradhana to help Kelly cover the bar. Since the Irish loved their perfect pint of Guinness, she stayed away from pouring it as she had struggled in the practice rounds with Kelly—the "head" was either too large or too small. Apparently, there was a perfect pint of Guinness, which was easily recognizable. She had tried a sip out of curiosity and almost turned blue in the face. It was thick and bitter and didn't taste like anything she'd ever had. Kelly had taught her how to make the regular cocktails—Rum and Coke, the sour drinks, martinis, and others. Kelly had also taught her about other drinks which weren't favored by this particular crowd. For example, the Cosmopolitan, Kelly explained, was probably too effeminate for their clientele. "But a Guinness never fails," she had said.

The first drink Aradhana ever mixed was a vodka martini. She stopped herself from staring at the customer as he tried a sip to see if he scowled or spat it out but nothing happened. As was the routine, he left her a couple of dollars tip before he even tried it. Gratification came when he pointed to his empty glass a little later indicating that he wanted one more of the same. She made over $50 in tips that night just at the bar.

She enjoyed her experiences behind the bar as it was always busy and time flew by. Still, she let fate and crowds decide when she could work behind the counter and did not request a steady position there.

After almost a month and half of working at O'Donnell's her savings account balance totaled a proud $1,121.

Pride and Prejudice

Sometimes while working at O'Donnell's, Aradhana would entirely forget that she was different from the rest of the people there while at other times, she was profoundly reminded of the fact. Growing up in India had given her a narrower view of racial differences. India was a diverse country with over 1600 languages—at least twenty-four of which were spoken by over a million people—spread across several regions. Most people within the regions looked different. A hotly contested theory is of the Aryan invasion of India by nomadic light skinned tribes from Central Asia. The theory contests that the Dravidians were indigenous to the country and were essentially pushed down to the southern part of the country by the Aryans invaders. The Indian culture had endured much enslavement and oppression at the hands of the fair-skinned people, including the Portugese, the Dutch, and the British. Over those years, the psyche of the people appeared to have developed contradictory offense and defense mechanisms. There was resentment against white people yet in some way there was still reverence and awe of them. This interesting quagmire manifested itself even within the Indian society. People from the north of India—the fairer complexioned, physically stronger Indians—subconsciously felt superior to the darker-skinned, traditionally more intelligent South Indians. On the surface all denied racism, but scratching the surface exposed significant internal conflicts and a struggle to establish an identity that could erase years of brainwashing.

Aradhana found herself no different from the many educated Indians who were trying to establish a sense of self minus the prejudices that had been handed down to them. None were directly exposed to any of that root contradiction in its original form. All experiences were driven by the subtle nuances and subconscious beliefs that were handed from generation to generation. Being ethnically from the north of India, but having culturally assimilated in the south had made Aradhana face the race issue in the Indian context some time ago. She credited herself as being beyond those shallow differences.

However, when Aradhana challenged her superego, she had to concede that this realization of righteousness made her feel superior. It was easy for her to make that decision because it was the right thing to do. But it was only when she was the recipient of prejudice that she

117

truly realized how it felt to bear the brunt of it. She knew that no one chose to be a victim of prejudice. No one ever believed that prejudice was ever right. Somehow it was easy to lapse into prejudice, but hard to be on the receiving end.

Nothing justified a feeling of superiority. If it did, it would change all balances in the world; the delicate balance that humanity was still trying to achieve between man and woman, animal and man, child and adult. There was a reason humans are considered evolved, Aradhana believed. Even thinking too much pushed this balance and had the potential to cause disruption.

Aradhana had decided some time ago not to challenge that balance. But working in O'Donnell's had set her mind's cauldron to bubbling again. This time she was on the receiving end of prejudice. There was an almost poetic justice to it. She believed it would ultimately help her become a better person.

There was one incident that made her acutely aware of the fact that it would never really matter to anyone that she was a deep complex person trying to evolve and be a better person every day. What they would always see was a young Indian girl hard at work in a place where she didn't really belong. They would also see the color of her skin before anything else. Aradhana had established a great rapport with everyone who worked at O'Donnell's. She stopped thinking of them as Irish-American and they stopped thinking of her as Indian. They were individuals who each had thoughts, feelings, and stories to share. Sometimes before the bar opened or on slow days they all sat around talking about life, their beliefs, and desires. There was an unspoken bond that what was said then would remain within the group and there was no offense to be taken. The two subjects that they decided to avoid were religion and politics as Patrick had commented that nothing good ever came from those two conversations.

Patrick was married but the rest weren't and one time the conversation landed on relationships. They insisted that Aradhana tell them about her love life, so she gave them a five-minute download about her relationship with Nirman and how it landed her in the States. Kelly spoke of a college sweetheart in the Marines who was on a two-year assignment in Germany. Peter and Paul were both recently out of relationships. Their conversations meandered to qualities they would look for in women as well as their general preferences. At first both joked about good cooks and looks. Peter quoted some source and said he wanted "Julia Child in the kitchen and Julia Roberts in bed." However, after some prodding they became more serious and even transgressed into the two forbidden topics of politics and religion. Both agreed that the woman of their dreams would have to be Catholic and have strong political beliefs. It was what Peter said next that took Aradhana by surprise.

He said, "She'd have to be white."

It really didn't offend Aradhana or make her judge Peter, but it made the fact that race would never go away very obvious. The look on Aradhana's face must have betrayed her because suddenly there was an awkward silence. Aradhana had a million thoughts going through her head, but she decided to salvage some pride and said,

"I understand completely. I would also only marry an Indian."

A White Christmas

$\mathcal{I}$n mid-December it snowed for the first time since Aradhana arrived. Locals complained that the snow was late and should have arrived a month earlier. The pundits blamed global warming. Aradhana didn't know the history and didn't really care that the snow was late—she was just excited to experience it. That day she ran outside and stuck out her tongue. This was the first time she had ever seen snow. She waited eagerly for enough snow to fall so that she could build a snowman. She had seen a healthy dose of English language movie classics while growing up and most had at least one snow scene in it and she had long fantasized about snowball fights and building a snowman. To her, the snow was romantic, pure, and free.

She was delirious with happiness when she got to play with snow for the first time. Giggling, she sang in Hindi what she thought were appropriate snow songs. Every now and then she scanned the environment to make sure no one was looking. She was in the Franklin Hill Apartments and the little cottages provided a perfect backdrop for what would typically facilitate a Bollywood movie song sequence. She had some interesting moments explaining to people why people sang songs in Hindi movies. Most Americans had a very limited understanding of Bollywood movies, but she found that Europeans, and of course other Asians, were better informed. She was extremely surprised when a friend from a small Estonian village said that he had seen many Hindi movies on cable television with subtitles.

It took an open mind for foreigners to fully appreciate a Hindi movie. The Hindi movie world, or Bollywood as it was called, had a culture of its own. It didn't truly represent all of India per se, but it was an undeniable part of it. It was most prolific in terms of the number of movies produced. The true stars of Bollywood were treated as demigods. The movies were fantastical, romantic, social, moral, and encompassed all other facets of human life. They showed people breaking out into song at the slightest indication of a romantic situation. The songs were romantic, musical, cheeky, foot-tapping or whatever mood the directors wanted to represent. Most often songs were sung in duet by the hero and heroine. Even the most romantic songs were supported by a large cast of extras who danced to the beat of the protagonist's singing. There was music for every occasion and a song for every mood. Raunchy numbers or "item numbers" as they came to be known, were cabaret-style numbers that were inserted without reason or situation into a movie. They were the crowd pleasers and the ones that made the movies money. The funny thing, though, was that no matter how awkward or misplaced the songs were, they became an integral part of the lives of Indian and so many worldwide Bollywood fans. The same songs would be hummed in bathrooms, played at parties, and blasted in the cars of the millions of non-resident Indians the world over. Bollywood music was an integral part of their fiber. Indians even had a game called Antashari whose entire *raison d'etre* was to have people sing songs. The game required teams of people who took turns singing a song beginning with the last letter of the song sung by the previous team. The industry had provided them with so many songs that it was really hard for the game to die of natural causes.

Songs in movies were the substitute for kissing or lovemaking scenes. One could assume without fear of being wrong that a song in the rain, or two lips coyly but dramatically pulling away from each other before bursting into song was meant to imply passion. For some reason the Indian audience seemed more able to reconcile this than a scene of actual kissing or sex. Aradhana always struggled with this dichotomy in a nation that gave the world the Kama Sutra and the bold frescos and sculptures at the various temples. It was the ultimate tribute to irony that the country with the world's second largest population chose to be so coy about its sexual interest. Nevertheless, no one in India actually sang around trees or in the rain. Clearly someone somewhere was making love. People did enjoy singing, though, and it formed a very important fabric of the Indian society. Pretending to sing in the rain was often satirical because it captured several conflicting moods in a simple action. As Aradhana play-acted the various songs, she smirked to herself. She had the song, the mood, and the background. The only thing missing was her hero.

She found herself leaning heavily on Nirman. It seemed that the more she became independent, the more she also became dependent on him. It seemed like she called Nirman more than he called her and when she got him on the phone, he was always on his way to a party. Either he fit into the core of the American society or he did a good job pretending he did. She was still holding on to the reason she had made this journey—that ultimately they'd get married.

It was soon after the first snowfall in December that Scott invited Aradhana to spend Christmas with him and his family. It was to be a huge family event with his parents, Uncle Jim, Kelly and the extended O'Donnell family. She had already met several members of Scott's family but had yet to meet his mother and father. Scott spoke fondly of them and from what she gathered, they appeared to know about her. Aradhana was sure that if Scott hadn't mentioned her then Kelly would have. So far all of her interactions with the O'Donnells except for Scott had been at the pub.

Scott had moved out of his parents' home almost a decade ago. During his undergrad years he lived in the college dorms and after graduating moved to the town of Somerville where the rent was cheaper than Cambridge. Aradhana always imagined that Scott's apartment would be chaotic and sparsely furnished. Scott had extended an invitation for Aradhana to visit him at one point but Aradhana hadn't been able to make the trip. So far he had not invited her again and Aradhana sensed that he almost seemed relieved that she had said no. Aradhana had told Scott about Nirman but had a hard time reading his reaction. Since on the surface he seemed unperturbed, she took it for face value. She hadn't told him about the difficulties that she and Nirman were experiencing of late, though. Instead she'd told him the short version about a girl who had never before left India following her high school sweetheart to the United States. Scott asked her why she didn't plan on visiting Nirman in California over Christmas. She gave an unconvincing answer of a too heavy workload and too little money. Even though it was partly true, she would have gone in a heartbeat if Nirman had invited her. In fact she had asked him to visit her. Alaya was spending winter break with her family in New Jersey and Laxmi was going back to India so she had the entire apartment to herself. She had begged and cajoled him, but he said that as the resident assistant in the dorms he could not leave. She knew this to be true, but doubted that there would be individuals in the dorm during over the break.

During the first few days by herself in the apartment, she felt lonelier than she had since first arriving to the United States. She knew she needed to distract herself. She had no on-campus jobs during break, only the job at O'Donnell's. She knew one sure way of attracting company in the Franklin Hill Apartments was food. Aradhana was a good cook and liberally used her skills to keep herself occupied. Every day Aradhana had five to ten people over who like her, had nowhere to go for the holidays, including Asad and the twins. She experimented with recipes Patrick had taught her as well as improvised with the Indian recipes she knew. Word spread near and far that good free food was up for grabs. She was five days into this ritual on December twentieth when early that evening the doorbell rang as she was busy cooking. Thinking it was one more of the much-welcome freeloaders, Aradhana moved lazily to the door. To her frustration, the doorbell kept ringing incessantly and showed no signs of stopping. As she opened the door with an angry look on her face, there stood Nirman in jeans and a grey and navy blue-checked sweater. Although he had sent pictures, she had not seen Nirman for three years and he looked more dynamic than Aradhana ever remembered him. The boy she loved had turned into a handsome man with tremendous confidence.

"You still mad at me?" he asked as he grabbed her in his arms and kissed her on the lips with a gentle fervor. Her lips quivered as she responded to the mastery with which his mouth sought hers. This was nothing like their first kiss several years ago that she initiated. After he let her go he smiled at her.

"I've had practice," he joked sensing where Aradhana's mind had gone.

Somehow she had a feeling that he wasn't joking. For now, though, she was delirious with happiness. Next to him were a duffel bag and a backpack. She quickly ushered him in. It was surreal— Nirman was standing in front of her. For the past three years, she had kept the same image of him in her mind of the day he had left. She knew she had changed and matured since he'd left and while she was quite sure he would have too, her mind never bothered with the progression. It was always more comfortable to remember him the way she knew him. He was like a familiar stranger. He had been skinny and tall before. During the last few years he had filled out and now looked like a man. She remembered him as awkward and a bit shy, but the guy who now stood before her was oozing self-confidence. Nirman had never been very comfortable around women but it seemed like he exuded a new magnetic energy. She could smell the fresh strong masculine cologne on contact. She was giddy with attraction and happiness as it had been too long since she had felt his tenderness. Too long since he had taken her in his arms. She felt vulnerable and realized that she *wanted* to feel vulnerable. She wanted to melt in his arms and never look back. She didn't want to face anything alone anymore. He was there and that's what mattered. He loved her—his kiss told her that. He had taken charge. He was in control of her at that moment, and that's the way she liked it. She was tired of taking charge. She wanted someone else to decide what was right for her.

Seeming to sense her vulnerability, he drew her closer. She hugged him tighter. Neither said anything for the next few minutes. Finally he kissed her lightly on her forehead.

"You've filled out," he with an impish grin.

"So have you," she said, returning the compliment.

"It's been too long," he said as he kissed her again, this time more passionately. She couldn't help but think of those years in India when they would meet on the sly, away from watchful eyes of both their families as contact was restricted and physical interaction forbidden. Yet for two years they had managed to find many opportunities, to touch, kiss and explore each other. Everything had been new. Neither knew any better, but they found immense pleasure and happiness in their journey. They had set barriers for themselves which would have been too easy to cross, but they never did. There was respect and honesty in that. In retrospect, there was not a thing she would have done differently.

The ringing of the telephone interrupted their passionate embrace. They smiled at each other as Nirman pointed to the phone, with an expression that said "go get that."

It was Asad asking when they should plan on being there. As Nirman made his way to the kitchen, Aradhana took the opportunity to explain the situation to Asad. All plans were cancelled until further notice. Teasing her, Asad insisted that they'd be there in ten minutes. "Just try it," warned Aradhana as she said goodbye. She knew they would more than understand. In moments of loneliness, she had told whoever would listen about her relationship with Nirman. She had never spoken of the emotional distance that had grown between them—only the physical distance. That was just something she struggled with internally.

Today, however, seeing him in the flesh as he examined the contents of the refrigerator, she felt no doubts. She snuck up behind him and grabbed his waist. In a move she didn't expect, and couldn't make sense of, he turned her around so that her back rested against the refrigerator door and began kissing her long and hard. She felt weak in her legs as he massaged her shoulders with the hand that had rested harmlessly just a few minutes ago against the refrigerator door. Gently he slipped it under her shirt and a button gave way with minimal resistance. She knew if she didn't stop him now, she would not be able to stop him tonight.

"Please stop," she said feebly.

"Do you really want me to?" he asked.

She didn't know where, the "No" came from, but that's what she said. She didn't want him to stop. She hadn't felt so secure and complete in a long time. She hadn't ever felt this close to giving in.

His lips followed his hands, starting with her neck, and made their way down. Aradhana responded with more passion than she knew herself to have. There was an aggression in her response that seemed to catch Nirman by surprise and he responded to her tempo. There were so many feelings going through Aradhana that she didn't know which one to address first. First she wanted to feel the warmth, and security, but close behind that was a need to mark her territory. Nirman was the only link with a world that she had left behind. He represented all things familiar, all things hers. He was hers; the life that she left behind was for him.

She hastily pulled his sweater off and, like a kid who was getting increasingly impatient with unwrapping a gift, ripped the shirt underneath. Before either knew what was happening, they were on the kitchen floor and she was on top of Nirman exploring the outline of his body with her tongue. She had never seen Nirman naked. As she unbuttoned his jeans, she felt weak. Where was this coming from? If she crossed this line, there was no going back. There never was. While this may not have been an unusual reaction here in America, her new home, this wasn't how things were done in India. The lines between morality and immorality as she was taught were black and white. There were no shades of grey. Now, however, it seemed like she was discovering that there was more grey than black and white.

Nirman had never seen her this way and responded with comparable passion. At that moment it seemed like she wouldn't be judged no matter what she did. She didn't need to be judged any more in life. She liked the control and he seemed to like her controlling him. She had always imagined that her first time would be gentle. The love of her life would be in charge, and would explore her. She would give in, grateful to be loved with such tenderness. This was nothing like that. There were no satin sheets, and no beds of flowers. In India, virginity was something you lost on the night you were married. Your bed was covered with flowers so you would make love on a bed of flowers. This was the kitchen floor. It didn't feel cold, but it was cold. Nothing mattered except this moment.

As her tongue began to explore forbidden territory, Nirman groaned. As he gently arched up from the kitchen floor, he kept massaging her back. Suddenly he flipped her over so that she was on the floor and he was the one doing the exploring. Aradhana responded loudly to the pleasure she felt and pulled him closer, not wanting any distance between them. She wanted to be one with him. Nirman wanted the same thing. She was afraid yet she had never been more confident. Today she was seeing a side of herself that was new even to her. Pleasure was not something you sought but today she was seeking, responding, appreciating. She didn't want anything to end. In her strength she was weak. She could just as easily have let go and not moved a single muscle but she wanted to give back to Nirman the pleasure she was experiencing. Almost without moving, Nirman took something out of his wallet. It was a condom. There was no looking back.

She then experienced a forbidden pleasure that transported her from being a girl to being a woman. Afterwards, she felt complete and honored. At that moment there was no shame but she wondered if she would regret it someday. The next thing she remembered was waking up at two in the morning in Nirman's arms, still on the kitchen floor. She kissed him gently on the forehead, woke him up, and took him upstairs to her room. It took him less than a few minutes to fall asleep again. This time, he rested his head on the crook of her arm.

• • •

After sharing a part of herself that she hadn't discovered yet, she wanted to share something else she was still discovering with Nirman—the city of Boston. She wanted to share the sights, smells, and sounds with him as it would be another experience that bound them deeper. The doubts and the acrimony she had been feeling over the last few months were forgotten. There were no pretenses and no games between them. They enjoyed each other for who they were. Aradhana took comfort in Nirman's confidence and his ability to find his way around. He represented all things she wanted to be. She wasn't sure that she was there as yet. She was confident yet there was still much insecurity in her whereas Nirman seemed to be very secure. She struggled with the two different sides of Nirman she had experienced.

There was no doubt that Nirman had changed a great deal since he had come to America. She couldn't seem to also reconcile the fact that he seemed so different on the phone from who he was in person.

Which of those sides was the real him? Was this just another instance of a shade of grey? Did distance make the heart grow fonder or did it separate people? She wasn't sure as yet. What attracted her now was that he let her be vulnerable. He pampered her and gave into her silly demands including wearing matching clothes, and singing her lullabies. He looked at her with goo-goo eyes, and every so often they spoke to each other in child-like voices. They rewarded each other for little accomplishments and kissed each other "boo-boos."

Over the next few days until Christmas, Aradhana enjoyed Boston more than ever before. One reason why was that Nirman seemed to see the broader picture of the United States experience. He didn't worry about school or money the way Aradhana did. In a few days Aradhana learned how many more things you could enjoy with money. Nirman had a boyish outlook on life. "Live for today, tomorrow will be okay," he said as he made Aradhana apply for the first credit card she ever had.

Aradhana decided to follow Nirman's example for at least the duration of his stay. The second night after his momentous arrival, they set out to walk the Freedom Trail but instead ended up getting food from Quincy Market and sitting by the Boston Harbor reminiscing about home. They ate dinner at a small Italian restaurant in North End and topped it off with some famous pastries from Mike's, the pastry shop that everyone frequented. She had tried them once before with Scott and was excited to share the experience with Nirman. After walking hand in hand through the North End, they made their way back home. For the first time since she had come to Boston, she took a taxi from the train station to her apartment, which cost them over twenty-five dollars. As with everything else that day, Nirman refused to let her pay, telling her that while he was here, he'd pay and when she came to California, she could pay. She was basking in the sense of belonging and comfort. She wanted to break every tie with this world and only be with him, not caring what it would cost her.

She was supposed to work the following day, but she couldn't get herself to go. Early in the morning, she called O'Donnell's, planning to tell Uncle Jim that she was sick and would be unable to work for the next few weeks. However, she couldn't get herself to lie to the only people who had welcomed her with open arms so instead she told him about the situation. She apologized for the extremely short notice but asked if it was okay if she took some time off while Nirman was here. Deep down she feared that they would lose respect for her as a dependable worker but Nirman's companionship was more important to her at that moment than what anyone thought of her.

Uncle Jim was very understanding and told her not to worry. He assured her that they would have it covered before giving the phone to Kelly. Aradhana explained the situation to her. Kelly didn't say much but assured her that she shouldn't worry. As she said goodbye, she added, "You should call Scott, though." Aradhana called Scott and as she had anticipated, he asked Nirman to join them for Christmas dinner. Nirman declined the offer, and said he'd rather stay home. Aradhana was not particularly disappointed but she could tell Scott wasn't too thrilled. He wished the two of them a Merry Christmas and happy holidays.

Over the following days, Aradhana and Nirman continued to discover each other as well as Boston. The explored almost every place in the city that the subway could take them. Among the places they visited were the Boston Aquarium, the Art Museum, the Science Museum, Harvard Square, Chinatown, Downtown, Park Street, the Charles River and the glorified educational institutions. She took Nirman to O'Donnell's but was adamant that they not go inside. She felt self-conscious about introducing Nirman to the O'Donnells although she wasn't sure why. Also, she did not want to go into the place she worked and be served. Nirman was content to view the establishment from outside, but then wanted to go to another Irish pub to share the experience.

The day before Christmas, Nirman insisted that they buy a Christmas tree with all the requisite paraphernalia. There were the red, white and green string lights, golden bells, angels with trumpets, and, of course, a star. They spent Christmas Eve decorating the tree and watching snow fall outside the window. On Christmas morning, for the first time since Nirman had been there, he was up before Aradhana. Aradhana's nostrils were tickled with the sweet smell of scrambled eggs cooked in milk and toast. She thought she was dreaming and didn't open her eyes but a few minutes later, Nirman came in with a tray complete with eggs, toast, and orange juice. Like Christmas, every day that followed was special. Nirman and Aradhana also spent a memorable New Year's Eve in Boston that started with making resolutions and ended with fireworks.

Aradhana made one resolution that year—that she would never let Nirman go.

Beyond Mediocrity

*N*irman left two days later. Aradhana felt she could not have started the year on a better note and the first few months only built on the way it had started. Everything was going amazingly well. Her efforts at taking notes and diligently working at her studies paid off. She had also learned the highly useful skill of networking and building relationships. Nepotism was everywhere only here it wasn't as crude and direct as it was in India. It was a little more disguised and sophisticated and cloaked under the innocuous robe of networking. Aradhana had spent the first semester observing the experts and figuring out how to make networking work for her. She regularly reached out to professors to ask if opportunities for scholarships and assistantships existed and went the extra mile to do research on topics she knew were of interest to the professors. Her hard work paid off and she succeeded in creating an assistantship for herself in the Philosophy department. It proved to be a better deal than she could have ever asked for. It entirely covered her tuition for work she was already doing plus provided her with a little extra. She occasionally assisted the professor in correcting undergraduate papers and supervising exams or projects. She continued to work at O'Donnell's because it made her feel alive and supplemented her income very nicely.

She and Scott took a couple of courses together over the next semester and got to know each other much better. Scott had depth and sincerity in everthing he did. He also seemed to keep his feelings close to his chest. Aradhana often joked that she didn't know what she needed to do to make him angry. She had never seen Scott show his emotions. She would tease him and tell him that he was cold-blooded and she was hot-blooded and never the twain would meet. All he'd do was laugh. Kelly was a lot more like her—hot-blooded and emotional. There was little that did not excite her. For two individuals that were so similar, Kelly and Aradhana got along famously. Aradhana just never opened her heart to her. Asad was really the only person apart from Nirman to whom Aradhana let her vulnerability show. To all other people, she came across as a passionate, strong, sometimes overly self-assured person. She did not want to expose herself; she just was not ready for it.

She was surprised by how much she missed Gauri. She spoke to Gauri more now than she had since becoming an adult. She had tried to get Gauri used to the computer but had failed. While the phone conversations were strained and not completely honest, Aradhana cherished them. Aradhana found that whenever she spoke of a struggle, Gauri got extremely worried and asked her to come back to India. Aradhana could not even think of talking to her about her other experiences. Still, she could tell that Gauri missed her. Aradhana was growing as a person but there was much to discover about her mother. She made Gauri promise her that she would come for her graduation. There was only one thing Aradhana was looking forward to and it was graduating. She couldn't wait to finish school and start the next chapter of her life. She wanted to give Gauri that feeling of pride she had robbed from her when she sabotaged her medical entrance exams. Somehow she felt that Gauri wanted her to be successful to compensate for what she herself didn't achieve. She promised Gauri that she would sponsor her trip to Boston for her graduation.

While she missed home, she could not afford to go back home yet. She was already saving to return the money that her father had given her, as her pride did not allow her to be indebted to him. She hadn't spoken directly to him since she had been gone. It was always her mother who communicated what her father said. Even through proxy, their conversations were limited to instructions and banalities. Aradhana wasn't particularly surprised as her father never really had much of a relationship with any of them. Somewhere deep down, though, Aradhana had hoped he'd say something nice to her. Perhaps he'd tell her how things were not the same without her. Perhaps he'd go out on a limb and tell her that he missed her. She knew better though. Mr. Kapoor was a bitter man. What caused him to be so bitter Aradhana didn't know, but he acted as if the world owed him. He was suspicious of most people, even his family. A quality that Aradhana, never really understood. Even though Mr. Kapoor didn't actively engage in doing things around the house, he laid down clear rules of how he wanted things done. There was structure in everything. There was a set time for breakfast, lunch and dinner. All her life, Aradhana saw him take the same food for lunch to work everyday—*rotis*, lentils cooked a certain way, and a spicy okra dish that never varied in taste. Dinner was elaborate and varied. There were always at least three courses and the food had to be elaborately presented on fine china. He wanted the entire family around the table but no conversation was allowed. The only time the family could talk was in response to his questions and to ask for something on the table. Because dinner was at the same time each day, there were no excuses for missing it. He expected the children to be dressed for dinner. Pajamas or night clothing wasn't allowed. Ashwin Kapoor was a mystery to Aradhana. Even though he was her father, she always thought of him as Mr. Kapoor. He was defined by what he was, and not by who he was. Though the family was obviously uncomfortable with his behavior, Gauri forbid the children from ever talking ill of him.

Aradhana had seen Gauri and Ashwin barely acknowledge each other as individuals. Their interactions were transactional; "Was okra added in the tiffin?," "Was dinner prepared?," "Were the monthly expenses deposited in the bank account?," "Would Ashwin, please make sure he's in time to attend the party" etc.

Aradhana never understood why her parents lived together. She was just glad that her relationship was nothing like her parents'.

Spring Break

*A*radhana decided to surprise Nirman over spring break. It was her turn to visit him in California. She was already saving for Gauri's ticket for her graduation but she pinched some money from that fund for her ticket to California. She and Nirman had been talking every day since his visit and he seemed to be more emotionally available to her than she had ever known him to be. Through their conversations, Aradhana knew that Nirman had no plans for the vacation and had hoped that he would ask her to visit, but he hadn't. Nirman had recently left his RA position because he felt it kept him away from his studies. He had just moved off campus to a two-bedroom apartment that he was sharing with a housemate and said he needed time to settle in. Moreover, he said he had to spend the break doing school assignments. Aradhana didn't mind. She rationalized that he was probably worried that he would have to spring for her fare. She knew Nirman would be ecstatic to see her. Plus, he would more than appreciate her help in setting things up in his new place.

She also worried about Nirman's health. She worried if his tumor would come back. Though the chances were slim, it did exist. She didn't want Nirman to take on more stress than he needed to. Nirman was an only child, and the apple of his mother's eye but he resented the extra attention he had received after his cancer. While his parents worked late hours, they went through great lengths to make sure Nirman had everything he needed. Nirman hated being constantly care for. Aradhana could somewhat understand that but she could not stop herself from asking him to slow down. The thought of transferring to Nirman's school had crossed her mind and she was hoping to discuss it with him during the trip. She was sure he would be pleased, but she also knew that she'd have to be careful not to give him the feeling that she was doing it to take care of him.

Aradhana got the address of his new apartment under the pretext that she wanted to mail him a jacket she had brought for him on sale at Macy's. Nirman chided her for spending money on him and said that she should save all her money so that she didn't have to work so hard. She really *had* bought a jacket for him, but she wasn't planning to mail it. She was going to deliver it in person.

She told him that she would be spending a few days of spring break with Alaya's family in New Jersey and then for the remainder, she'd be working at the bar and on her schoolwork. The truth, however, was that she had worked at the bar every single day for the past month in order to make some extra money and earn time off to visit him. Alaya had invited her to New Jersey but she had declined. She found it really hard to lie to Nirman. Because she couldn't afford a cell phone yet, he had asked for Alaya's number in New Jersey so that he could reach her during the break. She told him that she'd call him when she got there.

Aradhana had booked the airline ticket through Priceline.com. She didn't have a computer yet, and spend hours working in the school computer lab. She loved the fact that she could find a ticket within her budget but was worried about the flight timings. If the flight arrived late in the night she would have trouble finding her way to Pasadena. Moreover, she didn't want to disturb Nirman's housemate. She knew nothing about him except that he was a senior and his name was David. She was not disappointed with the itinerary except for the fact that she had to make a connection in Washington D.C. The United Airlines flight was supposed to leave at noon and arrive at approximately 5:15 p.m. The ticket cost her less than $200 which she assumed was a good fare coast to coast considering Nirman had spent close to $500 for his roundtrip ticket during winter break. She had done some research on the internet and knew there was an airport bus service that would take her to Pasadena after making one stop at a hotel in Los Angeles. Aradhana was very excited as this was the first time she was flying within the U.S. She departed on a Tuesday and had a return flight booked for the following Tuesday. She figured that she'd give Nirman whatever space he needed to do his assignments and would bring along her own assignments. She packed sensibly and was able to carry on her belongings. When she reached D.C., they didn't have to change planes but she did have an opportunity to de-plane. She ate some Chinese food and read a book. She became giddy when she thought about Nirman's face when he opened the door.

She wasn't sure if his housemate would be there with him or if he was away for spring break. Nirman had said that David was still deciding what he would do. She figured that even if he were around, he'd be glad to have her there as she planned to cook for him as well to make up for the inconvenience of showing up unannounced. Many people had told her that she was a great cook and most importantly Nirman loved her cooking. When he visited Boston, he had lovingly asked her to make his favorite dishes which Aradhana was only too happy to do. She smiled when she thought of the fun times they had in the kitchen with Nirman helping her out, which inevitability ended up with the two of them on the kitchen floor. Thanks to her working at O'Donnell's she had picked up some true Irish recipes. She had also perfected her vegetable lasagna which she was eager to cook for Nirman as he was also a vegetarian. He had stopped eating meat after he was diagnosed with cancer. To him it was a little sacrifice he was making to ask God for his own life back.

In addition to her culinary bribing, she hoped to impress Nirman and his roommate with her cocktail-making skills as she was sure that would win their hearts. She still didn't drink much but admittedly drank more than she did before she started working at O'Donnell's. She sometimes thought of how easy it was to take on drinking especially for someone who was struggling to find acceptance and their identity. She had to grudgingly admit that her confidence rose when she drank. In addition, It was easier for her to be social and fit into American settings when she did. She often wondered if she was compromising too much to fit in. For now, however, all she could think of was impressing Nirman.

She tried to imagine his face when he opened the door. He would be really surprised. In preparation for spring break she was wearing a sleeveless brown and cream floral print dress with a V-neck that exposed her ample cleavage. She wore brown carnation shaped earrings with a matching locket. She had even grown her nails for the trip and had them painted a luscious shade of brown. The cream and brown open-toed sandals exposed her toes with matching nail polish. A fake but very authentic-looking Burberry purse from Chinatown completed the ensemble. She had attracted more than a few glances on this trip, and was excited about it as she knew Nirman was becoming very Western. On his trip to Boston he had asked her if she would wear a bikini when she visited him. They had ended up fighting because Aradhana could not believe that he would want her to expose herself like that in front of everyone. The Indian in her wanted to be conservative yet the liberal in her was excited at the prospect. She herself had thought of the many liberties that being in the U.S. offered her. All the things she had to fight to do in India, she could do with no admonition here. However, Nirman asking her to do this had caught her off guard and her reaction to him was defensive. He had told her that she was a prude and had double standards. Aradhana had given it a lot of thought and finally bought an aqua blue bikini. When she modeled it for Nirman, he was more than overjoyed and credited her resourcefulness for managing to get her hands on one in the middle of December. She was bringing that bikini along on this trip. Aradhana realized that if she wanted to win Nirman completely over she would have to make some sacrifices. However, the only difference was that her own experiences lagged behind Nirman's as he had the advantage of being in the States for almost three years more than her. Moreover, as an undergraduate he was experiencing life through a completely different lens. Aradhana on the other hand was a graduate student forced to work many jobs and already had established concepts of morality and behavior. Still, Aradhana was young and eager to assimilate if it meant being closer to Nirman.

By the time they reached Los Angeles it was 7:30 in the evening and the airport was buzzing with activity. The walk from where they deplaned to the exit was a long one. Aradhana keenly observed people's increasing pace as they headed towards the exit and felt that she was lagging behind most of them by miles, rationalizing that her enthusiasm or urgency was lesser because no one was waiting for her. She had checked the printed bus schedule several times and knew that there was an 8 p.m. bus. Ten minutes into the walk, she too increased her pace, almost to the point where she was running. When she finally got to the sign that pointed to transportation she wasn't really sure if she was even in the right place. She looked around and found an information booth. An older African American woman sat behind the counter and tried to allay the fear in Aradhana's voice. Yes, she was in the right place and she had time. It was ten minutes to eight and Aradhana should have headed straight for the bus but her eye saw a little newsstand that was selling flowers. Instinctively Aradhana was attracted to the yellow roses that were prominently displayed and paid sixteen dollars for the bouquet. By the time she got on the bus it was already nearly full.

She saw people looking at her balancing the bag, her purse and flowers and giving her an all-knowing smile. She sat next to a Hispanic woman who struck up a conversation with her by commenting on the beauty of the flowers and introduced herself as Rosa. As always, Aradhana found it easier to pour out the story of her life to a stranger rather than to someone she already knew. She told Rosa about the little surprise trip and her journey all the way from India for love and nodded wholeheartedly when Rosa told her that long distance relationships were hard. Rosa herself was an immigrant from

Mexico who had been living in Arizona for thirty years. She was visiting her son who lived with his American wife and newborn daughter in Pasadena. Talking about her daughter-in-law, Rosa became overcome with emotion and started to describe how different "our" cultures were from the American culture. Despite being in the U.S. for thirty years, she said, she could never completely adapt to the American culture. Outwardly she may have changed, but inside she was still a Mexican.

"These people will never fully accept you even if they pretend to," she said.

The volume in her voice got lower as she sized up the white Americans sitting in front and behind her.

"They are hypocrites," she whispered. "They themselves are immigrants but don't want others to succeed even if they're too politically correct or scared to openly say it. You will always be an outsider no matter how hard you try."

Aradhana thought all this to be ominous but didn't take it too much to heart.

Through the rest of the trip Aradhana learned of Rosa's problems with her daughter-in- law. Apparently Aradhana was not the only person who found it easier to talk to strangers. Karen, Rosa's daughter-in-law, had vowed to not allow her daughter to learn Spanish or anything about the Mexican culture and had refused to let Rosa do her traditional Mexican customs when the baby was born. Moreover, Rosa felt that she judged her all along and never thought her good enough. Her son, she said, was too henpecked to say anything. Aradhana really liked Rosa and was more than willing to believe in the evil American daughter-in-law theory. Realistically, however, Aradhana wondered if Rosa may have been too overbearing and controlling to the woman.

Through this conversation she had picked up how similar the two cultures were. She had seen more than a fair share of overbearing Indian mother-in-laws trying to establish their territory with their sons. Mother-in-law and daughter-in-law relationships were strained by definition. Throwing different cultures into them would, almost without fail, strain things further. Rosa was nervous about this trip and wondered if Karen would treat her well.

"My son forced me to come, as I had sworn never to go to his house again, but I had to see my only granddaughter. This is the last chance, though. If she doesn't try, then my son is also dead for me.

You know, his father was a day laborer. We entered this country illegally through the desert. I had him strapped to my back. We hid for days with only a little food and water. We were able to file immigration papers and in ten years we had our green card. Now he is too much of an American to remember the sacrifices we made. His father never even got to realize his dream of being an American. I believe he died from sheer exhaustion. God bless his soul, he worked harder than any one I know. My son on the other hand has grown up with privilege. He has a Ph.D. and is some big researcher. He does not know the sweet joy of working with his hands like we did. See, my hands are like a laborer's. I own three Mexican grocery stores now, but my hands are still the same. We made sure our son never saw the hardships that we did. We were wrong. We should have let him struggle for himself. Only then he would have appreciated where he came from. Having a white wife doesn't make him white. He will always be a beaner or spic."

By the end of her five-minute summary on the life of two generations, Rosa was almost fuming. Aradhana had no idea what a beaner or spic meant by rightly surmised they were derogatory ways of referring to Mexican people. She made a mental note to research these terms on the Net.

In her impassioned conversation with Rosa, Aradhana lost track of time and before she knew it they were in Pasadena and she found herself hugging Rosa goodbye. Even thought it was after 9:30 p.m. when they arrived, the traffic was still heavy. As she was hailing a taxi she saw Rosa hugging a very attractive man, while a tall, stunning blonde looked on with a baby in her arms. She smiled, hoping only the best for Rosa.

She knew it was late and that she would need to rush to Nirman's house. It had been a heavy conversation and she needed to lighten up her mood a bit. She looked at her flowers and smiled. The taxi driver was a large black man who helped her load her luggage into the car. Years of bias made her a little fearful of him. As he smiled she saw a gold tooth in the molars. She chided herself for her biases and smiled back. On the way, she had hoped they'd pass a wine store but everything was closed. When the meter reflected twelve dollars, they entered a pretty townhouse community surrounded by tropical foliage. She gave Nirman's name and address to the security office at the entrance. After explaining to him that it was a surprise, she pleaded with the security guard not to buzz him. Both the taxi driver and the security guard smiled gleefully as the gate was lifted. She smiled back, and thanked him. As they got closer to Nirman's building, she asked the taxi driver to stop and gave him a generous three dollar tip to make up for her biased thoughts. She hoped that he hadn't noticed it. He wished her good luck and winked as he sped out of the community.

Aradhana found herself smiling like the Cheshire cat. She hopped, skipped and jumped down the stairs until it became too inconvenient to proceed with the tempo. The houses were arranged by odd and even numbers across both sides of the street. Finally she saw number 15, which was Nirman's apartment. It was a cozy entrance tucked away from the main road facing the rear side of the community. Judging by the other homes she'd just passed, the kitchen would lead to an outside porch used by most for barbequing. All the units had tall French windows on the left of the entrance that offered a view to the kitchen if the blinds or curtain were open. As she made her way to Nirman's apartment, she wondered if he would have blinds or curtains. She hoped that his bell wasn't too loud as she felt that it would take away from the mood she hoped for. She was sure her heart was beating a thousand beats a minute. She didn't want to be caught ringing the bell because that would make her entrance anticlimactic. Keeping the flowers but leaving her luggage outside the little gate that opened to the townhouse, she took her shoes off and held them in her hand so that they didn't make loud noises on the concrete.

Nirman's blinds were only slightly open, but it was enough to satiate her curiosity and plan her moves. She peeped into the apartment. The kitchen lights were on and she saw him in his red and grey-checked boxers rinsing a wine glass at the sink. Just as she was about to ring the bell, a tall red-haired woman walked into the kitchen and wrapped her arms around Nirman's waist. In horror, Aradhana watched as their tongues explored each other and Nirman gently pressed the woman against the refrigerator in the same way he had done to her just a few months earlier. Seconds later his hand began to find her breasts. Suddenly, the reality of it all hit Aradhana and she dropped her shoes and the flowers. To Aradhana, the sound that her shoes made as they hit the concrete sounded louder than a thousand glasses crashing. Nirman must have felt her presence because even in his infidel passion, he heard it, too. While Aradhana bent down to retrieve her shoes, the door opened and she found herself staring stone-faced at Nirman's boxers.

Coping

*A*radhana was losing the one thing that sustained her through everything in life—her self-respect. Not only had she lost the love of her life, but she also couldn't believe who she was becoming. The day Nirman shattered her trust she had exercised restraint and walked away. Nirman had run behind her but she kept going. When he finally stopped her, he had little to say other than he was sorry. Aradhana briefly remembered him saying something about how he was still young, and the relationship was tying him down. He was just an undergraduate and would never get these opportunities again. He loved Aradhana, but wasn't ready to settle down yet. They were growing up and growing apart. Aradhana was too needy, he said. She needed too much of him and he needed space.

Aradhana wanted to say a million things. She wanted to ask just how much space was enough space in America. Wasn't coast to coast enough? Had he forgotten that it was he who had pursued her against all odds? He was the reason that she was in the United States to begin with. Had he forgotten all the times they had spent at the temple, at his house, in her room? All those innocent times? And how much she had wanted him to succeed. Glimpses of her coaching him for his SAT whizzed before her eyes. In the few minutes that she was before him on that dark night, she felt like time was standing still. The minutes seemed like hours. How could she possibly walk away with any dignity after what she saw? She wanted to believe that it was all just a dream. She wanted to deny it ever happened, but something in Nirman's cold eyes told her that it did. In those few minutes she felt first denial and then indignation.

She didn't need him. For all she cared, he could go to hell, but she didn't say that. All she said was goodbye as she walked away. She would never forget the look of sympathy the security guard had for her when she asked him to hail her a cab, trying not to let her eyes tell the story that couldn't be stopped from being told. The ten minutes waiting for the taxi felt like an eternity. Once she was back at the airport, she asked whether she could get on the red-eye back to Boston and was told that with her ticket it would not be possible. However, if she wanted, she could pay for the ticket all over again. It would be $650 one way. She bought the ticket.

When she reached Boston, she took a taxi back home. She had not slept all night and her eyes were swollen and red. All through the flight she had cried silent tears. As there was no one in the apartment, she was free to cry loudly all day.

Over the next week, she called Nirman obsessively several times a day. Initially she got his voicemail and left him long messages. They varied from questioning to pleading to anger and to denial. She'd ask him why he had abandoned her and how he could do that to her. She pleaded for him to take her back. And then she asked him if the "white bitch" had given him pleasure. There were times she pretended nothing had happened. By the second week she got busy signals followed by a message saying that the subscriber had disconnected his service.

She began drinking heavily, staying in her room and drowning her feelings in cheap vodka and orange juice. She slept through the day and cried through the night. She got up with severe headaches. For two weeks she didn't see the light of day. After two weeks, her roommates were back. Laxmi, the confirmed vegetarian who said her prayers two times a day, was outraged at the empty vodka bottles in the room. The kitchen was full of empty ramen noodle packets and smelled of garbage that had piled up over two weeks. Aradhana looked ten years older than before they had left her.

Laxmi didn't care and just wanted the mess cleaned up. She went to Alaya and started complaining. She said that they didn't know Aradhana was a drinker, and didn't want a roommate who drank. She said that Aradhana was a bad influence and wanted her out. Aradhana heard the conversation and got belligerent. She asked Laxmi why she didn't have the guts to speak directly to her and asked her to do unspeakable things to herself. She pinned Laxmi to the wall and asked her if she had a problem.

Things with Aradhana reached rock bottom over the next month that followed. She missed work and classes and even quit her job at the bar. She told Scott that she couldn't work there because she didn't want to be around any families or couples. She didn't want to be around anyone. Everything she had based her life on was a lie. Her own identify and confidence was shaken. She pushed away anyone who tried to come close to her, most of all Scott. He tried to understand what had brought about this change in her, but she wasn't ready to talk. She even had problems with Alaya. The two of them had gotten along well because they both liked to socialize and share their experiences, but now that Aradhana did not even acknowledge the existence of anyone around her, there was a severe strain in their relationship. She and Laxmi shared a room, but ignored each other. She tried to avoid Gauri's calls and when forced to speak to her, responded with one-word answers. Gauri knew that something was wrong, but couldn't do anything about it.

Shutting everyone out from her life only made Aradhana feel worse. She wanted to abandon her schooling and go back to India, but knew that would make her a quitter.

It was exactly a month after the incident when Scott came to visit Aradhana. It was a little after noon and she was still in bed and therefore in no mood for entertaining anyone. As she opened the door, she saw that Scott had a look on his face that she had never seen before. He looked stern and in charge. He sat her down and literally shook her as he told her that he wasn't sure what Aradhana had experienced in California, but he had an idea. While it was none of his business, something in his heart just couldn't bear what was happening to her. He said that he wasn't a professional and was too close to the situation to give her any unbiased advice, but he knew she needed help. He couldn't explain why he had come to feel so protective and concerned for Aradhana in such a short time, but he did and therefore he had taken the liberty of setting up an appointment for her with the school counselor. He had also told her professors that Aradhana was going through a family crisis and was therefore unable to attend classes and to give her some time. What really touched Aradhana was the fact that he had done her assignments and handed them in, saying they were from her. She knew they'd be in serious trouble if anyone found out. The fact that he did all this for her without expecting anything back made her want to somehow make it up to him.

She knew she did not have the emotional energy to give Scott a chance in her life. She did not have the energy for any relationship. What Scott was asking her for was one of the most selfless gifts anyone could have ever asked her for—the gift of her happiness.

She didn't know how she found the energy but she hugged Scott tightly and cried on his shoulder for what seemed like eternity. In return, he did the best thing that he could by just being there.

• • •

Over the next few months Aradhana started seeing the school counselor and got her life back on track. She sometimes wondered if everyone in India would lose respect for her if they found out that she was seeing a counselor as that kind of thing was viewed as a last resort for a completely troubled mind. Surely, she would be judged and viewed as a failure. It had concerned her in the beginning as well. The first time she went out of a courtesy to Scott, but the next few times she went because she wanted to. She found herself talking to the counselor about a lot more than just her heartbreak with Nirman. She found herself talking about Gauri and discovered how important it was for her to get Gauri's approval. She also explored her relationship with her father. On the surface she harbored an intense dislike, if not hatred, for her father. Deep down, however, there was deep sadness. Because she felt rejected by her father, she pushed back by showing that she didn't care either. She also despised her father for not being available for her mother.

It was strange. Aradhana was learning many of the counseling skills herself, and was well aware of all the tricks in the books. Things that the counselor said to empathize or probe were apparent to her. However, it was like there was a flood of emotions that were being held to bay by a dam. As soon as a small outlet opened, all the emotions came spilling out. For the first time in her life, she tried to understand her relationship with her family and realized that they played a much more important part in her life than she had ever let herself believe.

The most shocking revelation, however, was her developing feelings for Scott. She was still hurt and vulnerable and could not give herself to a relationship but deep down there were unexplained feelings towards him. The fact that she found Scott physically attractive was not news to her but she had never thought that she could relate to a man who did not understand her culture and where she came from. There were many things that were important to her about her culture. For starters, she was fiercely patriotic and held the British single-handedly responsible for ruining her country and rendering it poor. This anger towards the British was easily transferred to all whites. She didn't think of it as racism, but just retribution for the feelings of white superiority they had infused in her country. Second, there were many nuances about her culture that she didn't expect anyone else to understand. India was a country full of paradoxes. Despite the poverty, the filth, the ignorance and corruption, there was an innocence about the country. That innocence could not be translated. Either you opened yourself and experienced India for all she was, or you only saw what was physically present on the surface. Aradhana ferociously defended her country and was not open to it being judged. After all, no matter how strange one's mother is, she's to be defended against all costs. Scott had never been to any foreign country except Ireland because according to him, he never had an opportunity. He could never understand where she was coming from. Moreover, she was still hurting from loving Nirman so intensly. There was no way she could love any one like that.

• • •

Aradhana gradually had resumed her routine. She was doing well in her classes again and work was as good as she could expect it to be. She had given up her job at the pub because she felt horrible about quitting after what happened with Nirman. She was now working full-time on campus. Money was still a little tight, so she had begun to work weekdays in the same Indian restaurant as Asad. She had taken a job as a hostess and was paid six dollars an hour, a pittance compared to how much she made at the pub. Moreover, she learned that at most Indian restaurants, the owners rather than the wait staff pocketed the tips. There was no "magic piggy" here. The good thing was that she got free food the three nights that she worked, which tided her over for a good portion of the week. The important thing to Aradhana was that she kept very busy and made enough money from her jobs to pay for her tuition and living expenses.

Her relationships with everyone around her had also evolved. Alaya and she shared a healthy relationship and cooked together at least two nights a week. Alaya would invite her if she was every going out into the city with her friends and Aradhana would reciprocate the courtesy. Even Laxmi and she had come to an understanding of silent cordiality. She was closer to Asad than ever before now that they spent several hours working together. She had also made several new acquaintances from different parts of the world, including Estonia, Ivory Coast, and Russia. Together they had potluck lunches and dinners, and went out together to explore the city. They were all from different parts of the world, but were united by the fact that they were all alien to this country.

Scott was now a permanent fixture in her life. There were many times that she felt vulnerable to him. There were times when they were studying until late in the night, and she wanted to ask him to stay. She wanted to rest her head in his strong arms and pretend that she was not in a foreign country. She wanted to feel his angelic face against hers, but something stopped her. The thought of being rejected so soon after the break-up with Nirman would be too much for her to take. Moreover, their cultural differences were too significant to ignore. Her feelings, however, were not as controlled as she was.

It was a cold night in late October when Scott drove her back to the apartment after an evening at the library. The heat was turned on in the Navigator and smooth jazz was playing on the radio. Aradhana and Scott were engaged in one of their deeply intense conversations on life, religion, morals, and philosophy. A half hour had passed, and both had little else to say. Leaving would have been the right thing to do but she was enjoying herself too much. She mentioned that it was late and she should probably leave but Scott suggested they sit in the car and listen to the music for a bit longer. Aradhana did not need her arm to be twisted. They both moved their respected seats all the way back and let the music fill the car. Neither said anything for a while and finally Aradhana said again that she should leave. As she leaned forward to hug Scott good night, she held on a few moments too long and when she moved away from the embrace, their cheeks touched. Aradhana did not pull away and when their eyes met, Aradhana lost herself in Scott's deep blue ones. They leaned close and Scott gently touched her on her lips, waiting to see if Aradhana would pull away. She didn't, so he kissed her gently. The petals of his lips traced hers as he put his arms around her. She embraced him back and with the passion and intensity from months of longing and imagining, kissed him deeply. Her tongue found his as the sweetness from the Altoids they had eaten less than an hour ago lingered on. Without a disruption, Scott pulled his seat all the way back, all along remaining engaged in a passionate kiss. Aradhana found herself leaning on top of him with her eyes closed shut. She felt tremendous security and trust. Scott gently massaged her back as their lips did the talking. It was only when a commercial came on the radio did Aradhana stop. She stopped, but didn't pull back. She continued to hug Scott.

Just then a car drove into the spot next to them. Aradhana was afraid it was someone she knew. Scott buried her in his arms and asked her not to look up. Out of nowhere, Scott asked if she'd like to come to his apartment and Aradhana found herself saying that she'd like that. He lived by himself not far from the campus, but she had never been there. All she knew was that she wasn't ready to say goodbye, and wanted to continue to melt in his arms.

Because she knew that her roommates would be worried if she didn't return home at night, she called Alaya and told her that she was staying at a friend's house. She gave her Scott's cell phone number in case of an emergency, but didn't mention that the number belonged to him.

144

She was nervous as they made their way up into Scott's brownstone condo. It was on the first floor and they went up a flight of carpeted steps with cone-shaped lights on the wall. The doors were black with gold numbers. As they opened the door to Apartment 10 she felt her heart race and her senses numb. They entered into a modern living room with squarely-cut white leather sofas, and metal and glass side tables. In the corner of the room was a white cylindrical vase probably a foot shorter than Aradhana with brightly colored wooden flowers. Hanging on the wall facing the entrance was a black and white picture by Robert Doisneau, which showed a man and woman in a passionate kiss.

Scott welcomed her in and they sat on the white leather couch. He saw that she was nervous and asked her if she was all right. Aradhana buried herself in his arms as she was getting used to doing. He hugged her tight and told her to relax. Tonight was all about her. He said that he was just happy to have her there with him, and that everything else was inconsequential.

"May I just sleep in your arms?" she asked gently. Afraid of what his response would be, Aradhana tried to cover her statement with humor, "See I said 'may' instead of 'can'—that would have made my third grade English teacher proud."

Scott smiled and put his finger on his lips signaling for her not to speak before he took her back in his arms and kissed her longer and better than even before. Before they knew it, they were lying next to each other on the couch. Because there was little space, Scott got up and led her to his room.

His bedroom had dark mahogany furniture in a straight square design, and colorful geometric prints on the white walls. "Welcome to my humble space." he said as he made the bed for her. He asked her if she'd like to change into something comfortable for the night, and offered her his New England Patriots t-shirt. Aradhana could tell that the shirt would probably go down to her knees. Something about wearing Scott's shirt was very sexy and familiar, so she agreed. When she returned donning her oversized attire, Scott had changed into a t-shirt and pajamas. She could tell that this was a courtesy he had afforded to her as she knew from past conversations that Scott liked to be in his boxers when he was alone.

He joked that he never thought anyone could look so sexy in a shirt that was two times her size and probably should long have been donated to Goodwill. Aradhana returned the compliment by saying that he didn't look so bad himself. They joked about it a little more and then sat on the bed. Scott could tell that Aradhana became uncomfortable as soon as they sat on the bed, so he told her to relax.

"Ary, please trust me," he said. It was stranger hearing Scott call her Ary. Only people at the pub had called her that since she came to the US. The warmth with which Scott said her nickname reminded her of home, and she burst out crying. Scott hugged her and as they lay down on the bed.

She hugged him but her body language said that she wasn't ready for anything else. Scott had learned to read Aradhana well. He hugged her back, and watched as she fell asleep, grateful for her love.

Under Attack

*I*t was a few days after Aradhana's one-year anniversary in the country when the attacks of September 11, 2001 occurred. She had studied late the night before and was sleeping that Tuesday morning when the lives of so many were changing. The first one to call was Scott, sounding frantic. He told her to switch on the television right away and see how the face of the world was changing. The country was under attack. No one knew what it meant or when it would end. Was this the beginning of something horrific? As Aradhana watched the continuous images of the two planes hitting the World Trade Center in succession, her head reeled. That was followed quickly by the attacks on the Pentagon and the fate of Flight 93. She wasn't sure what was happening around her. It was seemed surreal.

She knew the news would soon travel to India and she'd get some calls. She had no idea it would be so soon, though. She had scarcely hung up the phone with Scott when Gauri and Ashwin called, sounding scared and worried. They wanted to make sure she was safe. Like everyone else, they were watching every minute of the news and had trouble getting through to her as all the lines seemed jammed. They were insistent that she was not to leave her apartment under any circumstances. If things got worse, she was to come back to India. The irony that it would involve a plane ride was lost on them. They had heard that there were fears that other large cities or monuments would be next. They made her promise she'd stay home.

Scott was with his parents. He called again to ask if she wanted him to pick her up. Aradhana declined, trying to keep her promise to her parents. Scott's call was followed by more calls from India. Both her sisters and brother called and solicited similar promises. She was to take care of herself and not venture out anywhere.

She was lost in the madness unfolding in front of her eyes. The attack on ordinary citizens baffled her. She cried when she saw people jumping off the buildings and wondered what she'd do in similar circumstances. Acts of kindness and heroism always made her throat lumpy and her eyes water and today she saw many of them. She knew many Indians worked in the World Trade Center and around the New York area. Her mind immediately wondered as to what their fates might be.

As she was lost in her thoughts, the phone rang again. It was Alaya. Alaya had taken an internship in a large multinational corporation for the semester. Her office was in the Prudential Center building and the office had been declared closed and they were all sent back home lest a similar attack should occur. Normally, Alaya took the subway to work, followed by the Franklin Hill condo shuttle but that day she was stranded at the station and no transportation was in sight. She wanted Aradhana to drive her car and pick her up from the station. She sounded scared and confused and the fear in her voice was obvious.

Aradhana wasn't sure how to tell her that she had never driven a car in her life. She had an international driver's license, which to her, was an ill-gotten gain. She had to drive only a short distance in a pre-designated area that had no traffic to earn it. Though Bambi, her moped, had been a constant companion in her life, she had never driven a car on crowded streets. She wanted to oblige Alaya, but wasn't sure she was up for the job. Alaya pleaded with Aradhana, telling her she trusted her and knew that she'd do fine. Aradhana knew she had to get over her fear of driving a car and be there for Alaya.

As Aradhana started Alaya's Honda Accord, she saw a Koran on the passenger seat. For a second she thought of Baadshah, and a shiver passed through her body. She wondered if perhaps he was like those heartless terrorists. This wasn't a time for suspicion; it was a time for everyone to come together. Instinctively, she held the book to her head as a sign of respect. She needed blessings from everything blessed.

Thankfully the car was an automatic and therefore it wasn't very hard for Aradhana to figure out that "R" was Reverse and "D" allowed her to go forward. At first she tried changing gears without pressing the gas pedal and nothing happened. She then figured out quickly enough which of the pedals was the gas and which the brake. As she tentatively backed the car out, she prayed again that nothing worse happened that day. If she was blocking the traffic or driving badly, no one indicated so. Traffic en route to and from Boston was flowing heavily. She was glad that she watched Scott drive and stayed in the far right lane. Several cars overtook her from the left, as she was clearly not traveling fast enough. She realized she was sitting upright and leaning all the way up to the windshield, perhaps trying to mimic the proximity she felt to the outside world in Bambi. She felt that if she couldn't see the hood of the car then she was sure to hit something.

When she finally reached the T station, it was bustling with people greeting familiar faces with relief and enthusiasm. When Alaya saw Aradhana, her face lit up with relief as well. As Aradhana relinquished the driver's seat to Alaya, Alaya gave her a huge hug. She tried to make sense of the look she saw on Alaya's face, but couldn't tell what it was. As Alaya sat in the driver's seat, the first thing she did was put the Koran out of sight.

Giving Thanks

*O*ver the next several months, Aradhana's relationship with Scott evolved to a different level. He was the nicest, gentlest soul she had ever met—scarcely the Guinness-and whiskey-guzzling Irishman she had thought all Irish to be. Scott's family had been very supportive of Aradhana, which was more than she had expected from anyone since coming to the country. It was almost a year ago that she had been invited to Scott's home last Christmas which, of course, she did not attend because of Nirman. This time, however, when they invited her for Thanksgiving, she could not find a suitable excuse to refuse. It was not as if she did not want to go. In fact, she wanted to meet Scott's family in their own surroundings more than anything. It was more that she was afraid to find out just how different from her they might be. Plus, she felt terrible about telling Scott's mother Sarah that she wouldn't be eating any turkey.

She had barely gotten over her *faux pas* of calling Sarah "aunty" and her husband Sean "uncle" the first time they had been introduced at the pub. It wasn't because she hadn't already learned that you only called relatives that but because she didn't know any other way to give Sarah and Sean the appropriate respect she felt was due to them. They had accepted the salutation, but Aradhana knew that they were a little uncomfortable. Aradhana was conscious of that and the next time she saw Sarah she asked her directly what she would like to be called. She explained to her that in her country you didn't call older people by their first names. Sarah told her that she was comfortable with both Sarah or Aunty. Aradhana finally conceded and decided to address them by their first names.

Their house was in Newton. It was a large home with a huge pool and backyard. The house was tastefully decorated but in a traditional style as opposed to Scott's modern decor. Scott had already told Sarah that Aradhana was vegetarian, so in addition to the customary Thanksgiving side dishes of green beans, mashed potatoes, squash, corn and cranberry sauce, there was macaroni and cheese and a special baked tofu dish for Aradhana. As was tradition, Thanksgiving was about family. There were many familiar faces including Uncle Jim and Kelly. Also there were two aunts from Scott's mother's side of the family and some neighbors. Initially Aradhana was extremely nervous and stayed close to Kelly and Uncle Jim. However, Scott seemed to have told just about everyone about Aradhana because they all made a very conscious effort to include her in their conversations. In addition, they had several questions about the culture and people of India as well as Hinduism.

Scott rarely left her side. He casually put his arms around her a few times yet he made a conscious effort not to be visibly affectionate as he knew that it would make Aradhana uncomfortable. Even though they hadn't spoken about it, he knew Aradhana well enough by now to know how conscious she was of their different cultures. He understood that she came from a country where being romantically expressive was done only in privacy. Aradhana was complex and full of paradoxes. At times her views were extremely liberal and modern, but at other times she was conservative and reserved. From what Scott had come to understood so far, Aradhana could be very defensive when it came to her culture. Her approach to a situation could be diametrically opposite based on whether she thought she was representing her culture or herself. In this particular situation, he knew she was trying to represent her culture. She wanted Scott's family not only to get to know her, but also understand where she was coming from. Scott had never felt this way about someone and had never waited so long for someone. He had loved Aradhana from a distance for a long time and had let her go when he thought it was best for her. He had never felt such unselfish love ever. He was proud to be with her. His parents had never even socialized with an Indian before, let alone had one involved in their only child's life. They wanted to understand everything they could about a girl and culture they knew nothing about. More than anything, they didn't want to offend her.

Aradhana, too, did not want to offend anyone. Scott had already given her the Spark notes version of Thanksgiving's origins with a disclaimer that there were different versions of the history of the holiday. He chose to share the most common and widely accepted view on the holiday. He explained how the first pilgrims arrived at Plymouth Rock in Massachusetts from Plymouth, England in November 1620. After a harsh two-month journey and even harsher weather conditions, nearly half had perished before spring. However, their prayers were answered through help from the indigenous people (Because the explorer Christopher Columbus mistakenly believed he had reached India when he had landed in America over a century earlier, he called the indigenous people of the Americas "Indians," a name that despite its origin in mistaken identity, persisted until the more culturally sensitive years at the end of the twentieth century) who innocently offered food to the newcomers and taught them how to plant corn. They reaped a plentiful harvest the following summer and a three-day feast was declared by the pilgrims in November 1621 to thank God and celebrate with their native friends. Scott also pointed out the irony of the holiday intended to celebrate and give thanks to God and in some way to the Indians who were ultimately repaid for their initial kindness and generosity by being decimated and displaced out of their own country.

They had debated the pros and cons of blind tradition which both of their cultures seemed to have in abundance. Tradtions seemed to start for a reason and continued long after the reason was no longer valid. There were aspects of her culture that she didn't understand or agree with but continued because of its significance to her own history and life. In addition to the historical perspective of this holiday, Aradhana also learned about some cultural implications. It was Kelly who first pointed out that Thanksgiving and other big holidays were never complete without a family scandal or fight. This Thanksgiving was no exception, except that the scandal was innocuous and old news to everyone except Aradhana.

The O'Reillys lived next door to Scott's family. They had a beautiful daughter named Emily with dark curly hair and a porcelain doll-like face. Emily, who was one of the most beautiful girls she had ever seen, was friendly and warm to Aradhana and extremely friendly to Scott. In fact, she made several attempts to get Scott's attention. Aradhana couldn't help sensing there was some history between the two. She wanted to ask Scott about it but decided to ask Kelly instead. At first Kelly resisted, but then decided that it was best to fill Aradhana in. Emily and Scott had known each other since they were six. They had played together and grown up together. Emily had always idolized Scott. For his part, Scott treated her like a sister. Unfortunately, Emily thought of him as more than a brother. Though Scott never explicitly came out and said it, it was always clear that he didn't return Emily's interest. Emily went off to Stanford Law School and after she got her degree, she finally confronted Scott and told him how she felt. Scott broke her heart by telling her that because he always had thought of her as a sister, another type of relationship between them would never seem right to him. After that Emily moved to California and only came home for family holidays. During those times she avoided Scott. Even though Scott had had a

Split

couple of girlfriends over the years, Emily had never lost hope that someday they would be together.

Aradhana got the sense that Emily was not threatened by her because she did not expect her and Scott to last. She wanted to ask Scott about it, but she was sure that he would downplay it all. Despite how harmless it really was, she found herself struggling with the situation. Emily was beautiful and she was Irish. Scott was extremely attractive. If not Emily then he could have had his choice of many other suitable partners. She wasn't sure why he decided to pursue a relationship that was destined to be complicated. Scott had just begun to understand her. If she threw in the complexity of her culture and family into the mix, it was bound to be difficult at the very least. There was no telling what their future was. She had recently ended a relationship with a man who she had planned to spend her life. He had let her down and taken a piece of her away. She wasn't ready to let another man break her heart just yet.

However, she struggled with some complex emotions. Even thoughts of Scott being with someone else made her feel weird. Was she falling in love with him? She had to admit that there was nothing she wanted to do more than spend time with Scott. She waited for his calls or for him to stop by. Moreover, she felt a sense of pride at Scott's own achievements. Even looking at Scott's baby pictures this Thanksgiving made her feel proud. He was adorable and Aradhana was proud to be with him. Strangely she felt closer to Scott after looking through all his childhood photos. It was as though through the old photographs, she could share some of those moments that she had missed in his life and that maybe she'd get an inkling of what it must have been to be Scott. When she and Sarah looked at the pictures, she felt as though she had always been a part of the O'Donnells' lives. Every time Scott stole a glance at her, she felt her heart beating louder. She was definitely falling hard for Scott. Somehow it all felt so right. She realized that despite how conscious she was of their cultural difference, when she looked at him as an individual she never thought of him as white or Irish, but just Scott. Indeed he was the man who had been there for her when it mattered the most. She wanted to go back to Scott's apartment and take him in her arms and tell him that she loved him.

When they finally sat down for dinner, the mood at the beginning was somber as Sean started off by remembering those who had died in the horrific attacks of September 11th. He also thanked God for the heroism and virtue showed by those on that day. Then, elegantly changing gears and the mood, he thanked God for Aradhana's company and for the chance to learn about her culture. He added that lack of understanding was the cause of so much pain and hatred in the world today, and hoped that soon they could all appreciate each other's cultures in the spirit of this Thanksgiving.

Once the prayers were done, Sean carved the turkey. When Emily offered Aradhana some turkey, Scott jumped in and said that she was vegetarian. Scott was insistent that he serve Aradhana himself. Three times during dinner, Scott reached under the table and held her hand. Aradhana was brimming with eagerness to tell Scott what she had just realized—that she was in love with him. She wanted nothing more than to be with him. The conflict of culture seemed like an afterthought now.

After dinner, they all went down to the rec room in the basement to shoot pool and darts. That night Aradhana learned that she was a natural at pool. Emily looked adoringly at Scott on several occasions but each time Scott reached out to Aradhana in some way or the other. When the night was over, Aradhana found herself looking forward to going back to the place where she now felt most comfortable. After she hugged and kissed Sarah and Sean good night, she asked Scott if she could go to his apartment with him. When they got there, Aradhana told Scott that she'd like to give thanks as well. Sitting in the living room, Aradhana held Scott's hand and thanked God for the man she loved.

That night they made love for the first time. Aradhana was surprised that she had not only let herself fall in love again but that she had fallen so hard. Scott was more than good to her. She trusted him in a way she hadn't trusted anyone else and wanted to surrender to him. Scott asked her if she was sure and she told him that there wasn't a doubt in her mind. Letting their bodies do the talking, they made sweet, gentle love. They looked deep into each other's eyes and felt what the other was trying to say. There was trust and an understanding. At that point it didn't matter that they had grown up differently and spoke in different accents. They both understood each other's needs. Scott was tender and thoughtful. He kissed Aradhana all over her body starting with her forehead. His lips baptized her eyes. The tenderness of his touch made her shiver. It seemed like neither wanted the feeling of warmth to end.

As he finally became one with her, Scott said "Ary, I love you." She looked him in the eyes and told him that she loved him, too. After they had found bliss, Scott took her in his arms and played with her hair until they both fell asleep.

Keep the Faith

*L*ife was looking good for Aradhana and Scott. They were similar in more ways than they were different. Scott taught her all he could about his culture and heritage while Aradhana talked to him about hers. She broke him into Bollywood movies by starting with those in English, such as *Bend It Like Beckham, Monsoon Wedding, Mississippi Masala,* and *Fire (even though most of them were Hollywood productions)*. Then they graduated to Bollywood movies starting with the one she thought he should see for their pure wackiness. Scott had several questions about Bollywood movies. He had questions about the dresses, the songs, the rain, the parents, the villains, the predictability and just the sheer number of movies that were available.

She tried to explain the bundle of contradictions that made up the people in her culture. She spoke of the irony of a country with over a billion people, but who were prudish about sex. She tried to explain that even though the movies showed songs, Indians didn't go around trees singing songs. They did, however, like listening and singing songs but not as a replacement for a conversation or making love. She tried to explain that there was a huge disparity in incomes but it was no different than anywhere else. It was just that anything that involved a billion people just seemed like a lot more. Indians were emotional and expressive, yet in some ways they weren't. For example, while it was okay for parents to show affection in public to their kids, it was not acceptable for a young boy and girl or even a married couple to do so. There was reverence and an almost god-like respect for elders and especially parents. Even the thought of sending one's parent to an old age home was sinful.

However, just like her, India was undergoing a transformation. India was trying to rediscover itself. A lot had come full circle. There was a time in Indian culture when women held tremendous power. Even many of the gods of strength were goddesses. Then there was a black period when the culture and religion had been interpreted by a few, and the status of woman had changed for the worse. Now things were changing again. People in India were seeing more of the world, and had begun to question the status quo.

Aradhana believed it was easier for her to understand Scott than for Scott to understand her. Like most of the world, she had been exposed to American culture and language. For Scott, however, her beliefs and culture were completely new. Left to her own devices, Aradhana spoke mostly in English. However, having been forced to speak in English, a language that they both understood, she was tempted to express herself in Hindi.

Aradhana knew that she and Scott weren't the only or first multi-cultural or multiracial couple in the world but she was deeply grounded in her roots. Conflicted, but grounded. She believed that while she had the right to condemn and question her culture and traditions, no foreigner did—not even the man she loved. It was hard to defend things that she vehemently opposed to Scott. She felt she was being disingenuous to both her country and Scott, yet she didn't really know how to strike a balance.

Aradhana was religious and believed strongly in Hinduism. She viewed it as more a philosophy and way of life rather than a compilation of rituals. Her view was that Hinduism was the way she chose to live her life while her relationship with her God was personal and scared. She didn't blindly accept all the mythology that went with the religion. That to her, was the most beautiful part of her religion—it let her question everything. It was both flexible and firm. Above all, it spoke of attaining the ultimate inner peace and salvation. It didn't condemn materialism or even physical pleasure. It acknowledged that a good fulfilling life had everything in it.

Scott had grown up a strict Catholic. He attended Sunday school as a child, and had read both the Old and New Testament. He had attended YMCA camp with his family every summer. As he grew up, he became less involved with his religion and beliefs but nevertheless he still attended church on all the major holidays.

Scott was the first to ask Aradhana to visit church with him. It was for Christmas Eve. Aradhana had studied in a convent and was aware of basic church etiquette, but this was the first time she would be experiencing a complete mass. When it was time to shake the hands of those next to her and wish them peace, she found herself feeling awkward. She complied, but she wasn't sure if she was doing it right. She wondered if anyone would view her as a pagan. When they began to sing hymns, Scott pointed the hymn out to her in the song book, but when she sang she felt like her voice was the only voice echoing through the church. When she kept quiet, she felt like all eyes were on her. She wanted to do right by Scott as she respected him and what he stood for. Any religion that made him the way he was deserved her respect. Despite having more than a basic understanding of the religion, she felt like she knew nothing. When it was time to take communion, Scott asked her to join him. She knew that she couldn't because she wasn't baptized so she asked him to go ahead and waited for him. She stood uncomfortably as everyone around her went to take the communion and couldn't help but notice that she was the only non-white in the chapel. Could people see through her? Could they tell that she was Indian? She was dressed in a sober lemon-colored dress that brought out the gold in her own complexion. Scott came back with some bread for her. He smiled and put it in her mouth. Again, Aradhana felt like all eyes were on her.

Late in January Aradhana invited Scott to the temple with her. Scott joked that he never thought she would ask him. He had been reading voraciously about Hinduism and often times would ask her about things he had read. He wanted to know if there were really over a million gods and, if so, were they all equal? Which ones did Aradhana believe in and why? Aradhana explained the concept of the Trinity to him. Scott had already shared with her the Christian concept of the Father, Son, and Holy Spirit. She thought he might understand Hinduism better if she shared the concept of the Trinity within Hinduism. There was Brahma the creator—he was responsible for creating the world. He signified it all. There was Vishnu, the preserver—he maintained harmony in the world. Then there was Shiva, the destroyer—it was believed that he would destroy the world when it was no longer worth living. She likened it to the apocalypse. All other gods were reincarnations of them. Vishnu had the most reincarnations, including Lord Krishna and Lord Rama. Scott wanted to know how the Hare Krishna sect fit into Hinduism. Scott asked her many questions, but many of them she had no answers to. While she was a devout Hindu, she wasn't necessarily a very learned one. Often, she'd go to the Internet and do her own research so that she could answer Scott's questions.

When they finally went to the temple, Scott wanted to do it absolutely right. He wondered if he should dress up in something formal like a suit. Aradhana was amused. She had never really given much thought to what she wore to the temple. As long as it was decent it didn't really matter. She explained that they didn't have any specific day designated to go to the temple. Different gods may have had different days dedicated to them, but by and large most Hindus went to the temple as they pleased. No one really dressed up to go to the temple except maybe on festivals. She did caution him to wear socks with his shoes because to would need to remove his shoes outside the temple and walk around barefoot.

They went to the Vishnu temple in Ashland. Aradhana had been there half a dozen times before with Laxmi and the twins. Sometimes she'd pay her respects and spend hours sitting in the temple reflecting on her life. The temple wasn't necessarily quiet. The devotees rang big copper bells, pleading with God to hear them. The pundits chanted mantras glorifying the different gods. Children ran around the different sanctuaries. Mothers put their infants in front of the priests pleading with them to have God bless their child through the priests. Coconuts were broken to appease God and the sweet liquid from the coconut was distributed to the devotees. The devotees stood in line to receive the *Prasad*, or blessing, and be blessed by God's crown that the priest put on each of their heads for a split second. There was chaos, yet there was also tremendous rhythm and peace.

On this occasion Aradhana felt like she was giving herself yet a little more to Scott. By sharing this with Scott, she was sharing her innermost self. From the minute they entered the temple courtyard and parked Scott's Navigator, Scott followed Aradhana's cue. When she removed her shoes, he removed his. She touched the steps before entering the temple and kissed her hand to her lips. Scott wasn't sure whether he needed to do the same or whether that would offend Aradhana, but he did the same. The first sanctuary that Aradhana stopped in front of was that of Lord Ganesh. The elephant-headed god was her favorite. To her, he represented strength and cheekiness rolled into one. There was something lovable about his big round stomach and his penchant for good food. He was the god who was prayed to before starting any deed. Scott knew instantly that this was the god who lost his head during a misunderstanding with his father Shiva. Shiva, in remorse, asked that his son's head be replaced with that of the first creature that came by. It happened to be that of an ele- phant and that was how Ganesh the elephant-headed god was born. He also remembered the story where Lord Shiva and his wife Parvathi asked their sons to race three times around the world so that one of them could claim a large prize. Karthik, Ganesh's brother, raced around the world on his consort the peacock. Ganesh, though, made three cir- cles around his parents, claiming that they were his world. There was something mischievous about Lord Ganesh and there was scarcely any Hindu who didn't love all that he represented.

After they paid their respects to each of the sanctums and walked around each of them, it was time to take the blessing. Scott watched as Aradhana put her right hand on her left cupped it and accepted the *Prasad*. Scott did the same. The priest smiled as he gave him the *Prasad* and blessed him with the crown. There were two other token whites as Scott called them in the temple, presumably going through their first initiation ritual as well. Aradhana and Scott sat cross-legged on the temple floor with their heads rested against the pillar. As she leaned her head on Scott's shoulder, she felt closer to him than ever before. He smiled and rested his head back on hers. She didn't care or notice the glances that people gave them. She had accepted Scott in the house of God.

Super Bowl and Papadums

It was Aradhana's second Super Bowl, but she hadn't cared or known enough about it the first time. Scott was a die hard New England Patriots fan and had not missed watching a Super Bowl on television since he was five. He had painstakingly explained every single rule in American football to Aradhana. Aradhana wondered why it was called football as it was mainly played with hands and had originated from rugby. Kickoff wasn't really a kickoff and the foot was seldom used in the game. Several of the rules were lost on Aradhana. She was, however, interested in the psycho-social elements of a game recognized as one of the most popular sports within the country. She was especially intrigued by the fact that there were only a few black quarterbacks in the sport, which had over 70% black participation by some accounts. Scott tried vehemently to defend the honor of the sport by naming Philadelphia Eagles' Donovan McNabb and Tennessee's Steve McNair. He also referenced a September 2001 article in the *National Review* which had precisely addressed this question. The article concluded that the selection is race-neutral and in the eyes of the selectors "there are no white quarterbacks or black quarterbacks. There are just good ones and bad ones." Aradhana and Scott debated nonstop on race neutrality, a topic that was close to her heart. They both concluded that there was room for more race-neutral recognition of talent globally. Of course Aradhana didn't share the fact that she thought her own countrymen had little chance in the game save for some genetic abnormality.

By now Aradhana knew that several millions of dollars were spent on Super Bowl advertising. America was at a standstill during Super Bowl. Most people invited guests to their homes to watch the event with them and even cooking channels were talking about potential game day menus. Aradhana asked Scott if they could have their first Super Bowl party together. Most of her Indian friends who were new to America had never watched a Super Bowl, especially not on a large television like Scott's. Scott said that would be fine with him, as long as no one asked him to explain the game once it started. That worked for Aradhana. Scott's friends were invited for the game, while Aradhana's friends were invited for a pre-Super Bowl party as well. It was a small affair with Asad, Alaya, Laxmi and the twins. Alaya had watched the Super Bowl several times before and volunteered to

160

make papadums for everyone. So over papadums and Coke, Scott initiated the entire group as to the rules of the game. While Super Bowl XXXVI was being played in the Louisiana Superdome, Scott's bachelor pad was buzzing with a multicultural, multiracial crowd covering each of the continents. Scott had arranged for beer and other drinks and Aradhana was in charge of food.

"We're having papadums again, you know!" she had teased.

Scott teased back, "So big deal. I am with a papadum, right?"

Papadums were on the menu, but it wasn't the only dish. She had made a spinach and artichoke dip, nachos (*sans* the beef), shrimp, Buffalo chicken wings, and potato skins with cheddar and bacon. She knew that if Scott was with a Papadum, than she was with an Irish Potato.

Despite Scott's earlier concern about being disturbed during the game, he seemed eager to discuss the proceedings. In fact, he took great pleasure in quizzing his newly initiated comrades on what they thought about many of the referee's calls. When Aradhana went back and forth between the kitchen, he sternly directed her to sit down and watch the game. She found herself yelling and admonishing the players on the screen. The game between the St. Louis Rams and the New England Patriots was thrilling. The first three quarters saw the Patriots beating them hands down with a third quarter score of 17 to 3 in favor of the Patriots. The last quarter saw a dramatic finish with the Rams giving the Patriots a run for their money, but the Patriots still winning 20 to 17.

Aradhana felt so alive with Scott. He exposed her to many things that Aradhana had only read or seen, but had never done and she savored many of these experiences. Their relationship wasn't without its cultural challenges though. There were many things they didn't see eye to eye on. There were things where their interests were not aligned. When they went on a picnic for a summer production of *Macbeth* in the Boston Commons, it was Aradhana's idea. She knew every single line of the play, having had it assigned as course work, while Scott had never read *Macbeth*. Scott wasn't a Shakespeare fan and said he'd much rather read plain English. Aradhana had read and explained all of *Macbeth* to Scott prior to the Commons date and Scott had dozed off a half a dozen times as she prepped him. Aradhana preferred to think that Shakespeare not she was responsible for his lack of interest. On the flip side, Scott loved skiing while Aradhana couldn't have been worse at it. She spent over three quarters of her skiing trip with Scott tumbling downhill. At one point she was so embarrassed that she made Scott ski the more challenging black and blue slopes while she practiced on the yellow bunny slopes. Apart from the fact that she was bruised on several places on her body, her pride also took a beating. The day she skied, she was the only person of color on the slopes. Little kids stopped by to ask if she was okay, and if she needed help getting up. Some gave her a look that said skiing wasn't for immigrants from the tropics, but when she was horizontal, they'd help her up.

The other passion of Scott's that she couldn't share was bowling. Scott was the first one who exposed her to the sport, but after several gutter balls, and having migrated to the gutter guard, she decided she didn't particularly enjoy it. Scott called her the girl "who couldn't and wouldn't go skiing or bowling."

Going to New York City was her idea. She enjoyed Broadway and wanted to see a production of *Mamma Mia!* Scott thought Abba was way before his time, and would much rather have skipped it.

He called her a "culture vulture" and she called him a "fart at art."

Scott reminded her that it wasn't very long ago that she had prophesized that "never the twain shall meet," and yet they had. They still had a chance, he joked.

A Graduation Surprise

*A*radhana continued to work hard over the next year and a half and became an A plus student with a formidable grade point average. She had managed to save five thousand dollars that she sent back to her father for supporting her through her initial stages of college. Now that she wasn't bogged down by financial constraints, she was able to single mindedly focus on her studies. Before she knew it, her tenure at the school was over and it was time for graduation.

It was a sunny spring Sunday morning when Aradhana got a call from Gauri. It would have been past midnight in India, and Aradhana rarely heard from Gauri at this hour so she was expecting the worst. At this point the worst would have been not having anyone attend her graduation. Having Gauri there meant something special to her, but she was not sure what. She did not know if she was looking for graduation as an excuse to run into Gauri's arms and burst into tears for the loneliness and isolation she had felt over the years.

Aradhana knew she would not entirely be alone as she was graduating at the same time as Scott, Asad, and the twins. Scott's extended family had been a huge support through her assimilation into the American culture, and in helping her feel less alone. Even though she had said nothing to them, they seemed to understand her insecurities even without her voicing them. One random day Kelly stopped by to tell her to save her a seat at graduation. She joked that she would come to watch only her graduate, and not Scott. Aradhana was very touched by Kelly's white lie, but wondered if she had let her isolation show. Aradhana had prided herself for being able to hide her emotions from other people. It seemed like she had lost that skill, too.

With Gauri's call, Aradhana found her heart racing. Only last week her father had congratulated her and assured her that Gauri would attend. Instinctively she wanted to blame him for taking this joy aware fiom her. She was, however, worrying about the wrong issue. Gauri assured her that she would be attending. There was, however, a minor addition in the plan—Aasma would also be coming. Aradhana was taken aback. She had spoken to Aasma only once in her time in America, after the September 11 attacks. She was more than a little surprised, that the sister with whom she shared so little would be making this journey for her graduation. She asked if Pankaj, her brother-in-law, would also be coming and was told that for now, it was just Aasma. Since Aradhana didn't know what else to ask, she asked about Aasma's visa. Gauri replied that Aasma had an appointment at the consulate and Aradhana should FedEx the invitation letter immediately.

Aradhana found herself irritated at Gauri. First, for not bothering to ask if it was okay, and second, for rushing the paperwork. It was typical of her family to withhold facts until the last minute and then rush to get things done. Why were they so insensitive to her living situation? What if it was not convenient for Aasma to be there?

Gauri had no idea that her living situation had changed. As far as she knew, Aradhana still shared a room with Laxmi and the apartment with Alaya. Just where did Gauri think that Aasma and she would sleep? Even in her frustration, Aradhana knew it would be rude to ask how long they planned to visit. She knew she'd have to suspend any plans to live life normally for an indefinite period of time.

It was only by happenstance that her living situation had changed three days earlier when Laxmi had jubilantly announced that she had found a job in Texas. Aradhana's first reaction was shock as she tried to imagine Laxmi in Texas. Even in Massachusetts, a supposedly liberal and elitist state, Laxmi got more than her share of stares. Her well-oiled hair braided to perfection, a round maroon dot on her forehead, and a perfect traditional diamond stud in her nose being the primary drivers of the stares. Even though Aradhana came from the same part of the world, sometimes even she struggled with Laxmi's intensely spiced cooking, loud morning prayers, and thick South Indian accent.

In her heart, she really respected Laxmi for the courage she had to live her life without compromising. She knew that she herself didn't have what it took to sport that big dot and be stared at. Whenever she did add one to her forhead, it was as a statement of fashion than tradition. At any other time in her life, she would have loved to take inspiration from Laxmi, but this wasn't the right time.

Laxmi seemed more excited about leaving the apartment and Massachusetts than about her job. In her typical style she announced, "You will need to find roommate yourself." Without bothering to correct her grammar, Aradhana had argued that it was Laxmi's responsibility to find them a roommate, especially since she was the one breaking the lease. The discussion went on for an unproductive half hour and ended when both agreed to do their best to find potential roommates. It was decided that Laxmi would pay the rent until a substitute was found.

In speaking with Gauri, Aradhana regretted that wasted half hour. Now she would need to go back to Laxmi and tell her that she didn't need a roommate, and would find one herself when it was necessary. Aradhana was a little nervous about speaking with Alaya about this even though they got along well. Things had become a little strained between them because of Asad. Alaya liked Asad who, unfortunately, didn't reciprocate her feelings. Aradhana somehow felt personally responsible since Asad was her friend and only came to see her. She had given him numerous lectures on the suitability of the match. Alaya and Asad were both Muslim, which would have been perfect for their concerned families, but he just wasn't interested. Moreover, Alaya was extremely attractive and intelligent. Asad seemed to value intelligence over anything else so she wasn't sure what the problem was. Sometimes to get her mind off her own problems she'd try and psychoanalyze everyone around her. She wondered if Alaya intimidated Asad. She wondered if his traditional upbringing was driving him towards someone a little more docile. It was confusing to Aradhana because Alaya who was so independent seemed to become subservient and docile around Asad. In the end she knew better than to be a matchmaker. Ever since her own failed relationship with Nirman, she had taken the position that she had no right trying to manage the romantic affairs of others.

Her conversation with Gauri had been short. The papers would be sent first thing in the morning and Gauri would phone her again to confirm the ticket dates. Even trying to get her to email information was futile, so Aradhana reciprocated with a promise to call once the FedEx package tracked as delivered.

The conversation with Alaya was simpler than expected. Sure, her family could visit. That's what families did. She understood that Aradhana wasn't sure how long the visit would be. After all, even ABCDs knew that you can't ask your mother how long she would be visiting.

• • •

Aradhana could scarcely contain her excitement. It was just a week before her graduation and Gauri and Aasma's arrival. She had been extremely worried about how she would pick up both of them at the airport. She knew that if her luggage were any indication, they would both come with huge bags. She did not want to ask Priya to pick them up at the airport for several reasons, the most important being that Sanjay and Priya came as a package deal and she didn't want to subject anyone else to that torture. She then thought of asking Scott to help with his large SUV, which would be perfect, but something held her back from doing so. The thought of throwing a white guy in Gauri and Asasma's faces the minute they arrived seemed a bit too much. Sure, they were coming to his country but she thought it would be best if they first got used to seeing so many white faces and then gently slip Scott in. After all, he was her boyfriend. She wanted them to know him as Scott, rather than the white boy who picked them up.

After much deliberation, she finally asked Alaya. Fortunately, Alaya said she would be happy to drive Aradhana to the airport to pick up her mother and sister. It was the best option that Aradhana could have asked for. Alaya was a girl, she was her roommate, and she was of Indian descent.

Even though they got to the airport on time, they then had to wait for forty minutes before Aradhana finally got a glimpse of Gauri and Aasma trudging alongside a single trolley. Partly because she couldn't contain herself, and partly because it was expected, Aradhana rushed into the little corridor where only passengers were allowed. As Aradhana hugged Gauri, both let tears escape their eyes. Aasma also wiped a stray tear from the corner of her eyes. Aradhana was shocked to see how little luggage they had. If only they had let her travel so light! Aradhana took a step back and examined her visitors. Gauri wore a blue *salwaar kameez* and had her hair tied up in a knot. Gauri looked several years older and much thinner than Aradhana remembered her. Aradhana had asked her to email pictures many times, but Gauri hadn't complied. Her excuse had always been that she did not know how to use the computer, but now Aradhana understood that there was another reason. Aradhana gave Aasma a hug and felt a surge of warmth that she had rarely felt before for her sister. All her imagined competition with Aasma and any resentment she ever had seemed to evaporate at that moment. Suddenly she was genuinely happy to see Aasma, and was no longer giving her an obligatory greeting.

Aasma looked stunning in jeans and an orange polo shirt even after twenty hours of travel. For her part Aasma looked younger that Aradhana remembered her. It was probably because Aradhana now friends of all different ages, many much older then Aasma.

Aradhana felt great pride introducing her family to Alaya. Their confidence and charm made her forget her own insecurities. Gauri

166

kissed Alaya on her forehead, and thanked her for picking them up. Aasma shook her hand and murmured a soft, "Nice to meet you." Alaya seemed to sufficiently approve of the Kapoor family. She asked Gauri if she'd mind being called aunty. Gauri looked shocked and clearly baffled as to what any other alternative might be. The thought of being called her first name by someone her daughter's age was an alien concept to her. But she recovered well by saying "Call me whatever you'd like, *beta.*"

Aradhana tried to relive her first day at the airport and experiences through the Big Dig. Even before anyone could ask, she told them how expensive the parking was and about the Big Dig.

Neither Gauri nor Aasma looked as overwhelmed as Aradhana expected them to. In fact, they had little interest in the sights they were passing. They were more interested in finding out how Aradhana was doing, what she was planning to wear on her graduation, and the parties that she'd be attending. Only when they passed the Charles River and some of the Harvard buildings did they show interest.

It was late in the evening by the time they reached the Franklin Hill condos. Both Gauri and Aasma marveled at the closed gate condominiums. They were even more impressed with the size of the apartment. They did not comment on the lack of furniture. Aradhana got the sense that they had thought she was living in the lap of luxury. Aradhana had cooked lentils, rice, and two vegetable dishes the same way Gauri had taught her. There were two twin beds in the room. Aradhana had sprayed disinfectant on Laxmi's bed bought a year ago, and put two bed sheets over it. Just the thought of using someone else's bed was repulsive to Aradhana. The only comfort was that she knew Laxmi to be excessively hygienic, and never to partake in any activity that would involve any one else' bodily fluids. Moreover the fabric spray that she had purchased purely for this purpose did a good job of masking any remnants of the bed's previous owner.

Aradhana led them to the room and offered them each a bed saying she would sleep on the floor. Gauri had different plans, though. She intended to join the two beds, and have all of them sleep together.

The Sky (Aasma) Cries Too

A Lonely Cloud

As Aasma sat by herself next to the Charles River, the heaviness of her heart gave way to tears. She wasn't sobbing, but the tears rolled from her eyes. She'd wipe one, only to pave the way for the next. She had thought there were no more tears left within her. Here she was visiting her sister Aradhana, who she knew didn't care much for her. Aradhana always seemed to resent her for being a "goody two shoes" as she called her. If Aradhana only knew what had transpired in her life recently maybe she'd think differently about her. To be fair, she had always tried to be righteous in life. She had thought it that if she did good, only good things would happen to her. She had seen her mother suffer silently and, in her silence, had felt her pain. Over the years Aasma, too, had learned to control her emotions and not express herself. She tried to live life and base her morality along clear lines. Until her marriage, things were black or white, good or bad, right or wrong. There was no middle ground. Now, of course, her life had taken an ironic turn.

Today she was in America, a place she never thought of or wanted to visit. Yet at this point, it was the only option available to her. Gauri had made the decision for Aasma. For Aasma, Aradhana's graduation was only an excuse. Of course, she was proud of Aradhana's achievement. She respected Aradhana's strength, courage, and independence as it was something she did not think she had. Yet the years since her marriage had changed her and she wasn't sure of what she stood for anymore.

She felt heavy-hearted for not being able to share with Aradhana all that had happened. Aradhana was still young when she got married and they had never been close enough for her to expose her vulnerabilities to her. Now, however, Aasma felt like she owed it to Aradhana to tell her what she was going through. She was here because of Aradhana, and she could see that Aradhana was trying really hard for them to enjoy their time together. Every time Aasma let her inner feelings show, Aradhana took it personally to mean it was something she had said or done. Aasma and Gauri knew that Aradhana had nothing to do with it but Aradhana did not.

Aasma had always been naïve and gullible. She had been righteous and moral. She never hurt so much as a fly in her life. She had never been with any man in her life until she got married. She had

171

seen her older sister Amrita lead a happily married life and have a little boy after several years of trying to concieve. It was just too bad that neither Aradhana nor Aasma could really be there to share Amrita's joy. They both had their own reasons. Aradhana was too busy trying to come to the States. While Aasma had her own unique challenge. Aasma had entered marriage with great hopes and dreams. She was going to live with her in-laws and husband in a joint family. That did not bother her at all. She was happy to live in a large family and share the trials and tribulations of joint living. As prehistoric as it sounded, she was looking forward to taking care of her husband and in-laws.

She could still remember her wedding night. As was traditional in an Indian wedding, the girl and boy went to the boy's family home to spend the night. Pankaj's house was a beautiful three-story mansion. Pankaj's room—now her room as well—was on the second floor. The entire story was built as a separate living space. It had a separate entrance, a living and dining area, and kitchen. It seemed to have been built to accommodate an in-law situation. She was welcomed into the house with the traditions and ceremonies that were typical of a Hindu marriage. Some of the traditional icebreakers between the husband and wife shortly followed. They included fishing in a pot of milk for a ring and other trivial games whose main purpose seemed to be to have the married couple become comfortable with each other's touch. It was a perfect wedding day until the night.

The bedroom was decorated with candles and flowers. The Victorian bed was covered with a curtain of flowers, and their names lay written in flower petals on the bed. Giggling, his cousins and friends pulled the door shut. It was to be the day that their wedding would be consummated. It would be the first time that Aasma would even experience the touch of a man. All her life she had waited for this moment. She was exhausted, but tingling all over with excitement. She had always wondered what her first time would be like. Would it be gentle or passionate? Maybe gentle first and then passionate? She wanted to give her man all that he could possibly want. She knew that she had a lot to learn, but she was a willing learner. She sat down on the bed in her wedding finery. She had not covered her head like out of a scene in an old-fashioned Bollywood movie, but she hadn't changed either. She was hoping that Pankaj would initiate their physical union by helping unburden her of her heavy jewelry and clothing. She was already attracted to Pankaj who looked like a model in his embroidered wedding *sherwani*, and red *tilak*, or vermillion blessing mark, on his forehead. The combination of his chiseled Western looks and Eastern attire made Aasma long to be in his arms and beg him to protect her forever. He was the kind of man that Aasma had only dreamed about.

Pankaj, however, had different plans that night. He changed into his nightdress and went to sleep without even bidding Aasma a good night. Although she was disappointed, she didn't think too much about it as it had been a very long day and they barely knew each other. Aasma was hoping that he would at least turn around and hug her, but he didn't. She wanted to wrap her arms around him but decided that she'd let him make the first move.

The same thing happened the next night. This time, however, Aasma leaned towards him and hugged him and was shocked when he pushed her hand away. She bit her lip and let tears run down her eyes but Pankaj seemed not to notice and was asleep even before her tears dried up. A month passed and Pankaj had not even touched her yet. In all other ways he was decent to her. They ate as a family every day, and he spoke to her about his day at work. In fact, he even took her to the movies and shopping. He just never touched her. For a woman who had never been touched in her life, it should have been easy to accept, but it wasn't. She had abstained because she thought it was the right thing to do, not because she did not have physical needs. Moreover, the fact that everyone had asked her about her wedding night and how things were with Pankaj further made it difficult to accept what was happening. A girl who had never lied in her life was now lying to everyone, pretending that things were great between them. She wanted to ask Pankaj what was wrong but didn't know how to do it as she did not want to insult him or hurt his feelings. Thinking that time was all he needed, Aasma gave him some, but every night she was subject to the same anguish. After dinner when they got back to their bedroom, Pankaj would change, watch television, and fall asleep.

Aasma tried everything that she could. She wore sexy negligees, deliberately left the bathroom door open, sat in the sexiest postures she could think of, but she got no reaction from Pankaj. She was afraid to touch him because she still hadn't forgotten being pushed away when she hugged him a day after their wedding.

After an excruciatingly painful six months, Aasma still didn't know what she was doing wrong. In all other respects her marriage seemed decent. He spoke well to her and even occasionally showed affection, but it was never physical. Her in-laws had been as nice to her as she could possibly expect. She had married into a rich family and was scarcely asked to work, but, in fact, this bothered her as she had nothing to do all day. She would make her way into the kitchen and assist the cooks. She asked her mother-in-law what dishes Pankaj liked and made them, but she was bored and felt rejected. She had never experienced anything like this in her life. She did not have a perfect childhood growing up, but she always managed to keep a positive attitude.

She was even afraid to ask her husband what was wrong because she knew that if she did, it would be very difficult to recover from it. Once things were on the table, they could no longer pretend. At least now, she could make excuses for Pankaj. They ranged from Pankaj being too tired to her belief that days of doing nothing had made her unattractive.

She let a few more months pass, but she was dying inside. She hadn't spoken to a single soul about her strange dilemma. She almost viewed it as an insult to her own being. Telling anyone would only increase her humiliation. Why wasn't Pankaj able to see how devastated this was making her? She hadn't even seen her husband naked as he made it a point to lock the door behind him. The most she had seen was him shirtless, and that was only because he was in the midst of changing.

Soon it was their one-year anniversary, and as far as Aasma was concerned, she had nothing to celebrate. The fact that her in-laws and friends teased her consistently and asked when the baby was coming didn't help. Her in-laws had arranged a big party and before the party, Pankaj handed her a blue velvet box containing a diamond necklace, wished her a happy anniversary and left the room. Aasma stared emotionless at the expensive necklace, whose box bore the name of Delhi's most expensive and reputable jeweler. She would have taken his touch over a thousand such necklaces but it was not to be. She dressed in a sexy black sequined *saree* with a tube top blouse that exposed the stunning necklace on her fair skin. People oohed and aahed when she descended the stairs. Even Pankaj commented in front of everyone that she looked splendid, but there were no sparks, no fire emanating from him, only meaningless words being said for the benefit of others.

After eating an exquisitely catered six-course meal and cutting a large Black Forest cake, they bid their guests good night. As always,

Aasma played the perfect hostess. The only time Pankaj had bestowed any physical attention on her was after the cake cutting when he hugged her under obvious duress and prodding from the onlookers who had had one too many Johnny Walkers.

When they went to bed, Aasma broke down. She had stripped until she had nothing including her ego left on her self. When Pankaj came in, she grabbed him, and pointed to her naked, dejected body. She pulled a stunned Pankaj's hand towards her breast and asked him what she lacked. Was she not attractive enough? Were her breasts too small? Was she too fat? Too thin? Too fair? Too dark? What was it? After her voice reached an uncomfortable volume, she checked herself and fell on the bed crying. She wanted to speak, but no words came out. Mucous flowed from the nose of the ever-groomed and perfect Aasma and she shrieked like a madwoman. She demanded an answer from Pankaj. Any answer, something that would give her some sort of justification for this madness, this charade that they called marriage.

He looked at her with a strange expression on his face and came and sat by her and held her hand for the first time since their marriage. He looked her straight in her eyes and said,

"I'm sorry."

There was silence for a few minutes while he contemplated what to say.

"You are perfect. In fact, I have never seen anyone more perfect than you. You are beautiful, sexy, gentle, kind, and much more. I am sorry I haven't been honest with you. I don't know how to say this, but you deserve to know. I am not attracted to women."

The ground crumbled under Aasma as she listened to their heartbeats. She wasn't sure that she heard him correctly, but she knew in her heart that she had. There was no point in making him repeat what he said. She wanted to shake Pankaj, demand answers, and ask if things could be changed, but it wasn't going to be that night. She didn't know why, but she just held him in her arms. This time he held her too.

• • •

Over the next year, Aasma and Pankaj became best friends. He was a wonderful person. He had been trapped in a world of pretenses for so long that he had let his real self get lost. Aasma learned that Pankaj had never been with a man. He seemed to be attracted to them, but was too afraid to find out. All his life he had struggled with his identity. He had told his parents that he didn't want to get married, but they wouldn't listen to him. They had fallen in love with Aasma and wanted her as their daughter-in-law. Pankaj had never spoken to them about his feelings because he was sure his mother would kill herself if she found out that her manly, perfect son wasn't so manly or perfect after all. He knew all too well that homosexuality was extremely frowned upon in India.

Pankaj had thought that he could change and perhaps start being attracted to women, but that wasn't the case. Ever since he was a little boy, he had felt strange. He was drawn to feminine things. Once his mother had caught him applying her perfume and make-up. She laughed the whole incident off, attributing it to the fact that he had no sister but after that he learned to be more careful about getting caught. As he grew, his conflict increased. By all outward appearances, he was the perfect man. He was a star athlete who was bright, good-looking, poetic, sensitive, and any woman's dream. However, he kept his sensitivity at bay because it was what he feared most.

His upbringing, the expectations from his family, and the responsibility of being the only son forced him into a shell. For the sake of his own sanity and those around him, he let the status quo continue. If he was ever with a man and enjoyed it, there would be no going back. He tried to be honest with himself but couldn't find the strength to ruin the lives of so many around him. To him, it wasn't a choice. He tried to make it one by marrying Aasma, but he realized on the first night itself that he wouldn't be able to go through with it.

He began pushing her away and felt all the more miserable for it. It was her big heartedness that had stopped her from questioning him all this time. He was afraid that she would bring it up to his parents and he would be pushed to a corner. He had been living in constant fear of being exposed. He was so afraid of who he was that he did not even want to admit it. Being who he truly was had never been an option. What would he do? How would he face society? He would rather have lived the life of an asexual rather than confront the judgment and pain that came with being a homosexual.

As he opened up to Aasma, his guilt further increased. She was truly the nicest and most non-judgmental person he had ever met. There was more relief in the truth for Aasma than she ever thought possible. The truth was bittersweet. The bitterness was in the fact that her marriage was a lie; the sweetness was in the fact that it wasn't her fault.

With the burden off his shoulders he opened up to her more than he ever opened up to himself and she saw the sweet, sensitive human being that he really was. They shopped together, cooked together, ate together, and slept in each other's arms. He needed warmth and sensitivity, as did Aasma. The fact that they still hadn't—and would never—consummate their relationship was something Aasma had to accept.

As another year passed, Aasma worried for Pankaj more than she did herself. He shouldn't have to live his life as a lie, pretending to be something he wasn't around everyone who loved him. Even his parents commented on how happy he seemed over the last year, attributing it to his blissful marriage with Aasma. They even reminded him about how he didn't want to get married while all along the key to his happiness lay in Aasma. The irony in their words was strong. Aasma had indeed set Pankaj free and forced him to come to terms with who he was, but there was still a long journey ahead for Pankaj in self-discovery. His road to happiness would be long and treacherous.

Aasma had decided to focus on Pankaj instead of herself. She would try and bring happiness into Pankaj's life. It wasn't as if she hadn't given any thought to trying to convert him. Like every vulnerable woman, she thought that if she gave him true selfless love, he would change his mind. Aasma may have been naïve and vulnerable, but she wasn't stupid. Within the second year of their marriage she realized that it wasn't a choice for Pankaj. No matter how wonderful she was, Pankaj would never be attracted to her but she didn't want to give up the wonderful openness that she and Pankaj shared. Even their sexual relationship was starting to blossom just not with each other in the sense that people would expect a married couple to be.

Pankaj was exploring his sexuality openly in front of Aasma. It started with the two of them watching videos together that featured same-sex couples. Aasma never asked whom Pankaj bought the videos from, but Pankaj once volunteered that there was a large underground network for such things. For the first time since she had known him, as they watched the movies she saw Pankaj become aroused.

This self-gratification made Pankaj want more. Aasma knew there wasn't anything more she could offer him other than her support that he explore further. Hers was a lost cause. Pankaj was comfortable with the status quo and the companionship between the two of them.

The black and white lines that Aasma led her life by had blurred. This world of grey was not something she was accustomed to dealing with. Yet so far she had shown support to the man she was married to and a strength of character few could have demonstrated.

It was in fact Aasma who suggested that he do some further exploration with a man. She had given permission for the home they shared to be used. The only thing that mattered to her was Pankaj's happiness. The first time that he had a man over, she left the house. Even though it had been her idea, it broke her heart. She cried and cried until she could cry no more. She couldn't express herself in front of Pankaj as it would not have been fair. Sometimes, though, she wondered who was thinking about what was fair to her.

Even in a vacuum this would have been too much to take. Aasma's life, however, was not being lived in a vacuum. In fact, in all other ways, she was leading the life of a fairly traditional married Indian woman. Apart from the fact that she lived with her in-laws, she had other relationships in her life to tend. One that had become especially hard for her was that with her own family. She had always been very close to her sister Amrita and her mother Gauri; however, since her marriage she felt resentful of Amrita and too ashamed to speak to Gauri. It was nothing that either had done or said, it was just what she knew. Her feelings towards Amrita were especially hard to deal with after she had her first child, a boy. She knew she should feel ecstatic for Amrita especially since Aryan was born after over six years of trying to conceive and she knew how much her sister had always longed for a child. But this birth just made it harder for her to accept that it would never happen for her and Pankaj.

Aasma was physically present for Aryan's birth, yet she was emotionally absent. It was a joyous occasion, but she found it hard to find happiness. Everything reminded her of how miserable her life was turning out to be. She avoided holding the baby for as long as she could. When she couldn't get around it any more, she took the baby for a walk and cried her eyes out. What was even more painful to her was the fact that Pankaj was great with Aryan. He seemed to be one of the few men in their family that had the desire and patience to be with children. He willingly changed Aryan's diapers, sang lullabies, and patiently tried different tricks to amuse the baby. On two or three different occasions, he playfully put Aryan on Aasma's lap. Aasma found herself getting angry with Pankaj each time he did that. Did he not see the effect that this was having on her?

Pankaj was oblivious of all around him. For the first time in his life, he was truly happy. He loved Aasma and, in her, had found a best friend; someone who had accepted him unconditionally and supported him when no one else would. Just having Aasma in his life had made it better. This arrangement worked well for Pankaj. It was definitely better than openly being out of the closet.

The first time Aasma saw Gauri after learning about Pankaj's sexual preferences was at Aryan's birth. She tried her best to put on a happy face and not let Gauri know her pain, but she knew that Gauri suspected that something was wrong. It wasn't just this visit. Gauri had suspected something was wrong for some time now. Aasma had been evasive with Gauri since the beginning and never directly answered any question related to her happiness. This was the first time in her life Aasma had shut the door on her mother. She was afraid that acknowledging the madness of this situation to Gauri would be like acknowledging the madness to herself. If she did that, then she would have to do something about it. It would take great strength to make some changes and Aasma did not have any strength right now. She sometimes wondered what would happen if she left Pankaj. The answer was always that too many lives would be ruined. It wasn't just the fact that she would be divorced with little to no possibility of finding anyone else. It was more about what would happen to the lives of those connected to her. Most important, what would happen to Pankaj? He had escaped openly claiming his sexuality only because he was with a woman. That had kept even his harshest critics quiet. If he came out of the closet, his family would be ruined. His mother would most definitely kill herself.

And what about the shame this would bring to Aasma's own family? She suspected that somehow people might blame her. They may claim that she lacked what it took to make a man happy. Somewhere in her heart she was beginning to believe that. Maybe she *did* lack what it took to make a man happy. She was so distraught that the last thing she needed was to do something drastic.

A few more years went by. There was constant pressure from both families to start a family. Everyone but Gauri had mentioned it. Once Gauri had directly confronted Aasma and said that she suspected that something was wrong, but respected the fact that Aasma was not ready to talk about it. She promised Aasma that she would never bring it up again. She did, however, stress that whenever Aasma was ready to talk about it she would be there.

• • •

Then suddenly a ray of hope presented itself in Aasma's life. It was a promise of a new beginning. A promise that would give her the opportunity to reclaim some self-respect and establish an identity for herself apart from being Pankaj's wife. Granted this was an opportunity afforded to her by Pankaj, but at this point she believed she had earned it. Pankaj was a whiz with investments. He had taken his father's moderate textile business and transformed it into a force to be reckoned with in the textile import and export world.

His father, Mr. Khanna had opened a tiny textile shop in Delhi's busy Karol Bagh twenty years ago. His shop barely had enough space for five people to stand in it. He had a huge attic space where most of his merchandise was kept. The only convenient way to reach the attic was through a ladder. It took the slim frame of either of his two sixteen-year-old helpers to accomplish this. His typical customers were middle-aged housewives trying to match blouses for their *sarees*, or *salwars,* or *chunnis* for their *salwar kameezes*. One wouldn't know looking at him today, but the senior Mr. Khanna was born to be a salesman.

He had a quality that made women feel comfortable with him. The sale of a couple of meters of cheap *chunni* material always resulted in cross sales of the latest and most expensive material for a new dress for his customers. He complimented the women liberally, but within boundaries. The compliments weren't from him; they were always an advance proxy for what their husbands would say looking at the latest pending purchase. For a man who never in his thirty-five years of marriage remembered his wife's birthday, he remembered all his customers' names and special occasions.

Slowly he employed the services of a tailor so that the sales of materials were coupled with tailoring services. He had a keen eye for the latest fashions and colors. Lady luck, and his wife's daily prayers for his prosperity paid off. When the shop next to his own was having a hard time making ends meet, he acquired it. Now that his shop was a decent size, and to keep up with the increasing demand for his tailoring business, he retained the tailor from the newly acquired shop as well. His base of retail customers began to expand. He now had fashion students converging to his shop to ask what he though of certain colors and textiles. For a man from Punjab who had just barely passed his tenth grade exam, he had the business sense of a Wall Street investor. He teamed up with a no-name designer, and started to create and market women's clothing for every socially conscious Delhiite. It was not bare-all non-wearable designer ware for the skinny models. Rather, it was ornate and intricate hand-embroidered expensive silk dresses created to fit the buxom women who had paid him loyal patronage. His insights, the tailor's skills, and the designer's network spiraled them from out of oblivion into a force to reckon with in that niche. Plus, what was fashion in Delhi was just waiting to be explored in the rest of the country. His label now had real status and his own personal life began showing signs of prosperity. His wife now wore three diamond rings, and a pair of diamond solitaire earrings that were too large for her small face. He himself had a thick gold chain around his neck with a diamond locket of the goddess of wealth, Goddess Laxmi, and a bracelet with his name engraved on it. He wanted to dispel any doubts of his stature and splurged on the latest model of the Maruti Suzuki that was available in the market. They moved from their modest flat in Vayupuri to a large palatial home in Sainik Farms.

When Pankaj finished high school, the senior Mr. Khanna was keen for him to join the family business. However, surprisingly he was met with resistance from his wife even though she had never before questioned any of his decisions. She was keen that Pankaj study engineering. Where she picked up the concept of engineering as the education to pursue or why she was keen on it was never established. She put up a tough fight and Mr. Khanna ultimately consented. Pankaj went on to pursue engineering studies in the South of India with the clear understanding that this was just a degree and he would be required to come and join the family business later on. When Pankaj graduated from college, he took the business to a whole new level. He had visited the United States and United Kingdom with friends one summer and was swept away by the consumerism and abundance that he saw. He was fascinated with the large retail stores and malls. He had his father's gift for fashion and that, coupled with his exposure to the world beyond, began a new chapter in the family's business.

They began exporting textiles and later got small consignment orders for hosiery. Pankaj did not inherit his father's penchant for elaborate designs or desire for being ostentatious, so he breathed fresh life into the now-garish designs. He retained the old brand, but started his own labels for designer wear. During his travels he had learned about the power of private labels. He then applied that in his own business, designing and manufacturing clothing for some of the larger fashion houses in the country, who then slapped their own label onto it.

Business could not have been better. The new dream that Aasma was so excited about was also related to the family business. Like his father before him, Pankaj had started a fresh new round of acquisitions. He did not look for well-run profitable businesses—rather, he looked for sick industries with good fundamentals. When the loan sharks and bankers couldn't get what they wanted from the business and put it on the open market, that's when he grabbed the opportunity.

The latest acquisition was that of a garment factory called Jayanthi Enterprises. This wasn't a typical acquisition or even a sick company. It had an interesting history and just happened to choose him as the new owner. All he did was to show up to an open auction more out of curiosity than with a briefcase full of cash to purchase it. The factory had been a victim of its management's inability to reach an agreement with the labor union. On the surface the impasse had begun quiet innocuously with the labor union demanding increased benefits; however, underneath that a corporate scandal was brewing. It began with someone in middle management acquiring details on a lucrative export deal that the company had just acquired. The manager weighed how to best leverage this newfound information and finally decided that the highest bidder would be the union leader, Pran Aya. He leaked the information to the labor union leader for an undisclosed sum of money. The intention was for the union leader to use this information to incite the union workers to make increased demands, and when the pressure became too much to take for the senior management, he himself would betray his union and pocket a nice piece of change. No one would be hurt, his labor union would cool off soon enough, and everything would proceed as normal.

Pran Aya, where "Aya" translated to "elder brother," was an intimidating figure. He was dark-skinned with a large bushy mustache and always wore a white safari suit. Pran Aya had serious political ambitions. His day job was to look for opportunities to stir up unrest to small to medium size companies and fill his own coffers with money at the end of the day. He had the mind of a scheming genius. He'd make management make small concessions and play them off as big ones when it suited him. He was known to own several weapons, and rumor had it that had used contact weapons, namely a knife at least three times. He had been arrested twice, but had made bail each time. Many had seen the police chiefs and other inspectors share country-made liquor with him.

The erstwhile senior owner of Jayanthi Enterprises had recently passed away. His abroad-educated son had taken the reins a couple of years previously and had ambitious plans for the company. In the two years that he had managed the company, he got it ISO certified. He had implemented new stream-lined inventory management and manufacturing. All inventories were labeled and stacked in color-coded aisles and all workers had been given safety goggles, and hairnets. Helmets were given to those operating heavy machinery.

What Pran Aya had not anticipated was the idealism of the Six Sigma process re-engineer at the helm of operations at Jayanthi Enterprises. A sure sign should have been the numerous meeting requests that were turned down, but Pran Aya was persistent. When his good corporate behavior for meetings was not rewarded, he decided to use the time-tested formula. Wielding a knife, he went to the young entrepreneur's office. When his verbal threats weren't taken seriously, he began to vigorously knife through the air with his twelve-inch weapon. What he did not expect was that the in addition to being a black belt in process engineering, the young chief executive was also a karate black belt. He defended himself with the same calm and self-restraint that any trained black belt would—firm, yet restrained.

Pran Aya left with fewer broken bones than he deserved but was bruised on the inside. He made it his life's ambition to destroy Jayanthi Enterprises. He was successful, but it wasn't his doing. His second attempt to confront the CEO with an AK-47 and two goons was not taken lightly. The Ivy League-educated CEO used all his political connections and got Pran Aya behind bars for ten years without the possibility of parole. To prove that this behavior would not be tolerated, he put a big padlock on the gates of Jayanthi. Something about this incident made him realize that he was better off taking the partnership offered to him by the manufacturing consulting company in the United States so he packed his bags and moved part and parcel to the United States—but not before putting Jayanthi up for sale at a fraction of what it was worth. The MBA got sentimental and decided that the company named after his mother should go to someone who would nurture and care for it rather than to the highest bidder. He met Pankaj at the open auction and liked him instantly. They struck a deal that suited both of them.

Pankaj had promised Aasma that the factory was hers to run. While she had never run a factory before, she had a great business sense and it was the least he could do for her. They were planning to name it Aasma Fashions. The factory would manufacture men's and women's T-shirts that would then be exported to the United States and the United Kingdom. Aasma was very excited about finally having something worthwhile to occupy her mind and time. She had already begun searching the Internet for vendor, customer, and competitor websites. Even though she was not trained in fashion design, she had a keen eye for fashion and had sketched half a dozen designs. She had already visited the factory a couple of times and saw that processes within the company were already in great shape.

Her biggest task at hand was motivating the workers and erasing the company's recent unpleasant history. Already she had made big plans to create a socially conscious workplace. She had decided to pay for the education of two of each of worker's children. She hoped that not only would it mean that the workers' children were educated, but that it would also act as an incentive for having fewer children. Another surprising inequity that existed was that women were paid less per hour than a man who was doing the same job. That was the first thing that she would change. If she couldn't change her own life, she would try and change the lives of others.

• • •

It seemed that happiness was teasing Aasma. As she sketched out her ambitions for a new start in her professional life, life itself kept playing games with her. It was less than two months after sealing the deal for Jayanthi Enterprises. The name of the new company had been submitted and they were waiting on some legal paperwork to replace the sign at entrance and company logo. If Aasma couldn't have a baby, this would be her baby. Then, one day her life was shattered.

It was a cold rainy evening. Claps of thunder echoed through her large palatial home. Her day had been an ordinary one. As usual she had woken up early and tied her long hair into a bun before freshening up. Then she had made tea and scrambled eggs for Pankaj, a ritual she did not let any one else do as it made her feel close to him. She also packed the lunch that the servants had prepared. As was their routine, she had breakfast and tea with her husband as that was the time that they generally caught up on events. It was the only time in the day that she had his full attention and he was in a good mood. This morning was no different. They discussed the pending actions

required to formalize the name change and other business details. After hugging goodbye, Aasma got back to her ambitions for her
company. The rest of the day was spent sketching designs and brows-
ing the Internet for inspiration. She would have skipped lunch if her
mother-in-law hadn't come and insisted that she join them for lunch.
The day was ordinary, but the evening was not.

Her first feeling of uneasiness came when Pankaj came home and
didn't give her his now-customary hug. The one thing Pankaj and
Aasma had going for their relationship was warmth and companionship and Aasma always grew nervous when that was missing. Her
fears were not misplaced, as Pankaj looked troubled and anxious to
get something off his chest. His usual routine was to rush off and take
a shower after giving Aasma a hug, but today he grabbed Aasma by
her hand and made her sit on the bed. Aasma was anxious and knew
that this wasn't a good sign. Whenever Pankaj did this, it meant he
had a secret to tell. She didn't know if she had the capacity left to
keep any more secrets. Moreover, any secret that Pankaj held had the
capacity to change her life forever. For someone who had spent her
entire life avoiding conflict, conflict seemed to be seeking her as if to
make up for years of neglect.

While she braced herself for what Pankaj was about to say, she
could have never prepared herself for what she was about to hear.
Pankaj told her that he was had reached a crossroads of his life and
had to make a decision. He was very conflicted, and hoped that
Aasma might be able to guide him. Aasma was already nervous about
what she was hearing as any decision made at the crossroads of
Pankaj's life meant that it would alter the course of her own as well.
Maintaining a steady tone, she encouraged him to continue. He
started by saying that it didn't have anything to do with her but his
life had taken a turn that he hadn't expected. Aasma smiled to herself.
Because of him, her own life had been through more turns than she
would have ever chosen. What Pankaj then said shook the foundation
of her life as it stood. He was in love with a man. She had met this
man but hadn't thought of them as more than sexual partners. Somehow she had never explored the possibility that Pankaj would fall in
love. It took her a couple of years to reach the point where she had
finally accepted her marriage for what it was and now she had to deal
with this. This hurt way more than knowing that he wasn't attracted to
her. She had been able to accept this because she knew being attracted
to her wasn't a choice he was at liberty to make. He had told her that

he loved her and she believed him. What she had failed to grasp was that he loved her, but he wasn't *in* love with her. He loved her as one would love a best friend, but not the same way one would a lover.

Aasma felt a stinging pain in her stomach. This was just the beginning of the pain she would feel repeatedly in the months to come. She felt as if someone had taken her internal organs out while they were still connected to her and squeezed them tight. She had never felt this way before, not even when Pankaj had told her that he was gay. She wanted to say many things, but nothing came out of her mouth. Slowly, a tear fell from her eye. Pankaj pulled her towards him in an embrace, but she pushed him away. While she wanted Pankaj's warmth, she knew the conversation was not yet over—it was only the beginning. Pankaj had always been too afraid to come out openly and that was probably the reason that he had drawn close to Aasma so quickly. She was the reason that he got a chance to discover himself. He waited for Aasma to say something, to be mad at him, to scream and shout, but she didn't. When he felt the courage he had built inside himself for this conversation starting to ebb, he forced himself to continue.

He told her he was really sorry that their paths had crossed. Not for himself, but for her. If it hadn't been for her, he would still have been lying to everyone and never would have had the guts to discover himself. He was ashamed that he was doing this to her, which is why he needed her advice. He had an opportunity to move with his lover to Toronto, Canada. They had filed their paperwork six months ago and had just found out it had been approved. He hadn't taken it very seriously as he hadn't expected to have it approved so soon. This would be his only opportunity to come clean and stop living this life but he wouldn't make the decision without Aasma's consent.

Aasma wasn't exactly sure what emotions she was feeling. The pain was strong. There was anger towards Pankaj for keeping this secret for so long, then there was hurt, resentment, anguish, and finally sadness. She evaluated where her life now was. She asked Pankaj to at least give her the respect of time. She said she'd give him her decision very soon. Even in her pain, she slept with her arms wrapped around Pankaj that night. She held on to him as if it were the last time that she'd hold him that way. She wanted one last thing to remember him by. She knew that whatever decision she made would alter her life forever. If she stayed with Pankaj, she would lose the delicate balance they had cautiously reached together. If she walked away from it all, she'd have nothing to walk away to. Aasma was angry with herself and wondered if she could have done something differently. Had she let him get away with too much? Then again, she wondered if it really was her choice. All she knew for sure was that she would never have forgiven herself if she hadn't given the marriage a chance. Sure, it wasn't like other marriages, but it was *her* marriage. After all, when Aasma had walked around the fire with Pankaj during the Hindu marriage ceremony she had made a promise to herself and to him to give her all.

Theirs had been an Arya Samaj Hindu wedding, which was a simplified version of the traditional Vedic Hindu marriage ceremony. They had taken seven *mangal pheras*, or the ritual of making vows while circling the scared fire. With each of the pheras, they had made a promise to each other. Pankaj lead for the first four pheras, while Aasma lead for the remaining three. Hadn't she promised to come before him should any harm fall on him? Aasma had always been religious, but of late she had found herself questioning God. If God really did exist, why was there so much unhappiness in the world? Why was her own life being subject to this roller coaster? She had never hurt anyone or had a bad thought towards anyone in her life. One thing she was sure of was that she did not understand God's design for her life.

She spent the entire night clinging to Pankaj and thinking about promises made and promises broken. When she woke up in the morning she was clear on what she had to do. She went through the morning ritual of making tea and packing lunch. When Pankaj came down for breakfast, she kissed him on his forehead, took his hand and told him that she had made a decision. She was going to set him free. She would be out of his life come this evening. How he told his parents and what he did next was up to him. She told him that she was very happy that he finally had the guts to admit who he really was as the only shame was in the lies. Those who loved him would understand, and those who didn't shouldn't matter any way. She said that she would pray for him and that if he ever needed a friend she'd be there. At the same time, she implored him to respect her enough not to reach out to her now. She needed to come to terms with her life and everything she had been through. She walked away from the table even before Pankaj could say anything.

• • •

As Aasma recollected the last few years of her life, her blank eyes stared past the Charles from Cambridge to the Boston skyline. She didn't register the kids on bicycles whizzing past her, or the nanny pushing a six-month-old baby, or the three afternoon joggers. Even though it was the middle of an afternoon on a weekday, random people like her found their way to the banks of the Charles River. Each had their story and was alone with their thoughts. Even those in the company of others seemed to reflect on their own lives as they walked past.

A year had passed since Aasma had walked out from Pankaj's life and into Gauri's arms. Aasma had told Gauri what had happened but had begged her not to discuss it with anyone or even talk to her about it. It was a chapter from her past and that's how she wanted to keep it. During the months afterward that she spent at her childhood home, she was reserved and pensive. She did nothing all day except sleep and cook. Gauri encouraged her to read, but she couldn't find the strength. Her father said little to her. He showed support by not asking any questions and letting her believe that he knew nothing.

When Aradhana's graduation approached, Gauri made a decision. It was time Aasma went far away from everything. She needed some fresh air. Neither knew what would happen next, but the immediate step was clear. America was a reason for hope. Not because either knew what the country held or how it would serve as a balm, but because it was far away from the memories. In the beginning Aasma pushed back. She told Gauri that they couldn't impose as Aradhana was still studying, lived with roommates, and would probably be too busy but Gauri would hear none of it. Both Aradhana and Aasma were her daughters and they were sisters. They were meant to be there for each other, as that is how she had raised them. Them visting was a minor inconvenience for what it had potential to deliver. If Aasma could find even a little happiness it would be worth it.

That's when Gauri had called Aradhana and told her that Aasma was coming with her. She hadn't told Aradhana what had happened with Aasma, as it was Aasma's story to tell. When she was ready, Gauri was sure that Aasma would confide in her sister. Even Amrita who Aasma was so close to knew nothing except that Pankaj and Aasma had separated. Amrita had tried to reason with Aasma by telling her that a woman's true home was the one she made with her man and that whatever the problem was could be worked out. Aasma found herself getting angry with Amrita's self-righteousness. Granted Amrita had no idea what had transpired, but blanket statements like these made no sense to her anymore. The whole business of dedicated-to-husband theories made her sick in the stomach. As far as she was concerned, she had been as good a wife as she could have been. She walked away from it all without a fight.

When Gauri found out about the new acquisition of the garment factory that would have been Aasma's, she found herself unable to help herself. She cared about her daughter's security and Aasma deserved to get something out of the marriage. She wanted Aasma to fight for alimony and the factory, but Aasma would hear none of it. If she walked out of Pankaj's life, she did so for good. She wanted to have no memories of him. She would make her own future for herself someday. Gauri pleaded with her to be pragmatic. Aasma was now a single, soon-to-be divorced woman. Whether or not she would get another chance at marriage was uncertain as India was not the easiest place for a divorced woman. Sure, things had changed and Gauri herself knew of at least five recently divorced women, but acceptance was a process rather than an instinct. Gauri felt that financial security for Aasma was imperative. Moreover, the factory would give her something to aspire to. It meant that Aasma would need to live in Delhi, but Gauri was more than willing to live with her. Gauri insisted that even if they didn't move to Delhi, Aasma could sell that factory. Gauri was aware of the story behind the factory as Gauri was the first person with whom Aasma had shared the news of the acquisition. Aasma, however, had been determined. Her dignity was the most important thing to her. She had not said goodbye to anyone but Pankaj. She did not know how to face her in-laws. Somehow she felt shame for having kept Pankaj's secret from them. She felt like her whole life was a dirty lie. She felt unclean and humiliated and was genuinely scared for Pankaj. Did Pankaj have what it took to come out with the truth? He was afraid for his father and scared for his mother. Could he rock their world from under their feet? While it wasn't fair to his parents, living this lie wasn't fair to him either. Why should Pankaj have to choose between his happiness and the happiness of those that he loved?

It was three months after their separation that Aasma heard from her father-in-law. Instinctively, she still called him Papa-ji. He said he wanted to meet with her and would fly down to Hyderabad. He wasn't really asking for her permission, rather just for her to be there. Aasma went to the airport to pick him up and, out of routine, touched his feet. He blessed her to have a long life. Habits were always so hard to break. He wasn't carrying any luggage other than a leather briefcase. Aasma wanted to ask him why but didn't. Greetings were strained, but cordial. Mr. Kapoor wasn't home and was expected later in the day. An elaborate meal had been prepared. No one was sure why he was visiting, but it had to be important.

This man who had been the ultimate rule-giver in the house of Aasma's marriage looked pensive. The confidence he wore on his brow looked harrowed yet he carried himself with dignity like a man who was lost but not beaten. He had always been hard to read. Like her own father, Aasma had avoided him until it was absolutely necessary to speak to him. He seldom bore a smile on his face, but when he laughed, he laughed loudly and deep in his belly. He ate the lunch that had been prepared in his honor with polite appreciation and then asked if he could speak with Aasma privately. When they got to her room, he broke down. Aasma had never seen her father-in-law shed a tear, let alone cry inconsolably. After Aasma allowed him time to grieve, he started asking for forgiveness for the fact that his family had let Aasma down and had caused her pain and sorrow. He confessed that he felt personally responsible. If he hadn't forced Pankaj to get married, Aasma's fate might have been different. If it had been his daughter to whom this had happened, he said he would have killed the boy. Aasma had kept his family's dignity and respect and for that he was so grateful that he would give anything. He said he had disowned Pankaj and never wanted to see him again. It was through him that Aasma learned that Pankaj had packed his bags and had moved to Toronto. He said he had lost his son, but didn't want to lose his daughter. He knew that nothing he could say or do would make Aasma forgive him or his family.

Aasma then interrupted him. She told him she didn't hate anyone or hold anything against anyone. This was her fate and she accepted it. She asked him to forgive Pankaj, for it wasn't a choice he made. If Pankaj could have helped it or changed his life, he would have, of that she was sure. She said she knew Pankaj loved and respected his parents more than anyone else. This bold decision was his one chance to stop living a life that was a lie. No one in their family had ever mistreated her. In fact, they had all given her tremendous love. She had walked away knowing that.

Papa-ji was consumed with emotion. He told her that she had a very big heart. For that he blessed her to find true love and happiness. He had a small token for her. It wasn't much, he said, but it was they very least they could offer her. He opened his briefcase and took out a stack of notarized papers and handed them to her. When Aasma finished flipping through the papers her eyes got watery. She returned them to him and said that she could not accept them. They were transfer of ownership papers not only for Jayanthi Enterprises, but also for Pankaj's new labels. The Khannas had kept for themselves only what Mr. Khanna himself had built.

Papa-ji insisted that this was what Mummy-ji wanted as well. Aasma knew that Papa-ji would not take no for an answer but she could not imagine taking away from Pankaj all that he had worked so hard to build. Pankaj had been punished enough, and she did not want to add any more insult to injury.

When she was sure that Papa-ji wasn't going to take no for an answer she accepted the papers for Jayanthi Enterprises, and returned the rest. They rightfully belonged to Pankaj she maintained. Someday, she was sure they would find it in their hearts to forgive Pankaj the same way that she had.

As Papa-ji left that day, Aasma found herself the new owner of Jayanthi Enterprises.

Fate Intertwined

Graduate Summa Cum Laude

$\mathcal{F}$inally a day Aradhana thought would never arrive was here— graduation. She had graduated *summa cum laude* and was one of the top five in her class. It was surreal for Aradhana. She couldn't believe that she had actually spent over two years in America and that her life had changed so completely in this short time. She still hadn't introduced Scott to her family, as she didn't yet feel ready. They had been there for two weeks and Aradhana had only snuck out a couple of times to meet Scott. He hadn't been pleased as he couldn't understand what all the fuss was about. He said that he'd be fine with being introduced as a friend, but he didn't like the fact that Aradhana was just not willing to negotiate. Aradhana wasn't entirely sure why she was so nervous. The thought of Gauri not approving of Scott mattered more to her than she had ever thought. Suddenly the fact that Scott was so different from them was glaringly obvious. She loved Scott and didn't want him to be judged and, at the same time, she didn't want her family to be judged. She wasn't sure if there was a way out of this situation. All that she knew for sure was that she wanted the first time Scott met her mother to be perfect. Scott would be graduating as well, so she was in a strange dilemma. She wanted to be with Scott for the graduation and be able to hug and kiss him yet she was afraid that Gauri would see and disapprove.

Scott's family was going to be there as well. Aradhana was not sure how she was going to handle that situation. Scott was mad at her, and she understood why, but she was nervous at how upset Scott was. He wasn't one who shouted or screamed—instead he just gave people the cold shoulder. This was the first time she had experienced it herself. She wanted to give Gauri some more time to adjust to the country before she dropped this bombshell on her. Moreover, she was not sure about Aasma. There was a very distinct difference in her sister. There was sadness in her eyes and she said very little. Aasma was generally very self-righteous and she thought she'd have a lot of opinions about what she saw around, however she surprised Aradhana by showing very little interest. In fact, it seemed like she was in a world of her own. Aradhana was initially wondering how Aasma's black and white views would influence Gauri but now she wasn't sure at all about how Aasma being there would impact the situation.

The day of the graduation she called Scott and apologized for her behavior over the last two weeks and told him that she was ready to set the record straight and wanted Scott to meet her family.

Gauri was as excited as Aradhana was for her graduation, if not more. Even though it was her daughter's accomplishment, it felt like her own. Aradhana had achieved something that Gauri could never have achieved herself. She still hadn't forgotten how hard it had been for her to graduate with a bachelor's degree and now Aradhana was going to be graduating with a master's degree. She was really happy to have Aasma by her side and hoped that Aasma would find excitement in something. She had bought along two silk *sarees*. One was turquoise with silver polka dots, and the other was a brown Mysore silk *saree* with a gold paisley print border. She had insisted that Aasma wear the bright turquoise *saree* as she always told Aasma that dressing up made one feel better. She always maintained that getting dressed and going out made you feel alive. It made you realize there was an entire world out there that was larger than your own pain. On this day she insisted that both Aasma and Aradhana get dressed. She let Aradhana choose what she wanted to wear. She was aware that what she wore didn't really matter much as her graduation gown would cover it. Aradhana had purchased her first suit from a large store in the mall whose name she couldn't really remember. It fit her so beautifully that it made Gauri's eyes swell up with tears. When they were all ready, Gauri took both her daughters to the little temple Aradhana had created in her room, and asked God for happiness and peace for both of them. Aradhana gave both Aasma and Gauri hugs and then asked them to sit down, as there was something she wanted to share with them. She first asked for their understanding and made them promise that they would be objective. She then said that they owed her a graduation gift, and she was asking for their unconditional promise in the matter she was about to propose. Neither hesitated before agreeing.

Aradhana said that she had met someone very special. Even though she wasn't sure where the relationship would end up, she wanted her family to meet the guy and his family who had supported her through very hard times. Gauri looked shocked, but Aasma pulled Aradhana towards herself and hugged her. She said that she trusted Aradhana and was sure that she had made a good decision. Then she teased Gauri and told her that she should thank God that her daughter wasn't telling her that she was married or pregnant. Gauri saw the

196

humor in the situation, and was just happy that Aasma was finally smiling. She said that she promised not to kill Aradhana until she met the guy. Aradhana then announced that they would meet him soon as he was going to be picking them up.

The fifteen minutes from when Aradhana broke the news to when Scott arrived seemed like an eternity. Gauri insisted on making tea for Scott and was mad at Aradhana for not having given her more notice. She paced up and down adjusting the *saree* that she was already uncomfortable wearing. When Scott finally rang the bell all three rushed to the door. Aradhana wanted to brace Scott for the introduction, but she was to have no such luck. Suddenly Scott was face to face with three Indian women all scanning him intensely. He had two bouquets of flowers. One he handed to Gauri as he introduced himself and gave her a hug. Aradhana could tell that Gauri was completely taken aback but more than suitably impressed. He then shook hands with Aasma and handed the second bouquet to her. Aradhana could tell that the bouquet had been intended for her, and was inwardly impressed with Scott for his quick instinct.

Gauri insisted they sit down and have tea. It was after all, the first time they were meeting. Aasma went to the kitchen to get the tea and called for Aradhana to help her. Aradhana was nervous as being called to the kitchen was an indication that a serious matter needed to be discussed immediately. She realized that Aasma exerted significant influence over Gauri so she rushed to the kitchen without letting her anxiety show. Aasma grabbed her, hugged her and let out a little shriek. Her verdict was that he was cute beyond belief and she was thrilled with her selection. Aradhana felt that this was going to be the beginning of a very special relationship between her and Aasma. This was the first time in her life that she felt like she wanted Aasma's love and support and was overjoyed that her sister was responding.

Aradhana could tell that Gauri was on her best party behavior. She made sure to sit straight and spoke in a slight British accent, trying to accentuate her words. When they reached the college, Scott introduced them to his family. The O'Donnell clan exhibited the same warmth to Gauri and Aasma that they had to Aradhana. Gauri was surprised as she had not expected Americans to be warm and friendly. The all spoke very highly of Aradhana, which made her like them even more. They sat together and watched the entire ceremony.

Scott made a conscious effort not to publicly display affection. In fact, in all this time he had not so much as shaken Aradhana's hand. It was only when they made their way to the back room to line up for the graduation walk and instructions that he hugged her and told her to relax. She asked him to do the same and they both laughed. He said that this was a million times better and more relaxed than he had imagined. He really liked both Gauri and Aasma, and said he saw a lot of them in Aradhana. Aradhana felt proud. For the first time in many years, she was proud to have Gauri and Aasma as her family.

When Aradhana finally walked down the aisle to receive her diploma, Gauri stood up and clapped as tears of joy ran down her face. Aasma followed the cue of the several families of the students who had gone before and whistled loudly. As she did, Gauri stared at her in disbelief, quiet shocked that her little girl could made such a loud noise. Uncle Jim followed suit and Aradhana took her pretend diploma with more pride and grace than she had done anything else.

After the ceremony, the families convened for drinks and food under a designated tent. Scott's family then invited them all for dinner the following evening. Aradhana was hoping that Gauri would turn down the invitation. This had gone well, but she didn't want to push her luck. This afternoon the focus was on their graduation. Tomorrow, however, it would be different. All the cultural differences would again surface. Aradhana had a hunch that Gauri would refuse, but she was wrong. Gauri accepted.

Dinner at the O'Donnells'

Gauri had brought a couple of pairs of trousers and some skirts from India as she didn't get too many opportunities at home to wear "western dresses" as they called them. It was something that only young girls or very hip people in India wore. At her age, she could occasionally wear a pair of jeans to a picnic or a skirt during a special dinner, but that was about it. Both Aradhana and Aasma had forced her to buy at least half a dozen more ensembles during her visit so far. One of her recent acquisitions had been a long black skirt with a cream-colored sleeveless blouse, which is what she wore to dinner at the O'Donnells along with a delicate paisley shaped diamond pendant on a string of pearls.

Aasma wore a black and white polka dot knee-length dress with a white sash that she had designed herself. Aradhana couldn't believe how stunning the two of them looked. She had forgotten how attractive Aasma was and how much attention she had received from the boys while growing up. Aasma had insisted that Aradhana also wear a dress that Aasma had designed and Aradhana was surprised by how well it fit her. It was a simple yet extremely elegant dress made of lace with a satin lining. It had clean lines and flowed naturally on Aradhana's frame. The olive green color of the fabric brought out Aradhana's complexion. Aasma had even matched the dress with an elegant emerald pendent with a princess cut and small matching earrings.

Gauri was not sure what to bring for dinner. Aradhana had suggested they bring dessert. She didn't think of suggesting wine, because surely that would be a travesty. Gauri wasn't comfortable just taking dessert. It seemed like to little so she suggested that they bring a little something for the O'Donnells' home. Alaya drove them to the Burlington Mall where Gauri picked out a crystal vase from Mikasa. Aradhana was intrigued by the fact that Gauri wouldn't spend $12 on blouse for herself but parted with $59.99 for the vase without a moment's hesitation. At that point she realized that Gauri was a proud woman who would do whatever it took to keep her pride.

That evening Scott picked them up for dinner. He seemed genuinely enamored by how attractive they all looked this evening. As they drove over he suddenly became aware of his own family. He was hoping that they made as much of an effort for the dinner as Aradhana's family had. He had spoken to his mother four times during the day to remind her that there should be no beef. Of course they were already aware that Aradhana was a vegetarian, but he wanted to remind them that Aasma and Gauri were not. He insisted there should be a good balance between vegetarian and meat, preferably no beef or pork but something more neutral like chicken or fish. He also instructed that the food be flavored enough but nothing curried so it wouldn't look like they were trying to make a statement or accentuate their differences. He also asked them to curb their curiosity and not ask any culturally insensitive questions.

Scott wanted everything to be perfect. Aradhana made him feel alive. He felt that there was something special about her from the first day he met her. He just never thought that he'd fall so deeply in love with her. Aradhana was complex and different from anyone he had known. She made him feel things that he thought himself incapable of feeling. She was worldly, yet there was also a raw innocence about her. She didn't fall in love easily, but when she did, she gave her soul to it. She was vulnerable and could be hurt easily. He had seen what her relationship with Nirman had done to her. He had never met Nirman and was glad that he hadn't. He wasn't sure how he would have handled meeting him, especially since he had strong feelings for Aradhana from the beginning. He knew Aradhana cared for him as well and yet there was a fear in his stomach that she wasn't in love with him as much as he was with her. He knew she had some of her guard still up. Though she had seemingly moved on, sometimes he saw a void in her eyes and he worried that she was thinking of Nirman. Once she had called him Nirman in passing, but quickly corrected herself. Scott had pretended that he hadn't heard her as going there would do neither any good. He wanted her to take her time to heal and yet sometimes he wondered what it would mean for them if she didn't. As if life wasn't complicated enough, there was also the not insignificant matter of their two totally different cultures.

Scott had been nervous about meeting Aradhana's family. She had made them seem rigid and inflexible and had said that her mother would totally disapprove of their relationship. She hadn't spoken much about her sisters and brother. It was only after Aasma had arrived that she had shared some facets of their relationship. Scott knew that Aradhana missed her home and family but apart from talking about how much she missed them, and a little about her mother, she had shared little else. On the few occasions that Scott had met Gauri and Aasma he really liked them. They had made a conscious effort not to view him through the lens of race. He wanted them to know him as the person he was, not just as a white American who liked their daughter or sister. Aasma had been especially nice. Aradhana had shared the fact that Aasma was married, but he hadn't really had an opportunity to learn anything else about her yet. Aradhana had an advantage of knowing exactly what his culture was like due to the fact that she was living in the country and knew the exact extent of their similarities and differences. He, on the other hand, felt a little lost. He had made a conscious effort to learn about Aradhana's culture and yet he would never really know everything about it until he had had the opportunity to actually go to India. Given that this was unlikely to happen in the near future, the next best thing was to understand all he could about her family while they were here. He had asked Aradhana what he should call her mother and Aradhana had answered "aunty." Gauri would be shocked and would think it ill-mannered if he called her by her given name, so that's what Scott had been calling her so far.

This dinner would be a great opportunity to make Aradhana's family realize that deep down they weren't that different. Even though they called each other by different names, spoke differently, and looked differently, they held similar values. Both believed in strong and loving family structures and both wanted life to be a pleasant journey filled with laughter and joy. Those were the only two things that mattered. He wanted the dinner to be perfect in every way. The last thing he wanted was a cultural *faux pas* that would convince either Aradhana or her family that their relationship was a bad idea, which was why he was being so "anal," as Sarah called it.

When they arrived at the house, they were greeted by a warm hug from Sarah and a warm handshake from Sean. As Sarah gave them a tour, Gauri complimented Sarah on her beautiful home. Aradhana was pleasantly surprised by the tour as her stereotypes about Americans being private continued to be challenged. The fact that they sat for several hours in the family room chatting before they were ready for dinner was a great sign as far as Scott and Aradhana were concerned. Both were nervous in their own ways, though, as they were aware that their families had significant power and the capability to embarrass them, a power each family had not been shy to use in the past.

Dinner, however, was different. Sarah had slaved away for hours in the kitchen. For appetizers, she had made mushroom and chicken turnovers. She had also painstakingly followed the recipe from one of her numerous cookbooks and made vegetable kebabs on skewers as she thought it would be Eastern enough, without screaming so. She also made a spinach artichoke dip that she served with garlic bread and had pre-ordered a shrimp cocktail and a cheese platter from Costco. For dinner there was a starter of tomato soup on a pastry shell and a mixed green salad with goat cheese, cherry tomatoes and vinaigrette dressing. For the main course, she had made vegetable au gratin, chicken Kiev, mashed potatoes, and grilled asparagus. Dessert included a splendid apple crisp with pecans that was served with French vanilla ice cream.

Gauri was tremendously touched by Sarah's efforts. As someone who entertained frequently, she could only imagine the time it took. More than the gesture she was floored by how close Scott and Sarah were. She always took for granted that in Western cultures, parents and children were not close. From the shows she saw on television children had little time or interest for their parents but this inside look into their lives showed her how wrong she had been. The O'Donnells were no different than any happy cohesive Indian family. If anything, there was an honesty in their relationship that she had rarely seen before. The relationships between them were not held together simply because of conditioning or guilt, they were together by choice. In her view that was more than she could have said about many of the relationships she saw which were need-based and spurred by guilt.

The O'Donnells were delightful hosts and the Kapoors were gracious guests. Initially, everyone was formal and conversation was limited to safe topics such as the weather, shopping, and recipes. However, as the evening progressed, everyone became more comfortable and bold. Sarah insisted that Gauri try the fantastic bottle of Riesling that they had just opened and to everyone's surprise, Gauri consented. After that they spoke of their respective cultures. Aradhana was surprised as to how many questions Aasma and Gauri had and how similar they were to the ones she had when she arrived. They included questions about race, culture, familial values and a host of other topics.

Sarah for her part had her own questions about India. She asked about the caste system, the role of women, and other topics that at first made Scott cringe. He relaxed only when he saw the Kapoors passionately explaining the origins and the benefits of the caste system. They spoke about how it had originated from a division of labor and evolved into a segregation tool. They defended that broadly speaking, it had little room in the new India. All three Kapoor women were most passionate when defending the role of Indian women in the Indian society. Even Aradhana—who until this point had been quite tentative jumped in to defend their honor. The women knew the facts and went back to as far as pre-Vedic times to talk about Indian women scholars and priestesses. When they weren't discussing controversial topics, Sarah and Gauri were discussing food. The two acted like they'd know each other forever. If you put aside the difference in accents and appearances, you'd assume they had been best friends from school.

Unbeknownst to Aradhana, at one point during the evening Gauri took Scott aside. Scott would never tell Aradhana, but Gauri would. It would elicit an angry response from Aradhana, but Gauri countered that she had to be sure. She had asked Scott if he was serious about their relationship. Without hesitating Scott answered that he most definitely was.

Divine Secrets of Sisterhood

*A*lthough it had scarcely been a month since Aasma had been in the United States, she felt very much at home. Nothing in the country was hers and nothing of hers was the country's and in a strange way this made her feel very liberated. She suddenly felt unbound by the shackles that had bogged her down for so long. After a lapse of several years, she was finding pleasure in simple things. She felt closer to her sister than she ever had in her life. A couple of days after dinner at Scott's, Aasma broke down and let her little sister into her big secret. She had been very afraid of being judged. More than judgment of Pankaj, she was afraid that Aradhana would judge her. Perhaps Aradhana would chide her for sticking with Pankaj this long, and for letting him get away with breaking her heart. She was sure if it were Aradhana, she would have left the moment she was made aware of the situation. The inability to share her secret with anyone had made her feel heavy and helpless. Gauri knew and was supportive, yet Aasma was really looking for someone else's perspective on her life. Had she made a mistake? Could she have done something differently? Was she too weak? Or perhaps too strong? She didn't really know. Moreover, she felt like she owed Aradhana an explanation seeing that she had barged into her life without so much as a warning. Aradhana had been able to sense that something was wrong. She had even asked her a few times, but had backed off when no honest answer was forthcoming.

One evening Aasma and Aradhana went for a walk. They decided to catch their breath at a local park and found sanctuary on some benches overlooking the basketball court. It was late and while the sun had bid goodbye, darkness had not yet established its dominance. The night was clear except for a few stars that had front row seats to earthly performances. Even though the playground was off a road there was little to no traffic. Tall, well-trimmed hedges bordered the tennis and basketball courts. Flowers were in full bloom, and a mild fragrance filled the sky. As they sat on the benches neither said anything, both reflecting on their own lives. For Aradhana, hers was moving very fast and in a direction that she hadn't anticipated. Aasma, on the other hand, was thinking about her own failures and triumphs. Despite her pain, there was a feeling of freedom and liberty. Her life was now her own, to do with as she pleased. She just wasn't

204

sure what it was that she pleased. Little things would put a smile on her lips, yet big events and gestures did not.

She wasn't sure what exactly prompted her to confess at that moment, but something did. She told Aradhana about Pankaj and their marriage. She told her about how after five years of marriage, she was still a virgin. She told her that even after all her sacrifices, Pankaj left her for another man. She told her about Papa-ji and her inheritance. At first she focused solely on the facts to take attention away from her pain. It was what it was. The marriage, his homosexuality, his desire to find love, her setting him free, her moving back home, Papa-ji giving her the factory, Gauri bringing her to the United States and all details in between. But as time went on, facts gave way to deep emotions—her helplessness, her feeling of undesirability, her hope against hope, her strength, her weakness, her denial, her anger, her acceptance.

Aasma's feelings flowed like water gushing from a broken dam. She hadn't even shared these with Gauri. It was as if she was admitting her feelings not to Aradhana but to herself. At various points she bawled, wiping her tears on the sleeves of her shirt. She didn't care about anything at that point other than unburdening herself. It was therapeutic. Aradhana hadn't said anything so far. She had held her hand and Aasma had felt her squeezing it at some points when she was hysterical. She hardly felt anything because she was so consumed now by the power of her own emotions. After her tears had dried and she could cry no more, Aradhana cried. Aradhana cried for her sister. All she could say was that it wasn't fair. It just wasn't fair that all this happened to the nicest person she knew. It happened to someone who had never willed or done anything bad. After they both cried some more, they hugged in a long embrace.

After many moments of silence, Aradhana confessed that she would never have had the strength that Aasma showed. Aasma had emerged from this with dignity and had shown endurance and the ultimate respect for the institution of marriage. Aradhana truly admired her for it. Of late she had become aware of her own weaknesses. She told Aasma of her own failures—about her heartbreak with Nirman, her succumbing to the pain, her weakness, and her short but painful experience with the bottle. She talked about the feelings of loneliness that so often pierced her heart and left her immobile. She spoke about how her longing for her country consumed her and made her doubt her existence in America. She also spoke of her insecurities about the cultural differences between her and Scott. She said that she was afraid for their future, and wasn't sure that their relationship could sustain the trials and tribulations that came with their cultural differences.

A few hours passed without either of them saying anything, but neither was ready to leave the park yet. The constellations each told a story and Aradhana and Aasma each read the stories they wanted to in the sky. Both were apprehensive about the future. For the moment Aradhana's looked a little more promising, but she wasn't betting on it. Aasma saw in her namesake, the sky, hope for a new beginning. She was afraid to even ask for something least she jinxed it.

The sisters let their minds wander off into places they would be afraid to without this trance. Their reverie was interrupted by a mechanical intrusion,the booming sound of a Corvette taking off. On this celestial night, the sisters were connected by the same oneness and familiarity they had shared in their mother's womb at different times. The two sisters who had been nurtured in the same environment both inside and out had, until recently, felt like total strangers. It took coming to a land that neither had ever imagined nor dreamed of to understand each other. For most of their lives it was a land that they weren't connected to; a place that had been no more than a mass on the atlas or a subject in the news. They had felt nothing towards it— no love, no hate, and no indifference –yet, their lives were drawn to its boundaries. It was within its confines that the two had discovered the power of sisterhood. This was the beginning of their relationship.

It was finally Aradhana who broke their silence by announcing that they were going to have a big senseless desi party. She wasn't sure why she suggested a party. It had nothing to do with the topic at hand. She just felt like Aasma's life needed a little cheering up. Aradhana wondered for an instant why her mind had suggested a desi party versus a global party and concluded that it was simply because being "desi" came naturally to her.

Aasma smiled. Like Aradhana, she didn't know what brought about the party idea, but she liked it. It had been forever since she had been at a party that didn't involve forty and fifty year olds, diamond jewelry, designer dresses, lots of chicken, more alcohol than the bar could hold, and conversations that led nowhere. It would be good to have a party where she didn't have to be perfect.

Aradhana hadn't thrown a party or thought of doing so since she had arrived in the States. For one, it would have cost too much.

Secondly, she wasn't sure if she could. She had heard of neighbors calling the cops for loud music. That evening under the night sky, though, having a party seemed like an easy decision.

It would be a decision that changed at least one of their lives forever.

Bollywoodmania

Scott had been forewarned. He was welcome at the party and, in fact, he was expected to help. However, apart from periodic translations and some additional assimilation into the Indian pop culture, more would probably not be forthcoming. This was a Bollywood party—maybe some day they'd have a Hollywood one. Scott wasn't thrilled that their differences would so be highlighted during the party. He had started to get the hang of Indian culture and its nuances. The spectrum of beliefs ranged from highly conservative to highly liberal depending on whom you spoke with and on what subject. It was a culture full of paradoxes. It was not his or, as Aradhana had explained to him, even her place to judge it. As with every culture, there was good and bad. Once they had gotten into a passionate conversation about what they'd be if they weren't who they were. They were talking about nationalities. Both had a really hard time thinking of themselves as anything but who they truly were. Aradhana gave an impassioned and heartfelt soliloquy on why she would not trade being an Indian. Scott responded with his own tribute to the Stars and Stripes.

Scott asked her if she'd ever take American citizenship. She evaded the question by saying that the first stop was an H1 B work visa, which in itself was a pain to get and miles away from a citizenship. The conversion of an F1 student visa to an H1 B visa was an agonizing one for most immigrants. It involved sponsorships from companies and an entire list of requirements that Aradhana would soon experience herself. For now however, she philosophized, "One day at a time, Scott, one day at a time."

Bollywood was also a culture of its own. Aradhana shared with him all her thoughts on Bollywood films and the songs she had sang that day when it had snowed for the first time. She wanted Scott to understand just how uplifting a Bollywood party would be. She had asked Aasma if she could discuss her situation with Scott and Aasma had consented. Scott was becoming fond of Aradhana's family and he was looking forward to cheering up Aasma. Notwithstanding his lack of Bollywood knowledge, Scott was very excited about the party. He had little input into the menu or the music, but his help was invaluable. He happily chaperoned Aradhana and Aasma to the supermarket and Indian grocery store on several occasions. He helped blow up the balloons and arrange party favors. Aradhana and Aasma had never been to a store like Party City, a one-stop shop for all party needs. They were overwhelmed at the huge space dedicated to different themes and favors. As expected, there was nothing for a Bollywood theme, but with some creativity and customization they surprised even themselves. Glamour, glitz, and retro were the favors for the day. Blacks, whites, golds, and silvers dominated the color scheme.

To take their theme to another level they got posters from old and new Bollywood movies from the Indian store. For the rest of the posters they had used Scott's color printer liberally. Scott had also managed to get some old records that were out of commission and mounted them strategically on the wall. He was their social expert in residence. He had insisted they inform their immediate neighbors of the party. Aradhana had been shocked when cops had shown up to the party next door a few weeks earlier. She couldn't get over the concept that the neighbors could call the cops on you if they were bothered. She and Aasma discussed how in India if one complained about noise to their neighbor they'd have the door slammed on their face. That was, of course, after hearing that it was their house that they paid good money for and it was theirs to do as they pleased. Then there was the painful but frequently used insult in Hindi that crudely translated to "what does your father have to lose," meaning that it was not your business.

Now that she was in the United States she had to play by different rules. She had asked Scott to accompany her when she informed her neighbors whom she had never met. To her surprise they were all very gracious and thanked her for letting them know.

All the formalities were taken care of and both Aradhana and Aasma could not contain their excitement. Aradhana had spent more time with Aasma during this visit than she had in her entire life. Aasma was looking forward to forgetting her past for one raucous night and letting her hair down. Gauri was happy to see Aasma excited about the project at hand. She had provided her input on the food, but had determined that it would be best if she stayed over at Priya's for the night. Priya had been after her to come and visit, but until now Gauri had preferred to spend this precious time with her daughters. Priya and Briggs were invited to the party, but didn't plan to stay long since the babysitter was only available until 9 p.m. Gauri would go home with them.

Alcohol was going to be served. This was the first party that Aradhana had thrown where this would openly be part of the refreshments.

Gauri took the news reasonably well. She still had no idea that Aradhana had worked at a pub, but she did know that Scott's family owned some restaurants. For Aasma's sake Gauri did not want to put a damper on the party. Moreover, Gauri knew better than to tell her two grown children what to do. She enjoyed her children's inclination to listen to her and knew to choose her battles.

Songs from Bollywood movies and Indian pop music filled the sultry evening air. One of the nicer facets of Aasma's marriage to Pankaj had been a lot of partying. That, coupled with her penchant for fashion, had left Aasma with much glamorous party wear.

That evening Aasma and Aradhana both wore cocktail *sarees*. Aradhana's was a gold- sequined crepe *saree* in navy blue. She wore her hair in a bun and long gold earrings and her makeup was glamorous yet subdued. Aasma had spent time dressing her up as if she was a doll. She seemed to have an eye for detail and knew how to accessorize perfectly. As for Aasma, she wore a black chiffon *saree* that also had sequins, with a halter neck blouse that revealed her perfect back. She, too, had tied her hair in a bun, but it seemed to sit naturally on her head. That night many people remarked that Aasma and Aradhana looked like twins. The townhouse filled up quickly. Glamour and glitz were the themes of the night. Wine bottles were specially labeled thanks to Scott's printer.

Gauri had also been forced to wear a *saree* by both her daughters. She looked elegant and charismatic. She had worked hard on the food for the party but she was keen on making an early exit as she felt that the evening should be theirs. When every corner of the house was filled with people, music and drinks, she made an exit with Priya snd Briggs. Aradhana could tell that Priya and Briggs were having a really good time and weren't keen on leaving that early. Unfortunately, the unavailability of the baby sitter forced them to leave as scheduled. Aasma and Aradhana bade their mother goodnight with mixed feelings. Neither could deny that it was a little awkward having Priya, Briggs, and their mother there, especially since this evening was about letting their hair down.

With the house left to them and fifty other people who had nowhere to go, the party was about to reach new heights. They had removed the space furniture and had converted the dining room and living room space into a dance floor. Aradhana and Aasma danced like there was no tomorrow. Aasma dragged Scott to the floor several times. Like a jack in the box, he'd spring out for a number only to then retreat every time it was over. He was settling in slowly but surely. Aradhana knew, Bollywood or Hollywood, Scott was not a dancer. She was glad to see that Aasma liked Scott. Aasma's approval was important to Aradhana for reasons she couldn't explain. Scott had worn a black blazer with matching dress pants and a cream colored dress shirt. He looked dashing and got several compliments. Scott wasn't drinking, as he had made an executive decision to let this night be about the girls. He seemed to want to stay completely alert to protect the two Indian women entrusted to his care.

The women, though, seemed not to have a care in the world. Aradhana was surprised to see Aasma drink wine liberally. More important, she was happy to see that Aasma was mingling well with her guests which lifted a huge burden off her shoulders. She was dancing in superb tandem with Asad who had asked her for a dance. Aradhana had no idea that both were such good dancers. There was one number where both were so in the groove that everyone else left the floor. Alaya had a few dances with Asad, but he seemed more interested in getting Aasma's attention. Aradhana picked up on the vibe and brought it to Scott's attention before pulling her sister aside and teasing her about her new admirer. Aasma seemed to brush off the comments, but not the blush on her face.

It had been some time since Aasma had received attention from a man. Before she was married, Aasma received a great deal of it, but she never reciprocated. It was just not something she needed. But being denied attention changes a person and Aasma had changed too. All those years of marriage to Pankaj without admiring male attention had made her feel unwanted. The confidence that she didn't even know that she had been carrying all her life was lost. She longed for a loving word, admiring eyes, and for someone to crave her attention rather than she theirs. She didn't really know Asad but she knew that Alaya wanted Asad. That made him all the more attractive to her. Alaya was very attractive but Aasma was conventionally beautiful. Asad had a raw magnetism to him. It was something that even Aradhana had noted. He was five foot ten, but carried himself in a way that made him seem even taller. He was lean but muscular and his hazelnut complexion contrasted with Aasma's fair one. His eyes were gentle yet fierce. His lips were well defined and accentuated the angles of his face. When he leaned down to speak to her Aasma's could smell Davidoff's Cool Water on him. As the night progressed Aasma danced with him about a dozen times. She couldn't believe how well he moved. He was a natural and Aasma felt herself incredibly attracted to his powerful grace. He was confident, sexy, fun—all things Aasma wanted to be. As the night progressed and drinks flowed, the lights dimmed. The fast music was traded for the slower romantic Bollywood numbers, which were soon traded for non-denominational light instrumentals.

Aradhana and Scott were immersed in each other's arms. Scott found himself incredibly attracted to Aradhana in her clinging *saree*. The curves of her figure were fully visible and her navel came into view every time the wind blew through or she adjusted her *saree*. It was a good thing for Scott that Aradhana didn't know how to handle her *saree* well. Even though Aasma had done a stellar job of pinning it, Aradhana felt compelled to readjust it on an ongoing basis. Scott joked that he wouldn't have known if she wore her *saree* well or not—as long as it was wrapped something like a *saree*, then it was a *saree* to him. Hell, until he met Aradhana he didn't know what a *saree* was anyway. At one point while dancing he whispered in her ear that had he known he'd be so attracted to the *saree* he would have made all his girlfriends wear one. Something about his cheeky comment made Aradhana feel very proud of her national dress. In that moment as she felt like they had overcome yet another cultural barrier.

They kissed passionately, but Aradhana stopped suddenly when she thought of Aasma. She was trying very hard not to throw her romance in Aasma's face. She had periodically been checking up on Aasma. She seemed to have a new energy about her. Aradhana wasn't sure how she felt about Asad hitting on Aasma as she felt a strange protectiveness towards her sister. Then she thought about everything Aasma had been through and decided to let her live it up a little. When Aradhana looked up after the lights had dimmed, she didn't see either Aasma or Asad. Alaya was still dancing with someone she wouldn't have otherwise. She also had more tequila in her system than Aradhana had ever seen. When Aradhana asked her if she had seen Aasma,, Alaya murmured something about the two lovebirds flying away after wrecking her nest.

To Right a Wrong

*A*asma couldn't remember who had suggested that they go to Asad's house, but she remembered everything else because it was what she had being dreaming of for five years. She had been drinking but felt more aware of every sight and sound around her than she ever had. The merlot and cabernet had made her heady and prone to laughter. She was feeling bold. Asad was obviously smitten with her. All night he showered her with attention and compliments. If it wasn't her eyes, hair, or voice, it was her laughter. There wasn't anything that she could have done wrong. To him she was perfect.

Aasma was basking in the attention, but even more she was submitting to the contact. Asad was subtle which made every touch more exciting. It started with the planned accidental brushing against her hand and progressed to bolder contact. Throughout the party Asad's hands had explored Aasma's face. As they danced his hands traced her shoulders and then her hands. Aasma's body was on fire. Asad's touch was at first tentative but as he saw Aasma's body quiver with every touch it became more deliberate. Both knew they wanted more and there was an undeniable chemistry. For Aasma it was more than just the physical need. With physical warmth would come soothing of her soul. The balm could cure the years of pain and lack of self-esteem. Somehow she was sure that it would.

Asad's apartment was in the same community. His room was sparsely furnished and he took great care to adjust the lighting. Since mood lighting wasn't naturally built into the room he took a shirt lying on the floor and covered the bright camel colored lampshade. The red shirt bathed the room in a pink light. While Aasma surveyed the room, Asad filled the room with light jazz. As they both sat on the edge of the bed, Asad made the first move. He took the strand of hair that had freed itself from her bun and tucked it behind her ear. Then he whispered into her ear that he truly had never seen anyone quite so perfect as her. His fingers traced her face starting with her forehead to her eyes, and then her lips. Her lips parted naturally as his fingers moved over them. Her eyes were closed and she was savoring every trace his strong fingers made. She had never felt more alive. In that moment she experienced every perception. The sights, the smells, the sounds—they were all real, she was real. He leaned towards her. The sweet smell of wine infused with Cool Water tickled her senses. He

213

widened her parted lips with his own and his tongue explored the warmth of her mouth. She heard herself groan aloud. If this were all she got from him, it would be enough. Luckily for her Asad was just beginning.

The *paloo* of the *saree* that went over her blouse slid from her shoulder with one touch from Asad exposing her blouse and cleavage. Asad was in no hurry. He was with the woman he had been eyeing ever since she was introduced to him four weeks ago. As much as he wanted to caress every part of her body, he couldn't seem to take his eyes off her face. He came back to it again. This time he kissed her eyelids. Her lips parted into a smile. She tighly clasped his right hand and didn't release it for the rest of the night. She did not want to lose his touch even for an instant. All Asad had at his disposal were his lips and left hand. He made the best use he could of them. His touch was like fire. There was something magical and controlled in the way he moved his body. Aasma was a slave to his touch. At that moment there was nothing she wouldn't have given him. The magic of the moment had consumed them both.

Asad had been with many women. He had been told by many of them that he was the best they had been with. Looking into Aasma's innocent eyes that had become so alive with his touch made this moment magical for him as well. Like a conductor he directed their symphony. She responded to his every instruction however subtle. He continued to look into her eyes. He had seen the pain in them. He didn't know why she was so sad, but that night he saw nothing but pleasure. As he discovered her warmth, she groaned, her legs wrapping themselves naturally around his waist. Like their body movement, their breaths were coordinated. Their eyes smiled and both heaved a huge sigh as they both found the ultimate release of their pleasure.

Aasma was exhausted, yet she had never felt more invigorated. Here she was with a man she hardly knew. In that moment this stranger had given her more happiness than anyone else could have. She was finally at peace with herself. She knew it was wrong to put so much power and trust in the hands of a stranger and that her behavior tonight was reckless and diametrically opposed to the way she had lived her entire life. But if it was wrong, why did it feel so right?

Aasma knew it was late and that Aradhana would be worried, so after she had lain still for awhile and savored the the experience, she went to call her. With the lights turned on, Asad noticed blood. He was sure that his eyes were deceiving him, so he instinctively rubbed his eyes but when he looked down, he saw the same thing. He closed his eyes and thought about what had just transpired. He thought that Aasma was married and had suspected that either she was separated or was cheating. He never thought that he had just taken a woman's virginity.

He smiled—he wouldn't have planned her first night any differently.

• • •

As Gauri lay awake in Priya's home, she tried to get in touch with everything her youngest daughter would have been thinking and feeling over two years ago on that very same bed. Since Aradhana had left India, Gauri had dreamt every day of the day that she'd see her again. She had longed to understand her daughter better and knew Aradhana blamed her for several things—most of all, for not being strong. Somehow, Aradhana mistook her lack of strength and desire to protect her children as selfishness. Once when Ashwin had been in the throes of one of his mood swings and had insulted Abhay, Aradhana had confronted Gauri and told her she was selfish for not leaving Ashwin.

She knew that out of all her children, Aradhana blamed her most for the problems her marriage to Ashwin had subjected her children to. She knew she wasn't being selfish—she just had nowhere to go. This privilege of coming to the United States was something Aradhana could afford because of her seemingly selfish actions. All the education and comfort her children had received had been only because Ashwin had provided well for them. He had never let Gauri work. Slowly Gauri's confidence in her own ability to earn a living had diminished. Gauri had low esteem when it came to her own skills. She had long ago given up painting and even if she did take it up again, no matter how good she was, it would be a challenge to feed her family from it. Everything else she was good at—like cooking and housekeeping would probably not command enough dignity of labor in the minds of her society friends.

She had considered a better life several times. She did not expect Aradhana in her feminism to understand just how hard life for a single woman her age would be. Even if people didn't openly chastise her, they would judge her. Few doors would open for her. On the surface her high society friends would support her, but they would soon become distant. She'd have no life to speak of, she'd just exist. She had challenged herself several times on how that would be any differ-ent from her life with Ashwin. She didn't really care about the people who were her so-called friends but she couldn't lie to herself. She was afraid of what life would be like without what she knew. There was security in the known.

Things were coming to a head in her life. Abhay had grown up too, and with everyone out of the house, there was no one to shield him from Ashwin. As Abhay became stronger, fear gave way to anger. His resentment for his father had come to a boiling point. All of the years of bullying and chipping away at his confidence had made him despise his father. When she looked at her son, she saw pure hatred in his eyes and was afraid of what he might do. A few times she had to beg him to be calm. Once he had clenched a fist at his father after Ashwin had taunted him and accused him of showing his mother's genes. There was no tell-ing what Abhay would have done at that point if Gauri hadn't sent him to his room. She bore the brunt of Ashwin's anger and hatred towards the world on that night and many more.

After Abhay had graduated, he had started working in a call cen-ter. He worked U.S. hours and stayed away from home all night. He was out before Ashwin came home and asleep when he left. The two barely saw each other and for that Gauri was thankful. Gauri buried herself in books and housework throughout the day. Life was barely moving along when things went so wrong with Aasma. Her princess who had never harmed a soul was left alone in life. The pain in Aasma's eyes and soul was undeniable. She recognized it because it was what she had been living with for most of her life. She was weak when it came to her own life, but she was very strong when it came to her daughter. She would fight the whole world if it meant protecting her children. If Aasma never found someone, Gauri would still stand by her and fight the very society she couldn't fight on her own behalf. Her daughter deserved better—much better.

Unfortunately her children had learned well from her. They held their feelings close to their heart as she had taught them. Now that she wanted them to open up, they rarely did. Aradhana had never shared what her life was like in the United States. Now that Gauri was here, she realized how difficult things would have been for Aradhana. She was seeing her on an upswing and yet she could imagine the strug-gles. As strong and capable as she pretended to be, Gauri had heard fear in her voice several times when they spoke on the phone. Gauri was already feeling guilty about the money that Aradhana had spent on them. Aradhana had been offered a full time job recently, but there was limited cash flow now. Gauri had tried to offer her some money but Aradhana would hear none of it.

On a personal level she knew of Aradhana's relationship with Nirman. She was no fool. She knew it was love and not a Master's degree that had brought Aradhana to America. She didn't know what had happened between them, but she knew that whatever it was had devastated her daughter. Scott seemed like a wonderful person and Aradhana seemed to love him. Sometimes, though, she saw fear in Aradhana's eyes. Her motherly instincts told her it was fear about their future together. Perhaps even a fear of her own ability to fully forget Nirman. Aradhana never said any of this to her but she knew Aradhana like she knew herself. She knew all of her children. As she lay in the guest bed at Priya's that night with so many thoughts rushing through her head, she felt a shiver. Aasma. The shiver was for Aasma. Was she safe? Why did she feel this shiver? She looked at her watch and saw that it was two in the morning. She wanted to get home to her children, but she'd have to wait until the sun rose with all its glory.

• • •

The job at Swanson and Well was destined to be Aradhana's. She was quite sure that she did not want to work for a corporation and instead wanted to use her talents where they would make a difference in the world. She had often thought about pursuing child psychology or social work. She always believed that she hadn't had a normal childhood. Her parents barely spoke to each other and her siblings didn't seem to care much for her. She wasn't sure if it was normal or abnormal to be that way, because she never had the opportunity to discuss her life with anyone else. Gauri was a very private person and had insisted that they learn to keep their lives private as well. Tears never completed the lonely journey from Gauri's heart to her eyes. Gauri wanted her children to be so strong that they never had to battle the tears at all

When several corporations came to interview on campus Aradhana had decided to see what they were offering. She had not really spent too much time on her resume or researching the companies, but she knew she had to get a job because she would soon lose her student visa status. After speaking to several organizations, nothing appealed to her. She was about to give up when she saw the information booth for Swanson and Wells. They had a good pitch. She could make a difference. She could help make people's lives more rewarding.

She could help bridge the cultural gap. She could help make the playing field more level. She could pay off all her debts. They called her for an interview and a full day of interviews later, she was made a consultant.

That was two weeks before graduation. The Bollywood party had been a celebration of many things. Mainly it was a celebration to cheer up Aasma, but in Aradhana's mind, it was also a celebration for her own success.

When Aasma called her the night before, her heart was already racing. She knew she shouldn't judge Aasma—she wanted to protect her but she knew that ultimately Aasma was her older sister; a sister whose judgment she was learning to trust completely. If sleeping with Asad was what Aasma saw fit, then perhaps it was. Yet, she found herself angry and betrayed by Asad. She felt extremely conflicted. In her heart she knew she had no right to be angry with anyone. She imagined these conflicting feelings were what being a mother felt like.

When she received Aasma's phone call she felt butterflies in her stomach. Aasma was euphoric. She apologized for worrying her and asked if it was okay if she spent the night at Asad's. Aradhana scarcely had a chance to ask her anything when Aasma tactfully hung up.

That night, Aradhana sat up talking all night with Scott. For the first time she spoke nonstop about her family. Her overbearing father, her devoted mother, her blue-eyed sister, Amrita; her previously-goody two shoes-sister, Aasma, and her previously-little brother Abhay.

When Aasma came home the next morning, she found Scott and Aradhana waiting up for her. They looked like they hadn't slept all night. Apart from the decorations on the wall, there was no trace of what had transpired just a few hours ago. Aasma saw the disapproving look on Aradhana's face the minute their eyes met. She didn't expect her to understand right away. She knew that Aradhana meant well. Gauri had trusted Aasma's safety with Aradhana. She wished they didn't see the need to protect her. She was old enough to make her own decisions. Here in America, Aradhana felt she had the right to do as she pleased yet she was being judged for her actions. She had absolutely no regrets about what had transpired the night before. She knew she could make Aradhana understand. Walking in, though, she felt like a teenager who had stayed out way past her curfew and was confronted with the worrying, questioning, angry eyes of her mother. She knew this was only phase one. If Gauri were to find out, there was no telling how she'd react. Aasma had never been on the receiving end of such a situation and wasn't quite sure how anyone around her would react. Her own reaction had surprised her. At first, she wasn't sure what she should do. Should she make eye contact? Should she look down? Should she ignore them and walk upstairs? She let her heart decide. She did what came naturally to her. She walked up and hugged Aradhana.

Aradhana was taken by surprise. She hadn't quite contemplated how she would react, either. She was in a delicate situation. She was living her life by her rules. What right did she have to tell someone else how to live theirs? Yet she was perplexed by this strange blend of possessiveness and protectiveness that she was feeling. She didn't want Aasma to be hurt and wasn't quite sure what frame of mind Aasma was in. She didn't know what Asad's intentions were. In a way she felt as if she was responsible for the situation because Asad was her friend. A part of her also felt like this was probably the best outcome that could have been expected from the evening. At this point she wasn't even sure what had transpired. When Aasma hugged her, all her questions went away. She hugged her sister back and the smile on Aasma's face said it all. She was happy. Whatever it was that made her happy had to be right by Aradhana.

Scott stood at a distance, a little uncomfortable with the whole situation. He was beginning to understand the cultural dynamics. Perhaps this would have been a non-issue with most American families. After all, for the most part, consenting adults were free to do what they deemed fit. In this moment, though, he felt he understood the emotions. Through most of the night he had listened to Aradhana pour her heart out in a way he had never before experienced. This was special because it went to the core of who she was. She spoke about the things that had shaped her, but were buried deep within her. Secrets that she guarded close to her heart were brought to her eyes and lips. She had trembled and let the tears flow freely. She spoke of her insecurities, her failures, her struggles—everything that had made her who she was. She spoke of her journey for acceptance within her own family, and her quest to accept herself the way she was. She spoke of living in shadows, and her struggle to come out into the light. She spoke of the direction her journey with Aasma had taken. She spoke of the shock and pure pain in the realization that her sister had never experienced the touch of any man, despite sharing her bed with one for five years.

Standing in the kitchen watching the two sisters hug made Scott feel alive. There were no words exchanged but in their silence they told each other everything. Aasma was now a woman. The only thing that mattered was that she was happy. This was their secret. Gauri did not need to know.

•••

Asad was a devout Muslim. He was also extremely passionate about life. He was brought up in a very conservative middle class family in Allahabad. He was taught to say his prayers five times a day and maintain a fast during Ramadan. Like most boys in his community he knew the Koran by heart by the age of eleven. He had a head start with the local *maulwi*, or religious teacher, coming to his home to teach him and his older brother when he was just five. He remembered that mean-spirited man, who liberally beat them on their knees and backs. He learned early that complaining would not be accepted, either by the unkindly teacher or his family. It always puzzled him how someone who seemed to complain about everything around him could dispense words of love and learning.

As he grew older he frequented the mosque often. His life changed when he turned fourteen and his family moved into a modest apartment in Mumbai. He father was in the government and had been transferred to the "big city" as the family called it. He never forgot how all his friends warned him of all the evil that was just waiting to shackle him. The maulwi addressed the entire congregation but the words were meant for the men in his family. There was much evil in life. Everywhere you looked there was temptation. They were men of god and it was their duty to protect the women and themselves from evil eyes and intentions. He remembered leaving for Mumbai with a heavy heart.

He clearly hadn't been listening to the maulwi or to his friends because he let the "evil" get the better of him. He opened his mind to all the energy around him. He learned about other beliefs and cultures. When he first celebrated Holi, the Hindu festival of colors and victory of good over evil, his parents were appalled. He came home with yellow and green smeared on his face. In his hand he had a version of a squirt gun filled with bright pink colored water. His parents shook him—it was bad enough that he had stopped saying his prayers regularly and no longer visited the mosque as frequently, but now he was indulging in pagan rituals. He remembered washing himself immediately, but savoring every moment of his experience. He made friends from all faiths, and tried to learn as much as he could from them. He believed he was a good Muslim. He tried to do good by others and live the life of a good human being. He learned early on that his parents and several others interpreted the religion in ways that suited them. Unfortunately, as he was learning, that was true of almost all religions.

His greatest challenge was reconciling some of his early learning against how he enjoyed living life. He knew he was a decent human being and didn't hurt anyone and yet many around him continuously led him to believe that his actions were not in line with his religious beliefs. He didn't agree with them. He had reconciled to the fact that they were a hard bunch to convince so he did the next best thing that he could and lived with both his actions and beliefs.

He went to college in Mumbai and savored the experience. He was a charmer and attracted many woman. He used his charms liberally. He knew that if his inter-religious "sins" were ever discovered, he would literally be killed by several communities including his own. He always viewed them as women. To him it didn't matter whether they were Muslim, or Hindu, or Christian. He had no plans of settling with any of them. When the right woman came along, he would know. Perhaps then he would think of settling down.

After he got his engineering degree he had an opportunity to work in Dubai. Life in Dubai was scarcely different from his college life. He mingled in the expatriate scene and socialized often. It was easy for him to lean on his religion during trying moments and he continued to do so in an environment that encouraged it. When he felt like he had gotten all that he could from his Dubai experience he started exploring other options. Someone he knew was applying to American universities. He decided to give it a shot as well and was accepted into Sienna Fione.

The first year was hard and the second year was harder. September 11th occurred during his second year at school. He was far away in Boston but had felt the shift in people's perceptions of him ever since. He had never been a fanatic but had seen many around him take that road. He detested them then, and he continued to do so. He struggled to understand why he and his entire religion were being judged just because a handful had hijacked it. Everywhere he went people viewed him suspiciously when they discovered his religious affiliation. He had read the scriptures and quoted liberally from them when fanatic people from his own religion spoke of Jihad. He spoke of fighting the enemy within. He knew that some self-prophesied keepers of the faith even claimed Islam was inherently a violent religion. He shuddered to understand how that line of reasoning and interpretation was going to change the opinion the world had begun to develop about their community.

He was just a regular guy, out for a good time and good drink. He hoped that something as innate as that wouldn't bring his entire belief system into question. He reveled in the fact that at least he wasn't a hypocrite. He was who he was. He knew of several people from different faiths who spoke of God only in words. Their actions were far removed from theirs or anyone else's faith. They were actions not only against their religions but also humanity. He womanized, but only when the woman consented. He didn't hold a bad thought about anyone.

He was used to being popular for most of his life. He wrestled with how people automatically closed their minds in this country when they found out he was Muslim.

The first time he saw Aasma he felt a soothing sensation in his chest. When he made love to her, he felt whole. He wasn't sure what he was feeling, but it felt good. But he was also scared. He wasn't sure he was ready for this journey. The fact that Aasma was a Hindu bothered him. If she hadn't invoked such feelings within him, he wouldn't have cared.

• • •

Aradhana and Aasma spent several hours talking about the future. Aasma was infused with a new energy and wanted to start a new phase of her life. She wanted to return to India and crank up the machinery for Aasma Fashions. They both discussed how she might be able to get a headstart by contacting some buyers within the States. Even though it wasn't technically permitted by her visitor's visa, they both brainstormed how it might be okay as long as she didn't sign a deal while she was here. Aasma spoke so passionately about clothes, like a wine enthusiast might about wines. Like the different varieties and names for wine, she spoke of different materials, textures, and colors for fabric. Aasma wanted to have a commercially sound proposition. She also wanted to have a line that was hers.

Since she had come to visit she had been toying with an East-meets-West line of formal dresses. She wanted to use fabrics, colors and prints that were Eastern and designs that were Western. She had seen some examples at various stores, but nothing like she was imagining. She feared that with all the fabrics and dresses being made in China, she'd have a tough time penetrating the US market, but she savored the idea that such a collection could be just as welcome in

India. Her instinct told her that young women in modernizing India were looking for a perfect evening dress they could wear to that special occasion. A dress that was rich, charming, modest, and yet hip.

Both sisters were so excited at the prospect that they started drawing designs and taking notes in an empty notebook they found lying around. They also made detailed plans to study various stores and fashions. They made several trips to the mall and made extensive notes after each observation.

Aasma's tryst with Asad had changed things for her. She liked him. He was gentle with her and made her feel wanted, the one thing she had lacked in her marriage. She didn't know why she had drifted towards Asad that night. She couldn't even remember if she had drifted towards him or just responded to him. Destiny had somehow brought them together. It was as if something bigger than them both had determined the course of that night. As special and liberating as that night was for Aasma, she knew she couldn't make it a part of her life. She didn't know Asad, and didn't have the energy to find out more. She hadn't mourned her dead relationship fully. As much as a sham her marriage to Pankaj had been, she had truly loved him. She wasn't ready to be in love with anyone else yet. Moreover, she knew a relationship with Asad would be very hard work as their paths were so different. Neither of their families would accept the other's faith and she suspected neither would want to compromise. Any relationship with Asad would be too much work from the start. It was not a journey she was ready to embark on. Perhaps someday she would be in a relationship, but she suspected this would not be the one.

Asad had probably undertaken a similar soul searching exercise. When they met a few days later, they made gentle love again. As they lay in bed, they looked at each other as if to ask "Now what?"

It was Aasma who first proposed that this was probably where their intimate acquaintance ended. Asad didn't fight back. He was just glad that he didn't suggest it. He had thought that perhaps this would be the woman he took a chance on, for to him she seemed worth it. Notwithstanding this revelation he had envisioned in his mind's eye what their journey through mutual acceptance would be. As much as the romantic in him wanted to picture many more long passionate lovemaking sessions, the realist in him relented. He pictured what the conversation with his family would be like. They would no doubt die of shame and horror. If Asad married outside their community they would become outcasts. Already the fact that Asad was not yet married was a source of great anguish for them. His older brother had already contributed four daughters and two sons to the family tree. In a religion that permitted him four wives, he had not found himself one. His mother had shown him pictures of several women. Each woman was more beautiful than the next and they all were willing to go wherever Asad took them. However, these women did nothing for him. He wanted a thinker and feeler. He wanted a woman who would be able to challenge him mentally, sexually, and spiritually. He wanted a woman with a fire for life. He wanted a woman who would stir passion in him, and make him want to better his existence. He didn't just want to exist—he wanted to live.

He suspected Aasma could have been that woman, and yet when she suggested they end it, he was almost thankful that he didn't have to take on that challenging journey. They both parted amicably with the caveat that as long as she was there, they would seek out each other's warmth, with no strings attached.

Legacy Revisited

*A*radhana had been surprised that Aasma and Asad hadn't pursued their relationship further. The chemistry between them was undeniable and both seemed to make each other happy. Both were unattached and could probably make the commitment if they really wanted to. However, at the same time she admired Aasma's cool headedness and pragmatism. She knew if they had decided to take the path to a long-term relationship, it would have been a long and difficult one.

When Aasma had told Aradhana about where Asad and she stood, they talked for hours about it which was something they were now accustomed to doing. They spoke about what might have been, what should not be, and what would not be. They also spoke of Aradhana's plans. Unlike Aasma, Aradhana was not really sure what she wanted to do over the next few years. She had a job that she was due to start soon, but she missed India. She wasn't sure what she missed, but seeing Gauri and Aasma made her yearn to go back home. That being said, she had an undeniable connection with Scott. He made her feel safe, secure and happy. She was very conflicted and wished she had the same foresight that Aasma did.

Her family had been in town for a few months and were supposed to go back home in a few weeks. Aradhana was surprised that she felt so heavyhearted at the thought of them leaving. Over two years had passed without either of them in her life, and now imagining life without them was difficult.

She and Aasma discussed every thing, so it wasn't out of place when Aasma volunteered in passing that she had missed two periods. She indicated that she wasn't worried, as she knew herself to have irregular cycles. What caught Aradhana's attention was when she casually complained of continuous period-like symptoms and nausea. Aradhana immediately suggested she take a pregnancy test. At first Aasma laughed off the suggestion. The first time Asad and she had sex was without any protection, but ever since they had been very cautious about using condoms. She joked that both of them had to be very fertile for a virgin to become pregnant her very first time. Her irregular periods were proof that she definitely wasn't that fertile. However, when Aradhana persisted, Aasma agreed.

That evening they walked to the pharmacy to get a pregnancy test. After looking at several brands comparing the pros and cons of each, they agreed on one that required no interpretation and spelled the results out.

Once they got home after purchasing the test, they snuck the test upstairs and locked the door behind them. They wanted to be sure that neither Gauri nor Alaya caught them by surprise. Both studied the instructions long and hard. The test seemed to suggest that morning would be the best time to discover their fate. It would be the time that any HCG, or human chorionic gonadotropin which was the pregnancy hormone, would be most easily detected. They debated the pros and cons of waiting. While the literature suggested mornings were best, it also added that tests could be conducted at any time during the day. After much deliberation they voted to conduct the test that very evening especially since much time had passed since her missed period.

Aradhana stood outside the bathroom while Aasma followed the instructions. When five minutes had passed and she still hadn't come out, Aradhana began knocking at first gently and then rather violently when Aasma didn't answer. After a few rather loud knocks followed by loud whispering of her name, Aasma asked to be left alone.

It didn't require a sister to surmise what the results had indicated. Aradhana went for a walk, happy to be alone with her thoughts. What Aasma had probably just discovered was the single most important event in Aasma's life. The discovery had the potential to turn *all* of their lives upside down. She wasn't sure what Aasma was feeling. As for her, she was scared. While she didn't really care about what society thought, Aradhana was afraid of what Gauri would say. Her years of upbringing in a traditional society had taught her that people would not look kindly on a recently divorced woman becoming pregnant. The sin was worsened by the fact that the child growing within her was from a casual relationship that had no future. Surely a child like that would not be accepted into society. Perhaps they only way the child stood a chance would be with a blanket of lies woven by the family to protect its identify. She pondered about what kind of blanket of lies they could weave. They could still claim it was Pankaj's child. Perhaps they could raise the child in the America. Perhaps they could say the child was adopted. As her mind explored various options, a painful one pushed its way to the front of her mind. The merits of this option superseded all other ones. Perhaps it would be easiest to eliminate this seed before it caused any more disruption in Aasma's life. She wasn't sure of what Aasma was thinking, but she wouldn't have been surprised if the very same thoughts were going through her mind. Aasma had her whole life ahead of her. She was still young, at least by Western standards. Surely, there was no other viable option at this stage. She walked back home determined to convince Aasma to pursue this option, assuming Aasma wasn't convinced of it already.

When Aradhana returned home, Gauri was in the kitchen preparing an elaborate meal. Aradhana tried to avoid eye contact as she saw Gauri oblivious to the turmoil brewing within her daughters. Gauri, of course, wanted to engage Aradhana in conversation. Aradhana found herself bombarded with a barrage of questions and requests. How was the weather outside? Would she try the graham flour fritters and check if the spices were right? And, of course, where was Aasma?

None of these questions seemed out of place. It wasn't considered strange for Gauri to ask one of her children where the other was, even when she knew they weren't together. Gauri knew that Aasma was upstairs, but the question was more a frustrated statement informing Aradhana that Aasma should be down by then. Aradhana took this as an opportunity to excuse herself under the pretext of going upstairs to call Aasma.

Aradhana was half expecting to find Aasma where she left her, but Aasma had long left the confines of the bathroom and had now locked herself in the bedroom.

When Aradhana knocked, Aasma opened the door with a look that caught her off guard. If Aradhana hadn't been standing outside the bathroom, she would have sworn nothing had transpired. There were no tears or swollen eyes. If anything, Aasma looked radiant. Aradhana followed Aasma's cue and sat on the bed. Aasma shut the door behind her and pulled three test sticks from under the pillow. All three had the exact same reading. It was no surprise Aasma was pregnant. Aradhana said the first thing that came to her lips. It was a simple question, the answer to which she herself had been contemplating,

"Now what?"

Aasma repeated the question but her tone wasn't questioning. It was like that of a prophet who was just about to spill several thousand years of wisdom. Aradhana waited for what those pearls of wisdom would be. Perhaps Aasma had already come to terms with what needed to be done. It was, after all, the most logical decision. Aasma was pragmatic and hadn't been known to be a rebel. Aasma looked so content and at peace with her decision that Aradhana immediately relaxed her tensed shoulders. All through the walk and even now,

Aradhana had been stiff and upright as if she was afraid that any sudden move by her body would make the situation worse. She thought better when her body was tense.

What Aasma said next made her body stiffen again. She planned to keep her baby. Aasma's face lit up like a thousand watt bulb as she expressed how this was all she ever wanted in her life. A child would complete her. Nothing else mattered. In fact she was willing to fight the entire world to keep the baby she had been blessed with. Aasma continued on to express that her biggest regret with Pankaj had been the fact that they hadn't had a baby. If Pankaj had left her with a baby she would have experienced far less pain. She confessed that her biggest fear in life had been the fact that she'd never have the opportunity to be a mother. To her it didn't matter if she never had money or a career. The only thing she had both dreams and nightmares about was having a baby. The prospect of leaving this life without a legacy was painful to her. She had dreamt of this moment even when she was still a little girl.

Aradhana sat completed immersed and enthralled by Aasma's unabashed burst of emotions for this unborn baby. At that point all she could do was experience the pure flood of energy that overflowed from Aasma. She was so self-assured and confident that it almost made Aradhana forget the merits of her arguments. She felt mean, and little for even wanting to suggest that Aasma get rid of the baby. Aradhana knew that she had no selfish motive in suggesting this to Aasma. She just thought it was the best decision given the circumstances. But listening to Aasma, she felt it would be an insult to her sister to even suggest it now.

Aradhana let Aasma continue until she had nothing more to share but then she couldn't help herself. Though she didn't explicitly say what she had been thinking, she asked if Aasma had considered other options. Aasma seemed to sense where this was heading and, firmly, without leaving room for negotiation, she asserted that in her mind there were no other options. Even if she lost everything she had, she'd have the baby.

As Aradhana came to term with her sister's decision a thousand questions flooded her mind. The same question that she had asked Aasma at the beginning of the conversation was asked again,"Now what?"

• • •

Aasma was the one to break the news to Gauri. She didn't discuss it any further with Aradhana but she had come to the decision that this evening was as good a time as any other to tell her. She didn't expect Gauri to understand any of it. She knew Gauri would have many things to come to terms with. There were many details that didn't need to be shared. At the same time, there were many details that *did* need to be shared. Asad was a Muslim. Asad and she were not in a relationship. Even as the father of the baby, he would have nothing to do with the baby, she wouldn't want him to. It was her decision to keep the baby.

As confident as Aasma sounded about her decision, she was shaking inside. She didn't doubt that she wanted to have the baby. In fact, that was the one thing she was sure about. It was what it meant that scared her senseless. She was staying with her parents in India. She had no career to speak of or any source of income. If it hadn't been for her father-in-law thrusting the clothing factory on her she would have nothing to call her own. Even though she had papers that proclaimed her the owner, she still struggled as to whether it was ethical to keep it. Even if she decided to keep it, there was no guarantee that she'd make any money from it. She was most afraid of her father. He had been as supportive as he was capable of being, but surely this child would find no room in his heart or his house. Where would she find the strength or means to raise the baby? She had leaned heavily on Gauri and at this point she wasn't sure if she was even deserving of her support. She had been selfish and done what it took to make her happy but, strangely, she felt no guilt for doing that and that itself caused her guilt. Perhaps she should have been sorrier for her actions, but she wasn't. A chapter in her life had closed and a new one was about to begin. She was in a strange no-man's land between the closed and not-yet-begun.

• • •

Gauri continued to work in the kitchen despite having completed everything she needed to twice over. Her daughters were being very strange and abrupt. She pretended not to notice but she always did. Her country bumpkin style was more for their benefit than for her own. If they liked to think she had little idea of what was happening, than so be it.

She was thrilled that Aradhana and Aasma were close for the first time in their lives. She knew that Aradhana had always been uncomfortable in the presence of her sisters. It was great to see how much they had learned from each other. Aasma had become more confident and self-assured during the trip. She laughed a lot more and let her hair down more often. Aradhana put a lot less pressure on herself, let her guard down more, and smiled more. She believed she had so much to learn from both of them and she was eager for every lesson they unwittingly taught her.

When Aasma said she wanted to talk to her, she was concerned. As much as she complained that her children didn't confide in her, her experience as a mother had taught her that conversations that began with her children needing to tell her something never ended well.

• • •

Aasma wasn't sure where she should begin, so she started with her feelings. She knew that Gauri deserved to hear more than just the events, so she found herself reliving the pain and rejection as she talked about her feelings. She spoke of how the failed marriage had led to a sense of failed womanhood. She found herself talking unabashedly about her own desires and her yearning to feel the touch of a man.

Gauri held on to her daughter's every word. She was acutely aware that this was a prelude to a climax. She chided herself about being so pessimistic. Aasma had been through enough, she thought. In her eyes, she had possibly hit rock bottom. Surely she was reading too much into this flood of emotions that had caught her off guard. Yet, try as she may, she couldn't get rid of the heavy feeling on her chest. It was a feeling she had first experienced a very long time ago. Every ounce of her motherly instinct told her that her daughter was leading up to something that would forever change their lives. It was not like Aasma to pour her heart out without cause. A bomb was going to be dropped. As she tried to stop her mind from wandering, the bomb began to fall. The instant Aasma spoke of Asad and her attraction to him, Gauri thought she knew where it was heading. In her head, Gauri played out the scenario. Aasma was going to claim that she had found love and Gauri would then show her the error of her ways and the challenges she could expect to encounter if they stayed together. Then they could all move on. As difficult as that would be, she was sure she could talk some reason into Aasma.

When Aasma continued to tell her about what had happened after the party, Gauri's heart felt like it was locked in a lead container. She knew when she had experienced this feeling before. It was several decades ago as she lay in her own mother Savitri's lap talking about her own experience that fateful night that Amrita was conceived. This was the same, and yet it was completely different. As she saw this confident young woman talk authoritatively about what happened and taking complete responsibility for her actions, she knew this was different. As she spoke of her decision to keep her baby, Gauri couldn't help but respect the protectiveness that her little girl demonstrated towards her unborn baby. Aasma left no room for negotiation. There was respect in her tone, but fortitude in her voice. This was her decision to make, and she seemed to imply that she would stand strong in it regardless of whether Gauri supported it or not.

Gauri felt she was reliving her own pain, and yet she couldn't explain the pride she felt at her daughter's strength. Too many things were wrong with this situation but at that point nothing mattered except for the fact that Aasma couldn't have been clearer about the fact that this was what made her happy.

She wasn't sure she recognized the voice of the woman who said to Aasma,

"I'll be there for you."

• • •

Aasma knew that Asad deserved to know but she didn't know him well enough to know how he'd react. One thing she did know was that she didn't expect anything from him. She knew that if she were in his shoes, she would want to know. When Aasma called Asad he expected it to be for one of their rendezvous but he knew the minute she entered his apartment that this wasn't the case. Aasma looked uncharacteristically somber as she asked if they could talk. In the little time that he had known her, he knew this wasn't a good sign. They couldn't be breaking up because they were not a couple. He had no idea what this was about, but it didn't seem like a good thing.

Aasma didn't disappoint his instinct. She sat him down and simply told him that she was pregnant with his baby. He stared at her for a few minutes and then at her tummy trying to see the baby bump. Like Aradhana, he asked "Now what?"

By now Aasma was well-versed in the response to the question. She responded like a student who had crammed long and hard for a test and without stopping for breath gave him a soliloquy on how and why she planned to keep the baby. She emphatically added that she had absolutely no expectation from him but if he'd like, she would let him be a part of the child's life.

When she finally stopped for breath, she saw the struggle on Asad's face.

Asad was silent for a few minutes before he reached for her hand. When he thought she was going to say something else, he gently covered her lips with his fingers. When he was convinced that she got the message, he spoke. He wanted the baby too.

He got down on his knees and asked her if she'd marry him.

At that point Aasma wanted nothing more than to believe their life could have a fairy tale ending. If only she could say yes and they could sail into the sunset it would all be so perfect. However, she knew she had to be true to herself and to Asad. Nothing had changed between them. They were still from two different backgrounds and religions. Neither of their families would accept each other. In her mind there was no way this would work. She tried to tell him as gently as she could that she could not marry him. She had sacrificed her identity in her marriage to Pankaj and was not willing to do it again. Both were strongly grounded in their faiths and she didn't think he could accept her the way she was. It was especially harder for them than for Aradhana and Scott because of the history of conflict and hatred between their two faiths.

She thanked him for doing the decent thing but reiterated that she just didn't want to compromise again. She did not want Asad to marry her because he felt sorry for her or because he felt responsibility of the baby. Again she told him that she was just out of one pity marriage and had no plans to get into another.

Rediscovering Self-Respect

The night she learned of Aasma's baby, Gauri had a dream about her parents. In the dream her parents were walking hand in hand and looked as beautiful and youthful as she remembered them in her childhood. They kissed her on her forehead and told her they loved her. Before leaving they made her promise that no matter what happened, she'd protect the baby as her own. When she woke up she felt very strong. She knew she had to do right by Aasma and the baby and be strong for the two of them. She knew in her heart that she had to find the courage to face society yet once again.

She had called Ashwin in hopes that they could both put their differences aside and be there for their daughter. It had been years since they had shared anything that remotely could be considered companionship. Apart from the formality of checking in on him like a dutiful wife was supposed to do, they had hardly spoken during the two months she was away. Gauri had struggled long and hard with where their relationship was heading. Somehow coming to the United States had stirred something within her. She had so much time to herself that she found herself constantly thinking about her marriage. Every time they visited the mall, or walked down a crowded space, her eyes scanned the area for couples. She was especially interested in observing the dynamics of couple that were her own age. She also couldn't get Scott's parents out of her head. Looking at the dynamics of their relationship made her feel even more inadequate in her own.

Another interesting thing she had discovered since visiting the United States was that she was not afraid of being alone. It was like an epiphany. If there was one fear apart from the fear of society that had kept her from ending her relationship, it was the fear of being alone. She had never forgotten the feeling of complete and utter despair she felt when she lost Sidhant. She had lost her only living relative who loved her and she had been utterly bereft. Gauri remembered her fear and her loneliness. Ashwin had been in her life then, but he wasn't her flesh and blood. Still, she remembered clinging to the thought that at least she had Ashwin. She consoled herself with the thought that at least one person in the world cared if she was alive or dead. Since then she had developed a severe anxiety of being alone. Even though she and Ashwin didn't have a meaningful relationship, at least they were there for each other. They knew where the other was and would know if the other went missing. Sometimes Gauri would have nightmares and wake up drenched with sweat. She'd dream that her body was lying in an abandoned warehouse for days. In her dream her body was charred beyond recognition like her mother's had been and the smell of death and putrification would fill the whole warehouse. In her dreams no one was looking for her. Everyone's life went on as usual. Each time she'd wake up she would be able to hear her heartbeat. She didn't want to be alone. She didn't have the courage to do it.

When she called Ashwin, she wasn't sure what she expected him to say. Their relationship had been strained for so long that she didn't even know what a supportive partner should say. That day, however, she really wanted Ashwin to be there for her. She hoped that he would come through for his daughter and wife. She knew he was far away and it wasn't an easy story to tell. She knew Ashwin had a really difficult time with what happened to Aasma in regards to her marriage. She remembered preparing him for days before Aasma came to live with them.

"It wasn't her fault. She's our daughter. It's our duty to support her," she had chanted repeatedly.

He hadn't been convinced. He valued his position in society significantly. Once he had been a good father, but it had been decades since he had done anything to reclaim that title. Aasma's return from a failed marriage had made him feel like a failure as well.

Gauri had often wondered what he told other people about why Aasma's relationship had ended. Once when she asked him, he responded sullenly that there was nothing to tell. According to him, their daughter had left him unable to show his face anywhere. He was decent to Aasma when she returned but Gauri knew that it hadn't been easy for him.

When Gauri told Ashwin about how things had gone drastically wrong she wasn't sure how he'd react. For the first time she hoped that her husband would be strong for their entire family. Ashwin, however, was seething with anger.

He told Gauri to make sure the child was aborted. Gauri tried to calm him down, but to no avail. The clarity of the telephone connection was so clear that it made Gauri feel as if Ashwin was standing besides her. She could almost feel his hot fuming breath on herself and there were shivers up and down her spine.

After she found the courage to tell him that Aasma had decided to keep the baby, there was a long pause on the other line. The last thing she heard from Ashwin before the line went dead was "Like mother, like daughter. Both are wretched whores."

• • •

There was something is the silence after he hung up that stirred an emotion in Gauri that she had long forgotten. She heard her heart beat and felt blood rush to her head and the flush of her face. She hadn't felt this much rage in a long time. She had spent the better part of her life being abused by Ashwin. Her own self-respect had been kicked and beaten for so long that it never felt the need to awaken. She had tolerated worse things from Ashwin, but none had evoked such a strong a reaction in her. Every fiber in her being felt outrage for the words said about her daughter. It was one thing that her self-respect had been pulverized all her life, but it was another to hear a father vilify his daughter like that. She knew at that moment she felt so much strength and anger that had Ashwin been in front of her there was no telling what she would have done. Yet she was glad that he wasn't. She respected Aasma tremendously and had been struck by her decisiveness and courage. Weren't woman expected to have needs, or was that the sole bastion of men? The one undisputable instinct in a woman was the maternal instinct, and yet there was shame in a woman wanting that right for herself. Only in the confines of social conformity and marriage were these instincts respected. What about the right of a woman to be the ultimate symbol of womanhood outside of those boundaries? Were her instincts and needs just expected to vanish? As Gauri contemplated these things, it became clear what she needed to do. In fact, Gauri had never been so clear about anything in her life.

An invisible force compelled her to dial Ashwin's number. When he picked up, she knew he was expecting her to apologize as she had done so many times before in her life. Perhaps he expected her to apologize for her daughter's actions as well. The old Gauri would probably have also taken the blame on herself for being a bad mother.

This Gauri, however, was a completely different human being. Today she felt Savitri would be proud of her. For the first time since her marriage her mother would have felt like she stood up for herself and reclaimed herself. All Gauri said before she let the line go silent was, "Ashwin, I want a divorce."

A Sacred Promise

When Asad called Aradhana and Gauri to his home it was a week before Aasma and Gauri were due to fly back to India. Aasma had walked a few miles to the local library to read some textile magazines. Both weren't sure what Asad had in mind. Aasma had shared with them that she had spoken to Asad, but had told them no more than that.

Gauri had met Asad a few times and liked him, as he had a personality few could dislike. He was warm, funny, and full of life. She had seriously hoped that perhaps Aasma and Asad could raise the child together and that Asad would have come through and do the right thing. Gauri tried not to judge others in the way that Ashwin had judged her all her life. At the same time, Gauri was not naïve. Having lived in Hyderabad, which was a predominately Muslim city, most of her life she had heard her share of stories. The interfaith love stories almost never ended well. Entire communities went to war at the idea of two young people trying to start their lives with the ones they loved. Mostly it was the burgeoning middle class society who was most worried about appearances. It was they who felt the greatest need to conform and be accepted within the fabric of the already defined rules. In Gauri's view the same rules didn't apply to the very rich or very poor. They could probably live life on their own terms. It was indeed the middle class that faced the banalities and burden of social jurisprudence. She had some Muslim friends and had learned through them that you couldn't marry a Muslim unless you converted to Islam.

Asad knew Aasma better than Aasma thought he did. He had anticipated that she hadn't told anyone about the rejected marriage proposal. He knew Aasma was stubborn and that once she made up her mind it was hard to change it. He had given Aradhana very specific instructions not to tell Aasma about the visit. He had anticipated that Aasma would rather have not gone through the process of hearing others' views on his proposal.

Asad had thought long and hard about the day Aasma told him that she was pregnant. He had challenged himself to think about how he truly felt about Aasma and the baby. Was he compromising? Did he love her? Would the marriage between a Hindu and a Muslim be possible? Would they both need to compromise? Could there be a middle ground? Each time he got the same answers. He loved Aasma. He had never respected any woman as much as he respected her. In fact, in light of her decision to keep the baby his respect for her had gotten even stronger. Sure, he came from a conservative lower middle class Muslim family, and she from an upper middle class Hindu family, but in the end they both had similar values. Both were just looking to be better human beings and make the most of their time on earth. If religion was an issue, then they could both live in a neutral country where religious differences weren't as obvious or such a big deal.

When Asad told Gauri and Aradhana of his proposal and how Aasma had declined, both were taken aback. They had no idea of what had transpired a fortnight ago and how it had the potential to change Aasma's life. Asad proceeded to tell them the results of his deep introspection. He wanted nothing more than to be married to Aasma and raise their baby together.

Both Gauri and Aradhana looked at each other as they tried to digest the enormity and implications of Asad's proposal. When they were convinced that he was sincere, they got down to the tactical elements of the proposal. In rapid fire succession both fired questions to him that no doubt Asad had given much thought to; Where would they live? Who would convert? Where would they get married? How would they raise the child? What about his family?

Patiently Asad answered all their questions. He emphasized that he was open to modifying any of his proposals based on what Aasma wanted. All he really wanted was for her to say yes and for them to be married. He kept repeating that the incident had made him realize that he loved Aasma and wanted to marry her with or without the baby. They could live in the United States or Dubai. He had a job offer here that he could start soon. Neither would convert and both would keep their religions. They would have a non-denominational registered marriage in America. The child would be raised with an understanding and exposure to both religions. As for his family, he had their blessing. It was a difficult journey of acceptance, but in the end they only wanted to see their son happy. He said he was surprised they had blessed the union but was touched by the fact that they said they had never seen him talk with so much love and respect about anyone.

Asad pleaded with Gauri and Aradhana to also bless the union. He said he had prayed nonstop since coming to this decision for their blessing.

Gauri saw the sincerity and honesty in his eyes. Most importantly, she saw the love. She looked at Aradhana as if to ask what she thought. Aradhana nodded and smiled from left to right. Gauri gave Asad her blessing.

• • •

Aasma had struggled with her decision to turn Asad down. There was no doubt in her mind that she had feelings for him. When he proposed to her, she was surprised as she hadn't thought that he'd be willing to make a life long commitment to her. She thought of her situation as once bitten twice shy. She had rushed into marriage once for the wrong reasons and the fate of that marriage had left her overly cautious. She wondered if she would have accepted Asad's proposal under different circumstances but she wasn't sure. However, she was sure that Gauri would never accept the union. Gauri was deeply grounded in her faith and had raised her children to be dutiful Hindus. They were taught never to sacrifice the values of their religion. She knew she would never convert. As far as she was concerned there was no middle ground. She didn't know Asad's views on this, but had taken it for granted that he wouldn't compromise either.

Aasma wasn't a masochist. She didn't like inflicting pain on herself. Fate just seemed to be giving her choices to make that were resulting in her pain. She hadn't bothered telling either Gauri or Aradhana about Asad's proposal because she felt he had proposed to her more out of pity than anything else. Asad had been comfortable walking away from the relationship earlier. Surely it was his sense of duty that prompted him to propose. Moreover, she felt she owed Gauri more than that. She had already thrust one decision upon her family. She did not want to thrust another. This was her problem and she intended to take full responsibility for it.

Life had thrown several curve balls at her; Gauri and Aradhana's reaction just added to that list. When they told her they had blessed Asad and her union she was shocked. She could not believe that believe that Asad not only went behind her back, but also managed to sell them on the idea that this union would actually work. She wasn't sure how she felt about it.

Gauri was authoritative about it. There was no question in her mind; getting married to Asad was the right thing to do. Gauri had shared with her Asad's responses to their rapid-fire questions and believed in Asad's sincerity.

Aasma wanted so much to close her eyes and get transported to the promise of the new beginning that they had discussed. A beginning that came at a price, Gauri's divorce. The earth had shifted from under Aasma's feet the day Gauri told all her children that she was going to file for divorce. Try as much as Aasma and Aradhana did to talk her out of it, her mind was made up. Gauri wanted to reclaim her existence. Finally Aasma had told Gauri that they could live together and bring up the baby. What was at first a compromise solution had stirred within Aasma a strange excitement. She fantasized about her mother and herself raising a baby. She envisioned that she'd make up for all the bad things that had happened to her mother. She would be her mother's pillar of strength and she knew her mother intended to be the same for her.

Hearing Gauri talk about marriage to Asad and life in the United States, Aasma found herself getting angry. How conveniently her mother had killed their plans of life together. What would happen to Gauri? Where would Gauri live? In her heart she knew that Gauri would probably move out and live with Abhay, but Aasma wanted to be a part of the plan.

Gauri and Aradhana persisted. Aasma spoke to Aradhana at length as well. She was angry that Aradhana hadn't told her they planned to see Asad. Once Aasma moved past her anger, she poured her heart out to her sister. She was scared. She didn't know if she had the energy to make another marriage work. She was scared of the differences between them. What if she didn't have the maturity to work through the issues? Most of all, though, she was scared of being away from Gauri. Gauri was taking the most important step of her life. She wanted to be a part of Gauri's decision. She wanted Gauri to be a significant part of the child's life. She saw no reason to live in the United States. She didn't have a relationship with the country and didn't want to stay here just because her life would be comfortable. After they spoke for hours the answers became clear—it came down to whether Asad would be willing to kickstart their long list of future compromises.

When Asad came to see Aasma he was nervous. He was afraid of her reaction to the fact that he had gone behind her back to talk to her family. He was also really excited about the fact that however small it might have been, there was a chance that he could spend his life with the woman he realized that he loved.

Aasma wasn't sure what propelled her forward, but when she saw Asad she melted into his arms. A few minutes later she told him she was considering his proposal, but under one condition—they would marry and live in India, next to wherever Gauri chose to live.

For Asad the decision was easy. He would follow them to India if that was a way for him to keep Aasma close to him forever.

Homeward Bound

*A*radhana was still reeling from everything that had happened. Not only were things happening so quickly, but the lives of her family were changing forever. She wondered what their lives would have been like if they hadn't come to see her graduate. Scarcely three months ago she hardly knew how strong the women in her family were. All she knew was that her sister had married into a traditional affluent Punjabi family and that her mother was destined to spend the remainder of her days in a loveless marriage. Suddenly fate had changed the course of where their lives were heading.

After Aradhana had called her new job and asked to start one month later than scheduled, she and Asad booked tickets to India. Asad was traveling a couple of days earlier, so that he could visit his family. It has been over two years since Aradhana had been home and she couldn't wait to go back. Both Asad and Aasma were clear that they didn't want a big wedding. In fact, they had decided to have a registered marriage at a courthouse.

Gauri and Aasma had left as scheduled. As expected, Aradhana found the week without them challenging. She had grown accustomed to their familiar faces, their warmth, and their companionship. Without Aasma and Gauri there, her bedroom seemed empty and too large.

Her visit was going to be bittersweet. While her sister would be getting married, her mother was getting divorced. Like Aasma, Aradhana had tried to talk Gauri out of the divorce. As loveless as her parent's marriage was, at least it gave the family a nucleus. She worried what it would mean for their family if her parents were to be separated. One thing she was sure about was if they had to choose between both parents, the decision would be an easy one. Out of all the children, she was the one with the most unresolved feelings towards her father. Ironically, though, whenever she thought about her father there was a dull loyalty there. She worried what would happen to him. Gauri was unflinching in her decision, though, and it didn't seem like Ashwin cared about saving the marriage either. Aradhana knew that when she was got back home, her family structure as she knew it would be changed forever.

She thought of inviting Scott to India, but decided that this probably wasn't the best time. India could be overwhelming to the uninitiated and she wanted equilibrium when Scott visited. She could tell that Scott was hurt that he hadn't been invited, though. She told him she wouldn't be able to give him her full attention there the way she wanted to and promised they would visit India together at another more opportune time.

Aradhana wanted her first visit home to India to be utopian. She had spent several days and nights dreaming about returning and everything being perfect, but that wasn't to be the case. She bought fewer gifts than she had anticipated. Both Gauri and Aasma had done plenty of shopping and had bought gifts for everyone. Her visit after their recent trip and all that had happened would be anticlimactic. She felt guilty for thinking that it was taking away from her moment in the spotlight.

She flew Air India to Mumbai. The airline was not known for its service, but Aradhana enjoyed the familiar faces and the food. This time she was comfortably dressed and had checked in one bag and had one handbag with her. By the time she reached Mumbai it was late at the night. Her heart was racing at the familiar warmth, smells and faces she had grown up with. The air conditioning was turned off and the air was hot and humid. Under normal circumstances it would have irked her but she had waited too long for this day to let anything keep her from feeling anything but joy at being back in India once more.

She was still euphoric when the immigration officer beckoned to her from the immigration line. She proudly turned over her Indian passport to him. The first thing he was interested in was her U.S. visa and U.S. status. When he asked her how long she planned to visit, she was indignant and disappointed. She didn't like the thought of being asked how long she planned to stay in her own country. As a proud citizen, she voiced her irritation. The immigration officer didn't deem it worth his time to argue with her, so he didn't.

The bags were to be collected before heading to the domestic terminal. The wait for the bags was long. As she took them off the conveyor she was accosted by a baggage handler who tried to negotiate his help in dollars and she brushed him off. She walked confidently through the green line where she had nothing to declare. The walk through customs was uneventful.

As she made her way to the sea of people waiting in the humid darkness, she felt lost. She wasn't sure where she needed to go. She had to change from the International terminal to the domestic terminal to get a flight from Mumbai to Hyderabad. When she didn't see any signs, she asked the first person who looked like he knew the systems where she'd find the bus. She made it a point to speak in Hindi and not appear as having just descended from an international flight. In unison, a few people directed her to the bus. By the time she got there, she was told it was full and that she needed to return to a waiting room inside the terminal until additional buses arrived a little later. She pushed her unwieldy trolley back through the same route it had come from and found the waiting room crowded with people and buzzing with activity. There was no place to sit as all the seats were taken. Aradhana parked her trolley against a wall, tired from the long transatlantic journey, and sat on the floor.

Just when she thought she was done getting into arguments with people, she saw two people light up cigarettes even though there were "No Smoking" signs posted sporadically around the area. Smoke circles wafted through the already crowded room, but no one seemed to take notice. Aradhana walked over to the group of European tourists who were smoking and confronted them. Did they not see the signs? Why wouldn't they respect the rules when they clearly expected people to do the same in their country? Aradhana was feeling belligerent as she knew how keenly they adhered to rules in their own country. She was also angry with the group of expatriate Indians who were clearly living with a different set of standards in their adopted land as opposed to their native home. The same people who stayed silent in the face of authority were now spitting in the face of it. Those who were careful to throw trash in carefully designated areas were liberally strewing it across their own nation. When she found her rage reaching a climax, she walked over to the airport manager's office and gave him an earful. Although clearly amused by her rush of patriotism and morality, he promised he'd come in soon to handle the matter.

The manager didn't come in as promised and the bus arrived fifteen minutes after her encounter to cart people to the domestic terminal. Aradhana was exhausted. She still had five more hours before her domestic flight to Hyderabad. Like several other people, she sat cross-legged on the floor with her head resting against her bags and the marble pillars at the domestic terminal as well.

By the time she finally boarded, she was so exhausted that she promptly fell asleep and did not awaken until they were about to touch down at their destination. As she looked out the window, she saw the familiar land lit with morning light. As she stared at the kaleidoscope of colorful homes, a flood of emotion came rushing out. She wasn't sure why but she cried silently in joy.

Home Sweet Home

*A*radhana saw her father the day she arrived. Gauri and Aasma were still living at home. However, they had bought an apartment not too far away from the house where she had grown up and planned to move once Aradhana left. Gauri didn't think it was fair to subject Aradhana to a welcome diluted by her parent's separation. Aradhana was glad that she didn't have to deal with the inevitable right now.

Her father had stayed home when Gauri, Aasma, and Abhay came to pick her up. Abhay had worked all night and had come to greet her directly from work. He looked like a man now, different from when she left him. As she looked at her family and the surroundings that had once been so familiar, she was taken aback by how much had changed in two years. She wasn't sure if it was her imagination or reality. She'd find out soon enough what was what.

When she got home, her father came down to greet her. She didn't know why, but she cried when she hugged him which embarrassed her. She didn't typically hug her father and couldn't remember if he had ever seen her cry. The poignancy of the moment was not lost on him. He asked her to freshen up and pay him a visit at his office when she was ready. She was eager to follow him out as he headed for work, but didn't as she knew it would hurt Gauri. She was just as anxious to catch up with Abhay, but he seemed to be fighting off sleep, having worked with clients all night in her adopted country. She would have liked to make acquaintance with sleep herself as well but was too excited and didn't want to be jetlagged for the rest of the week. Gauri seemed to hear her thought process and gave her some advice: she suggested that Aradhana pull through the day and go to sleep at a decent time or else her body clock would be disturbed.

Aradhana was exhausted but fueled by excitement. As she went into her room, her heart became overwhelmed with warmth and security. She threw herself on her bed and looked around the room. It was exactly as she left it. The bright daylight still shone through the beige raw silk curtains. The built-in dark mahogany cupboards with their carvings gave the room a sense of drama. The bangles she had put around the tube light still reminded her of her attempted statement of art and freedom. The oil-painted leather lamps with Rajasthani prints shone brightly as she had instinctively flipped on the switches at the doorway when she entered. She checked her closet out of curiosity and was surprised as to how many of her old clothes were still there. She decided that she didn't have the energy to open her bags and would wear the first thing from her closet she approved of.

She was glad that in retrospect her clothes didn't look hideous. She couldn't wait to see if her old jeans still fit her. Once she put them on, she found that they were a little tighter than she remembered them but would do. She smiled thinking of how Gauri had commented that she had lost weight. Clearly, Gauri had seen her from a mother's eyes. She made a note to eat healthier once she went back to America, as she knew it was a promise she would be unable to keep while in Hyderabad. She was glad that Gauri had furnished the bathroom with everything she would need including a deodorant. There was nothing she needed to open her suitcase for, including underwear. She found the thought comforting that, apart from Scott, there was nothing in the United States that wasn't available to her in here at the family abode. The water pressure wasn't as strong as the one she had gotten used to and she missed the comfortable tub she had begun to spend significant time in. Still, she felt fresher with the shower than she had felt since she had embarked on the long flight.

When she got downstairs, Aasma had made stuffed potato *parathas*. The smell of butter melting on the hot crisp parathas made her instantly forget the tight jeans on her frame. Aradhana was so happy to see Aasma again that she insisted on eating the parathas in the kitchen as she watched Aasma cook. She asked about Aasma's health and how the baby felt. She also asked her how Gauri and Ashwin were handling the breakup. There were so many things Aradhana wanted to know. There was so much to catch up on after less than a fortnight of separation. Aasma tried to answer her questions as succinctly as she could between stuffing the parathas, turning them and loading them with real *ghee*. She was feeling fine. In fact, she had never felt better. She could hardly feel any symptoms of the pregnancy. She had seen a gynecologist and was scheduled for an ultrasound, but so far everything seemed to be going well. In light of the divorce, Ashwin was being elusive. He hadn't been rude to Aasma, but neither had he acknowledged her pregnancy and he had refused to attend Aasma's wedding. He was giving the same silent treatment to Gauri. They had spoken only once to finalize the details of the separation. He had suggested they not get divorced but merely separated as he didn't want to be made a mockery of in front of the

Arushi Sood Joshi

world. He didn't care about the material things—they were for Gauri and the children—but he didn't want to lose his pride.

Hearing Aasma talk made Aradhana finish her parathas quickly and hail an autoricksaw to Ashwin's office. She was not sure what she wanted him to say, but she felt a strong need to hear something from him. All her life they had had little to say to each other. There were times she was seething with rage at the treatment Ashwin doled out to the family, but, still, she was afraid for him. He was a loner—that much she knew—but she didn't know him to be strong. He hadn't left them wanting for any material things in the world and she felt like she owed him at least a shoulder. When she reached the office, it took the staff a few seconds to recognize her but then she got a very warm welcome. She wondered if Ashwin had even shared with them that she would be visiting. Probably not, because they looked very surprised to see her.

The office was modest but impressive. It was in a midsized commercial building with several small and midsize offices. The elevators were crowded at every point in the day, so Aradhana found that walking up the four flights was the quickest way to get to the office. The layout of the office was open and the desks were arranged in parallel lines making the space seem a lot larger than it was. A security guard at the entrance played the role of receptionist and often referred to the head accountant who sat close to the doorway when he needed guidance. Ashwin's assistant who answered the phone sat outside Ashwin's office rather than at the doorway. There were a few other rooms in addition to Ashwin's office. Aradhana rarely frequented the place but knew from previous tours that architects and designers shared one of the rooms while the second was a conference room. Ironically, all the back office functions were done in the common room up front which was called the front office. When the staff finally recognized her, they all rushed to be the first to knock on Ashwin's perennially shut office door. Ashwin always cited air-conditioning efficiency for his antisocial behavior.

Ashwin greeted her warmly and sent two people in two different directions to get her something to eat and drink. He wanted her to try the deep fried *pooris* and the potato curry from the little cafeteria that had opened in the building. They were to die for, he assured her. To drink, he had ordered *lassi* from a quaint little restaurant he had discovered. Aradhana was already stuffed with Aasma's parathas, but since Ashwin seemed so excited to share his world with her she didn't want to hurt his feelings. It seemed strange to her than Gauri still packed lunch for him like she had been doing for over thirty years. Aradhana knew that the contents would still be lentils, rotis and okra, cooked the same way as they had been eating for years.

Ashwin was refreshingly inquisitive about her life in the States. Did she like it there? What was life like? What was different? What was the same? He even threw a curve ball at her. In itself the question was innocuous, but coming from Ashwin not only was it unexpected and uncharacteristic, but frightening. She assumed Ashwin had never known anything about her life. When he asked how Nirman was, Aradhana was taken aback. For starters she didn't even know that Ashwin knew Nirman was the reason she went to the United States. She wanted to be truthful with him, but despite the sudden burst of intimacy did not feel comfortable sharing how her life had changed so she gave him the shortest answer she could and simply said they had broken up.

Aradhana was finding that the few years of separation had dulled her anger towards her father and she was struggling to remember why she disliked him so. She felt guilty for all the times she had asked her mother to leave him. Her guilt increased when he talked about his own break-up. In fact, he even joked that it was the season of break-ups. He admitted that he was glad it was over. Then he said things that reminded Aradhana of why she had such conflicting feelings towards him. What started out as some innocent venting of things that were wrong in Ashwin and Gauri's relationship turned into a list of all the things that were wrong with Gauri.

Aradhana's sympathy was turning to anger. She had no intention of being told just how inadequate Gauri was as a mother and wife. Aradhana was in a strange position. This was the first time her father had spent any significant amount of time with her, but unfortunately it wasn't the kind of time she had been hoping to spend. It was hard for her to walk away because it was obvious that she was the first person he was talking to about the break-up. She tried to apply all the psychological counseling skills she had learned and been subject to, but try as she might, she couldn't detach herself from the situation.

She found it hard not to judge Ashwin as she could easily prove every one of his accusations false. Gauri was a great mother, and as far as she was concerned, a good wife. In her opinion, no one woman would have survived or tolerated Ashwin's behavior for that long.

She didn't miss the sudden respect in Ashwin's voice as he asked her for advice on certain things. It was strange to her that just flying halfway around the world had elevated her status in her father's eyes. He, for one, had no idea what experiences she had been through. His respect was just by virtue of her non-resident status. He even commented on how much she had matured. Surely the old Aradhana would not have sat through five minutes of Gauri-bashing but here she was still seated fifteen minutes into the conversation. As much as Aradhana wanted to walk out of his office she stayed because she had a strange feeling that after this encounter, she would not be seeing him again for a long time to come.

Fifteen minutes into his ramblings, she asked him to stop and, strangely enough, he consented. When the lassi and heavy greasy breakfast finally arrived, Aradhana declined to eat it. When Ashwin insisted, she drank the lassi. As far as she was concerned she had paid her debt.

• • •

Aradhana then called on her friends, who had already been planning the details of her visit over email. She couldn't believe how happy she was to see their dear familiar faces. Her friends who had seen her in that comfortable phase of her life. Over the next week they lived like they were joined at the hip, visiting each others' home and their favorite places in the hometown that they all loved. The only difference from her younger days was that Aasma was now part of the group. They laughed and ate until their bodies couldn't support either activity.

They watched ten movies in a week, ate at two dozen street vendors, and even frequented the latest string of pubs and nightclubs that had sprawled across the city. Aradhana got to experience how far even her meager savings took her here. She was the queen. Everywhere she went she felt compelled to pay. People just assumed that she was from the land of dollars so she should foot the bill anyway. Aradhana didn't mind—she could pay for five restaurant meals in India for the price of one in the United States.

It was a week after she had arrived in Hyderabad that Asad followed suit. The tension was palpable when Abhay, and Aradhana went to pick him up at the airport. Everyone was nervous about what these unchartered waters would bring. Asad wasn't sure where he would be staying. Asad had spent a short time in his home town, and now was here with everything he possessed. He had sold everything he owned and was here with two large suitcases and a laptop computer. Abhay seemed to heave a sigh of relief when they finally saw

Split

Asad with his life contained in two suitcases. It was almost as if he wasn't expecting him to arrive.

Asad was set up in a new apartment that Gauri had purchased for herself. Until Aasma and Asad found a home they were all to live together. A few days after, Asad's brother arrived. He said that his parents were too old to travel but sent their blessings. Although not much older than Asad, he looked like he belonged to another generation. He wasn't wearing his skullcap, but he was still sporting a long unshaven beard for his visit. He was larger than Asad but his voice was a lot softer.

The wedding was a small affair with fewer than ten people in attendance. Amrita had flown down for the registered ceremony but her husband Kiran had not. The newlywed couple spent the night in an unfurnished apartment. There was nothing spectacular in it except an eight-inch thick layer of flowers that Aasma's well wishers had decorated in lieu of a bed.

Disruption

$\mathcal{A}$ radhana couldn't have planned her trip back home any better. That is, of course, until her doorbell rang one hot and sticky summer afternoon. The heat had made her uncharacteristically lazy and she wanted to lie in bed until the sun went down. There really was not all that much to do anyway. The novelty of her trip was wearing off and people needed to get back to their lives. Abhay and her friends were back at work, and Aasma was happily married. Aradhana knew she would soon set into her routine soon as well. She was leaving in less than a week.

She had spoken to Scott a few times but he seemed upset. Once he had commented that she didn't need him anymore now that she was in familiar territory. His comments hurt her deeply, but since it was so unlike Scott she let it go. She knew he wouldn't understand how soothing it was to be home after over two years away from her lifelong surroundings. She knew that no matter how much they cared about each other there would always be things about each other they would never understand. Scott had always been an insider in a community. What did he know about being on the fringe of society? What did he know about constantly feeling judged or evaluated? May be if he came in India, and realized what it meant to be different, he'd understand. Perhaps she was being too harsh on him. He had been there for her when no one had. Just as her mind was trying to justify Scott's reactions and her own unresolved feelings, the doorbell rang.

Aradhana was almost getting used to having people answer the doorbell for her. The doorbell rang for the second time when she realized that the help had the day off and Gauri was out at a kitty party. Gauri had wanted Aradhana to accompany her, but Aradhana begged to be pardoned from social niceties and insisted that Gauri attend the kitty party in order to make a statement. By now rumors about Aasma were circulating freely and some had even picked up on Gauri and Ashwin's separation. Aradhana had maintained that if Gauri didn't attend, people would talk. It would be better to go and deal with either the hundreds of questions that would come her way, or the complete neglect of the topic. Either way, Gauri had nothing to be ashamed about.

As Aradhana ambled towards the door, she tried to guess who it might be. The doorbell rang so often that she wished they'd just keep the door open. Everyone from the milkman in the morning to the electrician to the postman to someone looking to collect on a bill rang the bell. This would be the telephone repairman, she guessed, as Gauri had complained that there was static in the phone.

When she opened the door her heart skipped a few beats. She stood staring at the person at the door for a minute before he asked.

"Won't you at least ask me to come in?"

Aradhana thought she was dreaming, but Nirman touched her shoulder and shook her out of her shock. She instinctively pulled her shoulder away. The anger and hurt was still fresh and strong within her. She moved away from the door and let him decide if he planned to come in. He was familiar with the house and didn't wait for her to change her mind.

He walked to the beige and maroon-colored loveseat and sat down. Aradhana followed him and sat on the chair of the same custom-made living room set. She stared at him for a few minutes.

"What do you want now?" she finally asked.

"Just your forgiveness," Nirman replied.

Aradhana wasn't sure what was happening. She wasn't sure who told Nirman where to find her so, putting all niceties aside, she asked him outright. Nirman said that he had gone to Boston and finding only Alaya at home, begged her to tell him where he could find Aradhana. Shortly after, he got a flight to India. Aradhana didn't know if she should be angry with Alaya. Moreover, why didn't Alaya call her to tell her that Nirman was on his way to see her? Perhaps this was Alaya's revenge for what had happened between Asad and Aasma.

"Over a year is a little late, don't you think?" she asked, trying to continue the disrupted thread of conversation.

"I know. I screwed up. I wanted to come sooner but my cancer came back. I went through chemo again and should be completely recovered now. I was too ashamed to reach out to you. I didn't want your sympathy, but now I do want your forgiveness."

Aradhana felt like someone had taken her heart and grounded it with a pestle. She suddenly felt sick. Why was God doing this to her? She had loved Nirman more than she had loved anything in her life and he had broken her heart. Just as soon as she had gotten over him he was back in her life with a heart-wrenching tale. Her heart was beating loudly. She could smell the familiar cologne fused with Nirman's essence that she had dreamt of so many nights. Here he was sitting within touching distance and touching him would be a sin. Before Nirman could sense the grasp he had on her, she tried to answer his question.

251

"You broke my heart, Nirman. You made me doubt love itself. But I forgive you. What else do you want from me? This is all I can do for you," she said, trying to sound confident.

"I want you back in my life," Nirman said, doe-eyed.

Aradhana felt the ground moved under her feet. Even a year ago she would have died to hear those words from Nirman. Today, however, she felt her hands were tied. She told him she had moved on. She told him about Scott and how she was in love with him. Nirman reached for her hands. She wanted to pull away, but didn't. She was paralyzed. Nirman's touch made her forget everything. Everything between them came rushing back like a flood. Seeing that she didn't pull away, he got up and sat at her knees and rested his head again them. Aradhana's whole body was shivering. She could tell Nirman had lost a lot of weight. The signs of chemo weren't obvious, but he seemed weak. She stroked his hair.

"I'm sorry, Nirman. I've moved on. I had a really hard time getting over you, but now I finally have," she lied.

She knew she wasn't over Nirman. She never had been. She loved Scott, but she loved Nirman as well. Nirman understood her in a way that Scott never would.

Nirman sensed her dilemma. "I'm sure Scott is wonderful and I'd like to thank him for everything he's done for you. But he'll never understand you the way I do," he said.

Aradhana wanted to deny the truth in the statement. In a way she was angry with Nirman for dumping all this on her. But try as she may, she couldn't forget the beauty of their spiritual, physical and mental compatibility.

After years of dreaming about it, they made love in her childhood bedroom.

• • •

Aradhana felt cheap and vulgar for cheating on Scott. She knew she couldn't lie to him. Telling him about everything that happened would be the first thing she did when she got back. Now, however, she was conflicted about Nirman. After that fateful day, they met every day and made love more times in that week than they had in all their time together. It was fulfilling and pure and it completed Aradhana. At the same time she felt a strange heaviness. She wondered if this would be happening if Nirman hadn't told her about his cancer. Would she have still conceded to him? She felt sick for having more than a fleeting thought of whether the cancer had resurfaced at all. She realized that whether it was true or not, she had lost faith in Nirman.

Regardless of what the current situation was, that night in Pasadena had happened. He had slept with another woman. She wondered how that was different from what she was doing to Scott. She tried to justify it by saying this was her first true love and Nirman had cheated on her with someone he didn't have feelings for. She wondered if that actually made his situation more excusable. Surely knowing that the one you love was sleeping with someone they had deep feelings for was worse than getting over your love cheating purely for flesh.

If breaking up with Nirman was hard, then this was harder. She felt Nirman knew exactly what buttons to press and he wasn't coy about it. She felt he was taking advantage of the strong feelings she had for him.

The biggest difference between Scott and Nirman was that Scott set her free while Nirman controlled her.

• • •

Nirman wanted to change his flight to fly back with Aradhana, but she put her foot down. Aradhana wanted to be by herself while she evaluated just what a big mess she had made of own life.

She hadn't spoken to Scott since he told her that she didn't need him. She knew that he was upset and she shuddered to think how he'd react to her confession. She felt like she would be dumping her emotional load on him. She wasn't sure what she had started and how she planned to fix it. She was hoping that the twenty-four hours of flying and layover time would give her the answers she needed.

There were no guarantees that Scott would even want her back. In fact, she thought there was a pretty good chance that he wouldn't. In light of that, what she really needed to think about then was how she felt about Nirman. As close as she and Scott were, they had never discussed marriage and she wondered why. She knew she was partly to blame. For starters, she had made it clear to Scott than she wanted to work for at least a few years before she got married. She also wondered if she had projected some of her unresolved feelings about Nirman onto him. The fact that she wasn't sure whether she wanted to live in the United States or in India didn't help either.

Nirman, on the other hand, had proposed to her. He hadn't gotten down on his knee and given her a ring, but he had, however, told her that he wanted to marry her. He said he'd live wherever she wanted regardless of whether it was the United States or India.

Aradhana evaluated the situation. Scott may never ask her to marry him. Nirman already had. Scott was an Irish-American from a completely different culture than hers. Nirman was an Indian with a similar background to hers. Both she and Nirman were first generation immigrants to the United States and had gone through similar experiences. Nirman knew her inside out. He could complete her sentences and dodge an impending punch even before she made a fist. He knew what movies she'd like and what she'd dislike even before she saw them.

On the other hand, Scott had been there for her when no one else had. He hadn't judged her. He had given her significant room to grow and express herself. He made her feel safe. Most importantly, she trusted him.

How then could she break his heart this way? After twenty-four hours of flying she was no wiser than when she boarded the plane.

When she arrived, Scott was there to pick her up even though she hadn't given Scott her itinerary. In fact, this time around she had been hoping to take a taxi back to the apartment. She was still mad at Alaya for championing the start of this disruption in her life. She hadn't called Scott because she wasn't sure she could face him. It touched and surprised her that he remembered her arrival time from when she had booked her ticket. She almost let her cart fall over when she saw Scott rushing towards her to hug her. He didn't say much until they reached the car. She seemed off. Was it the jet lag, he asked. Why didn't she call him or confirm her flight? How exactly was she planning to get home? Why was she being so mysterious?

Scott was asking more questions that he normally did at a time when Aradhana had no energy to answer them. When they got to the apartment Aradhana said she was jetlagged and went to sleep.

She slept for a day and half. It was seven in the evening when she called Scott to the apartment. He must have known something was wrong because he seemed very pensive.

She gave him everything she had brought him from India including some clothes and artifacts. When she told him what had happened in India, he threw the clothes at her.

"Am I not hot-blooded enough for you?" he lashed out. "Perhaps I should sleep around like your precious Nirman and manipulate you the way he does"

Before slamming the door behind him, he said,

"Screw you, Aradhana Kapoor. Enjoy your life with your desi purebred ex. No sorry—your new boyfriend."

254

It's Been a Hard Day's Work

*L*ess than two weeks after Scott walked away from her life, Aradhana broke up with Nirman. Things would never be the same between them. Too much had changed. Most importantly, the trust between them had been broken. The last week she had spent with Nirman actually made her believe that they had both changed. Neither was no longer a lofty, idealizing eighteen-year-old. Both had faced enough adversity and were bitter in their own right. While the chemistry was strong, Aradhana felt something was missing from the relationship. Neither she nor Nirman had what it took to make a relationship stable. Neither could be an anchor for the other. As Aradhana described it to Nirman when she broke up with him, "We've grown up and grown apart."

There was nothing to do but move on. Aradhana had no face with which to go back to Scott. As far as she was concerned, Scott deserved much better so she did the most dignified thing she knew to do and let Scott move on.

She threw herself into her work and rented a two-bedroom apartment in Cambridge. Life as she knew it had changed. All her friends had moved on. Asad was the proud father of a little boy whom they had named Sameer, or "the wind." The name was non-denominational and both Aasma and Asad spent half their time chasing behind the wind.

Alaya and the twins were the only people still left around the Boston area from her grad school days. She had long forgiven Alaya and Alaya, too, had gotten over Asad. She had made a few friends at work and was active in the Indian community. When Aradhana felt lonely she'd spend hours writing odes to India about the hope that she'd return home someday. The money from her job was good. She still had bills to pay from school and was sending Gauri a thousand dollars a month. She had also started saving for some property in India so that she would have something tangible to return to.

Three winters had come and gone since she lost Scott. She thought of him a lot and realized she was still madly in love with him. She missed his cool headedness and in- charge personality. He complemented her passionate fiery temperament and had brought definition and meaning to her life. His counsel had been valuable through so many hard times. Whenever she was in a jam, she'd think in her mind "WWSD?"—What would Scott do?" Her love for him was precisely the reason she had let him go in the first place. She was certain that by now he would have found a nice Irish girl with whom he shared a similar background. Surely the whole relationship with her had soured him enough to be done with a more diverse love interest pool. Perhaps, he had even gotten together with Emily. May be her undying love had finally won him over.

She had avoided the family pubs altogether. She didn't feel kosher even talking to Kelly. She knew Kelly was a loyal cousin and would have expected no less loyalty from her own. She didn't want to put Kelly in a position that was awkward for either of them.

Spring was in the air and she had closed her first deal. It wasn't a large project but two hundred thousand dollars was a large enough amount for Aradhana. The partner for whom she closed the deal was also her mentor and insisted that Aradhana and a few more of his protégées celebrate the victory. For dinner he took them to the Top of the Hub restaurant on top of the Prudential Center where they ate an elaborate dinner and gazed at Boston shining in all its glory. After dinner, they decided they'd go pub-hopping in Quincy Market. Aradhana had downed two glasses of wine and was in her "happy zone" as she liked to call it. She knew better than to be drunk at an office party and decided to pace herself. The weather was wonderful and crisp and she had draped a black pashmina shawl over her sleeveless black dress.

They had stopped at so many places that she couldn't remember where they finally ended up. It was an outdoor bar, and they sat around a small octagonal fire pit. Clearly her colleagues didn't worry as much about their corporate reputation as she did. It was around 11 p.m. and Aradhana had a sudden urge to take a walk and take in what the market had to offer. She was gone for twenty minutes and was returning when she saw a familiar silhouette at the bar a few tables further from her office crowd. She changed her vantage point to see if she was imagining the familiar face, but she wasn't.

There was Scott in crisp blue button-down Oxford shirt and khaki pants sitting with two other gentlemen. As eager as she was to say hello to him, she didn't want to upset the balance it had taken her three years to create.

No point scraping scabs off a wound, she thought.

Just as she was planning her exit, her mentor and the bourbon inside him bellowed, "Aradhana where have you been?" Half a dozen people turned to see the object of his concern, including Scott.

Within seconds their eyes met and both walked over to each other at the same time. Scott was the first to speak.

"Hi Ary—sorry, Aradhana—how have you been? Thought you'd be in California with a nice handsome Indian baby by now."

He still sounded bitter which was surprising to Aradhana.

"Sorry—no Indian baby or husband," she replied. "Nirman and I broke up two weeks after you and I did. So, where's your Irish wife?" she asked, trying to keep the conversation light.

Their respective parties looked inquisitively at this new intrigue. Sensing half a dozen eyes on them, Scott asked what she was doing after drinks. Aradhana wasn't sure where this was leading but blurted out an excited

"Nothing."

After ditching their parties, they spent the entire night talking. There was so much to catch up on. Aradhana had come a long way and so had Scott. Scott was had become an independent consultant for entities opening Irish pubs throughout the United States. The work had kept him out of town and busy. Both were surprised to hear that neither had dated anyone else.

At the end of the night Scott was the one to break the awkwardness that had been lingering from the break-up. "You know, Ary, I was never mad at you. No matter how much I tried I couldn't get myself to hate you. Boy, did I try. I don't know why, but I never stopped caring about you."

Thank You, Amrrika

It hadn't taken too long for Scott and Aradhana to realize that they still meant a lot to each other. They took their time, but slowly they became a permanent fixture in each other's life. Aradhana and Scott both traveled a lot for work and both thought it was probably good for their fledgling relationship. If absence makes the heart grow fonder, then they both had had plenty of opportunities. Even Aradhana thought it was best for both to tread with caution. They both needed to be sure that they wouldn't end up in the same place as three years ago.

Aradhana wanted to be certain that there was no doubt left in her mind. She knew it was completely her actions that had caused the pain the last time around. She knew she had to make sure that this time she could honor the sanctity of the relationship. That said, she wasn't sure where the relationship was heading. She didn't know where life would take her next. She was on a H1-B work visa, but had filed for a green card. Even though, she intended to return back to India, before Scott came into her life, now she had wanted to keep her options open.

When the lease on Scott's apartment was up, Aradhana suggested he move in with her. He traveled most of the time anyway, and it had been two and a half years since they had been back together.

That cold December day when Aradhana headed for work, she thought about Scott as she looked at the undisturbed side of the bed. He had been in Chicago for a week, helping with the opening of another small Irish pub. Scott and Aradhana had been living together for six months. How she missed him when he was away. She couldn't believe that she broke the heart of someone she respected and cared about that much.

Scott's family had been even more magnanimous than she could ever have imagined and had welcomed her back with open arms. Kelly confessed that Scott hadn't been the same after they broke up. He seemed to have lost his spark for life.

Now Scott and Aradhana were an entity. No one said Aradhana without Scott, or Scott without Aradhana. With Scott by her side, life couldn't have been better. Thanks to Scott's constant guidance and support, she had progressed ever faster than before. She was in love with Scott, of that fact she was sure, but she worried if Scott would ever give her that undying trust again.

When she reached work she was glad she had taken the extra pair of shoes as her first ones were covered in snow. When she finally took them off in her cubicle, snow flurries flew everywhere. As she looked around the office, most of the cubicles looked like little snow globes as people dusted off their wet, snow-covered shoes. She was at the office earlier than usual. When Scott was away, she found that she couldn't bear to be home alone and therefore spent as much time as she could at work. It didn't work against her that was for sure. Scott joked that the path to her partnership was due to his absence from home.

At 10 a.m. all the cubicles around her area started to empty out as people headed to an apparent meeting. Aradhana checked her Outlook calendar, but there was nothing scheduled. She wondered if she had been left off an invite. That wouldn't have been good as it would have suggested that she was dispensable. When she walked over to the administrative assistant, the assistant seemed buried in work and brushed Aradhana off with a quick response that it was a performance evaluation meeting at which she was not required.

Aradhana was unduly hurt as she returned to her desk. She tried not to let things at work offend her, but this was a direct snubbing of her. She vowed to bring it up with the partners. It was highly unusual and it concerned her significantly.

As she sat dejectedly at her desk, a hand holding a bouquet of yellow roses suddenly appeared at the entrance of her cubicle. The hand belonged to Scott, who was now kneeling in front of her. Aradhana's face turned red as Scott opened a jewelry box holding a two carat princess cut ring and said,

"Aradhana Kapoor, will you marry this Irishman who has loved you since the first night he dropped you off at your apartment?"

A sea of her office colleagues appeared with grins stretching from ear to ear chanting and clapping as Aradhana replied,

"Scott O'Donnell, nothing would make me prouder than to be your wife."

Lightning Source UK Ltd.
Milton Keynes UK
19 August 2009

142848UK00001B/181/P

9 781605 943367